LOVE, HOLIDAY STYLE

ARI MCKAY

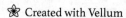

CONTENTS

GHOST OF A CHANCE

THE BOYFRIEND SWEATER CURSE

DANDY'S LITTLE GIRL

HOLIDAY HOOTENANNY

GHOST OF A CHANCE

1

"All right, let's see what we've got."

Mason Beaulieu stared intently at his laptop screen, impatiently waiting for the processing algorithm to finish analyzing the audio sample he'd selected. He'd written the program himself, so he knew how many complex calculations were being performed, but that didn't make him any less impatient for the result. Not that he expected there to be anything of interest in the recording. A small part of him -- one that he never acknowledged to anyone else on the team -- held out a tenuous hope that one day he'd be proven wrong. But after nearly twenty years of analyzing incidents of supposed "paranormal activity," Mason had never found even the tiniest shred of conclusive, irrefutable evidence that anything beyond the rational, mundane world existed.

He'd been fascinated with ghost stories since childhood. His grandfather had told him tales of how Beaulieu House was haunted by the spirits of British soldiers who'd died during the Battle of New Orleans and by an Acadian woman who'd been in love with a young man in the family and killed herself on the doorstep when he refused to marry her. Mason had absorbed the tales like a sponge, and he'd spent numerous nights in a sleeping bag on the front porch, waiting in shivery anticipation for the dead girl to appear, holding the bloody knife she'd stabbed herself with. He wasn't afraid of what he might see; he was eager for it, hoping he'd have his own stories to tell.

But nothing happened over the course of his childhood when all he'd had was a Polaroid instant camera and a cassette recorder at his disposal to document what he hoped he'd see. As he grew older and decided to study engineering, his equipment had gotten better, and he'd saved up for an infrared camera and a sensitive tape recorder. He expanded his hobby beyond the front steps of the family home, spending hours in the library reading up on local hauntings. He'd graduated from bicycle to second-hand car, then to a sleek Mercedes that had been his parents' gift when he'd graduated with his doctorate from Vanderbilt. His equipment had grown ever more sophisticated as he'd begun to design and build it himself, soldering his own circuits as he sought to construct something that would be sensitive enough to record the evidence he was still hoping to find.

Somewhere along the line, however, he'd somehow changed from wanting to prove the paranormal existed to wanting to debunk the claims of so-called "sensitives" and "psychics" who claimed their abilities put them in contact with the Great Unknown and to find rational explanations for people who were convinced their homes were haunted. Mason wasn't quite certain when it happened, but by the time he sold the patent he'd taken out on his high-speed infrared motion-activated video camera, enabling him to retire at the age of thirty-two, he was being called in to help debunk all manner of paranormal phenomena. In the area around New Orleans, that could sometimes feel like a full-time job.

"Hey, you have the results on the EVP from the DuFresne house yet?"

The voice of Laura, one of the other investigators of NOPI -- New Orleans Paranormal Investigations, the "ghost hunter" group Mason worked with -- distracted him, and Mason pulled his headphones off of one ear.

"Still working on it. It was a long file, almost two hours." Mason shrugged and pointed to the screen, where a progress bar crept up to the eighty-percent mark. "Another few minutes."

"Awesome." Laura flopped down on a futon sofa across from the chair Mason occupied, then pulled out her phone and began to tap out a text message.

NOPI had started out of the garage of the oldest member, Steve Monroe, but that had been before Mason had gotten involved. Now the six part-time investigators occupied a large bay in a commercial warehouse, which had plenty of storage room for their equipment and the racks of hard drives where they stored all their collected data. Mason had bankrolled a lot of the hardware, but he'd done it discreetly, not wanting anyone to think he was trying to buy control of the group. They were a democracy, although people did tend to defer to Steve, as the founder. If they often seemed eager to support investigations Mason wanted to do, he was pretty sure it was because they respected his abilities, not because they were afraid he'd take his toys and go home if they didn't cater to him. At least that was what he *hoped*.

At any given time, there was usually at least one member in the warehouse, partly for security, and partly because it was easy to get absorbed in analysis and end up crashing overnight from sheer exhaustion. Everyone but Mason had a job "outside", but Mason knew he couldn't spend twenty-four hours a day immersed in NOPI business or he'd quickly go nuts. He came from an "old family" in the area, which meant he had a certain number of expectations to fulfill, social obligations which had fallen to him after his father passed away. From time to time, he left the warehouse, donned a suit, and escorted his mother to hospital board meetings, society dinners, and charity fundraisers.

The progress bar finally hit completion, and Mason adjusted his headphones. The spectrogram display popped up, and he hit "play", watching as the plot moved in time with the sounds in his headphones. The recording had been made the previous night at the house of a normal suburban family, who were being haunted by "ghostly voices" waking them up in the middle of the night, terrifying their children, and leaving them nervous and upset. Mason had been there, running the recorder, and he'd actually heard the odd, whispered cadences in several rooms. He'd reserved judgment, and now, as he listened to the processed, enhanced, and filtered results, he was glad he had. Realizing what he was hearing, he began to chuckle.

"What? What is it?" Laura raised a brow, and Mason pulled the plug of his headphones out of the computer, so that the sound could be heard through the speaker.

"...yeah, the weather here is fine. Nothing like what you have down there, eh, but even in Canada, it can't snow all the time, y'know?"

Mason stopped the playback as Laura rolled her eyes. "Shortwave radio!" she said in disgust. "It must be damned close to their house, too."

"No more than a couple of houses away and possibly at illegal strength, since it's powerful enough to cause vibration in circuits that are off." Mason sighed. "Simple physics. Any radio receiver can resonate, even without power, if the input signal is strong enough. This one is probably bad enough that if one of those kids had been old enough for braces, they'd probably have been scared their teeth were haunted. So the family gets ghost whispers in the middle of the night while their neighbor is chatting with his buddies in the Great White North. Another mystery solved, thanks to NOPI."

"And you can't spell NOPI without the 'nope!'" Laura chimed in, using what had become the catchphrase for their group. She rose to her feet. "Thanks, that'll be good enough to wrap up the report. I want to be finished before six."

"Oh?" Mason smiled at her. "Got a date?"

Laura was a grad student in Psychology at Tulane and a very attractive young woman. Mason was aware she'd be quite a catch if he had any interest whatsoever in women -- which he didn't.

"Yeah. A cute med student. Too young for you, so don't get any ideas!" She stuck her tongue out at him teasingly, and Mason chuckled and shook his head. He wasn't interested in med students, no matter how cute. However, hot professors were quite another matter.

"Have fun. And say hi to Professor Woody for me next time you see him. Ask him if he's found a skunk ape out in the bayou yet."

"God, would you quit teasing that poor man?" Laura shook her head in exasperation. Haywood Fortenberry was one of Laura's instructors at Tulane, an assistant professor in the Psychology Department. He also happened to be a member of LaPS, the Louisiana Paranormal Society, a far more credulous group of researchers than NOPI. So Dr. Haywood -- who preferred to be called "Fort" -- was, unlike Mason, a believer. He also happened to be gay and damned attractive. Not that Mason had noticed, of course.

"Fine, fine, send him felicitations from one group of intellectual superbeings to another." Mason grinned wickedly. "Then ask him about the skunk ape."

Laura rolled her eyes and waved as she walked out of the room, and Mason chuckled as he closed his laptop. Another case closed, and a family could rest easy knowing they weren't being haunted by a vengeful ghost who was going to harm them in their sleep. It was a success by the standards of NOPI, and it would add to their reputation as the best debunkers in the state.

But it didn't keep Mason Beaulieu from feeling almost as let down as he had as an eight year old shivering through the night on the cold front porch and realizing as the sun rose that nothing really special ever happened to him.

2

At the Conference on Paranormal Research and Investigation held annually in New Orleans, Dr. Haywood Fortenberry took his place at the long table set up at the front of a small meeting room and shuffled through his notes left over from the brief talk he'd given earlier on parapsychology. Having studied at the Rhine Research Center in North Carolina, he was often asked to talk about the field of parapsychology and his experiences with it at various conferences and gatherings of fellow paranormal investigators. He'd also been asked to sit on this panel, which was called "Physics, Psychics, and Psychology: When Science and the Supernatural Collide." Since it would likely be an improvised Q&A session, he hadn't done much preparation for the panel, focusing on preparing for his talk instead.

He wasn't looking forward to the panel anyway; he hadn't been since he'd found out Mason Beaulieu was going to be on it, representing the physics part. Their paths didn't cross often, but when they did, Mason spent most of the time verbally poking Fort like he was trying to get a rise out of Fort for some reason. For his part, Fort thought Mason was attractive; he'd always been drawn to dark-haired men with glasses. But Mason talked too much, thought too fast, and seemed far too disdainful of what he called Fort's "credulity" when it came to the paranormal. He also never passed up the opportunity to make snarky comments about Sarah LaTour, one of the founding members of LaPS who was also a medium.

Fort preferred to think of himself as open-minded, not gullible. The team, even Sarah, looked for logical explanations for the things they experienced first, but sometimes, there *wasn't* a logical explanation. Fort had never seen or been touched by a ghost himself, unlike other members of his team, but he'd heard convincing Electronic Voice Phenomena, or EVPs for short. When he met Sarah, she had told him things about his deceased grandmother that she couldn't possibly have known, but he wasn't shocked. He considered her abilities to be similar to those of the people whom he'd worked with at the Rhine Research Center.

He hoped Mason would hold off on the jabs for once. The panel was supposed to be a collaborative event, and Fort didn't want it to degenerate into a verbal sparring match, or for Mason to take over and spend the whole time spreading his cynicism to the audience.

As if summoned up by Fort's thoughts, Mason sauntered through the door, wearing a black polo shirt that set off the width of his shoulders and well broken-in jeans that hugged his hips. Mason projected an aura that was part scientist and part badass, and there was always a gleam in his dark eyes, although it was difficult to tell if it was amusement or merely cynicism.

He approached the table, tossed a black leather portfolio down on it, and dropped into the chair next to Fort's, giving him a lazy smile. "Hey, Doc. Enjoying watching the Scoobies and the whackos?"

Fort suppressed a sigh, wishing Mason hadn't sat down next to him. Unfortunately, he couldn't bring himself to be rude enough to get up and move. Instead, he gave Mason a brief, polite smile.

"As a matter of fact I am," he said, trying to keep the irritation he felt at Mason's reference to "whackos" out of his voice. "Paying attention to people is part of what I do."

The conference did have its share of unusual attendees, of course. Most of them were like him and Mason: paranormal investigators who took what they did seriously. None of them had been tapped to host ghost hunting shows on the Syfy channel, which meant they had to hold down day jobs, but they were dedicated to the hunt for answers to one of life's biggest questions. However, there were a few colorful attendees in the crowd, some who were disassociated with reality enough that Fort had a difficult time not crossing the work/hobby streams and conducting impromptu therapy sessions with them.

Mason tilted his head and raised one eyebrow, his dark eyes intent on Fort's face. "I just saw a woman resort to speaking in tongues while she was arguing with a Vedun high priest over the 'true nature of spirits.' I almost wished he *could* hex her just to get her to shut up. Not exactly the kind of thing I enjoy observing, especially since the media focuses on crap like that, making it harder for people to take this kind of research seriously."

"Extremists get the attention in any field, not just ours," Fort pointed out, focusing his attention on his lecture notes in the hopes that Mason would get the hint and not try to draw him into yet another ideological argument. "They're what boosts the ratings."

"Yeah, but they also try to convince people that perfectly ordinary phenomena are signs from the Great Beyond." Mason rolled his eyes. "It sure makes investigations more difficult when you have either True Believers or outright scammers trying to twist everything to make it come out to their advantage."

Fort inclined his head to acknowledge the point. "It does, but fortunately they're a minority, if a vocal one. The rest of us are professionals who take the job seriously, and that's what I prefer to focus on."

Mason sighed. "Yeah, I know, but it can be hard when they get in your face about it." He smiled ruefully. "Sometimes I feel like the only atheist at a church picnic or something."

Fort glanced at Mason and offered a sympathetic smile. No doubt it *was* difficult and frustrating for Mason at times, and Fort sometimes wondered why Mason remained in the field when he seemed so adamant that everything was either a hoax or had a logical explanation. Most investigators Fort knew, himself included, had a sense of wonder to balance out the scientific detachment, but Mason didn't seem to have anything but determination to prove there were no paranormal explanations for anything, merely normal explanations.

"Interesting choice of words there," he replied. "Atheist rather than agnostic. Should I invoke my day job and call it a Freudian slip?"

Mason's eyes widened, and he gaped at Fort for a moment, obviously taken aback. Then he chuckled and shook his head, giving Fort a surprisingly warm glance. "If you want to analyze me, Doc, I'm game. Maybe you'll find out some things that surprise you."

"I don't think you need therapy." Fort paused and smiled self-deprecatingly. "No more than any of us who wander around dark houses in the middle of the night, talking to ghosts."

Besides, he wasn't sure he wanted to delve any deeper. Mason Beaulieu was handsome, intelligent, and gay, but Fort didn't think they were at all compatible. Maybe he was as credulous as Mason claimed he was, but he'd rather be credulous than cynical, and he didn't think their conflicting world views would mesh.

People had started filing into the room, and Mason leaned closer as the third panelist, a local radio psychic, approached the table. His voice dropped low so that only Fort could hear him. "That's too bad. I kind of like the idea of you poking around inside me."

Fort sat up straight and stared, his full attention riveted on Mason for the first time during their conversation. He felt heat rising in his face, but he told himself sternly that Mason couldn't have possibly been throwing around innuendo. Not with *him*. Mason had always seemed to look down on him, which meant attraction and flirting were out of the question. Obviously, it had been too long since Fort's last date if he was reading too much into something *Mason* said to him.

"Uh. I think it would be a conflict of interests. Or something."

"Yeah, I'm sure would be *something*, all right." Mason gave him a wicked smile, then turned to look out at the gathering audience. "Hello, everyone! Find your seats and settle in. I suspect this is going to be a rather stimulating discussion." He turned to look at Fort again, dark eyes gleaming. "Don't you, Dr. Fortenberry?"

Mason was poking fun at him again, and Fort kicked himself for being momentarily flustered. He smiled politely once more, putting on his best professional demeanor.

"Of course, Dr. Beaulieu. Psychology always is, as far as I'm concerned."

Surprisingly, Mason winked at him, then turned to the audience again. "So is physics. And let's not forget the third 'P' in this discussion and our psychic representative, Mr. Ken Carnadine. Tell me, Mr. Carnadine, who's going to win our little debate? Inquiring minds want to know."

_____

"Hey, Mason! Got a moment?"

Mason looked up from the circuit board he was soldering, watching as Steve lowered himself onto one of the stools around the workbench. "Of course. What do you need?"

The older man smiled. "We've had a request come in, and I think you're the best one to take it."

Laying the soldering iron in its cradle, Mason raised one eyebrow. "An investigation? I thought it was Derek and Todd's turn to take the next one. I don't want them to think I'm hogging all the opportunities. I know they've been eager to get a good assignment."

"Well, see, here's the thing. This is rather special, and they only want a single investigator."

"What? We don't do solos. That's your first rule!" Mason shook his head, frowning. It was a rule he happened to agree with. Not only did it mean that there were multiple observers for any phenomena -- which gave it more credence -- but it was safer as well. Some of the places they investigated were old, and there was always the risk someone could be injured, so it was best to always go in pairs.

"I know, but it won't be solo," Steve hastened to explain. "We had a call from KITN. They're sponsoring a webcast of an investigation at

Wisteria Grove Inn on Halloween night. It's partly for publicity for the town of Boulard Crossing, to help promote tourism."

Wisteria Grove was one of southern Louisiana's more famous "haunted houses", and Mason rolled his eyes. "Oh, no. Please tell me this isn't some gimmicky 'ghost tour' thing! I hate those, because people want to see things, not do a real investigation. If that's what it is, please count me out."

"Now don't jump to conclusions!" There was no mistaking the twinkle in Steve's eyes, and Mason realized Steve had been baiting him, and he'd fallen for it hook, line, and sinker. "What they are proposing is a joint investigation with a member of LaPS. A *real* investigation, showcasing the strengths of both groups, and showing cooperation. Access to the entire inside, no one else present. They're shutting the place down, and they're locking you in. This is real, and we might never get a chance like this again to do such an in-depth investigation of the place."

"Oh, lord. Please don't tell me LaPS is going to send their psychic!" The thought of working with someone who claimed to have "special powers" didn't appeal to him in the slightest, even if the opportunity itself was appealing. "If it is, I'm definitely not the right person."

Steve smirked at him. "Actually, they're sending Dr. Fortenberry. What do you think of that?"

Mason sighed and shook his head; judging from the smirk, Steve had guessed Mason was interested in Fort. "I think you're an ass. That's what I think. Good thing I like you."

"So you'll do it?" Steve sobered. "Look, Mason, we've known each other a long time, and all kidding aside, I think you're the best one for this. I know you'll do us proud, so... what do you say?"

For a moment, Mason hesitated. He wanted to do it, partly because it was a unique opportunity, and partly because it would give him a chance to spend time with Fort. Unfortunately, he was starting to get the feeling Fort didn't like him, and spending hours locked in a house with someone who couldn't stand him wasn't something he thought could lead to a successful investigation.

But Mason wasn't the kind to back down from a challenge, and perhaps he could change Fort's opinion of him. Teasing and flirting hadn't worked, so maybe if Fort saw Mason really was a professional, not just a skeptic, he'd see Mason was worth getting to know better.

It might only be a ghost of a chance, but it was one Mason wanted to take.

Fort parked his fifteen-year-old pickup in the guest parking area of Wisteria Grove, an antebellum plantation house that had been turned into a bed and breakfast. It was a popular wedding venue, thanks to the massive live oaks dripping with Spanish moss, the lush gardens, and of course the wisteria trees for which it was named. It was also popular with ghost hunters, who came from far and wide to investigate what was touted as one of the most haunted places in Louisiana.

Fort hadn't investigated Wisteria Grove before, so when KITN had pitched the idea of a representative from both LaPS and NOPI performing a joint investigation that would be streamed live on the internet on Halloween night, Fort had immediately volunteered. The rest of the group had agreed to let him represent them, partly because he'd never been to Wisteria Grove before and partly because he would make them look good on camera in more ways than one.

His professional credentials were strong, but he suspected the team had picked him because he was also easy on the eyes. At six feet tall, he was broad shouldered and narrow hipped with wavy auburn hair and dark blue eyes. Even in front of a class, he was usually seen in jeans and well-worn cowboy boots, and he moved with a rangy grace and the air of someone comfortable in his own skin.

As he mounted the wide porch steps, Fort looked around in admiration at how well the house had been maintained, stately and beautiful despite its age. Once inside, he veered right into the living room that had been turned into a reception area, and approached the young woman at the desk.

"Hi, I'm Haywood Fortenberry. I'm here for the Halloween ghost hunt walk-through."

There was no mistaking the appreciation in the receptionist's eyes, and the smile she gave him showed off her dimples. "Of course, Dr. Fortenberry, they're expecting you." She pointed to a set of glass double doors. "The director and Dr. Beaulieu are in the sitting room. Go right on in!"

Fort nodded and went through the doors, glancing around the small room. His gaze immediately fell on Mason, and he nodded politely.

"Sorry if I kept you both waiting," he said as he claimed one of the chairs near them.

Mason returned the nod, removing his glasses and favoring Fort with a long, intent look, his dark brown eyes oddly warm. He was lounging in one of the wingback chairs, long legs stretched out in front of him in a pose of indolent grace. He gave Fort a slow smile, teeth very white in his tanned, square-jawed face.

"No problem, Professor," he replied. "We were just chatting."

"Yes, Dr. Beaulieu was telling me about the equipment he'd like to bring." Catherine Bollier, a director from KITN, smiled at him in welcome. She'd served as the liaison between the station and both LaPS and NOPI for the special. "I'm quite excited about the show. We're already garnering quite a lot of buzz on the internet."

"Is that right?" Fort was quite pleased to hear it. Perhaps the exposure would bring in new interest and maybe even new members for both groups. "I'm looking forward to it myself. I've never investigated Wisteria Grove, but I've wanted to for a long time."

"I was here several years ago, before I joined NOPI, but the equipment I had wasn't as refined as what I have now." Mason raised a brow. "Were you planning to bring anything special?"

"Just the usual. Digital recorder, EMF meter, Flir camera, that kind of thing. We don't have an engineer on the team, so I'm sure your equipment will be better than mine," Fort acknowledged without any resentment. He envied NOPI having such a gifted tech person, but he didn't begrudge them at all.

Mason nodded. "I was telling Catherine I want to put some motion-activated cameras in the rooms reputed to be most active. I think we should stick together at all times so we can both witness any occurrences that can't be verified by the recorders."

"That sounds fine to me." Fort nodded, amenable to the idea not only because it would allow them to corroborate their experiences, but also because it would be safer.

"Excellent." Catherine smiled and rose to her feet, then pulled a tablet from her purse. "Let's get started on that walkthrough, shall we? I have a short blurb about each of the rooms you can use when describing them for the audience if you want. We can make sure there are extension cords available in any location you want to leave equipment in so we don't have to scramble when you're ready to set up tomorrow."

Mason got up, stretching languidly. "Sure, we can get going." He slid his glasses back on. "Coming, Fort?"

Fort stood up, shooting a mildly quizzical look at Mason, who hadn't called him "Dr. Woody" once the entire conversation. Maybe Mason was exercising a little professional tact in front of Catherine, but whatever the case, Fort was just as glad not to hear the nickname for once.

"I'm right behind you."

A gleam of amusement flashed in Mason's eyes before his expression turned bland. He made a sweeping gesture. "Oh, no, after you. I insist."

That was taking professional courtesy a little too far. Fort might be gay, but there was no reason to treat him like a Southern belle. He didn't think it was worth kicking up a fuss over, however, so he shrugged and sauntered ahead of Mason.

Catherine led them into the foyer, and they began a quick tour of the inn, spending time in the rooms with the most alleged activity to make note of what equipment would best suit the various locations. Mason tapped notes into his smartphone, muttering to himself from time to time as he looked behind chairs and dressers for power and phone outlets. He also peered behind curtains and checked the frames of many of the windows, as well as taking note of any creaking floorboards they came across.

Fort recognized that Mason was gathering information in order to debunk whatever claims might have been made about the area or whatever experiences they might have during the investigation, which was fine with Fort. If something could be explained easily, that gave more weight to the experiences they *couldn't* explain.

For his part, Fort paid more attention to Catherine's descriptions of the rooms and the stories associated with them. He'd heard most of the stories already, but it wouldn't hurt to refresh his memory. If nothing else, it might make interesting color commentary for the audience. After they made a full tour of the areas they would be investigating, Catherine led them back to the sitting room where they'd met. After making sure they didn't have any other questions or concerns, she excused herself, saying she needed to get back to the station before the evening news broadcast, leaving the two of them alone.

"Seems straightforward enough to me," Fort said, preparing to take his leave as well. "I guess I'll see you back here tomorrow night."

"I'll bring coffee and snacks along with the gear." Mason smiled at Fort. "How do you take yours?"

"Two sugars, no cream. I can bring the snacks if you bring the coffee," Fort offered. "Sounds like you're already bringing more equipment. I'd like to carry my weight, even if it just means providing some MoonPies."

Mason grinned. "So long as the MoonPies are banana, you've got a deal. So I guess that's--" He looked past Fort as if something had caught his attention. "Good afternoon, ma'am."

Fort turned to see who Mason was talking to and saw an elderly woman entering the room. She was short and stooped, her white hair styled in a neat bun. She wore a dress the color of violets with a silver knitted shawl draped over her shoulders, and she carried a bag that was bulging with balls of yarn.

"Hello, ma'am," he greeted her politely as well, wondering if she was a guest at the bed and breakfast or part of the staff.

She smiled at them, a particularly sweet smile that lit up her face. "Such nice young men and so handsome! I do beg your pardon if I'm intruding. I like to sit by the west window to do my crochet in the evenings. The light is better for my old eyes, you know." Her accent was a soft, slow drawl with a surprisingly girlish lilt for someone who appeared to be in her eighties.

"Of course," Mason replied at once, returning her smile. "It's no intrusion, ma'am. We were just about finished anyway, weren't we, Dr. Fortenberry?"

"Yes, we were, Dr. Beaulieu." Fort smiled at the lady as well as he took a step toward the door. "You have a nice evening, ma'am."

"Oh, two doctors! Now isn't that interesting?" The lady moved toward a carved wooden rocker, placing her bag beside it as she settled in, and primly adjusted her skirt. She favored them with a speculative look from eyes as blue as delphiniums. "And such gentlemen, too. My goodness, one rarely sees such fine manners these days, more's the pity. I do see a lot of people, you know. All manner of folk come to Wisteria Grove these days. I'm Miss Violet Duvall, by the way. I am pleased to make your acquaintance."

Mason looked at Fort, giving him a crooked smile. It was obvious the old lady wanted to talk, and Mason Beaulieu was too finely bred to be rude to his elders. "Pleased to meet you as well, ma'am," Mason replied gallantly. "My colleague and I are quite interested in the house -- and in certain people who've been through it, too."

Fort couldn't bring himself to rush off either, and so he moved closer to Mason again. "Dr. Beaulieu is an engineer, and I'm a doctor of psychology. We share an interest in history and ghost stories, and Wisteria Grove has both in abundance," he said with a warm smile at Miss Violet.

Miss Violet returned the smile. She reached into her bag and pulled out a piece of intricate white crochet work, settling back in her chair with an air of sage wisdom. "Wisteria Grove does have its share of spirits," she replied, lowering her voice to a confidential tone. "There's the parlor maid who fell in love with the master of the house back in... oh, I think it was 1843. Before The War of Northern Aggression, you know. He got the poor girl with child, though not many folk know that, and when his wife found out... Lord a mercy, it was a sad thing. The wife -- that was the former Miss Allison Carruthers, and lands, did she have the temper to go with her red hair -- she had the girl whipped by the foreman. Hurt her so bad she died and the baby with her. Jealous Allison was, if you ask me, not so much of her husband but that the maid was carrying his child. Allison never had a baby of her own, you see, but not for lack of trying. The maid walks in the garden where she died, crying out for her unborn son to this day, poor thing. Such a sad, lost soul." She shook her head and sighed.

Mason stared at Miss Violet, then looked at Fort with a slight frown. "Have you heard that one before? I don't remember reading about it anywhere."

Fort was perplexed as well. He'd done a lot of research on Wisteria Grove, but he'd never run across that story either. "Can't say that I have. That name rings a bell, though," he said, making a note to check the records to see if there was indeed an Allison Carruthers attached to the house. "Where did you hear that story, Miss Violet?"

Her smile became crafty. "Gentlemen, a lady can't reveal her secrets! But you can trust me, every word is as true as the Gospel. The maid was Miss Lucy Finch, and she's buried out at the Saint Louis cemetery in town. Allison wouldn't stand for her being in the family plot, you know. I think if her husband had outlived her, he would have had the grave moved, but the Rouxchambeau family always did have short lives and powerful bad luck in love."

"Is that so?" Mason was looking speculatively at the old lady, but then he sighed. "Miss Violet, I'd love to stay and chat with you and hear more of these fascinating tales, I truly would, but I have to escort my mother to a charity masquerade. I do hope to talk with you again sometime."

"As do I," Fort agreed. He didn't have a charity masquerade to attend, but he thought it would be unfair to sit and listen to her stories without Mason present, since they both were curious. "But I need to be getting on home myself."

"I appreciate you fine young men spending a little time listening to an old lady rattle on." Miss Violet smiled again, revealing dimples in her wrinkled cheeks. "I have a good feeling I'll be seeing the two of you again, however, and my feelings are never wrong. Oh, yes. A very good feeling about the two of you."

Mason blinked, seeming a little taken aback from the certainty in Miss Violet's voice, but then he smiled and gave her a courtly, old-fashioned bow. "It would be an honor to speak with you again, ma'am."

Fort shook his head, amused by Mason's over-the-top antics. "Come on, Rhett. Let's get on out of here before they smell all that ham and throw you in the pot with the black-eyed peas."

For a moment, it looked as though Mason was going to retaliate in kind, but then he smiled beatifically. "Of course, Dr. Fortenberry. I'll go anywhere with you."

Miss Violet gave a girlish giggle, and Mason gave her a polite nod before turning and walking toward the door.

Fort resisted the temptation to roll his eyes at Mason's back, but just barely. Instead, he smiled at Miss Violet and followed Mason outside.

"I'll see you back here tomorrow. What time would you like to get started with the set-up?"

Mason turned and pulled out his phone, consulting the calendar. "I'm going to come by around one. Setting up the equipment is going to take a while, then we have to calibrate it and make sure the feeds are working correctly." He looked at Fort. "What were you planning to wear?"

"Something loose, comfortable, and warm. I'm not dressing up for the camera, and I don't want to get cold once the sun goes down." Fort pulled his keys out of his front pocket and turned toward the parking lot. "I'll be here at one, too. I don't have much equipment to set up, since mine is mostly hand-held, so I'll be glad to help with yours if you want me to."

"Sure. And don't forget the MoonPies!" Tucking his phone back into his pocket, Mason smiled. "'Til tomorrow, then."

Fort nodded and headed off to his pick-up, his mind already busy with lists and plans for the investigation ahead, along with a mental reminder to do some follow-up research on Miss Violet's story about the maid. If there was any possible truth to it, they might want to add the garden to their list of places to concentrate on. With any luck, their investigation would give the viewers a Halloween treat to remember.

5

Halloween morning dawned bright and sunny, but by the time Mason had finished loading equipment into the trunk of his car, clouds had started to roll in from the north, heralding a cold front and possible thunderstorms by the evening. While thunder and lightning would no doubt add to the atmosphere of Wisteria Grove and boost the number of watchers for the show, it could play hell with the recordings and invalidate most of the data. He reminded himself this was more about theater than science anyway; the real hope was that the show would help promote tourism in the area, drawing visitors from the bright lights of New Orleans to the quieter countryside. Mason supposed he could stand to deal with spurious electrical readings and unusable EVP recordings if it meant more people would visit Wisteria Grove and the little town of Boulard Crossing.

When he arrived at the plantation, the sky was completely overcast, and he cast an anxious eye upward as he opened his trunk. He wanted to get everything inside without it getting ruined, even if he might not get any good readings.

Not five minutes later, Fort's battered truck pulled up, and Fort parked beside Mason. He climbed out of the truck and sauntered over to Mason's car, greeting Mason with a smile. As he'd said, he had dressed casually in dark cargo pants and a zippered Tulane hoodie with a thermal shirt peeking from the neckline.

"Looks like we're going to have to move fast," he remarked as he peered into the trunk. "What do you want me to take?"

"Talk about riding to the rescue!" Mason smiled at Fort in relief, while surreptitiously taking a moment to admire Fort's tall, rangy body. "If you can take that big case in the corner, it would help a lot. You don't have to carry it. It has wheels on the bottom and a handle. It has the infrared cameras, so it's probably the most fragile of the bunch."

"No problem." Fort reached in and hauled out the case, setting it carefully on its wheeled bottom and pulling out the handle. Mason was pleased to see he treated the case with care, making sure to jostle it as little as possible as he wheeled it into the hotel -- and the cargo pants gave Mason a nice view of his firm ass as he walked away.

It was a pity Fort never seemed to show the slightest bit of interest in him, and Mason sighed as he lifted out a heavy crate of audio equipment, putting it on the wheeled folding cart he'd brought along. His verbal sallies -- like calling Fort "Dr. Woody" -- rarely got more than a raised eyebrow in response. None of the teasing or light-hearted flirting he'd done when they'd met at conferences seemed to faze Fort at all. Mason was self-aware enough to know he was considered rather attractive, so all he could figure was he simply wasn't Fort's type. Nevertheless he'd dressed in jeans and a snug black pullover, hoping that by the end of the night, perhaps Fort might decide he was worth a second look after all.

He hurried to load the rest of the equipment onto the cart, then closed the trunk and hurried toward the building as the first fat rain-drops began to fall. He got everything piled on the porch, then shook water droplets from his dark hair before transferring everything inside.

Catherine, the director, was in the foyer. "Good timing," she said when he finished hauling in his equipment. She pointed to two head-mounted, wearable camera rigs on a side table. "I'm just here

to get you two wired up and do the audio and video checks. The
crew has swept the premises to make sure everyone else is gone, and
we've locked all the exterior doors and windows so no one can sneak
in on you. There's a central alarm panel behind the reception desk
that can monitor everything, too, so if you get worried about
someone trying to crash the party, you can figure out how they
got in."

"Sounds good. Let me get my stuff out of the truck right quick,
okay? I'll be right back." Fort disappeared out the door, and he
returned quickly, carrying a medium-sized reinforced bag. His
clothes were spotted with wet splotches, and his auburn hair was
flecked with raindrops.

For a moment, all Mason could do was stare. Part of it was
because Fort had come to his aid before dealing with his own things,
which was incredibly nice of him, but a larger part was because a
damp, flushed Fort was even more appealing than Mason could ever
have imagined. He wanted to run his fingers through Fort's wet hair.

He got a grip on himself, deciding to return Fort's kindness.
"Would you like me to get you a towel? You might get chilled if you
don't dry off."

"I'd appreciate it." Fort smiled at him, a more open and warm
smile than Mason usually saw. "I'd hate to spend All Saints' Day laid
up with the sniffles."

Mason nodded, then turned and walked down the hall to where
he'd noted a linen closet the previous day. He took out a big, soft
towel and returned, handing it to Fort, wanting to see that warm
smile again. It was the most hopeful sign he'd seen yet that Fort
might consider him more than a skeptical rival who didn't believe in
anything he couldn't record or quantify.

"We definitely don't want you getting sick," he said teasingly. "If
you sneeze too much, you might scare away the spirits."

Fort made a scoffing noise as he toweled off his face and hair and
blotted his clothes. "No more than you running your mouth all
night will."

"Oh, there are things that will shut me up." Mason gave him an innocent look, trying not to feel let down by Fort's comment. "You just have to find out what they are."

"Duct tape, maybe?" Fort matched his innocent look easily.

"Duct tape has its uses, some of them quite interesting," Mason agreed, offering Fort a brief, wicked smile. Then he looked at Catherine. "Shall we get started on wiring us up? Then you can get out of here before the thunder and lightning move in."

Catherine hooked up their head-mounted cameras with brisk efficiency, did a check with the technicians back at the station who would be monitoring the feed, and nodded with satisfaction when everything seemed to be working properly. Then she ran them through the schedule. "You'll need to turn the cameras on shortly before seven o'clock, and we'll begin live streaming right at seven. It'll be broadcast on our website, with occasional cut ins on channel ten, and the cameras will record everything so you can review the footage later. We'll turn off the feed at one o'clock, so it'll be up to you whether you continue investigating after that, but no one will be here to unlock the doors until six o'clock tomorrow morning. Unless there is an emergency, of course, in which case we'll deal with it as best we can." She glanced back and forth between them. "Any questions?"

"I'm good," Fort replied.

"So am I." Mason removed his camera. "I don't want to mess it up while I'm crawling around hooking up the other equipment, but I'll have it back on by seven, don't worry."

With a nod and a cheery goodbye, Catherine departed, locking the front door from the outside as she left. There was an emergency exit through the French doors to the veranda, which the fire marshal had insisted upon, but other than that, they were locked in with only each other and any supposed spirits.

After a glance at his watch, Mason rubbed his hands together. "Shall we get started? I can't wait to see what you think of my toys."

Fort's blue eyes were alight with genuine interest as he nodded. "I'm looking forward to seeing what you've got. I guess you've done a lot of customization?"

"Oh, yes." Mason smiled, pleased to be able to talk about his equipment. He was rather proud of the modifications he'd made, and Fort's interest was gratifying. "I modified the camera design from the one I sold a few years ago. That one was for things like military ops and security applications, with an internal processor to track and enhance human-sized creatures. But the kinds of things we might be looking for could be any size and actually might be *colder* than the surrounding air. So the processor I used for this model looks for both heat and the absence of heat, and it will track and lock on both."

Fort listened intently, looking impressed. "That sounds amazingly useful for investigations. Have you had any luck catching unusual images with it?"

"Nothing that we can't logically explain." Mason walked over to the case Fort had brought in for him, knelt down, opening it up to display the cameras. He held one of them up so Fort could see the various modifications. "But if there is ever anything for them to catch, these babies will do it. Here, if you take this one, I'll get another. I brought four, because I figured we'd only put them in rooms that are supposed to have spirits. That way we can catch any possible manifestation from the very beginning, not miss it because we're off in the opposite part of the house."

Fort accepted the camera Mason offered him and examined it closely, obviously pleased with the device. "Have you thought about selling these? There are investigation groups all over the world who'd pay out the nose for something like this. Hell, I'd take out a second mortgage on my house if I had to."

Mason looked at him, debating with himself about what he should say. He knew what he *wanted* to do, but he didn't want Fort to think he was looking for quid pro quo, or even worse, that he was throwing his wealth around. Then an idea occurred to him, and he smiled.

"Tell you what. I'll give you a couple of them, just for your use or for LaPS if you want to share. Subject them to all the rigors you think they should be able to undergo, and we'll see how they hold up. Then if you like them, maybe you'd be willing to write up an endorsement?"

"I'd be glad to." Fort's face lit up like a kid at Christmas at the offer, and he nodded eagerly. "Thanks, Mason, this is really generous of you."

It was all Mason could do to keep from reaching out to touch Fort. He looked damned appealing when he smiled, but Mason forced himself to simply shrug. Just because Fort was the first man to attract his interest, both physically and intellectually, in quite a while was no reason to act like a desperate teenager with a crush.

"I'm glad to do it. Just because we have different attitudes in our approaches to the paranormal doesn't mean I don't think what you and LaPS do isn't worthwhile. I used to believe, you know. But after so many years of natural phenomena and outright hoaxes, I'm afraid I've lost my sense of wonder about it all."

"That's too bad," Fort said softly, his expression turning sympathetic. "I admit, I was curious about your attitude. I got the impression that you looked down on us at LaPS, and I didn't know if it was because we don't debunk enough for your liking or because we have a medium and you think she's a fake."

"Neither, really." Mason looked down at the camera in his hands, fiddling with the mounting bracket. "I'm not saying I accept what your medium says, because I'm an engineer. I have to approach this from the standpoint of only accepting what can be proven scientifically. But as far as credulity... it's really more that the investigators in your group are 'the glass is half full' types, while NOPI sees the glass as being half empty. Believe me, if you can produce real scientific proof, I'll be the first one in line to congratulate you. But you can't quantify what your psychic does, and most of the time, you can't prove it, right? It's like Miss Violet's story yesterday. Yes, it sounds plausible, and possibly it did happen just the way she says it did, but there are no records and no proof, so it's a story, not history."

"I can't quantify it, no, but Sarah has told me things about my family that she couldn't possibly know." Fort shrugged and smiled slightly. "Maybe I just want to believe too much and that colors my judgment, but I've experienced things I can't explain, even if I can't prove it well enough for it to hold up in a court of law."

"I'm envious," Mason admitted with a crooked smile. "I've been able to explain everything I've encountered. I'd love to experience something special. Something that could make me believe again." He cleared his throat. "I guess we should get busy setting all this stuff up, or we won't be done in time."

"I guess we should." Fort gave Mason a long, measured look before his usual easy-going smile returned. "I've done set-up work a time or two with LaPS, so just point me in the direction you want me to go. We'll get done quicker if we work separately."

Fort was right, but Mason felt a bit disappointed. There was nothing he could do about it, of course, so he nodded. "If you can set that up in the dining room, I'll put this one in the Green Bedroom. I think the other two could go in the library and in the Pink Bedroom. How does that sound? Catherine should have had the crew run extension cords already."

"Works for me," Fort drawled as he began gathering up coils of extra extension cords and other necessary equipment. "Meet you back here when we're done?"

"Yes. Then we can figure out where to put the audio pick ups." He picked up a second camera, nodded to Fort, and turned toward the wing where the guest rooms were located to set up the cameras.

The Green Bedroom was a charming room, decorated in soft spring green with white eyelet curtains. It was too feminine for Mason's tastes, but he could admire the old-fashioned appeal of the decor. The room was supposed to be haunted by a young daughter of the Rouxchambeau family, who'd succumbed to a wasting sickness, possibly consumption. It was said the girl could be heard coughing in the middle of the night and that she could sometimes be seen standing at the window, staring outside at the world beyond that she could never enjoy.

After placing the camera on a dresser and pointing it toward the window, he plugged everything in, then moved on to the Pink Bedroom. This one was definitely too frilly, the wallpaper featuring dark pink roses on a lighter pink background and frilly little pillows dotting every flat surface. But the owners of Wisteria Grove kept it true to the history of the room, which had been the favorite place of the spinster sister of the Grove's owner during the Civil War. According to the stories, the lady had been a happy person who had been loved by the whole family. Supposedly she stayed close to this room, unwilling to leave the place where she'd been so happy.

Once he'd deployed the second camera, Mason returned to the foyer, closing the camera case and opening another case. This one held his computer equipment, his laptop and several hard drives where he would store the recorded audio. The microphones he used were very sensitive, and he winced as a rumble of thunder caused the glass of the windows to vibrate in their frames. It was going to play havoc with the recordings, but there wasn't anything he could do about it.

Fort ambled in a couple of minutes later. "Okay, I think we're good to go. Are you going to stream feeds from the cameras to your computer or just record everything since we don't have anyone around to monitor for us?"

Mason glanced up. "Oh! I forgot to mention the cameras have an integrated solid state hard drive for recording. Each one is five hundred gigabytes, and the processor has a real-time compression algorithm to maximize the amount of data that can be stored. We should be good for the whole night. There's even an onboard battery, but it's only good for about two hours. It's for power outages or operating in areas where we don't have electricity."

Fort let out a low whistle, his eyes widening as he looked at Mason. "Are you sure you want to hand over two of them? They're sounding more expensive all the time."

"We have a deal, and I won't let you go back on it." Mason was glad he hadn't mentioned how much the cameras could do before Fort had agreed to take them, or he might have turned them down. "I built them myself, if that makes you feel better, so it's mostly just the cost of the components. We're not starving grad students anymore, remember? Don't worry about it."

"Let's just say I'm glad all you want is an endorsement, because I think I really would have to take out a second mortgage to pay for one." Fort chuckled. "Although to be honest, if that thing could brew coffee, I'd marry it. It's that perfect."

Mason reached into the pile of equipment, pulling out a canvas bag and opening it. He smiled as he held out a large thermos to Fort. "It can't brew coffee, but I can. Perhaps we can talk about taking the two of us as a package deal."

Fort shot him a startled look and raised one eyebrow questioningly as he accepted the thermos. "Are you serious or are you just running your mouth, trying to get a rise out of me again?"

For once, Mason wished he had kept his big mouth shut, but he hadn't been able to resist the opening. He *had* been half joking, but in a flirtatious way. He wasn't a man who took big risks when it came to other people, and his teasing probably covered up more insecurity than he was comfortable admitting to, but he was attracted to Fort, and he wouldn't mind seeing where it went.

"I'm not trying to get a rise out of you," he said quietly. "I think you're a very attractive, intelligent man, and I already know you're gay. We have a lot in common, and I wouldn't mind at all getting to know you better. I've always gotten the feeling you don't like me very much. That's the only reason I haven't asked you out."

"Only because I thought you didn't have a lot of respect for me." Fort watched Mason intently, his expression unusually serious. "Calling me Dr. Woody, all those times you tried to get under my skin, all the comments about LaPS."

"I was teasing you, but I wasn't trying to be mean," Mason protested, rising to his feet and facing Fort directly. "Hasn't anyone ever flirted with you before? I'm sorry if anything I said was hurtful to you. It wasn't meant to be. I only tease people I like; no one else is worth the effort."

"The men who've flirted with me before called me names I *like*," Fort pointed out, although a smile tugged at his lips. "I wasn't hurt. I assumed you didn't really respect me or the group I investigate with, so you poked fun at us. I just let it roll off, because there isn't any point in getting all riled up over a difference of opinion. If all you meant to do was tease, well, I'll look at it in a different light from now on."

"I swear, Fort, I was only teasing. I told you I was envious of you, didn't I? I never meant you to think I didn't respect you." Mason smiled sheepishly. "I confess I do have reservations about the psychic, but if that's the way you go about things, I don't knock it. Well, I don't knock it *much* and never to anyone outside of our little community."

Fort laughed and reached out to clap his hand on Mason's shoulder. "It's fine. I know plenty of people think mediums are as full of shit as a Christmas turkey."

Mason grinned, relieved that Fort wasn't offended, and he was encouraged that Fort had actually touched him. Maybe he could talk Fort into going out with him after all. "My, my, I don't think I want to be invited to your house for Christmas supper if that's what you cook with."

"If you're invited to my house for Christmas supper, we won't need a turkey to have something full of shit," Fort retorted, but his voice held a lighter note than Mason had ever heard in his rejoinders before.

"Why, Dr. Fortenberry, are you flirting with me?" Mason batted his eyelashes playfully. "If you keep saying such sweet things, you'll turn my head."

Fort made a scoffing noise, but he smiled at Mason, and there was a gleam in his eyes Mason hadn't seen before. "I'm just trying to figure out how to speak your language so we can have a meeting of the minds. Seems we've both been pretty far off the mark until now."

Mason's breath caught, and he turned more serious. "If you have any questions, just ask. I know I spout a lot of nonsense at times, but I can speak plainly."

"I might have a few questions, but not right now." Fort glanced at his watch and held it up so Mason could see the time. "We should start getting ready for the investigation."

For the first time he could remember, Mason was annoyed at having work interfere with his personal life. Perhaps he was being overly optimistic, but after almost four years of crossing verbal swords with Fort, it seemed they might finally be ready to lay down their arms. He had no idea how this night would end up, and it was entirely possible he'd open his big mouth and say something that would alienate Fort again. He'd prefer to reach an understanding with Fort before that happened, but they *had* made a commitment to this investigation, and since other people were depending on him, he couldn't screw it up.

"I suppose so," he replied with a sigh. "Let's get these microphones deployed. I think we should try to avoid the windows and not put them close to anything crystal or metallic that might resonate with the thunder."

"Good idea." Fort cocked his head, listening to the growing rumble overhead, and frowned. "That's going to play hell with our audio. But it adds to the creepy atmosphere for the audience, so maybe it's a good thing."

"That's what I was thinking earlier, actually. It's less about the investigation and more about garnering interest for the town." Mason returned his attention to the microphones, handing three of the rigs to Fort. "We have enough to cover every room and the hallways, if we can find places for them. The audio will stream back to the computer for time encoding and storage. I guess we'd better hurry if we're going to have time to run a systems check and eat before we go live."

Fort took the rigs and headed out, pausing at the door. "Save room for the dessert. I brought banana MoonPies." He gave Mason a smile and a little wink, and then he was gone.

Had Dr. Haywood Fortenberry actually *winked* at him? Mason stared after him for a moment, then shook himself and hurriedly gathered up the rest of the mics. He was far more interested in investigating this new understanding between him and Fort than any non-existent ghosts.

6

"Hey, y'all, I'm Fort from the Louisiana Paranormal Society, LaPS for short." Fort spoke directly to the audience watching them on the live stream. In some ways, it was odd because he wasn't accustomed to narrating an investigation other than to mark times, locations, and things to pay attention to during the review. But he had recorded podcast lectures for his classes, so he was more familiar with the idea of speaking to an invisible audience than Mason was.

"This is Mason from New Orleans Paranormal Investigation or NOPI," Fort continued. "We're here at Wisteria Grove for our first joint Halloween investigation. Wisteria Grove is a former plantation that's been renovated as a bed and breakfast, but it's more famous for its ghosts than its room service. Wisteria Grove has been called the most haunted house in southern Louisiana, and people come here all year round, hoping for some chills and thrills. Some guests even swear they were driven away by ghosts. We'll talk about where we are and the kind of equipment we use throughout the night, and you can also find more information on our groups' websites."

While Fort provided the commentary, they made their way through the darkened hallways to the kitchen with only flashlights and small lights on their head cameras for illumination. Every light in the house had been turned off along with every appliance and electronic device that could safely be deactivated to minimize the electric interference with their equipment. The result was near total darkness and an eerie silence throughout the house, making their breathing and their footsteps seem louder.

"Mason is going to start off using a camera of his own making," Fort continued. "I'll let him explain all about it in a minute. I've got a digital recorder, which I'll use to try to pick up what we call EVPs or electronic voice phenomenon."

Once they reached the kitchen, he stopped and shone his flashlight around for the audience's benefit. "We're going to begin our investigation in the kitchen, where people claim to have seen a woman in a maid's uniform and where pots and pans allegedly move around by themselves. As some of you may know, the kitchen wouldn't have been inside the house when Wisteria Grove was first built. The kitchen was in a separate building at a safe distance away to decrease the risk of a kitchen fire spreading to the main house. We know that in the early twentieth century, the back of the main house was expanded to incorporate the old kitchen building."

He moved to the far side of the room, where a large brick fireplace took up most of one wall, and pulled out his digital recorder. "Records show the kitchen building burned down and was rebuilt at least three times that we know of. Although there's no evidence of any fatalities, there's a chance someone might have been injured or killed in one of the fires, which may account for the spirit activity."

Mason had his head camera pointed at Fort, picking up what he was doing. He smiled, giving Fort a playful wink. "Kitchens also have a great deal of pipe in the walls, as well as metallic pots and pans, and a lot of electrical current in the various appliances. Those things can't be discounted as possible causes of unusual occurrences."

"Of course not." Fort smiled back at Mason and inclined his head to acknowledge the point. "We'll make every attempt to find a rational explanation for any allegedly irrational experience we have tonight."

He fully expected Mason to try to debunk everything, and maybe

Mason *would* be able to. Fort had been on plenty of investigations that turned up nothing. Either no one on the team experienced anything and none of the equipment provided any information, or everything was easily proved to have some normal, logical cause. If that was the case tonight, so be it, although deep down, he hoped it wasn't. He wasn't ashamed to admit he was sentimental enough to hope they experienced something that would let Mason regain his sense of wonder about the world and about what they did.

Mason held up the camera in his hands. "While Fort tries to get EVPs, I'm going to scan the kitchen with this camera. It's designed to detect variations from background temperature, whether positive or negative. It's a handheld version of the motion-sensor ones we have set up elsewhere in the house. We'll need to turn out the lights to use it, but I've slaved the camera output into my video feed, so all of you will be able to see what we see in the viewfinder." He motioned to Fort. "The screen is big enough that you can see, too. Want to come over here and turn of the flashlight and your head light?"

Fort didn't hesitate to join Mason, and while he knew they probably wouldn't be so lucky as to have some unexplainable form pop up on the screen as soon as the camera was turned on, he couldn't help but feel excitement and anticipation at the possibility. He doused his flashlight and head light as he stood close to Mason, close enough to feel Mason's body heat radiating through his clothes, and it made Fort shiver slightly.

"Ready when you are," he said huskily.

"Right." It might have been his imagination, but he thought Mason sounded a little breathless. Then Mason turned off his own head lamp, and the room was completely dark.

Mason held up the camera, the view screen's faint luminescence glowing eerily in the darkness. "What you're seeing is even more than what we can see, since you're looking in the infrared spectrum which is invisible to the human eye. You can see how some of the appliances glow in a different color, showing they're a slightly different temperature than the air around us. And of course Fort and I glow like Christmas trees." He turned the lens of the camera on himself, and

Fort saw the red, yellow, and green of the heat signature of Mason's body in the view screen. Then Mason turned the camera again and began to slowly pan around the kitchen, his arm brushing against Fort's. "See anything unusual, Fort?"

"No, not yet, but the night is young." Fort felt a little twinge of disappointment that nothing had popped up on the screen, but perhaps one of the other rooms would yield better results. "Do you want to keep looking around in here with that while I try for some EVPs?"

"That works." Mason stepped slightly away and turned the camera to point at Fort. "Go ahead. I'll keep you in frame, just in case something decides to snuggle up to you while you're talking."

There's only one thing in here I'd like to have snuggled up to me. The thought rose up in Fort's mind unbidden, and he was glad Mason couldn't see his face, because he felt his cheeks growing hot. Now that he knew Mason was teasing rather than mocking him and he understood the disappointment behind Mason's cynical attitude, Fort wasn't as wary, which apparently meant the attraction he'd been ignoring all this time intended to cut loose at last.

"Good idea. If there's something here, it might get closer when I'm trying to communicate with it," was all he said aloud.

He flicked on his digital recorder as he moved away from Mason; with all their lights off, he had to rely on his own night vision to keep him from bumping into anything, so he moved slowly and carefully around the room.

"I'm going to ask some questions," he explained to the audience. "It's pretty simple. You ask basic questions to establish communication. Be sure to wait a few seconds between each question in case something answers you. You might not be able to hear it with your ears, but the recorder might catch it. Anything you want to add before we get started, Mason?"

"Only that after the playback, we'll also be analyzing the results to see if anything we've picked up has a natural explanation. We'll be sharing our findings, so folks can check on either the NOPI or LaPS website in a few days if they want to see what we've found."

"Right, because sometimes the strange voices people hear or that are picked up on tape can come from things like shortwave radio and other electronic devices. What we're hoping for are responses that are clearly answers to our specific questions." Fort held up his recorder, looking around even though he couldn't really see much of anything. Normally, he began by announcing the team members, but since it was only him and Mason that night, he decided to skip that formality. "We're in the kitchen of Wisteria Grove. Is there anyone with us right now?"

Fort waited a few seconds, then ran through the gamut of his usual questions, but if there was a response, it wasn't in range of human hearing. The kitchen remained silent and still. Fort wasn't a medium, but the room *felt* empty to him. Sometimes, a room with spirit activity felt different, as if there was energy present beyond that of the human occupants, but not this room.

"End session," he said and turned the recorder off. "I think we can head out. It doesn't seem like there's much going on in here. Is there anywhere you're particularly interested in checking out?"

"I wish it wasn't raining, so we could check out the garden. I'd love to verify that story Miss Violet told us." Mason turned off the infrared camera and clicked his head lamp back on, blinking in the sudden brightness. "But since that isn't on the table, why don't we try the main hall? People claim they've seen a bride on the stairs. The story is she fell and broke her neck on her wedding day."

"Poor girl," Fort murmured. He remembered hearing that story, and the family records backed it up. The bride in question had caught her heel on the hem of her wedding dress on her way down-stairs to be married in the gardens. If there was any truth to the theory that ghosts lingered at the sites of tragedy, surely those stairs qualified.

He turned on his head lamp and flashlight and rejoined Mason. "That sounds like a prime area to me. Let's go."

Mason led the way out of the kitchen. "One of the really inter-esting things about being a paranormal investigator is doing research on the location you're investigating. Wisteria Grove is interesting because of the number of deaths that have occurred here. Of course, any old house tends to have a couple of deaths associated with it, but Wisteria Grove has a particularly large number of tragedies in its history. There's no way to prove it, but some people believe certain places attract tragedy the way they attract spirits. Bad luck does seem to cling to some places, doesn't it?"

"Indeed it does." For some reason, Fort found himself reaching out to rest his hand on Mason's shoulder as they walked along, and he told himself it was to help him remain steady while his eyes adjusted to having some light again. "Battlefields are supposed to have a lot of spirit activity, for example. There's a reason why Gettysburg is called the most haunted place in the country."

"Now that's a place where I'd love to take my equipment." Mason turned his head and grinned at Fort, apparently not minding the hand on his shoulder. "There's actually a couple of ghost photos from there that even I haven't been able to completely explain. But I want to collect my own data, so I know it's done scientifically. It's harder to accept someone el--" He stopped suddenly, looking back over his shoulder with a frown. "Did you hear anything?"

Fort froze in place as well, and he tightened his fingers on Mason's shoulder. He thought he heard footsteps coming from the direction of the main staircase, but he couldn't quite be sure since they'd been talking. "I think so," he whispered. "Footsteps?"

"Yes." Mason tilted his head to one side, listening intently. A rumble of thunder sounded, rattling windows in their frames. "Damn. You might want to turn your recorder back on, just in case. Although it'll be a chore to edit out our own footsteps later."

Fort turned on his recorder as he moved more quickly toward the stairs, his heart beating faster with anticipation. "We're in the entrance hall, heading for the stairs. Check for footsteps that aren't ours. Is there anyone here with us?" He began his litany of questions, deciding to make them more specific since they knew who the spirit might be. "Are you a bride?" he asked, pausing before asking the next. "Did you fall on these steps?"

"Turn off your headlamp. I'm going to pan the staircase with the infrared," Mason whispered close to his ear, warm breath ghosting over Fort's skin.

Fort's skin tingled in response, and he had to fight back a soft moan. It had been a long time since he'd been with anyone, and apparently, his latent attraction to Mason had been unleashed in a stronger rush than he'd expected. He reached up to turn off his head lamp and doused his flashlight -- and all thoughts of attraction and arousal vanished at the sound of a crash from upstairs.

"What the hell was that?"

"I have no idea." Mason's headlamp was still on, and he looked up. "I think it was the Green Bedroom. Come on, let's go!" He reached out and grabbed Fort's hand, urging him up the stairs.

Fort clutched Mason's hand as he used his long legs to full advantage. His heart was pounding now, and he felt his adrenaline surging as he thought about what they might find in the bedroom.

The door to the room was open, and flickers of lightning were visible through the sheers over the window. Mason stepped into the room and groaned.

"Oh... fudge." He pointed to the floor, where one of the expensive motion-sensor cameras lay in pieces. "I don't know how that could have happened! I put it on the dresser, and it wasn't near the edge."

Fort stared at the remains of the expensive camera in dismay, not only because they would lose the opportunity to film in this room but also because of the personal loss for Mason. "I'm really sorry." He knelt and turned on his flashlight, training it on the pieces. "Do you think it's salvageable? Not tonight, but in general."

"Possibly, but that's not the important part." Mason knelt beside him and reached out to pick up the hard drive, and there was an odd tension in his movements. "This is. I hope it recorded whatever happened is on here. I can't believe that camera fell on its own."

"You're sure?" Fort didn't really doubt what Mason was saying, but they couldn't discount the possibility of human error. "You're positive you didn't put it anywhere near the edge? It wasn't sliding or moving at all?"

"I'm pretty sure," Mason said slowly. He rose and looked at the dresser. "It seems level, but I'm willing to entertain the notion that it isn't and the thunder rattled things enough to make it slide off. But I still want to check the hard drive." He drew in a deep breath. "Rest assured, I'm going to scrutinize this very, very carefully."

"We could check the dresser now," Fort suggested. "I've got some stuff downstairs. We could get the measuring tape and a bubble level at least."

"Works for me." Mason left the other pieces of the camera where they were. "Let's do it."

Fort stood up and waited for Mason before exiting the room and going back downstairs, finally remembering to turn off the digital recorder as he did. It didn't take long to rummage through his equipment and find the tools they needed, and they were back upstairs in the Green Bedroom in just a few minutes. He held out the measuring tape and bubble level out to Mason.

"Want to do the honors? This seems like your mystery to solve."

"Sure. Catch this on the voice recorder, okay?" Mason took the tools and set about measuring the distance from the dresser to the pieces of the camera, calling out each number. Then he drew in a breath and picked up the level. "Okay, moment of truth." He put the level on the dresser, watching carefully as the bubble moved. "Damn. It's not level. It's at least five degrees off true in the direction the camera fell."

Fort tried valiantly not to look or sound as disappointed as he felt. "I guess it was a slow slide, helped along by the thunder."

"Probably. But we won't know anything conclusive until I check the hard drive. Unfortunately, with the camera itself broken, I'll have to do that tomorrow back at NOPI. I don't want to sacrifice one of the other cameras to look at it right now." Mason actually seemed disappointed as well.

"No, it can wait." Fort flashed his light around the room, remembering the original noise they'd heard. "This doesn't explain the footsteps we heard."

"True." Mason straightened. "We can come back for this later. Shall we go back to the staircase? I still need to film it."

"Sure, just leave the level and the tape measure in here as well," Fort suggested. "We'll get everything when we take up the equipment in the morning."

"Right." With a brief smile, Mason turned for the door, then paused and waited for Fort to join him. "Well, this hasn't been a boring investigation, at least."

Fort laughed and shook his head. "No, definitely not," he replied, reaching out to touch Mason's shoulder again, although his hand landed more toward the middle of Mason's back, and he couldn't resist sliding it down briefly in an almost-caress.

Mason glanced back at him quickly, eyes wide, before his lips quirked in a rather naughty smile. Fort could practically see Mason holding back from saying what he wanted to say.

"If things are jumping this much before midnight, I can't wait to see what the main event is going to be like." Mason said at last.

Although Fort knew Mason was referring to the investigation, the naughty look made him wonder if Mason had another level of meaning beneath his words. Maybe it was the illusion of safety offered by the dark and of privacy offered by being locked in alone together, but he couldn't resist replying in kind.

"Maybe we're having a slow build to something explosive," he said, keeping his expression innocent.

"I sure do look forward to finding out." Mason grinned, then reached out and took Fort's hand, tugging him forward. "Come on. Let's get started."

Privately, Fort thought they already had a pretty good start, but he simply nodded and clasped Mason's hand. "Let's go, partner."

7

As he descended the stairs back down into the foyer, Mason could barely believe Fort was still holding his hand.

Apparently their little talk earlier in the day really had changed Fort's opinion of him, and Mason was very glad the news station had put together this little adventure. It had given him an opportunity to clear the air between them, and if Fort holding his hand, in addition to the caress down his back was any indication, Mason could probably talk him into a date before the evening was over. That was well worth spending Halloween locked in an empty house, even without the questionable presence of ghosts.

Unfortunately they still had several hours to fill for the watchers, so when they reached the bottom of the stairs, he released Fort's hand, but not before giving it a little squeeze. "I guess we should pick up where we left off, right? We still haven't tried to get the bride on a video recording."

"Right, and I didn't finish my EVP session," Fort replied. "Even if we don't see her, maybe she'll talk to us."

As though Fort's words were some kind of bizarre trigger, a woman's anguished scream of pain reached them from outside, rising over the rumbling thunder. Mason froze in place, the hair on the back of his neck standing up and a chill running down his spine. That had never happened to him during an investigation before, and pure shock held him immobile as the scream died away into choked sobs.

"What in the--" he gasped finally, and he ran toward the front door.

Fort raced to the door with him, and they both crowded around the windows, trying to see out. Neither of them bothered with the door since it had been locked, but Mason wondered how much trouble they would be in if they broke a window in case someone really was out there and either injured or in danger.

"Do you see anything?" Fort asked, looking worried as he kept trying to peer through the darkness.

The rain was slashing down, and flashes of lightning illuminated the sky, throwing the live oaks lining the drive into relief and highlighting the sodden plants of the front garden. Mason stared out, trying to see if anyone -- or any*thing* -- was moving, but other than the branches swaying in the wind, there didn't seem to be any possible source for the scream.

"No, nothing," he replied, still peering out. "Could it have been an animal? A loon is supposed to sound like a woman, or maybe a bobcat? I just can't--"

A particularly bright flash of lightning lit up the entire garden, and for one unbelievable moment, Mason could have sworn he saw a woman standing near a stone birdbath. She glowed almost as brilliantly as the lightning, and her image seemed seared on his eyes. With her hands over her face, she seemed to be sobbing, and her hair was in wild disarray around her shoulders.

Then the thunderclap sounded, and Mason felt the glass beneath his palms vibrating so strongly he was afraid it was going to shatter. He snatched his hands away, and when he focused again on the garden, the glowing figure was gone.

"I did not just see what I thought I saw." He looked at Fort, eyes wide. "It had to be an illusion of the lightning and shadows."

"Well, I don't know about you, but *I* saw a woman out there." Fort sounded as shaky as Mason felt, and his eyes were wide with shock as well.

"There's a logical explanation." Mason tried to inject a firm tone into his voice. "Plenty of people knew about this broadcast and knew we'd be locked in. The most likely thing is that some kids are trying to freak us out, knowing we can't get out there to prove anything."

"Good job, kids," Fort muttered as he took a couple of steps back from the window.

Mason's heart was still pounding, and he drew in a deep breath. "Yeah. Nice try, guys, and I'll admit you gave us a start, but no proof is still no proof. Back to the stairs for us. Maybe the third time will be the charm."

Fort seemed to shake off being spooked and grinned at Mason. "Maybe, although now I'm kind of curious about what else could happen to distract us from investigating the stairs."

"We're going to film those stairs if it kills us," Mason muttered, then snorted in amusement. "Okay, given that a woman died on them, that was a rather macabre thing to say, I admit. Anyway, let's do this."

Fort returned to the foot of the steps and turned his recorder back on. "We're in the entrance hall again. If anyone is with us and was trying to communicate with us earlier, we're sorry for all the interruptions, but maybe we can have a little chat now." He glanced over at Mason. "Want me to douse the lights?"

"Yes, please." Mason turned off his own head lamp and raised the camera. "Let's do this."

When Fort turned the lights off, Mason activated the camera again and panned the staircase. "Go for the rest of your EVPs. Maybe if your questions don't get an auditory response, something will show up on the video."

Fort began asking questions, tailoring them toward the specific entity that allegedly lingered on the stairs, but there were no more crashes or screams, and nothing showed up on the camera screen. When he finished his session, Fort turned his head lamp back on and turned to Mason.

"I didn't hear anything, but maybe we'll catch something on the playback. Did you see anything?"

"Only some flickers from the lightning." Mason turned off the camera and looked at his watch. "I don't know about you, but I'm ready for some coffee. After that fright, I think I need it to calm me down."

"Coffee and a banana MoonPie?" Fort flashed a teasing smile at him. "I brought a couple of those unnatural things for you and a couple of normal, *original* MoonPies for me."

"Nothing unnatural about banana." Mason grinned in return. "Let's get our snack and discuss what we want to do next."

Once they'd opened the thermos and Fort had produced the promised snacks, Mason settled down on one of the chairs near the reception desk and smiled at Fort in invitation. "It's been an exciting evening so far. Not that we have conclusively seen anything we can verify, but the place is definitely jumping."

"I'm already looking forward to examining the evidence." Fort nodded as he sat down and snagged one of the MoonPies. "If we don't have some decent EVPs, I'll eat one of those nasty banana abominations."

"You heard it here, folks! We have a wager!" Mason grinned and bit into his MoonPie, humming with pleasure at the sweet, familiar taste. "If we *do* get something that I can't put a rational explanation to... Hm. I like regular MoonPies, too. So what kind of forfeit would do in exchange?"

"Well, it needs to be something you wouldn't necessarily want to do." Fort gave Mason a long, measured look as he sipped his coffee. "Okay, I've got it. If we do collect evidence tonight that you can't find a logical explanation for, you'll let Sarah, our medium, read you."

"Sure." Mason shrugged easily, returning Fort's regard steadily. "Since I'm a skeptic, I'm not worried about her seeing any deep, dark secrets. She'll find me rather hard to convince."

"Then it shouldn't be any worse than me having to eat a banana MoonPie." Fort lifted his cup in a silent toast.

"Indeed." Mason sipped at his own coffee, glad for a moment's respite before they started up again. "What's next? The Master Suite where old Colonel Rouxchambeau murdered the Yankee general who occupied Wisteria Grove after the Fall of New Orleans? Or would you prefer the Red Bedroom, where Miss Serafina Rouxchambeau supposedly entertained her Yankee lieutenant lover until he left her and she hanged herself?"

"Hmm... Let's try the Master Suite first. Isn't that where guests have reported feeling the bed shake and having their covers pulled off?"

"It certainly is." Mason put aside his coffee cup and stood, brushing a few crumbs from his shirt. He picked up his infrared camera. "Let's get to it!"

For the next three hours, they made their way through the house. Fort did EVPs in each room, while Mason used the infrared camera. They heard sounds a few times, but since the storm was continuing outside, Mason was unwilling to admit that any of the bumps, taps, or groans they heard could have a supernatural origin. At one point, they heard a prolonged creaking and scratching from the attic, but the owners of the inn had asked them not to go up there, since it was full of junk and they weren't certain it was safe for anyone to go poking around in the dark. Mason had dismissed it as probably a tree limb scraping against the roof, although he waited patiently while Fort recorded a segment of the sound for later analysis.

"It's coming up on midnight now. The witching hour," Mason said in a deep, theatrical voice. "Where should we spend it? None of the motion-sensor cameras have alerted any activity, so I think the dining room, the library, and the Pink Bedroom aren't worth more effort. Other than the owner's office, I think all we have left is the sitting room, although no activity has been reported there."

"We might as well cover it," Fort replied. "We can do a thermal sweep and maybe an EVP session just for the sake of thoroughness."

"Sounds like a plan!" Even if the investigation hadn't yielded anything worthwhile, the evening, in Mason's opinion, had been quite productive. Despite the fact that they had to keep their words innocuous, Fort had often touched him, not intimately perhaps, but in a way that Mason couldn't deny was flirtatious. Mason had responded in kind, resting a hand on Fort's back while he did the EVPs or pressing his shoulder against Fort's as he shared the viewfinder of the video camera. It was enough to keep Mason a bit wound up and a little frustrated, and now they were coming to the end of the investigation, he was eager for it to be over so he and Fort could talk without an audience. Or even better, *not* talk.

He led the way back downstairs, and they entered the small sitting room they'd been in the day before. "Even though there are no ghosts associated with this room, we're going to give it a look-see anyway," he said to the listening audience. "It's a very restful room, so I can imagine that if there were spirits here, they'd be very laid back, and--"

Mason stopped abruptly as the light from his head lamp fell on the chair by the window. Unbelievably, there was someone sitting in it, the light gleaming on her white hair and sparkling in her blue eyes.

"Miss Violet?" he gasped. "What in the world are you doing here?"

"Hello, boys!" she replied gaily, her smile full of mischief. "Are you surprised to see me?"

"Well, yes ma'am, we are." Fort was staring at her as well. "This whole building is supposed to be closed off to visitors and staff until tomorrow morning. We weren't expecting anyone to be in here but us."

"I'm not a visitor. I live here," the old lady said complacently. "So I can't leave. I hope that doesn't interfere with your plans."

"Uh... No, ma'am." Mason gave Fort a wry smile. It was too late to do anything about it, of course, but Miss Violet's presence would probably invalidate a lot of their data, since they couldn't be certain the footsteps they'd heard weren't hers. But it was hard to argue with someone old enough to be his grandmother, and it was possible the staff had overlooked her when they were clearing the building. "We'll manage." A thought suddenly occurred to him. "Did you hear a scream in the garden a few hours ago? I hope that wasn't you out there in the rain!"

Miss Violet laughed. "Oh, lands no, child, that wasn't me. It was Lucy Finch, crying for her son. Didn't I tell you she died on October 31st? Poor lost soul, she'll never rest." She sighed and shook her head sadly.

"What about the camera in the bedroom upstairs?" Fort asked, looking dismayed. "Were you up there? Did you accidentally knock it over?"

"No, that wasn't me." Miss Violet shook her head and folded her hands primly in her lap. "Little Katie doesn't like people staring at her. It makes the poor thing self-conscious. She was so thin at the end, just a wasted shell, and she couldn't bear for anyone to look at her."

Mason blinked. "Little Katie? Is that the girl who is supposed to haunt the bedroom? Have you seen her? Are you saying *she* knocked the camera over?"

The old lady laughed. "Well Lord a'mercy, of course I've seen her! I've seen all the spirits who live here at Wisteria Grove. I've been here a long time, and they have all gotten to know me."

Fort nodded, as if he understood. "You must be sensitive to the presence of spirits."

For a moment, Miss Violet's smile became far too innocent to be innocent. "Oh, I think that's safe to say, Dr. Fortenberry. But the spirits here are mostly tragic ones. Give me a good, hot-blooded romance over a woebegone soul any day! I never married, but I do have an eye for seeing when folks are suited for each other."

"Oh, really?" Mason was surprised by her comment, and he cast a sidelong glance at Fort. "You must see a lot of couples come through Wisteria Grove, then."

"It's a romantic place, sure enough." She nodded, and her smile was suddenly that of a naughty girl. "Don't tell me the two of you haven't felt it. The Rouxchambeaus might have been unlucky in love, but neither of you will be."

Fort glanced away and rubbed the back of his neck. "No offense, but I wouldn't exactly call the dead of night in the middle of a storm romantic. That seems more like a 'June in broad daylight' thing."

"Perhaps for most people, but then, you two aren't most people, are you?" She laughed. "Oh, you're not the first pair of men I've seen, but you certainly are two of the most interesting. June in broad daylight is fine for brides with stars in their eyes, but I'm thinking October and thunderstorms suit the two of you much better. It's the thrill of the hunt, isn't it? Ghosts and ghouls and things that go bump in the night."

Mason blinked in surprise, unable to believe she'd nailed his own preferences so exactly. "Well... I can't deny that, ma'am," he said slowly, then turned to look at Fort, wanting to hear what Fort had to say. Mason might not believe in psychics, but perhaps someone as old as Miss Violet had developed a keen insight into people. "Can you?"

"No, not really," Fort admitted, glancing sidelong at Mason.

"There, you see? Sometimes it's that simple." Miss Violet nodded sagely, picked up her bag from beside the chair, and rose gracefully to her feet. "Well, it's time I was going. It's nearly midnight, and you boys have things to do." With a wave she moved past them, trailing the scent of lemon verbena behind her.

Mason drew in a breath. "Yes, ma'am. Goodnight. It was a pleasure talking to you again."

"Good night, ma'am," Fort echoed, waiting until she was out of the room to turn to Mason. "Well, that's not good."

"What?" Mason stared at him, wondering if he'd read Fort incorrectly after all. He'd thought Fort was interested in him, and surely Miss Violet's words were an almost blunt encouragement. He swallowed his disappointment, not wanting Fort to think he was some kind of mushy romantic. "I'm sorry you see it that way."

Fort looked at him like he'd suddenly sprouted two heads. "How am I supposed to see it any other way? Our entire night's work is compromised because someone was in here the whole time and we didn't know it. We might as well pitch everything out the window and go home."

"I..." Mason suddenly realized Fort was talking about the investigation, and he chuckled, breathless with relief, looking into the camera mounted on Fort's head. "Well, it's not a complete loss if Miss Violet is right about the camera being tossed by a ghost. We'll get on that analysis tomorrow and see if there is evidence that the ghost in that bedroom did it." He paused suddenly. "Wait a minute, speaking of bedrooms, where exactly is Miss Violet staying? I mean, we've been in all the bedrooms, haven't we?"

"Yes..." Fort said slowly, rubbing his chin as he frowned. "But maybe she's been moving around, and we missed her until now."

"I suppose that must be it." Mason frowned, something about that idea bothering him. "Come on, let's go ask her where she's staying. Lord help us if she's in the Pink Bedroom. The camera might give her a fright when she goes in there and it starts tracking her!" He began to move quickly to the double doors, opening them and stepping out into the hallway.

Fort followed close behind, but when they entered the hallway, they found it empty and silent. "Huh." Fort peered into the darkness, his frown deepening. "I didn't think she could move that fast."

Mason shrugged. "I suppose she's as spry as she is smart." He smiled at Fort teasingly. "Come on, let's check on the Pink Bedroom, just in case."

They went up the stairs quickly, but the door to the Pink Bedroom stood open, and the room was dark and empty. Mason didn't want to disturb the camera, so he motioned for them to go back downstairs, and they returned to the sitting room.

"Well, we'll have to process all the data with an eye toward Miss Violet's presence, but we still might find something." He glanced at his watch. "Damn, we missed midnight! It's almost a quarter after now!"

"We've got forty-five minutes until the official investigation ends." Fort looked down at the digital recorder in his hand and then tucked it in his pocket. "At least it sounds like the storm is moving off finally."

Mason became aware that the thunder wasn't crashing, and that the flares of lightning had gotten fewer and farther between. "I guess it has. Well, folks, I won't say this has been a typical investigation, because it hasn't, but it's been interesting. One of the things we learn in doing paranormal investigations is that we have to roll with the unexpected, no matter what it is."

"Exactly," Fort agreed. "Sometimes we get pleasant surprises. Sometimes not. Either way, we have to adapt and move forward."

"Hopefully everyone has enjoyed watching and getting to see how we do our research. What you've seen tonight is only a small fraction of what goes on, however. We'll be posting the results of our analysis of the recordings as we complete them, so be sure to check the NOPI and LaPS websites. If anyone is interested in taking part in either organization, you're always free to contact us, or if you have a house you believe is haunted, we'd love to hear from you."

Fort shot him a questioning look, one eyebrow raised, but he didn't offer to stop Mason from wrapping things up early. "I believe the TV station said they would put up links to our websites on their site, or you can find them with a web search. Thanks for joining us. Happy Halloween!"

Reaching up, Fort turned off his camera and removed the headset, finger-combing his hair back into place. Mason watched as he removed his own camera, then reached out to turn on one of the table lamps, providing a soft, low light, which was still bright enough to make him blink after being in darkness for hours.

"Sorry about the abrupt ending, but you were right. There wasn't much point in continuing, not with Miss Violet in the house. It's only a bit early, and we missed anything that might have happened at midnight anyway. Although I can't say I found the evening entirely without merit, to be honest."

"Oh?" Fort regarded him quizzically. "Is it because you're a lot more confident about making me eat a banana MoonPie now?"

"No. I don't give a damn about the MoonPie." Mason gave Fort an inviting smile, deciding to be forthright. If Fort wasn't interested getting to know each other much, much better, Mason wanted to know right now. "There are much better things I'd like you to do with your mouth."

Fort's shocked expression quickly faded into something softer and warmer. "I'm certainly open to any suggestions you might have."

Well, *that* was certainly encouraging, and Mason stepped closer, lips quirking into a wicked smile. "Then come over here, Dr. Fortenberry, and let's see if you kiss as sweetly as you talk."

Fort didn't hesitate to accept the invitation, sliding his arms around Mason's waist and snugging Mason up against his tall, lean body. Bending his head, he brushed his lips against Mason's lightly before returning for a deeper taste.

Mason wrapped his arms around Fort's shoulders, moaning softly and parting his lips in invitation. Fort's body felt wonderful against his, firm and warm, and he pressed closer, liking the way they fit together. He slid his fingers into Fort's hair, enjoying the way it felt as silken-soft as it looked. Fort continued the kiss at a leisurely pace, seeming to savor the taste and feel of Mason's mouth, and he slid his hands down to Mason's ass, bringing their bodies into even closer alignment.

When they broke apart at last, Mason looked up into Fort's eyes, managing a breathless smile. "Dare I hope that was better than a banana MoonPie?"

"I ought to be the one asking you that since I don't like banana MoonPies." Fort gave him a teasing smile. "But I sure did like *that.*"

"Oh, I can easily say you're much, much better than a MoonPie, no matter the flavor." Mason ran his fingers through Fort's hair again, enjoying the way Fort felt, still firmly pressed against him. "You feel good, too. I scored the best treat for Halloween. Eat your heart out, kids."

Fort laughed softly and gave Mason's ass a playful swat. "Here we are, locked in a dark, mostly empty house together until morning. I guess continuing the investigation is out of the question, so what do you suggest we do to pass the time?"

Mason knew what he'd like to do, but he wanted more, too. "Well, before we do anything at all, I want to make sure you aren't just looking to pass some time. Up until tonight, you didn't have a very high opinion of me. I don't want to turn into a pumpkin when the sun rises."

"Up until tonight, I didn't think you had a very high opinion of *me*," Fort pointed out. "But that never stopped me from finding you attractive. I think it's a given we have a lot in common. Maybe we'll never see eye to eye on the credibility of mediums, EVPs, and orbs, but I think we can agree to disagree if we want to try dating and seeing where this goes."

Now *that* was what Mason wanted to hear, and he grinned. "That sounds like an excellent plan, Dr. Fortenberry. In that case, I see a perfectly nice sofa right behind you. I don't mind acting like a teenager and giving you an opportunity to see what base you can get to."

Fort began walking Mason backwards until they reached the sofa. He dropped down on it and pulled Mason after him, getting them both caught in a delicious tangle. "On the first date? I had no idea you were that kind of boy."

"Is this our first date?" Mason grinned as he pressed Fort down, enjoying the hardness of Fort's body beneath him. "Whether it is or not, I'm willing to be exactly that kind of boy for you." He batted his eyelashes.

"Well, we're in a public place and I provided MoonPies, which might technically count as taking you out for dinner. If we're okay with a very loose interpretation of the concept, this is our first date." Fort grabbed a throw pillow and tucked it under his head as he shifted to stretch out on his back. "Lucky for you, I'm that kind of boy too."

"Perfect. Except you talk too much," Mason said, leaning down and capturing Fort's lips again. He shifted slightly, moaning against Fort's lips at the friction of their bodies rubbing together, the clothing between them muting the sensation. But it was still enough to turn Mason on, and he deepened the kiss, wondering if he could tease Fort to the edge of losing control.

Fort slid his hands down the length of Mason's back in a leisurely caress and let them come to rest on Mason's hips. He parted his lips as he rocked his hips up, teasing Mason with more friction. Mason slipped one leg between Fort's, rocking back against him, enjoying the slow easy rhythm. He broke the kiss, but only so that he could nibble his way along Fort's strong jaw, then up to his ear, nipping playfully at the lobe to see how Fort responded. Fort made a rumbly noise like a growl in his chest and retaliated for the teasing bites by slipping his hands beneath Mason's sweater and caressing Mason's warm, bare skin as far as he could reach.

Mason arched up into the slide of Fort's hands. He loved to be touched, and he hummed in pleasure, not ashamed to let Fort know he liked it. Kissing his way down the side of Fort's neck, he managed to get his hand between them, tugging down the zipper of Fort's hoodie.

"Too many clothes," he complained, sliding one hand under the hem of Fort's thermal shirt. He splayed his fingers against the skin of Fort's side, then scraped lightly with his nails. "I want to touch you too."

"You can touch whatever you want." Fort's smile was lazy, and his eyes were half-lidded as he gazed up at Mason, but he lifted up enough to help get the hoodie and shirt off. "I just hope Miss Violet doesn't decide to come back down here anytime soon."

Fort's skin was pale, but he was lean and fit, and Mason greedily ran his hands over Fort's warm body. "Miss Violet is a smart woman. I'm sure she's fast asleep by now." He drew in a deep breath. "God, you're gorgeous. You look good enough to eat."

"Is there anything in particular you'd like to taste?" Fort grinned wickedly and waggled his eyebrows.

"Oh, yes." Mason returned the grin, then lowered his head, running his tongue over one of Fort's nipples. Fort's skin tasted clean and salty, and Mason flicked his tongue, teasing Fort's nipple into a taut peak.

Sucking in a hissing breath, Fort arched his back, and he tightened his arms around Mason. "Feels good," he said huskily, a heated gleam in his eyes.

Mason looked up and grinned, pleased at the reaction. "Good." He moved his hand over Fort's chest, pinching the other nipple as he bit down lightly on the one between his lips. He didn't know if Fort liked to play rough or not, but this was a good way to find out.

Mason could feel the vibrations as Fort made that rumbly noise again. "You don't have to play nice if you don't want to." A ragged edge had crept into Fort's voice. "I can take it."

That was all Mason needed to hear. He gave a little growl of his own and bit down harder, then laved the swollen bud with his tongue. Shifting slightly, he gave Fort's other nipple the same attention, then sucked on it hard, turning the pink skin darker. At the same time, he raked his nails down Fort's sides, hard enough to mark but not break the skin. Beneath him, Fort moaned and writhed, his pale skin growing flushed with arousal.

Lifting his head, Mason grinned. "Like that?" he purred, running his hands soothingly over the skin he'd scratched. "Want more?"

"Damned right I do." Fort's normally laid-back demeanor was replaced by a startling intensity as he grabbed the hem of Mason's pullover and unceremoniously stripped it off. He captured Mason's mouth in another deep kiss as his own fingers went to work, tugging and tweaking Mason's nipples mercilessly.

Mason was very glad he was lying down, because he didn't think his knees would have been able to hold him up. His toes curled hard inside his shoes as he kissed Fort back hungrily, his arousal inflamed by the sensual onslaught. He didn't know where this forceful side of Fort came from, but he liked it a lot.

Cradling the back of Mason's head in his palm, Fort continued the slow, searing kiss, seeming to savor the taste and feel of Mason's mouth. He slid his splayed fingers down the length of Mason's torso to the fastening of his jeans, working to pop the buttons with one hand.

Moaning, Mason helped, desperate to feel Fort's hands on him. He couldn't remember anyone arousing him so quickly before, making him feel like the randy teenager he'd teased Fort about earlier. Fort's answering chuckle was wicked as he helped Mason shimmy out of his jeans just enough to let Fort slip his fingers beneath the waistband of Mason's briefs and tease Mason's cock with too-light strokes.

"Oh, God." Mason clamped his hands on Fort's shoulders, breathing hard as he looked into Fort's blue eyes. "You're evil. Don't stop."

"I don't plan to." Fort's eyes were dark with need as he pushed Mason's briefs down and curled his fingers around Mason's cock, stroking it harder. His touch was confident as if he was certain of his ability to give Mason pleasure.

"Good." Mason had to move, pushing into Fort's hand, desire threatening to make him spiral out of control. He groaned, feeling need tightening like a coil within him. "Fort... oh, that's so good..."

Fort smiled with fierce satisfaction as he began working Mason's cock with a deft skill that made Mason's eyes roll back in his head, and he tweaked Mason's nipple with his free hand. "Tell me what you want, Mason, and I'll give it to you."

There wasn't a single thing Mason could think of at the moment; his brain had turned to mush, and the only thing on his mind was how good Fort was making him feel. He swallowed hard, wanting to let go and yet not wanting the pleasure to end as he stared down at Fort, seeing the desire and satisfaction he felt reflected in Fort's eyes.

"You!" he gasped, then shuddered as he came completely undone, unable to hold back any longer.

Fort watched avidly, and he continued to stroke Mason throughout his release until the pleasure ebbed away at last. He brought his hand to his mouth and lapped at his fingers, humming with pleasure. "Mm, you taste as good as you feel."

Sated and breathing hard, Mason relaxed against Fort, watching him with lazy satisfaction. "Mmm... does that mean I get to taste you?" he asked, tracing circles around one of Fort's nipples with his forefinger.

Fort shivered pleasurably and leaned back against the throw pillow, gazing at Mason with heat in his eyes. "I certainly don't have any objections to that."

Chuckling, Mason dropped a kiss on the corner of Fort's mouth. "Well, then, let's see if I can manage to make you feel as good as you've made me feel."

After pulling a handkerchief from his pocket and cleaning Fort up, Mason rose to his feet, since the sofa wouldn't give him enough room to do what he wanted to do. He pulled up his briefs and jeans, then dropped to his knees, giving Fort a wicked smile as he unfastened the button of Fort's cargo pants and slid the zipper down.

Mason's eyes widened as he caught sight of the black boxers Fort wore. A touch proved that they were indeed silk, and Mason gave a low whistle. "Why, doctor, I do believe you've got the cure for what ails me."

Fort shifted to sit up straight and swung his legs over the edge of the couch, one on either side of Mason. "You can have as much of the cure as you can handle. I wouldn't want you to feel poorly on my account."

"I can handle a lot," Mason replied with a smirk. "Lift up a little." He tugged Fort's cargo pants down, but left the boxers in place for the moment. He leaned down, pressing open-mouthed kisses against the hardness of Fort's cock, enjoying the slide of silk against his lips.

Fort groaned and reached down to comb his fingers gently through Mason's hair. "Now who's evil?"

Mason gave Fort a heated glance. "Quid pro quo. Accept your fate."

He ran his hand over the silk boxers, caressing Fort's hard cock through the fabric for a moment, before unfastening the button which held the fly closed. He licked his lips as he pulled Fort's cock through the opening, humming with pleasure at the sight of it, flushed and hard. Leaning down, he engulfed Fort completely in the wet heat of his mouth, wanting to give Fort as much pleasure as he had been given. Fort cried out, his hips bucking slightly, and he tightened his fingers in Mason's hair.

"Yes! Feels so good, Mason...."

Mason started humming again, relaxing his throat so that he could take Fort in deeper. Fort tasted salty and musky, and Mason pulled back so he could swirl his tongue around the tip, getting a better taste. Moaning, Fort let his head fall against the back of the sofa as he gave himself over to Mason's ministrations in a display of utter trust. His body grew taut as his need built, but he refrained from rocking his hips.

Pulling back, Mason looked up. "You can let go," he said. "You don't have to hold back with me." He leaned down, brushing a kiss to the tip of Fort's cock before taking him in deeply once more.

Fort apparently took Mason at his word, because he began to rock his hips, and he gazed down at Mason with a warmth that was deeper than mere desire in his eyes. "Okay, I trust you," he murmured.

Since he couldn't speak, Mason gave Fort a wink, then turned his attention to driving Fort crazy. He moved to meet the thrusts of Fort's hips, taking him in deep, enjoying giving Fort pleasure and wanting to drive him over the edge into complete incoherence. It wasn't long before Fort's moans escalated to wordless cries; his face was flushed, and his damp hair clung to his skin as he gave himself over to need and pleasure. With a wild shout, he snapped his hips up and came hard.

Mason swallowed around Fort's cock, not wanting to miss a single drop. He ran his hands over Fort's thighs, caressing him, feeling intense satisfaction in having made laid-back, mild-mannered Fort go wild for him.

After a few moments, he released Fort's cock with a little lick and looked up with a grin. "Mmm... You do taste good. Better than Moon-Pies. Maybe better than coffee too."

"Better than MoonPies *and* coffee?" Fort grinned back at him, sprawling on the sofa in boneless satiation. "Damn, I'm good."

That made Mason laugh, and he crawled up next to Fort, throwing one arm across him with a sigh. "Yes, you are. If you're that good on the first date, in fact, I think I'll be dead by the third. Maybe the fourth."

"Hmm." Fort eyed him speculatively. "If I'm really on my game, I could try for the second. It could be fun to find out."

"I'm more than willing for you to blow me away whenever you feel up for it." Leaning close, Mason pressed his lips to Fort's. "Can't you see it? I die, and you'll have to do the EVPs when I haunt you. Everyone wants to know why all my ghost says is, 'Harder! Harder!'"

Fort burst out laughing as he wrapped his arms around Mason and held him close. "No livestreaming *that* investigation for an audience!"

"It wouldn't embarrass me, since I'd be dead," Mason pointed out, snuggling unashamedly into Fort's embrace.

"I wonder if it would embarrass you if you were alive," Fort retorted, giving Mason a little squeeze.

"Very little embarrasses me." Mason sighed in contentment. "I wonder if ghosts do exist, do they still feel anything or are they just echoes? If I was to end up as a spirit, I think I'd still want to feel things. Wouldn't you? Do you think a ghost can feel something like satisfaction or amusement?"

"If it's an intelligent haunting, maybe it can." Fort looked thoughtful as if he was giving the question serious consideration. "I suppose it depends on how connected they are to the world or how much of their humanity they have left."

"I suppose." Mason yawned suddenly, feeling warm and content. He rubbed his cheek against Fort's shoulder. "You make a good pillow."

"Then go to sleep." Fort caressed Mason's back gently. "We've got time to get some rest before they come to open up in the morning."

"Good. Just a nap." Mason yawned again, then blinked and looked up at Fort as an odd sound reached his ears. "Did you hear a chuckle?"

"Just now? Yeah. I thought it was you."

"Wasn't me." He should probably be more concerned than he was, but he already knew they weren't alone, so he closed his eyes and sighed. "Maybe Miss Violet is watching television. Must be a good show."

"I hope it wasn't *our* show," Fort grumbled, sounding disgruntled, but he didn't move except to lean his cheek against the top of Mason's head.

"That sweet old lady isn't interested in us," Mason murmured, feeling sleep beginning to pull him under. He let it, but just before he dozed off, he thought he heard another chuckle, as though someone had heard his words and was very amused.

8

F ort was still groggy when the alarm he'd set on his phone went off, giving him and Mason just enough time to freshen up and make sure there weren't any telltale signs of their tryst either on themselves or on the sofa. Mason looked as bleary as Fort felt, so they didn't talk much, but sleepy smiles were exchanged, and they helped each other clean up and straighten their clothes.

They were presentable by the time Catherine arrived along with a woman she introduced as the current owner of Wisteria Grove, Eugenia Rouxchambeau Clermont.

"Great show last night!" Catherine beamed at them. "We've gotten a lot of positive feedback, so I think we'll see some payoff with increased tourism. I had no idea you two were such good actors, though," she added, bracing her hands on her hips as her expression turned stern. "That was an amazing stunt, but if you wanted to wrap early, you could have just said so. You didn't have to pretend someone had gotten in here with you."

"What?" Fort stared at her in confusion, his sleep-deprived brain trying to process what she was saying. "We didn't pretend anything."

Catherine tutted and shook her head. "Nice try, but we could see there wasn't anyone there. How long did you two have to practice that conversation to make it look so real?"

Mason glanced at Fort, his eyebrows climbing. "We didn't practice anything. Miss Violet was right there with us. She said she lives here and couldn't leave."

"Ah, yes, we should talk about that." Eugenia, a smartly dressed woman in her fifties with blond hair fading to silver, smiled at them, and something about the twinkle in her blue eyes was very familiar. She turned to the director. "I can't tell you how pleased I am with the response last night, Catherine. The Inn's website had an all-time high number of hits, so I'm sure we'll recoup the loss of revenue for last night very quickly. And business for Wisteria Grove means business for Boulard Crossing. Thank you so much."

"Well, KITN has always been a proud supporter of local businesses and events," Catherine replied, apparently willing to drop the subject of their "act", which was fine with Fort since he was still confused about the whole thing. "Maybe next year, you could use this investigation as the basis for some kind of special Halloween event, maybe a costume party."

"We'll definitely consider it. I brought coffee for the boys, and I'm sure they have to get their equipment together." Eugenia gave Catherine a charming smile, softening what was obviously a dismissal. She turned and linked her arms through Fort's and Mason's. "Now come along, I'm sure you could use something to fortify you after the night you had."

"That would be very welcome, ma'am." Mason smiled tiredly.

"The cameras are packed up." Fort glanced over at Catherine, wanting to make sure she knew where to find the equipment from the TV station. "We left everything at the reception desk."

"Thanks, I'll get it and be on my way, unless you guys need anything else?" she asked.

Fort shook his head. "No, we're good."

Nodding, Catherine turned and headed off, and Fort let himself be led away with Eugenia and Mason.

"Coffee does sound good. Thanks for bringing it, ma'am."

Eugenia smiled up at him like they were old friends. "Trust me, coffee and beignets is the least I could do for the two of you. Especially since I have to ask you for an enormous favor."

"A favor?" It was obvious Mason was suddenly on guard. "What kind of favor? No disrespect, ma'am, but if you're wanting us to say we saw a ghost when we didn't, I'm afraid I won't be able to accommodate you."

Strangely enough, Eugenia didn't seem offended. Instead she laughed as she pulled them into the sitting room. "No, no, nothing like that. Go on, have a seat, and let's get some caffeine into you both. I think you're going to need it."

As they seated themselves, she slid a very large tote bag off her shoulder and placed it on the coffee table, pulling out a big thermos, a stack of foam cups, and a pile of napkins. She added a white sack, and the warm, sweet smell of beignets reached them. "Help yourself, please. I need to make sure you're totally awake."

Fort wasn't shy about pouring himself a cup of coffee and snagging a couple of beignets, relishing both as he let the caffeine bring him up another level or two of wakefulness. Once he felt the fog dissipating from his brain, he finished off his first beignet and turned to Eugenia.

"What's the favor?"

Eugenia crossed her ankles and folded her hands in her lap. She had taken a chair across from the sofa, while Mason hadn't hesitated to settle himself right next to Fort, close enough that their legs were touching, a fact which seemed neither to surprise nor bother their hostess. "First, let me explain something to you both, because you'll see the footage for yourself when you review everything. Your conversation with Miss Violet was quite real to the two of you, I know. But you have to believe me when I say that what everyone else saw was the two of you talking to an empty chair."

Mason stopped with his coffee cup raised to his lips, staring at her incredulously. "That's impossible. She was right there, and it wasn't the first time we met her."

"That's right." Fort nodded, ready to fully support Mason's version of what happened. "We saw her the day we did our walk-through, and then she showed up around midnight last night. We talked to her both times. She told us stories about the house and some of the ghosts that allegedly haunt it."

"Of course she did. I've met Miss Violet myself, you see." Eugenia smiled at them warmly. "But she only appears to certain people, since she's a hopeless matchmaker. But I assure you, Miss Violet Duvall passed away quite peacefully in her sleep in 1887. She was as real to you as I am, I know. But she's a ghost, gentlemen. A genuine spirit who lives here at Wisteria Grove."

Fort stared at her, scarcely able to wrap his sleep-deprived mind around what she was saying. Miss Violet had appeared so real -- so solid -- and he had never experienced any kind of spirit activity that was so vivid. He doubted anyone on his team had experienced anything like this before.

"Are you serious?" He half-expected her to start laughing at pulling one over on the ghost hunters or for someone to pop out with a hidden camera and announce they were being pranked.

"Quite serious, actually. I know it's hard to believe, but you wouldn't be the first not to realize Miss Violet is a ghost." Eugenia chuckled and shook her head. "We get mail for her from people who've met her and think she's my maiden aunt, which she is, but about six generations back. She was the spinster sister of my sixth great-grandmother, who came here in the eighteen-twenties and never left."

"Impossible." Mason was staring at her, his brown eyes intense. "I simply can't believe that. You have to be trying to put one over on us. I've looked for ghosts for most of my life, and not once have I seen anything I could believe was a bona fide spirit. And you're trying to tell me that we conversed with one, not once but *twice* and didn't know it."

"That's exactly what I'm telling you." Their hostess gave a solemn nod. "You'll see it on the recordings, you know. I'm just trying to prepare you for that because I would be very grateful if you pretend you really were pulling a prank on the viewers. I never expected Miss

Violet would appear to the two of you, or I wouldn't have permitted the broadcast in the first place."

Fort frowned and shook his head, not understanding her request. "Why? I thought you wanted us to investigate the house and find out if the claims are real so you'll have an extra tourist draw. Why would you want us to suppress information about one of the most vivid manifestations either of us have ever seen?"

Eugenia smiled. "That's easy. I didn't agree to the investigation for you to prove that ghosts exist. After all, *I* know they do. Other than Miss Violet, all the spirits here are like the ones I've heard about everywhere else. Echoes of poor souls caught in the tragic circumstances of their lives and unable to move on. I figured you would get a few sounds, maybe catch sight of Lucy Finch and perhaps even old Colonel Rouxchambeau and the man he murdered. Mere hints and echoes, tantalizing enough to draw the curious. Tourists, perhaps a student of history or two, maybe even religious-minded folk looking for answers."

She grew more serious, her blue eyes full of entreaty. "What I don't want, and never planned for, are a bunch of scientists, spiritualists, skeptics, crackpots, exorcists and heaven knows who else descending on my home and turning it into some kind of circus sideshow. I love this place, and I love Miss Violet. I am responsible for making certain that this house -- which truly is her home, perhaps eternally -- remains here and isn't vandalized or worse by someone because they want to destroy a 'real' ghost. I'll even beg you if it will help, but please don't tell anyone what you really saw. You were blessed with something very special, something not many people see. Please don't ruin it for everyone who will come after you."

Hiding evidence went against everything Fort stood for as an investigator and an academic, but he couldn't ignore the earnestness of Eugenia's plea. Wisteria Grove was her property, and she had the right to privacy. Despite his researcher's instincts, he respected her right not to be overrun as she'd described. Having a few extra curious tourists hoping to hear voices or feel their bed shake was different from becoming the focus of a media circus and the center of attention in the world of paranormal investigation.

"I won't tell anyone." Fort glanced at Mason questioningly. "Are you okay with that?"

Mason hadn't lost his intent look, and his eyes gleamed with something Fort couldn't quite identify. Given that Mason had revealed he'd secretly longed to find his belief again, it seemed likely he wouldn't be so easily swayed from shouting to the world what they'd experienced, even by so eloquent a plea as the one Eugenia made.

"I have a question, first," he said, giving Eugenia a piercing look. "You said you wouldn't have invited us if you'd known she would appear to us. Assuming I do buy that Miss Violet really is a ghost in the first place, I want to know why you didn't think we'd see her."

"Because I had no clue either of you were interested in each other," Eugenia said, not trying to evade the question. "Catherine indicated you two were acquainted, but on opposite sides of the paranormal question. Rivals, in a way. I never thought you'd see Miss Violet because she's a matchmaker. I never saw her before my boyfriend Philippe came to pick me up for a date. He waited for me here in this very room, and I came down to meet him. Then Miss Violet walked in and greeted us both, and I could hardly believe my eyes. I thought my grandmother had made up the story, but I couldn't deny what I was seeing, and I was thrilled. Philippe proposed, and we've been happily married for thirty years. You see, Miss Violet only appears to people who are meant for one another. Not just lovers, not just people who fancy each other, but those who are destined to be real love matches."

She smiled gently at them, blue eyes so like Miss Violet's regarding them with hope. "I think something that special is worth keeping in the family, don't you? That's why you are now part of the family. My family. Won't you help keep Miss Violet's home safe for her? Please?"

EPILOGUE

"**F**ort! Hey, did you get the camera set up?"

Mason stood atop one of the large boulders that were strewn about the part of Gettysburg National Military Park known as Devil's Den. He shielded his eyes from the rays of the setting sun, straining for a glimpse of his partner. Fort was deploying one of the motion sensor cameras they'd brought with them, hoping that the device would catch some glimpse of the numerous spirits who were supposed to haunt the site.

He could barely believe they were actually here, having gotten permission to camp out overnight in one of the most allegedly haunted places in the country. They'd been in the area for a week, having done investigations at the Farnsworth House, the Jenny Wade House, and the Culp Farm. They'd gotten some EVPs that looked promising, and the motion-sensor cameras had captured *something* walking across a room in the Farnsworth House, but everything would have to wait for final verdicts until they got back to New Orleans and could do the post-processing of the data.

A year ago, he'd have been skeptical that even their most promising recordings held anything of worth, but that had been before he'd gone to Wisteria Grove and encountered Miss Violet. It

had taken him seeing the recording of him and Fort on Halloween
night to finally convince him, but he'd been convinced at last. But in
some ways, it was less the proof what had happened and more the
fact it had happened to *him* that had changed him. He'd meant it
when he'd told Fort he'd lost his sense of wonder, having run across
too many things which were explainable or even outright hoaxes
while looking for that tantalizing, elusive glimpse of into the
unknown, but Miss Violet had changed all that. Even though he and
Fort hadn't seen her again despite several hopeful visits to Wisteria
Grove, Mason was content with what they had. He'd agreed with
Eugenia and Fort that Miss Violet's home had to be protected, even if
it meant that he and Fort took a great deal of flak for their "hoax".

Fortunately their professional reputations hadn't suffered, since
everyone seemed willing to chalk it up to a Halloween prank, especially since they hadn't even tried to pretend it was "real" after they'd
talked to Eugenia. Other than the actual webcams they'd been wearing, they didn't have any other recordings of Miss Violet anyway,
nothing they could produce as evidence. But Mason didn't need it,
because at long last, he truly understood why some things couldn't be
measured, evaluated, or quantified. There was wonder in the world,
and Mason and Fort had been gifted with the opportunity to experience it, something just for the two of them. Something they would
always share.

Fort loped over to join Mason, catching him around the waist and
pulling him close. "Camera's set up and ready to go. Are you ready to
have a sleepless night?" He snugged Mason against his lean body and
leered playfully.

Smiling, Mason wrapped his arms around Fort's shoulders,
savoring the contact. The passion they'd discovered in the sitting
room at Wisteria Grove had only grown stronger in the last year, and
Mason couldn't imagine how he'd managed without Fort in his life.
"As long as there are no webcams involved, I'm more than ready," he
replied in a husky drawl. "It's cold up here in the north, so I hope
you're planning to keep me warm."

"Mmm." Smiling, Fort leaned in and nuzzled Mason's nose. "I've got a couple of ideas about how to do that. I think you'll like them. There definitely won't be any webcams this year, so you can strip and scream all you want. No one but me and the ghosts will know."

"You've become an exhibitionist." Mason returned the nuzzling happily. "Last year, you were clutching your pearls at the thought of Miss Violet watching us, and now you don't care if a bunch of phantom soldiers watch you pounding me into incoherence?"

Fort chuckled, his smile turning sheepish. "Well, I guess she helped me get used to the idea that you never know when someone is taking a peek from the other side, so you might as well not worry about it."

"Good. Because it's supposed to drop down into the thirties, and I think we're going to have to generate plenty of heat to keep from freezing." Mason gave Fort a coy look from beneath his lashes. "We might even scare the ghosts away. I do hope you don't mind contenting yourself with my attention rather than the attention of a bunch of specters."

"I vastly prefer your attention to anyone else's, living or dead." Fort cupped Mason's cheek in his palm, his eyes growing warm with affection. "Happy anniversary, babe. I love you."

Mason never grew tired of hearing Fort say those words, and he leaned against Fort's hand. "I love you, too. And this is a very happy anniversary. The happiest. Now shut up and kiss me before I die of longing."

Fort didn't hesitate to comply, and Mason responded eagerly, putting all of his love, all of his desire, all of his gratitude for what they had together into the kiss. He was grateful to Miss Violet for bringing them together, and for opening his eyes to wonder again. But he was even more grateful to Fort for sharing his life and giving Mason his love and most of all for showing him that he didn't have to experience anything supernatural to feel like the most special man in the world.

THE BOYFRIEND SWEATER CURSE

1

S ix years ago –

GABRIEL SUTTON LEANED FORWARD in his chair, watching eagerly while Jack opened his present. They were celebrating together on Christmas Eve since Jack had plans with his family on Christmas day. Gabriel had set the mood by dimming the lights in the living room of his apartment so the white lights on his tree illuminated the room with a cozy glow. His tree was decorated with an array of ornaments that reflected his various fandom interests, and he loved it.

Jack tore off the shimmery red wrapping paper, opened the oblong white box, and peeled back the tissue paper to reveal the sweater Gabriel had knitted for him. They were both *Star Wars* fans, and Gabriel had spent almost six months knitting a sweater in fair isle colorwork using *Star Wars* images. The pattern consisted of five horizontal rows repeated on both the back and front; he'd used black yarn for the background so the images would pop, and he'd added a ribbed crew neck and cuffs.

The first row alternated with the Rebel Alliance symbol in white and the Empire symbol in red. The second row X-Wing and TIE fighters in charcoal gray. The third row was a line of AT-ATs in white. The fourth row was a line of R2D2s in white and blue, and the last row was a row of Death Stars in white and gray. In between each row was a thin border made of lightsabers with either a blue, green, or red blade. It was by far the most intricate colorwork project Gabriel had ever knitted, but he thought the hours he'd spent on it were worth it. *Jack* was worth it.

Jack held up the sweater, his eyes growing wide. "Wow, that's really something!"

"Do you like it?" Gabriel scanned Jack's face for signs of enthusiasm, but while Jack was smiling, he didn't seem overwhelmed.

"Of course I do, babe." Jack kissed him lightly, then put the sweater aside in favor of retrieving Gabriel's present from under the tree.

Gabriel didn't see Jack wearing the sweater over the next couple of weeks, but they didn't spend every day together, so he assumed maybe he missed seeing Jack when he wore it. Then in late January, Gabriel stopped by Jack's apartment to pick him up for a date. A new restaurant serving Ethiopian food had opened in downtown Asheville, and they both wanted to try it. Jack opened the hall closet to get his coat, and Gabriel saw the *Star Wars* sweater still in its box and half-obscured with tissue paper on the floor next to Jack's hiking boots.

A heavy sandbag lodged in the pit of Gabriel's stomach as he retrieved the sweater and held it out to Jack, who looked sheepish. "You haven't worn it?"

"It's a little busy. I prefer simpler designs," Jack said, offering an apologetic smile. "Do you want it back?"

Gabriel ran his hand over the soft wool stitches, disappointed that he had misjudged what Jack would like. He didn't like taking back gifts, but if Jack didn't want it, fuck it. He'd wear it himself. In fact, he wore the sweater to his knitting group's next meeting at the local independent yarn shop. They gathered each month in the cluster of comfortable secondhand chairs by the large picture window at the front of the shop, and they spent two or three hours knitting and chatting over sweet iced tea when it was warm and coffee when it was cold.

"Isn't that the sweater you were knitting for Jack?" Miss Hilda May asked.

"He didn't like it, so he gave it back," Gabriel said, his lips twisting in a moue of annoyance, and the circle of ladies made sympathetic noises. They all knew how it felt when a handmade gift went unappreciated.

"Better be careful," Miss Betty said. "You might have triggered the boyfriend sweater curse."

"The what?" Gabriel put down the cabled hat he was knitting and turned to her.

"The boyfriend sweater curse," Miss Oleta said, nodding sagely. "It's real. I knitted my first boyfriend a sweater for his birthday. We broke up less than a month later. I didn't knit my husband a *thing* until we were married, and we'll celebrate fifty years together this summer."

"Wait, what curse?" Gabriel frowned as he looked around the circle of older ladies.

"You haven't heard of the boyfriend sweater curse?" Miss Betty's penciled eyebrows climbed to the roots of her dyed blond hair. "Oh, shit, honey. I guess we should've told you when you started working on that sweater, but we thought you knew. *Never* knit a sweater for your boyfriend, or you'll break up for sure."

Gabriel shook his head and scoffed. "We've been together almost a year. I think we're solid."

Jack broke up with him by email the day before Valentine's Day.

~

FOUR YEARS *ago* –

GABRIEL STILL DIDN'T BELIEVE the boyfriend sweater curse was real, but he was a little more cautious about investing a lot of time and effort into the sweater he was knitting for Ben. He used ivory wool and chose a pattern that featured wide vertical row of Aran cables down the front and moss stitch sleeves. The sweater was more traditional than the *Star Wars* sweater – which Gabriel still wore – and it seemed to fit Ben's taste in clothing.

They exchanged gifts after Christmas because Ben went home to Georgia for the holidays every year. He claimed he couldn't take Gabriel with him because he wasn't yet out to his parents, and at the time, Gabriel believed him.

Gabriel had indulged in a Yoda tree topper with a lightsaber that lit up that year, and he wasn't in a rush to take his tree down, so he kept his decorations out until Ben returned to Asheville. He queued up a playlist of holiday music on his iPod, and he prepared cups of generously spiked eggnog so they could rekindle the feeling of Christmas even though it was after New Year's Day.

Ben reacted with far more enthusiasm to his sweater than Jack had, but the next time Gabriel saw the sweater, it was being worn by a blond twink who didn't look old enough to buy his own alcohol. The twink had rolled up the ribbed cuffs, and the bottom of the sweater hit him at almost mid-thigh. The twink was tucked under Ben's arm and gazing up at Ben with a besotted expression that made Gabriel's stomach churn.

Ben looked horrified to see Gabriel standing in the door of the coffee shop where he and the twink were waiting in line. "I can explain," he said.

"No," Gabriel said. "You really can't."

This time, he didn't get the sweater back.

TWO YEARS ago –

"I'M NOT sure I should even be doing this," Gabriel said, looking at the circular needles and skein of heather dove gray yarn in his lap. Christmas was three months away, and he wanted to knit a sweater for Will. At thirty-two, he was ready for a stable relationship, maybe even marriage and buying a house together. He had dreams of restoring an older house, and there were plenty of those in and around Asheville. But even if he didn't get his fixer-upper, his club and bar days were behind him. His job as an antiques conservator at Biltmore Estate required focus and attention to detail, and he couldn't party like he had ten years ago. Hell, not even like he had five years ago. His auburn hair was as thick as it had always been, but he'd found a few gray hairs to go along with his decreased tolerance for late nights and hangovers.

"Third time's the charm, right?" Miss Hilda May said, giving him an encouraging smile.

"It's the curse," Miss Betty said, her tone dire.

"I don't believe in curses or superstitions," Gabriel said, casting on the stitches defiantly.

This time, he was sure he'd done everything right. He'd chosen the color based on his observation that Will seemed to prefer basic, neutral colors for his wardrobe, and he was keeping the style simple – not too busy, not too heavy. He picked the most beginner level sweater pattern he could find, one that would go with anything and would be suitable for layering.

When Will opened it, he immediately checked the collar. "I don't see a tag," he said, giving Gabriel a puzzled look.

"I knitted it myself," Gabriel said, his stomach starting to sink.

"Oh, I guess you can't exchange it then." Will laughed as he refolded the sweater and put it back in the box.

"Is something wrong with it?" Gabriel reached for the box, and Will didn't stop him from taking it back.

"Well, it's a crew neck," Will said, shrugging. "I prefer V-necks. I was going to see if I could exchange it, that's all."

Gabriel stroked the front of the sweater, tears stinging his eyes. Sure, it had been basic enough that he only needed about three weeks to knit it, but it was still thousands of stitches and hours of his time invested in someone he cared about, someone who didn't give a shit about the thought and effort behind the gift.

Three sweaters. Three mistakes. Maybe there was something to the boyfriend sweater curse after all – or maybe Gabriel was doomed to spend the rest of his life alone, knitting his days away.

"Hey," Will said, caressing Gabriel's cheek. "I didn't mean to upset you. I like the sweater."

Gabriel retreated from the touch and rubbed his eyes. "It's okay. I should've asked about the neckline."

But Gabriel had a difficult time forgetting Will's reaction to the sweater, and his friends in the knitting club were indignant on his behalf.

"He said what now?" Miss Oleta's dark fingers stuttered and dropped a stitch as she gaped at Gabriel.

"He wanted to *exchange* the sweater?" Miss Betty's faded blue eyes widened in horror.

"You broke up with him, right?" Miss Hilda May asked, frowning at him over the top of her horn-rimmed glasses.

"Not yet, but at this point, I feel like it's almost inevitable," Gabriel said, his needles resting still in his lap, the scarf he was knitting all but forgotten.

"It doesn't sound like it would be a big loss," Miss Hilda May said.

"Dump his ass," Miss Betty said. "If he can't appreciate a hand-made sweater like it deserves, he sure as hell can't appreciate *you* like you deserve."

In the end, Gabriel kept the gray sweater, but not Will.

Present day –

"Happy birthday," Gabriel said, holding out his glass of Cabernet Sauvignon to toast the man sitting across from him.

He'd been dating Noel Rivera since January after Miss Betty finally wore him down about meeting her nephew. She was convinced they would hit it off, but Gabriel hadn't been so sure. Noel was a financial planner, which Gabriel thought was a snooze-fest of a job, and when they did meet, he hadn't been blown away by Noel's appearance either. Noel was around 5'10 – the same as Gabriel – so neither of them had to crane up or down when they kissed. He had thick black hair and soulful brown eyes behind his glasses, but nothing stood out about him.

And then Noel smiled, and it was one of those wide, genuine, whole-face-lights-up kind of smiles that transformed him from "average at best" to "*wow.*"

They didn't have much in common career-wise, but beneath Noel's suit and silk tie beat the heart of a true nerd, and they had spirited discussions about their favorite movies, shows, and books. On the night of their blind date, they had talked until the restaurant closed, and their chemistry was so sizzling hot that Gabriel had broken his own rule about not inviting a guy home on the first date.

But after his last three awful relationships, Gabriel was inclined to proceed with caution – and he wasn't about to knit *anything* for Noel, especially not a sweater. He didn't want to admit to believing in curses, but the longer they dated, the more he wanted this relationship to work out, which meant he didn't want to take any chances.

They had been together almost ten months by the time Noel's birthday rolled around in early October, and Gabriel had gotten a dinner reservation at the Biltmore Estate's Inn. It was the priciest of all the restaurants on the estate, but he got an employee discount, and besides, he wanted to treat Noel to a fancy formal dining experience since Noel tended to be frugal.

"I hope you're enjoying it so far," Gabriel added as they touched glasses.

"It's fantastic. Thank you," Noel said, his eyes crinkling at the corners as he smiled at Gabriel, not hiding his pleasure. "It's definitely the best place anyone has ever taken me for my birthday. You're spoiling me, and I love it."

"I enjoy doing it," Gabriel said as he took a sip of wine and admired how good Noel looked in his suit. Usually Noel wore more casual clothes when Gabriel saw him, but they had both dressed up for this occasion. Gabriel had dusted off his one nice suit – the one he wore to weddings and funerals – and tied his shoulder-length auburn hair in a neat ponytail. "Now the question is, do you want your present before or after we eat?"

Noel chuckled and shook his head. "You've known me how long, and you can ask that? Have you ever seen me able to resist a surprise? You're lucky I'm not already making grabby hands at you. I've refrained only because of the surroundings."

Grinning, Gabriel bent to retrieve the gift-wrapped package he'd stashed under his chair. "Yeah, I probably should know better than to ask by now," he said as he slid the package across the crisp white linen tablecloth to Noel's side of the table.

He'd debated about whether to knit something simple like a hat. Noel was a huge *Firefly* fan, and Gabriel could have knitted a replica of Jayne Cobb's infamous hat in less than a week, but he didn't want to risk it. Besides, his last three relationships barely made it past the first anniversary. He and Noel still had several months to go before they reached that milestone, and Gabriel was waiting for something to go wrong with Noel like it had with Jack, Ben, and Will. Thus he'd bought Noel a book about the history and restoration of Biltmore Estate, one that talked more about the role of conservators than most books about Biltmore did, since Noel seemed interested in learning more about Gabriel's job and what it entailed.

Noel ran his long, sensitive fingers over the wrapping paper, then untied the bow. He lifted away the lid of the box and looked down at the book. Gabriel thought he saw a flash of disappointment cross Noel's features, but when Noel glanced up at Gabriel, he was smiling. "Thank you so much! I've been meaning to pick up a book about the estate, because everything you've told me about your work seems so fascinating." He rested his hand on top of Gabriel's and squeezed it gently. "I'll enjoy reading this."

"I hope so." Gabriel studied Noel, wondering if he'd imagined the disappointment. "I hope it's not too boring a gift. I was debating between this and the Captain America t-shirt you've been eying in the comic shop for the last few weeks."

"Of course it's not boring! You know how much I love books," Noel said. "You've also brought me to this wonderful place for dinner." He opened the front cover of the book and read the message Gabriel had written inside that wished Noel a happy birthday. "Thank you for personalizing it. That means a great deal to me."

"I thought it might be something to remember me by if... Well." Gabriel shrugged and smiled wryly. He didn't want to sound like a pessimist, but when it came to his romantic life, he was a little less optimistic now than he had been when he was younger.

Noel looked at Gabriel intently. "It's my intention to have *you* around to remember you by," he said, his tone somber. "Aunt Betty mentioned some ridiculous curse thing with you and your previous relationships. I don't believe in superstitions. I believe in *you*."

Warmth bloomed in Gabriel's chest at Noel's reassuring words. Noel sounded so certain about their future, but Gabriel had had conversations about the future with his exes as well, so he couldn't bring himself to jump into the deep end yet.

"The boyfriend sweater curse," he said. "Some knitters believe that if you knit your boyfriend a sweater, he'll break up with you. I don't really believe it either, but I knitted a sweater for my last three boyfriends for Christmas, and now they're my ex-boyfriends, so make of that what you will."

"It seems to me they're ex-boyfriends because they were wrong for you," Noel replied. "Let's see, there was the first one, who sounds like a self-centered jerk. The second one was a cheating jerk, and the last one... well, just plain old jerk seems to cover it." He grinned. "Fortunately, I'm not a jerk. My aunt even says so, and from Betty Johnson, that is high praise indeed. Even though the one time she ever tried to teach me to knit, she said my little dishcloth looked like I'd knitted it with my feet instead of my hands."

"She does speak highly of you," Gabriel said, inclining his head to acknowledge the point. "She started trying to set us up as soon as Will and I broke up."

"Really? I think she played it a bit more subtle with me." Noel shook his head. "Though I will say she did keep mentioning a very charming young man she knew who did the best colorwork she'd ever seen."

"Well, you've seen the *Star Wars* sweater," Gabriel said. "That was the first cursed sweater. Jack thought it was 'too busy,' so he asked if I wanted it back." He paused, debating whether he wanted to go into detail about the other two sweaters, but he supposed there wasn't any reason why he shouldn't. "The second sweater was cable work. I didn't get that one back because the twink Ben cheated on me with was wearing it when I ran into them. You've seen the third cursed sweater too. It's the plain heather gray one – straight stockinette stitch with some narrow ribbing around the cuffs and the neckline. I made it a crew neck, and Will preferred V-necks."

"What did I tell you? Jerks, all of them. I would have been proud to wear something you made me." Noel's expression became a little sheepish. "Maybe I *am* a bit of a jerk, after all. I had a rather wistful hope you'd made me something I could wear to the Pride events next week."

"Sorry." Gabriel offered an apologetic smile. He felt a twinge of remorse for not giving Noel something handmade, especially since Noel was the first out of all his boyfriends to express any real interest in receiving a knitted gift. But superstition aside, he was hesitant to invest too much too much of his time – too much of *himself* – into someone who might be out of his life in a few months. He felt bad that Noel was affected by damage caused by other men, but at the same time, he didn't think being careful was a bad idea for either of them. "Curse or no curse, I need to be absolutely sure about you and about us together before I commit to handmade gifts again."

Noel didn't seem upset. Instead he lifted Gabriel's hand and leaned across the table to press his lips against Gabriel's palm. "Then I'll have to make sure you have no reason to doubt me, won't I?"

A pleasurable shiver rippled through Gabriel at the feel of Noel's warm lips on his skin, reminding him of the dessert they would share later in the privacy of his apartment or Noel's condo. "That's what I'm hoping for," he said, sounding a little breathless. "I'm not looking for reasons to distrust you, I promise."

"Good." Noel smiled again, this time slowly and seductively. "Because I want us to look back on this night years from now, maybe on our fiftieth anniversary, and think 'Ah! Remember talking about silly superstitions? We were so young, and we know much better now!'"

Gabriel thought about Miss Oleta, who had been married over fifty years now, and the times he'd been envious of her long and happy marriage. She always sounded so certain when she spoke of her husband – as certain as Noel sounded now.

"I'd like that," he said. "More than anything."

"Then you'll have it." Noel nodded. "Trust me, it's like money in the bank."

"You're sure you want to do this?" Gabriel gestured to the stacked plastic bins that held his Christmas decorations. There were nine total, each one of them stuffed full. Most of them held his ornament collection, which took up a lot of space because he kept them in their boxes for safekeeping, but he also had a lot of ornaments because he'd begun collecting the fannish Hallmark ornaments when he was a teenager.

His tree was already set up. He'd purchased a live tree from one of the local tree farmers and gotten it delivered the day before. The delivery men had even helped him fit the trunk into his tree stand, so all he had to do was water it. He'd invited Noel over to help him decorate, but he hadn't expected Noel to accept. His previous three boyfriends hadn't been into decorating as much as he was, and he'd expected Noel to have the same attitude.

"Of course I do." Noel smiled, giving Gabriel a quick, one-armed hug. "I can't wait to see all your ornaments. I never got into the collectibles myself, but I inherited my grandmother's stash several years ago, so my tree is always in the wooden toy and ceramic angel style. This will be fun."

"Okay, but do you want the full Gabriel Sutton tree decorating experience?" Gabriel asked, giving Noel an arch look. "Or should I try to keep it cool since this is your first time?"

Noel wrapped his arms around Gabriel and met Gabriel's gaze with a direct look. "What I want is to be part of what you love. I want to see your enjoyment, because seeing you happy makes me happy. So I want the full ride – all the ornaments, the Christmas music blaring over the speakers, dancing, drinking, naked revels. Whatever you want to do. I'm just happy you're letting me participate, rather than decorating by yourself and inviting me over afterward."

Although Gabriel's cynical side warned him not to get his hopes up, his heart melted at Noel's apparent sincerity, and he slid his arms around Noel's waist in return. "It starts with Christmas music and my special hot chocolate. The naked revels are for after the house is decorated. That part of the festivities is *very* exclusive. VIP access only."

"Dare I hope to qualify?" Noel asked, widening his eyes in appeal. "I'll do anything."

Gabriel found it difficult to say no to Noel when he turned on the big, brown puppy eyes and gave Gabriel that soulful, pleading look, but Gabriel pretended to consider the question. "Well, I suppose I could put you on the waiting list."

Noel's lower lip quivered slightly, but there was a flash of amusement in his eyes. "I'll have to find a way to weasel in front of everyone on the list, because I don't want to share you with anyone."

"It's a short list," Gabriel said, sliding his hands down to grope Noel's firm ass. "You're the only one on it."

Noel wriggled against Gabriel's hands. "Well, then, I think we should get started as soon as possible."

"First, we have to set the proper mood." Gabriel released Noel's ass with reluctance and moved away, his heart feeling more buoyant than it had in a long time. He woke up his computer, found the two-hour yule log video on YouTube, and set it to full screen. "Crackling fireplace, check," he said, grinning at Noel.

Noel laughed. "That's brilliant! I've had the fish tank one up before. It's mesmerizing. But the fireplace is much more in tune with the season."

"Sometimes I wish I had a real fireplace, but this is much cleaner and safer," Gabriel said as he went to turn on the music. "I have a Christmas playlist that my iTunes says is two days' worth of music." He hit Shuffle and then Play, and the first song that popped up was by Alvin and the Chipmunks, and he gave Noel a sheepish smile.

"I suppose it can only get better from there, right?" Noel asked, a teasing note in his voice. "Do you have David Bowie and Bing Crosby's version of 'Little Drummer Boy?' I love that one."

"I do," Gabriel said. "If it doesn't play before we're finished, I'll queue it up for you. Now you have a choice. You can start unpacking the bins and unboxing the ornaments, or you can watch me make the special hot chocolate."

"I vote for the hot chocolate," Noel said, rubbing his hands together. "I want to know all your secrets."

"But are they safe with you?" Gabriel asked lightly as he led Noel to the galley kitchen. It was smaller than he liked, and given how much he enjoyed cooking, he looked forward to the day when he could afford a house with a spacious kitchen.

"Of course they are." Noel propped one hip against a counter, looking completely at home. "I'm very good at keeping things private. Accountants have to be. But if something is important to you, Gabriel, it's important to me, too."

"And the things that are important to you are important to me too," Gabriel said, squeezing Noel's hand briefly. "I don't want this to be all one way. I've been on the receiving end of that enough to know it isn't fun."

Noel smiled and returned the squeeze. "I appreciate that, and I know things aren't one way. But I haven't had anyone hurt me the way you've been hurt, babe. I know you're not completely sure of me, not yet. That takes time, but like I told you, I'm here for the long haul."

"You're good to me." Gabriel leaned in to press a lingering kiss to Noel's lips, and then he smiled against them. "For that, I'm going to make your special hot chocolate extra special."

Noel returned the kiss. "Oh? Will it be Gabriel flavored? Mm…"

"Sorry, but you don't get anything Gabriel flavored until the naked revels at the end," Gabriel said, drawing back at last.

"Darn. I guess I'll settle for extra special hot chocolate." Noel gave Gabriel's ass a quick grope, then released him.

Gabriel made a show of bending over to get the pot he needed, and he gave Noel a coy look over his shoulder as he put his ass on display.

"I like this already," Noel said. "Though too much teasing isn't fair, since we still have a tree to decorate."

"True, and I would like to get it done today." Gabriel smiled wickedly and gave one last shimmy before he turned his attention to the hot chocolate, which he made from scratch using slabs of dark chocolate, milk, and heavy cream as a base. It was a more time-consuming process than heating up some milk or water and stirring in a powder, but he liked the richer taste, which he augmented with a shot of Fireball whiskey in each mug. He topped the hot chocolate with a generous dollop of whipped cream and a sprinkle of cinnamon, and then he handed one mug to Noel. "For you."

Noel closed his eyes and breathed in deep. "Oh, that smells wonderful," he said. Then he smiled and raised his mug. "I think this calls for a toast, don't you?"

Gabriel picked up the second mug and touched it to Noel's. "To special hot chocolate and decorated trees."

"To that, and to our first Christmas together," Noel replied. "The first of many."

"I hope so," Gabriel said softly, gazing at Noel with far more of his heart in his eyes than he realized. "I really do."

～

GABRIEL TUCKED his arm through Noel's as they waited at the Bryson

City depot to board the Polar Express Train, unable to keep the silly grin off his face. He'd heard about the excursion, which was part of the Great Smoky Mountain Railroad, but he'd never done it before, and he'd been excited about the trip ever since Noel said he'd gotten tickets for them.

The crowd around them consisted mostly of children – some of whom were wearing pajamas like the characters from *The Polar Express* – and their parents, but he and Noel weren't the only childless adults waiting for the train. He didn't want to go so far as to wear pajamas, but he did put on one of his knitted Christmas hats for the occasion. His was a red and white striped stocking cap with ribbed brim and a pompom on the end, and he let Noel borrow a colorwork beanie featuring a row of green trees with tiny gold stars on top between two rows of white snowflakes, all against a red background.

"Thanks," he said, hugging Noel's arm. "This was a great idea."

"I'm glad you don't think it was silly," Noel said, his gaze full of warm affection. "I thought it might be fun, and maybe a way to start a new holiday tradition? One that's not just yours or mine, but ours."

Warmth bloomed and spread in Gabriel's chest, and he slid his hand down Noel's arm to twine his fingers with Noel's. Whatever doubts Gabriel had about the longevity of their relationship, Noel obviously didn't share them, and Gabriel was starting to believe this was the one that might last too.

"I like that idea," he said.

"Good." Noel gave Gabriel's fingers a squeeze, and his lips curved in his familiar, heart-stopping smile. "And just so you know how much I love you, I'll let you have the window seat."

"Wow, that *is* love," Gabriel said, slanting a teasing smile at Noel. "Or maybe it's just an excuse to hang all over me on the pretense of looking out the window."

Noel hadn't been shy about voicing his feelings for Gabriel, but Gabriel couldn't quite bring himself to say the L word yet. As much as he wanted to go all in with Noel, his doubts and insecurities were holding him back from approaching this relationship with as much openness and trust as he had in the past. It wasn't fair to Noel, and he knew it, but he was trying to move past his reservations, albeit slowly.

"Is that an objection?" Noel grinned back. "Shall I keep my hands to myself?"

"Of course not," Gabriel said, elbowing him playfully. "Just don't scandalize the kiddies."

"I would never," Noel said, solemnly crossing his heart with his free hand. Then he gave Gabriel a wicked look and tugged him over to the sales register.

"Can I help you?" The cheerful young woman at the register didn't seemed fazed by the sight of them holding hands.

"I'd like one of those plush throws," Noel replied, pointing to the wall behind the sales assistant. The throw in question was about five feet square, and it depicted the Polar Express climbing a snow-capped mountain against a moonlit sky.

After Noel paid for the throw, he handed the bag to Gabriel. "What do you think? Will it suffice for hiding any wandering hands – yours or mine?"

Gabriel laughed as he accepted the bag, and he leaned in to kiss Noel's cheek. "I think it'll do the trick."

An image of himself snuggling with Noel on his couch under the fleecy blanket popped in his mind, and he was struck by the domesticity of it – and by how much he *wanted* to make the fantasy happen in reality.

"It'll be good for cuddling under later," he said, trying to sound more casual than he felt. "Maybe with all the lights off except for my tree lights and some of my special hot chocolate."

"I like how you think," Noel replied. There was a long, deep whistle outside, and Noel pulled Gabriel toward the door, apparently as excited as any of the children. "Oh, look, the train's arriving! Let's get our seats."

In keeping with the theme of the excursion, the train that pulled up to the station was an old-fashioned steam engine. Noel had purchased First Class tickets, which meant they had seats in the caboose. The conductor escorted them to a pair of seats with their own small table, and most of the other passengers in the car were also adults and mainly couples, both old and young.

"Window for you," Noel said gallantly.

Gabriel felt like a kid again as he looked around at the festive decorations. The climate controlled car was decorated with wreaths and swags that filled the air with the fresh scent of pine, and it was lit by electric candles. He took the window seat and beamed as Noel sat down beside him. "This is *so cool*."

"It is," Noel said. He moved close to Gabriel, pressing against him. "They'll serve us cocoa and cookies and read us the story. Just like we were kids again, eh?" He stroked one hand along Gabriel's thigh. "Only better."

"*Much* better," Gabriel said, covering Noel's hand and squeezing it gently. "I think I've thrown myself so hard into making new holiday traditions to make up for my family pushing me out. It hasn't always gone as well as I'd hoped, but this year..." He gazed at Noel for a moment, unable to hold back a besotted smile. "This year is shaping up to be pretty good."

Noel leaned in, kissing Gabriel tenderly. "I'm glad you've let me be part of it. Thank you."

"Thank *you*," Gabriel said softly.

It wasn't long before the train pulled out of the station, and Gabriel turned his attention to the scenery passing outside the window. It was too soon for him to call this the best Christmas he'd ever had, but if things kept going as they were, it would definitely be at the top of the list.

It was the second week of December, which meant it was officially time for Christmas movies. Gabriel didn't have as many holiday movies as he did holiday albums, but he had enough to keep him entertained for the rest of the month if he wanted.

In lieu of going out somewhere that Saturday night, Gabriel had invited Noel over to watch a movie or two. He'd carefully curated a selection of movies for Noel to choose from – a mix of black and white classics and modern feel-good films – and he'd promised pizza with grilled chicken, spinach, and olives with beer from Burial Beer Company for dinner.

Noel had chosen *It's a Wonderful Life*, which was one of Gabriel's favorites as well, and Gabriel started the movie as soon as they were settled with their pizza and beer. After dinner, Gabriel tugged the Polar Express throw Noel had bought him off the back of the couch and draped it over them as he snuggled against Noel's side, content to settle in and enjoy the movie.

Noel wrapped his arm around Gabriel and leaned against the cushions, but he crossed and uncrossed his legs several times, and he didn't even chuckle when Clarence made his first appearance and the associated mayhem began to unfold on screen.

Gabriel glanced at him, curious about the lack of response. Noel said he loved the movie, but maybe he'd seen it often enough that he didn't laugh at the antics anymore?

Noel met his gaze and smiled ruefully. "Sorry. I was thinking about something and got distracted."

"Anything you want to talk about?" Gabriel stroked Noel's thigh soothingly.

"It's nothing important. Something I'm working on," Noel said. "Feeling a bit of a time crunch, that's all. Don't worry about it."

Gabriel frowned slightly, puzzled by Noel's unusual reticence. Noel didn't divulge specific information that could identify any of his clients, but normally if he was stressed by his workload or had a frustrating case to deal with, he didn't hesitate to vent to Gabriel about it.

"Okay..."

"Honest, babe, it's nothing," Noel said. "Sorry, I just zoned out and started mulling over what I needed to do to get things wrapped up before Christmas."

"I'm not taking up too much of your time, am I?" Gabriel asked, worried that in his holiday zeal, he'd monopolized Noel's time and caused him to get behind. He didn't know what times of year things got hectic in Noel's line of work, but maybe he needed to give Noel more space to get work done.

"Of course not!" Noel grabbed the remote and paused the movie before turning to face Gabriel. "You are the most important thing in my life, believe me. I love every minute we spend together. If anything, I resent the other obligations in my life that keep me away from you. I'm just not used to being... stymied, I suppose. Usually things go smoothly for me, but I'm dealing with something that's a bit trickier than I expected."

Gabriel studied Noel. "Is there anything I can do to help?"

For the briefest moment, it seemed as though Noel's eyes widened in alarm, but it might have been the low light playing tricks, because Noel smiled and leaned in to kiss Gabriel lightly on the lips. "No, this is something I have to handle on my own, but I appreciate the offer. It's fine. I'll figure it all out."

In Gabriel's experience, fine *never* meant fine, but Noel seemed determined to keep whatever was distracting him to himself, and Gabriel wasn't comfortable pushing.

"Well, if you change your mind, let me know," he said, settling against the cushions again.

"I will," Noel replied, clasping one of Gabriel's hands and holding it tight. "Just two more weeks and it will all be over. Promise."

The words sounded ominous, but Gabriel told himself he was filtering them through his bad experiences in the past. Noel loved him and wanted a future with him. Whatever was going on now was temporary.

He hoped.

～

GABRIEL SANG "SANTA BABY" along with his iPod as he rummaged through his closet in search of something to wear on his date with Noel. They were going a bar near Gabriel's neighborhood that was hosting a holiday party. All the drink specials were holiday themed, and a local band was going to perform a set of nothing but holiday songs. Gabriel had gone alone last year and had a great time, and he couldn't wait to share the experience with Noel this year.

He pulled out his black leather pants, which he hadn't worn in at least two or three years. They were a relic of his twenties, and he wasn't sure he could fit into them anymore even though he did make time to go to the gym and keep himself fit. But if they *did* still fit, he could pair them with his red silk shirt and maybe leave the top two buttons unfastened and forego underwear so he could tease Noel about what he would find when he peeled off the leather pants.

Hopefully Noel would find the sight of Gabriel in tight pants sexy and appealing. Other than Noel's distraction during their movie night, Gabriel thought things had been going pretty well between them, but he'd thought the same thing about his previous relationships. No doubt he was jittery because things had taken a sour turn over the holidays with his other boyfriends, and despite Noel's assurances, Gabriel was worried about history repeating itself this year even though he hadn't knitted a sweater. Once the holidays were over and their relationship was still intact, he'd be fine. In the meantime, he'd try on the leather pants.

He was surprised but pleased to find they still fit, and he got out the red silk shirt to go with them. He left his shirt untucked because he was trying to entice Noel, not trawl for a hookup, and he put on black boots and a wide black leather wrist cuff studded with silver to complete the look.

Studying himself in the full-length mirror on his closet door, Gabriel wasn't satisfied. He checked his phone, and since he still had about ten minutes until Noel was supposed to pick him up, he went into the bathroom and dug up his navy-blue eyeliner pencil. Gabriel didn't wear eyeliner except when he went to a bar or club, which he and Noel hadn't done yet, so this would be another surprise for Noel. Hopefully Noel would like it.

This time, Gabriel struck a pose in front of the mirror, feeling confident and hot. He planned to get Noel worked up the whole time they were out and make sure the night ended *very* well for both of them.

He still had a few minutes, so he dropped onto the couch and pulled out his phone to play solitaire until Noel arrived. But after several games, he glanced at the time again and realized Noel was ten minutes late, which was unusual. Noel was always punctual, and if he *was* running late, he called.

Still, it was only ten minutes, so Gabriel tried not to worry. Noel probably got stuck in traffic and would be there any minute. He closed the solitaire app and checked the weather to see if he needed a jacket or his heavy down coat. He checked his email, and then he checked Twitter.

No Noel.

After almost half an hour, Gabriel gave in to his worry. What if Noel had gotten into an accident on the way over? He called Noel's cell phone, and his anxiety increased when the call went straight to voicemail. Unable to sit still any longer, he jumped up and began to pace, staring at his phone as if that would make it ring. Another five minutes passed, and then his phone rang. Noel's number popped up on the screen.

"God, babe, I'm so sorry," Noel said, sounding breathless and a bit harried. "I was in the middle of something and totally spaced on the time. Give me ten minutes, and I'll be right there."

"Was it an idiot client?" Gabriel asked, worry giving way to sympathy. He'd heard enough about some of Noel's more high maintenance clients to know the kinds of demands they could make on Noel's time.

"Umm... no..." Noel hesitated, and Gabriel could almost envision him biting his lip. Noel had once admitted he tried to never lie, because he was so bad at it and his ears turned pink whenever he did. "It was... something I'm... er... struggling with. But it's not important. We have a date, and I promise I'll be right there."

"It was important enough to make you late," Gabriel said, his tone a little sharper than he intended. This was the second time Noel had taken refuge in vagueness, and that wasn't like him. "If you need to stay put and work on whatever it is, that's fine. I can go by myself. I did last year."

"But last year you didn't have me," Noel said. He was quiet for a moment. "Are you angry with me? I really am sorry, Gabriel. When I saw you'd tried to call, that's when I noticed the time, and I got off the phone to call you as quickly as I could."

"I'm not angry," Gabriel said, although he was annoyed to find out Noel was on the phone, but apparently not with a client. "I was worried. You're never late, and then when I called and it went to voicemail, I started imagining terrible car accidents."

"Oh, babe," Noel said, his voice laced with remorse. "No, nothing like that. I was..." He hesitated again. "I was talking to my Aunt Betty." He made the admission with what sounded like reluctance.

Gabriel frowned, even more puzzled than before by this new information. "Seriously? That's what made you forget our date?"

"You know how Betty is, right? I mean, I was asking her something, and she... well, I got a dissertation." Noel chuckled, but it sounded forced.

"Yeah, I know." Gabriel couldn't argue with that. He knew how Miss Betty was when she got on a roll. "Okay, well, if you still want to go, we can. We can probably catch about half of the set."

"Yes, I want to go," Noel replied. "Like I said, ten minutes. Love you!"

"Ten minutes," Gabriel said, a growling undercurrent in his voice. "If you're not here by then, I'm calling Miss Betty myself to complain about you."

"No! Please don't do that!" Noel begged. "I'll be there. Bye!"

"Bye," Gabriel said, and then he ended the call and went back to the couch to wait.

Noel's explanation made sense, and yet on some level, Gabriel wasn't completely satisfied by it. But Noel sounded genuinely contrite, and so Gabriel pushed his doubts aside. They would go to the party, and if Noel made it up to him well enough, he'd give Noel the chance to peel off the black leather pants after all.

GABRIEL WANTED to think it was his imagination making him feel like Noel's time for him – for *them* – was getting scarcer as Christmas drew nearer. He wanted to, but he couldn't because Noel had started cutting back on the number of times they saw each other during the week and was calling him less as well. When they did talk or text, Noel seemed distracted, like his full attention was never focused on Gabriel the way it used to be. But Noel still said he loved Gabriel, and he hadn't been late for another date, so Gabriel tried to tell himself it was due to an end of the year rush at work, not the slow deterioration of their relationship.

On the weekend before Christmas, Gabriel went to get Sunday brunch at his favorite bakery. He and Noel had gone out the night before, but they didn't have any plans for that day. Noel had seemed more harried than usual, so Gabriel hadn't pushed, thinking maybe Noel needed time and space to get work – or whatever had been stressing him out lately – finished before Christmas.

But the bakery was selling gingerbread cheesecake, and the slice Gabriel tried was so good, he bought two more before he left – one for himself for later and one for Noel. He thought about taking the cheesecake back to his place, but he wasn't sure when he'd see Noel again. Besides, he wanted to do something that might help lift Noel's spirits or at least let him know Gabriel was thinking about him. Thus Gabriel headed over to Noel's condo to deliver the cheesecake and maybe a kiss or two under the mistletoe he'd hung in Noel's foyer when he'd helped decorate Noel's tree the week before.

It took a few moments for Noel to answer the door, and when he opened it, he didn't smile as he normally would have. Instead he stared at Gabriel, eyes wide. Noel was barefoot, dressed in sweatpants and a sleeveless t-shirt, and he looked flushed and tousled, as though he'd been running his hands through his hair – or someone else had been doing so.

"Gabriel? I didn't know you'd be stopping by," Noel said.

That wasn't the reception Gabriel expected, and he felt a lead weight forming in the pit of his stomach. "If it's a bad time, I'm sorry," he said, holding out the plain white pastry box. "I won't stay. I wanted to bring you this, that's all."

Noah's expression softened as he took the box. "Thank you, that's so thoughtful," he said, offering a crooked smile. "Sorry, the place is a wreck and I was working... but come in. Please. Just give me a second."

He didn't wait for Gabriel's reply. Instead, Noel dashed – there was no other word for it – back to the living room. Frowning, Gabriel closed the door behind himself and walked slowly into the living room.

As he stepped around the corner from the foyer, he saw Noah shoving something into the storage ottoman in front of a leather recliner. Noah straightened and gave Gabriel a searching look. "I've been letting the housework slide, I'm afraid."

Indeed, the room didn't look as neat as it normally did. There were a few plates and cups on the coffee table next to Noel's computer. The sofa cushions were askew, and it didn't look as though the rug had been vacuumed in a few days.

Gabriel looked around, concerned by what he saw. Noel was an innately tidy person, and Gabriel had to wonder if there was something more serious than a work-related crisis involved.

"What's going on?" He fixed Noel with a worried look. "Is something wrong?"

"No, of course not!" Noel ran his fingers through his hair, mussing it further, and his face grew a little flushed. "Christmas is soon. Santa has to keep his secrets, you know."

"Uh-huh," Gabriel said, but he wasn't convinced. The strange greeting, the recent evasiveness, and the blatant hiding of something – someone else's boxers, maybe? – were giving him flashbacks to all the signs he'd missed, or perhaps willfully ignored, with Ben. "Well, I won't keep you from your secret strategizing with Santa."

Noel approached Gabriel and slid his arms around Gabriel's waist, pulling him closer. "I'm sorry I've been so busy lately," he said, his expression contrite. Leaning forward, he pressed a kiss to Gabriel's lips. "It'll all be over soon, I promise."

"I hope so," Gabriel said quietly. He slid his arms around Noel's shoulders and nestled close, allowing himself the comfort of the embrace while he had it. His stomach knotted up at the thought of Noel breaking up with him, and he realized with dismay that losing Noel would hurt more than losing Jack, Ben, and Will combined. He drew in a ragged breath, fighting the urge to cry. "I've missed you."

"Oh, babe..." Noel stroked Gabriel's back tenderly. "I've missed you, too. Would you like to come to the bedroom and let me show you how much I love you?"

Gabriel's cynical side urged him to say no and start distancing himself now to lessen the impact of heartbreak later, but that wasn't what he wanted to do. Instead, he nodded. "Please."

Noel smiled as he led Gabriel toward the bedroom. "You've been very patient with me, and you deserve the best. I'm going to make certain you get it."

This was more like the Noel Gabriel was familiar with, and he relaxed a little as he followed Noel into the bedroom. Maybe he was just being paranoid because of Ben. Maybe Noel was frazzled because work was driving him crazy and he was getting behind on Christmas shopping. Maybe they would survive the holidays and everything would be okay.

It had to be, because the alternative was something Gabriel didn't even want to think about.

Gabriel slowed his pace and glanced at Noel, his eyebrows climbing, when he heard Noel's phone go off again. They were barely thirty minutes into a leisurely walk around downtown Asheville after dark, taking in the lights and decorations, and Noel's phone had already rung twice, which was unusual.

"Do you think it's an emergency?" he asked.

Noel pulled out his phone and glanced quickly at the screen before pocketing it again. "No, definitely not an emergency," he said, reaching out to take Gabriel's hand.

"Are you sure?" Gabriel gave Noel's hand a little squeeze. "I don't mind if it's something you need to deal with."

Noel smiled as he returned the pressure. "It's fine, really. I'll return the call later."

Gabriel nodded and turned his attention back to the scenery. A lot of the shops had put up lights and decorated the front windows, and he always enjoyed looking at all the decorations. Their plan was to walk around until they were ready for dinner, then pick a restaurant, maybe one they hadn't been to before. Gabriel hoped a low-key evening focused on soaking up the festive atmosphere would help Noel decompress from whatever had been stressing him out lately.

But not ten minutes later, Noel's phone rang *again*, and this time, Gabriel stopped and tugged Noel to one side, out of the path of other pedestrians on the sidewalk. "If it's the same person, I think you should answer it. Is it someone from work?"

Noel resisted at first, but then he sighed. "No, it's not work," he replied, pulling out his phone with an air of resignation. "I'd rather focus on you, but if you really want me to..." He pressed a button and raised the phone to his ear. "Hello?"

For several moments Noel just listened, but then he shot Gabriel a sideways glance and moved a few steps off. "No, I haven't. Look, this isn't the best time, okay?" Noel listened again and took another couple of steps away, lowering his voice. "No. No. It's complicated, you know that. I'm doing my best, but... it sucks. It's terrible and he's not going to be happy... Fine. Look, I'll call you later, okay? I know. Yes, I know. Me, too. Bye."

Noel tucked the phone away, then walked back to Gabriel. He smiled, but it was weak. "See, no emergency. Shall we continue?"

"Um. Sure." Gabriel started walking, his mind full of static as he tried to process what he'd heard.

Who was "he?" Not a client, because Noel said the call wasn't work related. A relative? Gabriel didn't want to think it referred to him, because if it did, that whole conversation sounded like bad news waiting to happen.

What if Noel wanted to break up and was waiting until after

Christmas to drop the bomb in order to avoid ruining Gabriel's holiday? What if there really was another man and Noel was cheating on him just like Ben had? The only way to find out was to ask, and Gabriel didn't want to do that. He might be wrong, after all. There could be a reasonable and innocent explanation for all the weird shit that had been going on lately. Gabriel had no idea what it was, but surely it was possible.

Noel drew in a deep breath and reached out for Gabriel's hand once more. "Do you know where you'd like to go for dinner? Something light, something filling?"

Gabriel's stomach was tied up in such tight knots that he wasn't sure how he could swallow a single bite and keep it down, but he mustered a smile. "Maybe something light. I'm not that hungry."

"All right." Noel glanced at him again. "Is everything all right, babe?"

"Everything's fine," Gabriel said.

Everything was fine, aside from the realization that it wasn't the sweaters that were cursed but Gabriel himself. If the signs were indeed pointing to a breakup, Gabriel thought he might as well take himself off the market for good. Obviously he was a failure either at picking the right man or at relationships or both. Either way, after four failed relationships, he got the message the universe was sending: stay home and knit.

ON CHRISTMAS EVE, Gabriel put on his favorite Christmas sweater, one that his maternal grandmother had knitted for him almost twenty years ago back when he still had a family that acknowledged him. It was dark green with stylized Scandinavian motifs in white, including large snowflakes and reindeer. She had taught him to knit when he was eleven because he expressed interest in a lace scarf she was knitting, and they had bonded over yarn and pattern books. He'd thought they had a close relationship, but then he came out at eighteen, and he learned how easily his family ties could be unraveled. But he still loved the sweater as a remembrance of the woman who had given him the gift of knitting, which had helped keep him sane during the most difficult time of his life.

With it, he wore a pair of old, faded jeans and a pair of red socks with the Grinch on them. He had at least a dozen pairs of more cheerful Christmas socks, but these reflected his state of mind more accurately.

He went through the motions of creating a cozy atmosphere – dimming the lights in the living room, turning on the lights on the tree, starting up his Christmas playlist – but he wasn't in a festive mood at all. He was still waiting for Noel to drop the breakup bomb on him, and he was starting to wish Noel had done it before Christmas. Sure, it might have made him sad during his favorite holiday, but at least he would know what was going on and could start dealing with it. This way, he was living in dread.

A glance at his phone showed Noel was due to arrive in a few minutes, and Gabriel went into the kitchen to prepare some spiked eggnog. They were having their private celebration that evening because Noel was spending Christmas Day with his family. Gabriel planned to do what he did every year: spend the day watching Christmas movies in his pajamas.

Precisely on time, there was a knock at the front door, and Gabriel opened it to find Noel on the doorstep. Noel was dressed in a black leather jacket which was partially unzipped to reveal a red silk shirt beneath and black jeans that clung to his hips. He looked as if his hair had just been trimmed, and Gabriel caught the subtle scent of a spicy cologne. Noel was holding a medium sized package in his hands, wrapped in glittery red foil and topped with an enormous silver bow.

"Merry Christmas, babe," Noel said. He looked both nervous and oddly hopeful, and his expression seemed pensive.

Gabriel stood aside to let Noel in and mustered up a smile, trying to pretend everything was normal and fine. He had a gift for Noel under the tree, but considering how things had gone downhill so quickly, he was even more glad he'd been cautious about knitting anything.

"Hi," he said. "Come on in. I've got some eggnog if you want it. Spiked, of course."

"Sounds good to me," Noel said fervently. He stepped inside and paused to brush a kiss to Gabriel's cheek. "I could use it."

Uh-oh... Gabriel tried to quell the flare of nerves he felt at that. What if Noel was gearing himself up with liquid courage to dump Gabriel tonight?

"Sure, have a seat, and I'll get it," he said, and then he made a hasty retreat to the kitchen.

His fingers trembled as he poured two glasses of eggnog and placed them on a plastic tray with a big Santa Claus face in the center along with a plate of gingerbread cookies he'd picked up from the bakery. He'd bought two dozen so he'd have plenty for his Christmas Day movie marathon.

"Here we go," he said as he entered the living room and carried the tray over to his coffee table.

Noel had placed the package he'd brought under the tree and seated himself on the sofa. He smiled, quick and nervous. "Thanks. I haven't eaten all day."

"You should probably have something more substantial than eggnog and cookies," Gabriel said. "I could make you a sandwich. I've got a small turkey breast for tomorrow. I can slice it right quick."

"Thanks, but not right now," Noel replied. He reached for the eggnog and touched his glass to Gabriel's. "Here's to a happy Christmas for both of us."

Noel's antsiness was unusual, and Gabriel wondered if Noel wanted to rush through their gift exchange. Frowning, he put his glass aside untouched.

"Is something wrong?" he asked. Fuck it, he couldn't go through the rest of the night like this. If their relationship was over, he wanted to know sooner rather than later. "If there's something else you'd rather be doing, then just tell me."

Noel's eyes widened, and he put his glass back down on the tray.

"What? No!" He reached for Gabriel's hand and clung to it tightly. "I'm nervous. I know I haven't been around as much as either of us would have liked in the last few weeks. You've probably wondered if I'm losing my mind. But... I've never done anything like this before, and I'm scared about how you're going to feel about it."

Gabriel's frown deepened as he stared at Noel, trying to make sense of what Noel was saying. "Done what before? Broken up with a boyfriend?"

Noel stared at Gabriel, and his expression of complete shock might have been funny in other circumstances. "Break up? You think I want to break up with you? Oh, God... do you really mean you want to break up with me?"

"No!" Gabriel shook his head vehemently. "That's not what I want. I thought that's where you were headed. You've been so distant and secretive lately, and it's not like you. I was seeing the same signs that I saw with Ben. I thought maybe you'd found someone else and were waiting until after Christmas to tell me."

"God, I've probably screwed this up beyond hope. No, babe. Nothing like that." Noel stopped talking and swallowed hard. "I think I'd better come clean and hope you don't end up shoving me out the door."

With that, Noel stood up and went over to the tree. He picked up the present he'd brought, then carried it over to Gabriel and held it out to him. "There is no one but you, Gabriel. If you want to know why I've been distant and secretive, open this and you'll find out."

Gabriel took the package, hardly daring to let hope bloom beneath all his bewilderment. He had no idea how the contents of the box could explain Noel's behavior over the last couple of weeks, but he was curious enough to open it and find out.

The present looked as if it had been professionally wrapped with a sleek ribbon tied around all four sides and a poufy bow on top. He slid the ribbon off and tried to take off the shiny paper with a minimum of tearing. He put the wrapping paper aside and held the plain white box, regarding it for a moment. There was some weight to it, but not enough to be a book, plus the box was too big for that.

Finally he pried off the lid and peeled away a couple of layers of tissue paper to reveal... a sweater.

It had been knitted with a bulky weight yarn in a medium, heathered gray. As Gabriel lifted it from the box, he could feel the yarn was also soft, probably a blend of wool and silk, maybe with a touch of cashmere. But the stitches were uneven – some tight, others loose – and there were dropped stitches that had been inexpertly repaired. The neckline was wide and straight, and he could tell the sweater had been knitted by someone who had neither the experience nor the talent for knitting.

"It sucks, I know," Noel said. He was twisting his hands together. "If you hate it, that's okay. Just... no curse, okay?"

"You made this?" Gabriel stared at Noel with wide eyes, scarcely able to believe what he was hearing. "For me?"

"Yeah." Noel looked miserable. "It's terrible, isn't it? I've been at it for weeks, and I had to start over like five times, despite all of Aunt Betty's help. But every sorry stitch in the ugly thing is mine. Because like I said, I believe in you."

Gabriel's breath hitched, and he stroked the sweater with shaking fingers. All this time, he'd thought Noel was distancing himself, but instead, he was *knitting*. Relief and joy collided within Gabriel, overcoming him until he could do nothing but press the soft folds of the sweater against his face and sob.

"Babe?" Noel dropped to his knees and stroked Gabriel's hair. "I know it's horrible, and I didn't want to give it to you because it's ugly. I don't care if you never wear it, honest. You can put it in the box and we'll go find a bonfire to throw it in."

"No!" Gabriel clutched the sweater against his chest, not letting it go even long enough to wipe his eyes. "It's *perfect!*"

Noel looked nonplussed. "You don't have to pretend, Gabriel, honestly. I do have eyes in my head and I won't be upset to hear the truth. Betty said it was the worst sweater she'd ever seen in her life, but then she said I had to give it to you anyway."

"She was right," Gabriel said, still hugging the sweater. "And I'm not pretending. I know exactly how much time it takes to knit a sweater, and I know how difficult it is for a beginning knitter to tackle something like this." He was tearing up again, but this time, he didn't hide his face. "I also what it means to knit someone a gift like this. It means you think they're worth the time and effort it'll take to finish the project. It means you want to make them something special and personal just for them." Unable to hold back any longer, he flung his arms around Noel's neck and clung to him. "It means you really do love me, and I love you too!"

Caught by surprise by Gabriel's enthusiastic hug, Noel gasped and fell backward, carrying Gabriel with him. But he wrapped his arms around Gabriel in return, and his smile was wide and joyous. "I do love you," he said. "More than anything. Are you sure you love me? I can't knit and I screwed up so badly that you thought I was going to break up with you."

"You've got plenty of other qualities that make up for your lack of knitting skills," Gabriel said, leaning down to kiss Noel. "And I forgive you for the screw up. Part of it was my own insecurities messing with me, so it wasn't totally your fault."

Noel blushed, but his eyes were alight with happiness. "I knew you'd been hurt badly, maybe even worse than you were willing to admit. I knew you had doubts about *us*, too. I foolishly thought knitting a sweater wouldn't be nearly as hard as it is, but I had to keep going, even though it was costing me time with you. I could tell you weren't happy about it, but I couldn't stop. I had to finish, if for no other reason than to show you I don't believe in any stupid curse and that you would be safe with me."

"I know that now." Gabriel sat up and straddled Noel's hips, and he pulled his Christmas sweater over his head. "I'm going to wear my new sweater," he said as he tossed the old sweater aside.

His new sweater was loose around the neck, and one sleeve was too long, but he rolled up the cuff. He stretched his arms out and showed off the new sweater proudly. "See? It's perfect, and hell, yeah, I'm going to wear it."

Noel chuckled. "The sweater is ugly, but you're gorgeous," he said, resting his hands at Gabriel's hips. "Crazy, but gorgeous, and I love you with every breath in my body."

"I love you too," Gabriel said, smiling widely. He was safe, he was loved, and he could say the words now without any fear. "The curse is broken."

"So it is." Noel moved his hands around to grope Gabriel's ass. "Now that we've reached an accord, I have a request. Gabriel Sutton, would you do me and my family the honor of spending Christmas Day with us? I don't know if Aunt Betty will believe everything's all right unless you accompany me and reassure her."

"Are you sure?" Gabriel was surprised by the offer, and as much as he liked the idea of spending the day with Noel and his family, he didn't want to impose. "They won't mind?"

"Not at all," Noel said. "We're in love, aren't we? Now that you trust me, maybe we can start thinking about a future, can't we? A future together?"

Warmth bloomed in Gabriel's chest and spread its tendrils throughout his entire body, and he couldn't hold back the foolish grin curving his lips. Noel was different from his exes in every way, and he felt far more secure now with Noel than he ever had with them.

"Yes and yes," he said, leaning over to kiss Noel with all the love he felt. "We're definitely building a future together. I don't have any doubts about that anymore."

Noel returned the kiss tenderly and caressed Gabriel's cheek. When Gabriel pulled back, he smiled. "I want it all, just so you know. I've been saving up for years, waiting for you to come along. And I do mean *all* – the house and the dog and the picket fence. But we can talk about that later. What do you want to do right now? I'm all yours. In any and every way."

"Well..." Gabriel sat up and slanted a playfully coy look at Noel. "You could open your present, or we could have some gingerbread and eggnog, or you could unwrap your *other* present," he said, slipping his hands beneath the hem of his sweater and pushing it up just enough to give Noel a peek of his bare stomach. "And we could celebrate taking our relationship to the next level."

"Oh, I like that last option," Noel said. He wriggled under Gabriel. "Floor or bed? For you, I'm easy."

"I'm aware," Gabriel said dryly as he rolled off Noel and climbed to his feet. "How about bed? It's far more comfortable and better suited for cuddling afterward." He held out his hand to help Noel up.

"I like how you think." Noel grasped Gabriel's hand and let Gabriel haul him to his feet, and then he gave Gabriel's ass a playful grope. "You might want to turn off the music, though, or put on a different playlist. I can't promise what might happen if the Chipmunks started up at the wrong moment."

Laughing, Gabriel went to turn off the music, putting an enticing sway in each step along the way. He could scarcely believe how quickly what he'd thought was his worst Christmas ever had turned into the best Christmas of his life, and he smoothed his palms down the front of his sweater to remind himself that this was real.

"There," he said as he returned to Noel. "We won't be interrupting by singing chipmunks."

"Perfect." Noel clasped Gabriel's hand and led him to the bedroom. "As fetching as you look in the sweater, I'm anxious to get it off."

As soon as they reached the bedroom, Gabriel released Noel's hand and headed to the nightstand to get lube and condoms. Normally, he had them out and ready before Noel got there, but given he hadn't been sure how the evening would go, he hadn't prepared this time.

"Do you want to do the honors?" he asked, lifting the hem of his sweater a little as he gave Noel a come-hither look.

"Absolutely." Noel slid his fingers under the sweater and caressed Gabriel's stomach with feather-light touches. Then he grasped the bottom of the sweater and lifted it up slowly, letting the soft fabric slide over Gabriel's skin. "The sweater may look ugly, but I did like how the yarn felt, all soft and sensuous. It reminded me of your skin."

"It was a good choice." Gabriel's eyes went half-lidded as he focused on the pleasurable feel of the fabric gliding against his skin, and he lifted his arms to help Noel get the sweater up and off. "I won't need to wear a t-shirt under it if I don't want to because the yarn isn't scratchy."

"My thoughts exactly." Noel lifted the sweater off, chuckling when he had to tug the over-long sleeve free. Then he tossed the sweater onto the overstuffed chair by the window, his dark eyes taking on a heated gleam as he splayed his hands on Gabriel's chest. He smoothed them over Gabriel's skin and circled Gabriel's nipples with his thumbs. "Your skin is much better than any yarn."

Gabriel's chest hitched with a gasp, and he grabbed Noel's shoulders to keep himself steady. "My skin has missed the feel of your hands lately," he said, leaning in to nuzzle kisses along Noel's jaw.

"I'm so sorry about that," Noel said as he tilted his head to accommodate Gabriel's kisses. He wrapped his arms around Gabriel and drew him close. "You'll never have to doubt me again, I promise."

"I believe you." Gabriel slid his arms around Noel in return, enjoying the simple pleasure of holding Noel and being held by him. "I trust you," he said, and he meant it. Noel wasn't like his exes, and he could – and would – put all of his worries and doubts behind.

Noel's whole face lit up with happiness, and the warmth in his eyes was for Gabriel alone. "That means so much to me. You can love someone without really trusting them, and I know how much your trust has been abused. Thank you."

With that, he captured Gabriel's lips in a tender kiss, one that quickly became firm and seductive as Noel moved his hands to Gabriel's ass, urging him closer, molding their bodies together and leaving Gabriel in no doubt as to how much Noel desired him. Gabriel parted his lips and moaned into the kiss, eager to surrender – to give to Noel without reservation.

After a time, Noel pulled back from the kiss with a groan. "I want you so much," he said. He gave Gabriel's ass a smack. "You want to top or me? I don't care as long as it involves getting naked right now."

"I'll bottom," Gabriel said, sliding his hands down to grope Noel's ass in return. "I'm in a giving mood. We can see how long it takes before one of us screams 'ho ho ho'," he added with a mischievous smile.

Noel laughed, and then he kissed Gabriel again, fast and hard. "Okay, then. Off with the jeans and anything under them. You can leave the Grinch socks on, if you'd like, though it won't just be your heart that grows three sizes if I have anything to do with it."

"It's grown a size or two already." Gabriel leered playfully at Noel as he unfastened his jeans and pushed them down along with his red boxers, which had three tree ornaments across the front with "nice balls" above them.

"Oh my God, that's great!" Noel laughed as he cupped Gabriel's crotch with his hand. "Truth in advertising! They really are nice balls." He fondled Gabriel playfully.

"I'll let you play ball all night long if you want," Gabriel said, shifting his stance to offer Noel better access. He couldn't remember desiring his exes as much as he desired Noel, and he didn't remember their touch arousing him like Noel's. He'd finally found the right man for him, the one who complemented him best, and he wanted to kick himself for not realizing it sooner.

Noel kept up the teasing for several moments, then kissed Gabriel and stepped back. "Okay, onto the bed before I come in my jeans like a teenager." He shrugged out of his leather jacket and let it fall to the floor, and then he unbuttoned his silk shirt, smiling evilly. "I have to make a confession. I don't have on any clever boxers. In fact, I don't have on any boxers at all."

Gabriel climbed onto the bed and sat back against the two rows of pillows piled against the headboard, eager to watch Noel strip. A sharp zing of arousal shot through him at Noel's admission, and he whimpered softly. "It's probably a good thing you didn't tell me that sooner. We might not have made it to the bedroom."

Noel finished unbuttoning his shirt, then parted the red silk, giving Gabriel a glimpse of his furred chest and the well-defined muscles of his abdomen. He let the silk slide off his shoulders, then stepped out of his loafers, bringing him closer to the bed. "I wasn't a Boy Scout, but I thought it best to be prepared." With a sultry smile, Noel unfastened the button-fly on his black jeans, doing a teasing little bump and grind. When he finished with the final button, he hooked his thumbs under the waistband, and slowly peeled the tight jeans down his hips.

"More, more!" Gabriel whistled and applauded, his gaze riveted on the slow descent of Noel's jeans.

His face flushed, Noel slipped the denim down past his cock, then pushed them the rest of the way off. He stood in front of Gabriel, naked and aroused, and wrapped his fingers around his cock. "See what you do to me, Gabriel? Do you see how much I want you?"

"I want you too," Gabriel said, the words underscored by a moan. He let his gaze travel up and down the length of Noel's body, drinking in the sight, but he was ready to touch too. "Come here and take what you want!" He held out his arms and beckoned to Noel.

Noel didn't hesitate to move into Gabriel's embrace and settle between his legs, aligning their bodies. He captured Gabriel's lips in a deep kiss as he rocked his hips enough to arouse but not nearly enough to satisfy. Gabriel hummed with satisfaction at the welcome weight of Noel's body atop his, and he hooked one leg around Noel's hips as he matched Noel's slow, teasing rhythm.

Gabriel could feel the way Noel's heartbeat sped up, and Noel broke the kiss and gazed down at Gabriel with his dark eyes gleaming with heat. "I want you," he said, reaching toward the nightstand. "I need you right now."

"You can have me." Gabriel arched against Noel, a flush of need washing over his skin as he thought about Noel fucking him. He wanted to feel Noel buried deep, to be joined, to celebrate this newfound level of commitment. "I'm yours."

"And I'm yours."

Noel opened the bottle of lube and coated his fingers before returning the bottle to the nightstand. He pressed his fingers to Gabriel's opening and prepared him with loving care. Then Noel wrapped his free hand around Gabriel's cock, stroking him slowly to keep his arousal close to peak. "You're so gorgeous, babe. So beautiful, inside and out. You take my breath away."

Tension coiled tighter in Gabriel's belly, and his body quivered with need as he gazed up at Noel. He saw the love in Noel's eyes, and he felt as if his heart, like the Grinch's, had grown three sizes.

"I love you so much," he said, resting his palm against Noel's cheek. "I *need* you so much. Please, Noel!"

Noel rubbed his cheek against Gabriel's hand. "If you're ready, so am I," he said huskily. He took a moment to retrieve the condom and roll it on, then applied extra lube to his cock. Positioning himself, he looked down at Gabriel, and Gabriel could see Noel's love and desire naked in his eyes, as if Noel held back nothing, offering Gabriel every bit of himself.

"I love you," Noel murmured, then claimed Gabriel's body, taking him in one slow, deep thrust.

Gabriel wrapped his legs around Noel's hips and rocked up, wanting to send him deeper. He clutched Noel's shoulders and moaned his approval of Noel's claim.

"That's it. I want to make you feel good," Noel said, stroking Gabriel's cock in counterpoint to the movement of their hips. He sped up the rhythm, driving himself deeper and faster, the bed rocking as they moved together.

Each thrust chipped away at the fear, doubt, and loneliness Gabriel had carried for so long until his heart was left bare of all defenses. He'd never opened himself so much – never felt like he *could* – but now he wanted to give Noel everything he'd never shared before. He let go of his inhibitions and let Noel see all the desire and love he felt as he shattered beneath Noel, unleashing his pleasure with a wild cry.

"Yes!" Noel continued to stroke Gabriel through his release, and then he groaned, burying himself deep one last time as pleasure overcame him as well.

Breathing hard, Noel lowered himself onto Gabriel, his skin warm and damp as he relaxed in the aftermath. He pressed his lips to Gabriel's, the kiss a tender benediction.

"My beautiful Gabriel," he said. "All mine."

Gabriel slid his arms around Noel's shoulders, holding him close and tight. "All yours," he said, and then he flashed a mischievous smile. "I have the sweater to prove it."

"Indeed you do," Noel said, chuckling and rubbing his nose against Gabriel's. "Anyone who sees you wearing it is going to think you're either crazy or crazy in love. Or maybe a little of both, eh?"

"Maybe, but if anyone dares to say a word about it, I'm going to tell them my partner made it for me, and I love it," Gabriel said, returning the affectionate nuzzling with a happy little sigh.

"Then maybe I'll knit you a scarf to go with it," Noel teased. "It certainly can't be any worse looking than the sweater, eh?"

"I'd say you can't go wrong with a scarf because there are such simple patterns available, but I might regret those words," Gabriel said, teasing Noel in return. "But if you knit a scarf for me, I'll wear that too."

"It's definitely love," Noel said, grinning down at him. Then he moved away and collapsed onto the mattress. He pulled Gabriel into his arms and cuddled him close. "Mm... how about a nap, then eggnog? Even though I've already gotten what I wanted for Christmas, I'd like to kiss you under the mistletoe at midnight. For luck."

"I'd like that." Gabriel nestled closer, feeling safe and happy in Noel's arms.

The boyfriend sweater curse was broken at last, and Gabriel was already planning what special gift he would knit for Noel for Valentine's Day.

DANDY'S LITTLE GIRL

1

———

"I'm making my list and checking it twice!" Andy Lane's rich baritone carried through the aisles of Kaufman's toy store, making heads turn and children's eyes grow wide. He sang in a loud, clear voice as he took the long way to the escalator, the showman in him unable to resist the temptation to draw a crowd.

By the time he arrived at Santa's Workshop on the second floor, he had a string of children behind him, dragging their parents to the already lengthy line. Pretending to conduct, Andy led his audience in one last chorus of "Santa Claus Is Coming to Town" before he took a seat on Santa's gilded throne and let out a hearty "ho ho ho". His deep laugh was one of the reasons he'd been chosen to take over as a substitute Santa, since he'd been told he sounded like Santa Claus ever since his voice had changed.

Kaufman's spared no expense with their annual Santa's Workshop, which looked like something out of a Hollywood set. They paid attention to detail, right down to the hand-stitched gold embroidery on the red velvet Santa suit. It was no less than their patrons expected. Kaufman's had been upholding its exacting standards in customer service and merchandise since 1945, and it had paid off in a loyal customer base that kept the store thriving in Highland Park, IL, even when the chain toy stores began encroaching. By now, Christmas at Kaufman's was a local legend, and people traveled for miles to see the window displays, the lights, and the decorations throughout the store. But Santa's Workshop was the best of all.

Even if he hadn't been asked, Andy would have volunteered to take over when their regular Santa called in sick with the flu last week. As one of the store managers, he could have delegated the job to someone else, but he loved kids and he loved performing.

"Merry Christmas!" Andy waved to the crowd while the photographer "elf" finished setting up the camera. "I hope you've all be good boys and girls this year!"

Most of them screamed "Yes!" but Andy heard a few parents' voices adding "No" to the mix, making him grin behind his fake white beard. As soon as the camera was ready, Tinsel the elf (whose real name was Bruce) opened the white gate and ushered the first child of the day up to Santa.

Judging by the length of the line, Andy knew he wouldn't have any lulls in his shift, but it would go quickly. He had a high success rate with reassuring nervous children and even coaxing the frightened ones into sharing their Christmas wishes with him, letting them use Tinsel or their parents as intermediaries if that made them feel safer. Sometimes, he held a child in his lap and felt a wistful longing for a family of his own, but being single and gay made the likelihood of that ever happening remote.

For now, he immersed himself in the moment, enjoying his brief connection with each little girl and boy -- even the ones who tried to pull his beard off.

About an hour into his shift, he glanced up to see how the line was moving, and he did a double-take when he saw a familiar face. Noah Coleman. Older, of course, and filled out from the baseball star he'd known in high school. With blond hair and piercing blue eyes, Noah had been attractive as a teenager. As an adult, he was sexy as hell, especially with those horn-rimmed glasses he was sporting now. Andy had always had a weakness for men with glasses.

Even more surprising was that Noah was holding the hand of an adorable little girl with blue eyes like his but with a head full of gorgeous red curls. Andy had considered himself too cool for relationships in high school, but that hadn't kept him from getting a gay vibe from Noah. He wondered if his youthful gaydar had been wrong. Then again, the little girl could be Noah's niece or the daughter of a family friend. There was only one way to find out, and Andy couldn't wait until Noah reached the head of the line.

It took some time, but at last Tinsel escorted the little red-haired girl -- and her big, buff guardian -- up to Andy. Unsurprisingly, no hint of recognition showed in Noah's eyes as he relinquished the little girl's hand. She smiled at Andy shyly, hanging back against Noah's legs.

"It's all right, Princess," Noah said quietly, his voice deep and pitched to a soothing tone. "I told you your grandmother used to bring me here when I was a little boy, right? Wouldn't you like to have your picture taken with Santa just like daddy did?" Well, that seemed to settle the question of whether she was Noah's daughter or not.

The little girl turned and wrapped her arms around Noah's leg, burying her face against his thigh. She said something Andy couldn't catch, but Noah must have heard her, since he smoothed a gentle hand over her curly hair. "Why don't you ask him?"

Big blue eyes peeped at him, although she didn't release her stranglehold on Noah's leg. "Are you *really* Santa?" she asked breathlessly.

"I really am." Andy leaned forward so he could meet her more on her level, grateful that Kaufman's splurged on a makeup artist to apply his wig and beard so they looked as natural as possible. No over the ear hooks for Kaufman's Santa! "In fact, I can prove it to you. I remember when your daddy was on my naughty list."

Two pairs of blue eyes were suddenly fixed on him. The little girl's were wide with surprise, while Noah blinked and tilted his head to one side, obviously curious. "Now, Santa, are you trying to get me in trouble?"

"Not at all, Noah." Andy grinned and winked at him. "I just want to reassure your daughter that I'm the one and only Santa Claus." He

turned his attention back to the little girl and gave her a conspiratorial smile. "Once when your daddy was in school, he dressed up as a
werewolf, hid in a trashcan at school, and jumped out at a very nice
teacher named Ms. Evans. He scared her so badly that she screamed,
and the school almost went into lockdown."

"Did you really do that, Daddy? You scared a *teacher*?" The little
girl gazed up at Noah, wide-eyed.

Noah flushed and shot Andy an aggrieved look. "I did. It was
Halloween, Princess, and I wasn't trying to be mean, I promise. I liked
that teacher very much. It was just a silly joke."

"Oh." She seemed to mull that over, and then she frowned at
Noah. "You were a bad boy, Daddy!"

"Never mind that, Emily," Noah replied hurriedly. "Don't you
want to tell Santa what you want for Christmas?" From the way Noah
looked at him, Andy rather thought that what *Noah* wanted was a
chance to punch Santa right on his jolly red nose.

Apparently that was enough of a distraction, and Emily, who
seemed to decide Andy must be the real Santa after all, nodded. "Yes,
please."

Andy held out his arms, inviting Emily onto his lap. "It's very nice
to meet you, Emily. I'm sure you've been a very good girl this year."

This time she didn't hesitate, going right to Andy and letting him
pick her up. She smoothed the skirt of her green velvet dress primly.
"Yes," she nodded solemnly. "I had to get shots at the doctor and I
didn't cry. An' I didn't cry when I fell of the swing, neither."

Andy listened and nodded solemnly. "That was *very* brave," he
replied as he studied her, looking for other signs of Noah in her face.
He felt a twinge of envy that Noah had such a gorgeous little girl.
"Brave girls definitely qualify for the nice list. What would you like
for Christmas this year?"

Emily looked quite satisfied, beaming at him with a wide smile
that showed off a missing front tooth. "I want a Susie Sunflower doll
and a doctor kit. I want to be a baby doctor when I grow up!"

"That's wonderful!" Andy smiled at her, pleased that she had high
goals already. "Will Susie be your first patient?"

"No, I have a Baby Betsy, and I take care of her, too. Don't I, Daddy?"

"You do a good job, Princess," Noah said, gazing at his daughter with obvious love.

"Ah, so you're expanding your practice." Andy nodded again, trying to ignore the little zing of attraction he felt at the sight of Noah. God, was there anything sexier than a loving father -- in glasses? "It's good to start early. Is there anything else you'd like?"

"Well...." She glanced at Noah, then held up one small hand as she craned around to whisper in Andy's ear. "I wanna baby sister. But don't tell Daddy."

Andy glanced over at Noah, his eyebrows climbing. He couldn't help but wonder if there was a Mrs. Coleman who could help with that request. "I won't tell him," he assured Emily, keeping his voice low so Noah couldn't hear their conversation. "Baby sisters are a little out of Santa's purview. That's Mother Nature's area, but I'll put in a good word for you."

Emily smiled and nodded, seeming satisfied, and she gave Andy a hug. "Thank you!"

Noah waited during this exchange, his eyes intent on Andy's face as though he was trying to see beneath the beard and makeup. "Okay, Princess, we should take your picture now and let Santa talk to the other kids, okay?"

"Yes, Daddy." She turned to face the camera and grinned widely. "CHEESE!"

Andy smiled for the picture as well, letting his delight over Emily's precociousness show. Hopefully this would be the best photo with Santa she ever took. Then he helped her off his lap and waved as she hurried back to Noah. "Merry Christmas, Emily!" He flashed a teasing grin up at Noah. "Merry Christmas, Noah. Try to stay off the naughty list this year, okay?"

"You do the same, *Santa*," Noah replied easily, scooping Emily up in his arms. Tinsel handed her a candy cane, and with a cheerful wave, she turned to Noah and began chattering happily about how Susie Sunflower was going to need her own bed. The last glimpse

Andy had of Noah was an intent blue gaze that seemed to promise that Noah was going to remember this occasion quite well.

Andy chuckled as he turned his attention back to the next child in line. Even if Noah did some digging, Andy doubted he would associate Kaufman's second floor manager with the young man he'd known in high school. They had never run in the same social circles, and Andy had been quite different back then.

But if Noah did figure out who "Santa" was, Andy wouldn't object. Maybe he'd been wrong about Noah's orientation, but that didn't mean they couldn't reconnect as friends. At the very least, he could pass along Emily's secret wish so Noah and his wife could consider whether they wanted to make it come true.

2

"   nd they all lived happily ever after."

". . . "A   "The end!" Emily laughed, as she did at the
conclusion of every story. Noah smiled as he closed
the well-worn copy of *Sleepy Beauty*, reaching out to stroke Emily's
curls back from her face as she gazed up at him. He felt a pang, as he
often did, that Jeff wasn't there to see her, to watch as she grew and
blossomed from a baby, to a toddler, to a small girl who was bright
and happy and everything a father could possibly wish for. He was
well aware that he was biased, but Emily was a lovely and loving
child, and Noah was inordinately proud of her. It hadn't always been
easy, raising her alone, but that hadn't been the plan, of course.
Unfortunately, as the saying went, life was what happened when you
were making other plans -- and death was, too. But Noah really
couldn't complain, as long as his daughter was happy and healthy.

Emily yawned, clutching Baby Betsy close, and he could see she
was on the verge of falling asleep. Tucked up in her bed with the
Princess and the Frog comforter, she looked content, despite the recent
upheaval of their move to Chicago. They still weren't completely
unpacked, but Noah had made Emily's room a priority, wanting her

to have familiar things around her so she wouldn't feel the change of moving had taken anything from her.

Looking at the doll reminded Noah of their visit to Kaufman's earlier that day. "Hey, Princess, what did you whisper to Santa? Is it a special toy you would like?"

Emily shook her head. "It's a secret."

"Well, if you tell me, maybe I can help Santa out a little," Noah said, trying to cajole the information out of her. He tried very hard not to spoil Emily, but Christmas was special, and if there was something she really wanted, he'd do his best to give it to her.

But his daughter shook her head, lower lip coming out in a stubborn little pout that managed to be adorable. "You don't tell secrets, Daddy."

A little dismayed, Noah smiled. "Are you sure? Not even a hint?"

"Nuh-uh." Emily yawned again and rolled to her side, closing her eyes. "'Night, Daddy."

"Good night, Princess." Noah leaned down and kissed her cheek, then stood. "Sweet dreams."

Emily mumbled something, but she was already out, falling into the easy sleep of the innocent. It still amused him, the way she could be laughing and chattering one minute and then collapse in a boneless heap, sound asleep the next. He turned out the light but left her door cracked open so that he could hear if she got up in the middle of the night. The head counselor of the single parent support group he'd been going to in California had indicated that young children who faced uncertainty and upheaval in their lives, such as during a move, could sometimes sleepwalk, and he didn't want her to wander around and get hurt. They'd been in the house for almost a week, however, and nothing had happened, but Noah didn't take any chances when it came to Emily. She was the only thing in his life that really mattered.

Making his way down to the living room, he sighed and rubbed his forehead, thinking about all the things he still needed to do. Their furniture had arrived and had been put in place, although there were still boxes stacked here and there that he hadn't gotten to yet. But the

Christmas tree was up, the twinkling lights reflecting in the glass of the front window. Noah gazed outside, part of him still marveling at seeing snow again after so many years out west. He'd brought Emily back to Chicago for visits since his parents still lived here, but they'd come during the summer when the weather was good, not during the potential misery of a Midwestern winter. Now they were going to be living in it, but with his parents getting older, Noah wanted to come back and help take care of them. He was an only child, and he loved his folks, and they loved him and Emily both. He knew it was the right thing to do, even though it had been hard to leave Palo Alto and the house where he and Jeff had lived together. But it had been almost five years, and Noah realized there were far more reasons to leave than to stay, so he'd finally asked for a transfer from his company, and with surprising speed, he'd pulled up ten years worth of roots and gone back to the city of his birth.

Emily had been fascinated with the snow, and so far she didn't seem to miss their old house. He thought moving at Christmas time was actually a good thing, and the Christmas tree had been one of the first things he'd set up, even before unpacking their dishes. Emily was worried that Santa wouldn't be able to find her, so he'd told her the tree would help Santa know it was their house. Then he'd taken her to Kaufman's so she could be reassured that nothing was going to come between her and her Christmas presents.

Noah sank down on the sofa, thinking back to the store visit. It was obvious that "Santa" was someone who knew Noah from high school, given the incident he'd brought up to Emily. Noah had maintained few ties to anyone in Chicago other than his family, and he'd not even bothered to come back for his ten-year reunion. It had been scheduled right around the time Emily's birth mother was due, and six months after that, Jeff had died, so there had been more on Noah's mind than reconnecting with a bunch of people he hadn't seen in a decade. He had no clue who was behind the beard and padded suit, although he found himself curious. Given Emily's refusal to tell him what she'd asked Santa for, Noah knew he had two good reasons to find out who had played Santa to his daughter.

Which was why he went back to Kaufman's the next day. He was on leave from his job until after the first of the year. Emily was at kindergarten, and Noah's mother was picking her up afterward and taking her for a girl's afternoon out. So Noah had time to drive back to Highland Park and see about finding Santa and prying Emily's Christmas wish out of him.

He made his way to Santa's Workshop, but one look at the man in the big chair proved it wasn't the particular Kris Kringle Noah had met the day before. This man was older, and his belly was quite real. So Noah went over to Tinsel the Elf -- who was the same one from the previous day -- and waited until he had a moment.

"Excuse me. I need to find whoever was playing Santa yesterday. Can you tell me where to find him?"

The burly elf glanced over at the line of children waiting to see Santa and gave Noah a pointed look. "It was *Santa*, of course," he said loudly, and then he lowered his voice. "Not so loud. You're breaking the fourth wall here."

Noah blushed. "Oh, God, I'm sorry," he whispered, then ran a hand through his hair. "I'm not usually so clumsy. But can you please tell me who it was?"

Tinsel gave him an appraising once-over. "If you're looking for an older bear, he won't be your type. He's young and skinny under the makeup and fat suit."

Noah gaped at Tinsel, then he felt his face grow even hotter as the man's meaning sank in. "No! I mean... I was here yesterday with my daughter. He said something that made me think I went to high school with him, and my daughter told him a Christmas wish that she isn't sharing with me. I just want to find out what she wanted, that's all."

"Oh!" Tinsel smiled apologetically. "Sorry, I thought maybe he flirted with you. Yesterday, one of our managers served as a substitute Santa. You'll find him on the second floor, usually in the video games department. Ask for Andy Lane."

"Does he flirt with many customers?" Noah asked, unable to keep a disapproving frown off his lips. Then he shook his head. "Never mind. None of my business. Thanks for the help."

He turned and looked up at the direction signs hanging from the ceiling until he found the one pointing to the video games. The name sounded vaguely familiar, but Noah couldn't seem to put a face to it.

Once Noah reached the video games department, a sales clerk approached him, smiling, but he couldn't be Andy Lane; he was far too young, appearing to be in his early twenties at most. "Can I help you, sir?"

"I'm looking for Andy Lane," Noah replied. "Is he here?"

"Sure, he's in the stockroom. We don't usually let customers back there, though. Is there something I can help you with instead?"

Noah shook his head. "Sorry, no." He lowered his voice, glancing around to make sure no children were within earshot, having embarrassed himself enough for one day. "He was Santa yesterday when I brought my daughter, and I need to know what she asked him for so I can get it."

"Oh!" The young man nodded and beckoned Noah to follow him. "In that case, I'll let him know you're here. Come on back."

He led Noah to the far end of the room and approached a set of double doors. He opened one and leaned into the room beyond. "Andy! You've got a visitor!" With that, he gestured for Noah to go ahead inside.

Noah did, glancing around at the boxes that were stacked everywhere. No doubt the store went through a phenomenal amount of stock at this time of year, but the sheer amount of stuff was overwhelming. He didn't stray from the door, not wanting to knock into a stack and send things crashing to the floor.

A figure came around the corner of a large pallet of boxes and approached, and as the man drew nearer, Noah could see he was slender and of average height with light brown hair tied back in a neat ponytail. The man stopped short when he saw Noah standing there, his blue eyes growing wide.

"Huh! I thought it would be at least two or three days before you showed up, if at all," he remarked casually. "Was it the high school stuff or the whispering that got you?"

"The whispering, mostly," Noah admitted, tilting his head to one side, trying to fit the man before him into some memory of high school. "Though I find myself at a bit of a loss. You obviously know me, but...." He stopped, eyes widening, as it suddenly hit him. It was the eyes that finally did it, because in high school, Andy had spiky black hair and wore black eyeliner and black lipstick. But Noah had a thing for eyes, especially blue ones.

"*Void*? Is that you?"

Andy grinned and swept a theatrical bow. "I'm impressed! I didn't think you'd remember."

"I almost didn't. You look different without makeup." Noah shook his head in wry amusement.

Andy didn't much resemble the teen he'd once been. "Void", as he'd insisted on being called in school, had been one of the Goth crowd, with their pale skin, black everything else, and gloom and doom attitudes. But Void -- Andy -- had been in several of Noah's classes, even though Noah was part of the Future Business Leaders of America set. Andy was bright, but Noah had sometimes wondered how Andy could turn his head with the size of the chip on his shoulder. Still, Noah had found him intriguing and sexy, in a rather bad-boy sort of way.

"This is my real hair color too." Andy raked his fingers through the length of his wavy ponytail. "I haven't dyed it jet black in years."

"Well, it suits you better anyway." Noah's attention was captured by the slide of Andy's slender fingers through his hair, which was ridiculous, even though he knew Andy was gay. Noah hadn't exactly been in the closet himself, but he had been so intensely focused on school and getting a scholarship that he'd not dated often until he got to Stanford.

Not that it mattered if Andy was gay or not, he reminded himself. Andy was incredibly good looking, but Noah didn't have time to be interested, no matter how rich and sexy Andy's voice was.

"Anyway, sorry to bug you at work, but I really would like to know what Emily asked for," he said, offering a slight smile. "I've put her through a lot, moving back to Chicago, so if she would like something special, I want to give it to her if at all possible."

Andy gave him a wry smile. "Well, it's possible, but you and Mrs. Coleman will have to act fast if you want to tell her the news by Christmas."

Noah blinked, confused by the apparent non sequitur. "My mother? What's she got to do with this?"

"No, not your mother." Andy shook his head, looking confused as well. "Your wife. Emily's mom."

It took Noah a moment to process that, and then he sighed, reminding himself that this was something he was going to be hit with a lot. Back in California, there were enough non-traditional families that people didn't tend to make too many assumptions about parentage of a child. "There is no Mrs. Coleman, and there never has been," he said patiently. "Emily's mother was a surrogate my partner Jeff and I hired to carry our child."

"Oh!" Andy's pale eyes widened again, and Noah thought he saw something like disappointment flash in them. "So you have a partner."

"He passed away not long after Emily was born." Noah had had to explain Jeff's absence enough in the past that it no longer gave him as much of a pang as it used to.

"I'm sorry for your loss," Andy said softly. "It looks like you've done a great job raising Emily, though. She's a bright, personable little girl."

He nodded to acknowledge the condolences, but Noah also couldn't help smiling, pleased at the compliment. "Thank you. She's the light of my life. Which is why I wanted to know her Christmas wish. So... what is it?"

Andy gave him a sympathetic look. "She wants a baby sister for Christmas."

Noah winced, sliding his hand through his hair in a nervous gesture. "I thought I'd explained it to her well enough, but I suppose she can't really help wanting what she wants, despite the... impossibility of it."

"I told her baby sisters were Mother Nature's area, not Santa's, but I said I'd put in a good word. That was when I thought you were married," Andy explained.

"It's not your fault." Noah gave him a wry smile. "She's been asking me for a baby sister for over a year. I thought between starting kindergarten and moving, she might have forgotten about it, but apparently not. I'm just going to have to explain it again, I suppose." He drew in a deep breath. "Thanks for telling me. You were a great Santa, by the way. Emily chattered about you all the way to school this morning. But I won't take up any more of your time."

Andy's face brightened at the compliment. "I'm glad she enjoyed the experience. I loved doing it." He paused, watching Noah speculatively. "I should get back to work, but maybe we could get together sometime?"

Noah felt his eyebrows climbing. "Get together?" He wasn't certain what Andy meant by the invitation, and he didn't want to leap to any conclusions. They hadn't had much in common during school, but Andy had been really great with Emily, and Noah was starting over from scratch with everything, including friends. "What did you have in mind?"

"We could get a beer, catch up on what's been going on since high school, maybe facepalm over our yearbooks." Andy gave him a teasing smile. "You weren't at the reunion, so you missed all kinds of gossip, and I've got photos too."

"Sure, that sounds good." Noah nodded, pleased with the suggestion; it might be easier to pick up old friendships than form entirely new ones, especially if some of his former classmates were still in the same neighborhood and had children Emily's age. "I haven't kept up with anyone, I'm afraid, but it would be cool to hear what everyone has been up to." He pulled out his smartphone. "Why don't we exchange numbers? If you let me know when you're available, I can get my mother to babysit for a few hours one evening."

Andy pulled out his phone, and once they had exchanged phone numbers, he checked his calendar app. "Let's see... Maybe right after Christmas? I hate to sound like I'm putting you off when this was my idea, but the store gets crazy during the last few days before Christmas, and my band's got a couple of holiday gigs lined up. I'll be free from the twenty-sixth through the thirtieth, and then we've got a New Year's Eve gig."

"I'm pretty free after Christmas, too, since my company gave me time off until the beginning of January to get settled with the move. How about the twenty-seventh? That's a Friday." Noah raised a brow, smiling slightly. "Dare I ask what kind of band you're in? If you were still Void, I'd have guessed death metal or maybe a Bauhaus tribute band."

Andy laughed and shook his head. "No, far from it. I'm in a bluegrass band, actually."

Noah's mouth fell open in surprise. "Bluegrass. Are you serious? Really?" He couldn't reconcile his mental image of the teenager Andy had been with plaid shirts and banjos, and he found himself joining in Andy's laughter. "Wow, people really do change, don't they?"

"To be honest, I liked Bluegrass, folk music, and even sea shanties back then, but I was far too cool to admit it." Andy winked, his blue eyes sparkling with amusement over his teenage self. "I grew up listening to a healthy mix of all of that plus big band, jazz, and swing thanks to my grandparents, and my mom turned me on to The Rolling Stones, Jimi Hendrix, Janis Joplin, and of course, Motown, so my musical tastes are all over the place."

"That's a relief," Noah admitted, shaking his head in amusement. "I don't have to worry about you suggesting a bar where I'd wind up with a headache from the music or have to worry about the lack of leather in my wardrobe."

"No, leather is optional but certainly appreciated." Andy grinned impishly at Noah before turning his attention back to his phone. "Anyway, yes, the twenty-seventh sounds great to me. What time? I can meet you as early or as late as you want after six."

Noah snorted at Andy's nonsense. "Emily is usually asleep by eight. How about eight-thirty? That way I don't miss reading her bedtime story. With the move, I'm trying to keep things as routine as possible for her to help her feel secure. My mother can come over, and Em won't even know I'm gone."

"Eight-thirty it is." Andy typed the information into his phone. "Do you have any preference for where? If not, there's a great bar in the old neighborhood. It opened about three years ago, and I've made it my default ever since. It's smoke-free, and there aren't any TVs blaring sports games all the time, plus their wing sauce is amazing."

"That sounds fine with me." Noah typed in the bar's name and address when Andy gave it to him, then slipped his phone back in his pocket. "Sorry, I know you need to get back to work. I'll see you on the twenty-seventh."

"I'm looking forward to it. It's good to see you again, Noah." Andy smiled warmly at him and waved good-bye before he turned and headed back into the depths of the stockroom.

"Bye." Noah watched Andy walk away, then turned and headed back toward the main part of the store. If anyone had told him back in high school that he'd be planning to meet Void to reminisce fifteen years later, he'd have told them they were nuts. But he found himself actually looking forward to it. This would be his first real move to settle into his life here, rather than floating along, doing what he needed to do to take care of Emily and make her comfortable without really thinking about himself and what *he* needed. It had been pure chance that Andy had been the first person he'd reconnected with, but in a way, he was glad. They had enough common memories to be able to talk comfortably with one another, but they hadn't been so close that there would be awkwardness about not having stayed in touch over the last fifteen years.

This would be uncomplicated, and that, Noah knew, was what he needed most. A nice, easy friendship. He chuckled and shook his head, once again recalling Andy in leather and eyeliner. Who would have ever dreamt Void would grow up to be Santa Claus?

3

Andy arrived at the Laughing Spirits Bar shortly after eight o'clock to secure a decent booth and ordered a Goose Island's Nut Brown ale, which was one of his favorites. He held off on ordering food, not wanting it to be cold by the time Noah got there. He was a little nervous, and he'd gone out of his way to spruce up even though this wasn't a date-date. He'd chosen jeans and a cobalt blue sweater that did nice things for his eyes over a plain white tee shirt, and he'd brushed his hair back into a neat ponytail.

The music that played over the amazing sound system each night depended on who was working, and tonight the bartender was playing mellow jazz, which was perfect. Hopefully Noah would like the atmosphere -- and him. Andy was treating their get-together like a pre-date; after fifteen years, they were practically strangers, and while he found Noah even more attractive now than he had as a teenager, they needed to get to know one another again and see if their adult selves gelled. If things went well, he planned to ask Noah out on a real date instead of covering his interest with the guise of catching up with an old classmate.

The server brought his beer quickly, and he sipped it, keeping an eye on the door as he waited for Noah to arrive.

Just before eight-thirty, the door opened and Noah stepped inside, shaking snowflakes out of his hair. He glanced around the bar as he removed his gloves, sliding them into a pocket of his coat, and he smiled as his blue eyes found Andy. He crossed to the booth.

"Hi, hope I'm not late," Noah said, as he put a messenger bag down on the seat, then removed his coat. Like Andy, he was wearing jeans, with a silvery gray sweater that made his hair look like burnished gold. "Princess Emily wanted two stories tonight, so I had to rush to make sure I made it on time."

"No problem." Andy gave Noah an appreciative once-over, admiring the view. "Are you hungry? I haven't ordered anything but this yet," he said, holding up his glass. "I was thinking wings and some homemade potato chips, but they have sandwiches and burgers too."

"Wings and chips work for me. It'll be a nice departure from spaghetti." Noah smiled wryly. "I'll have whatever you're drinking. I can't think of the last time I had a beer."

Andy signaled the server and ordered another Nut Brown ale, a platter of wings, and a large basket of potato chips with extra bowls of ranch and blue cheese. Once their order was in, he turned his attention back to Noah and regarded him curiously.

"Really? You didn't get together with your friends wherever you've been for the last fifteen years?"

"Of course I did, but most of them were either into health food, so they drank nothing but water or juice, or they were wine snobs." Noah shrugged lightly. "I don't drink when I'm by myself, so yeah... it's been a while."

"Health food and wine." Andy decided to take a shot in the dark about where Noah had been. "California, maybe?"

Noah nodded. "Palo Alto. I went to Stanford, then started working in marketing for a computer company in Silicon Valley." The waiter returned with Noah's ale, and he raised his glass to Andy before taking a sip, then smiling in satisfaction. "Oh, that's good."

"Isn't it? It's a local brewery." Andy smiled, pleased he had guessed correctly, although he was surprised to hear Noah had ended up out west. "Somehow I thought you'd end up playing ball professionally. It's hard to imagine you as a computer geek," he teased.

"Baseball was just a hobby, and I'm not a computer geek, really." Noah chuckled and shook his head. "I have an MBA, so I'm the one convincing the public to buy what the geeks produce. Fortunately for me, my company is big enough that they have regional offices in New York and Chicago. My folks are getting older, and I realized how much of Emily's life they were missing out on, and I came back."

"That's great," Andy replied, smiling with warm approval. "Family is important, whether it's by blood or by choice. I'm a big believer in setting down roots and creating close ties."

"Really?" Noah sounded surprised, but then he gave Andy a swift smile of apology. "Sorry, I didn't mean that as an insult. It's just... well, remembering you in school, you seemed to be the Angry Young Man rebelling against the world. I figured if you had a molecule of sentimentality in your body, you'd have driven a stake through it." He grinned. "Or maybe skewered it with a piercing."

Andy laughed and inclined his head to acknowledge the point; he'd had nose, eyebrow, and lip piercings in addition to multiple piercings in both ears, but he'd let the holes close up years ago. "I *was* an angry young man back then." He paused as the server approached with their wings and chips and waited until they were alone again to continue. "My father dumped my mother for a younger woman when I was nine, and he never wanted much to do with me after that. I harbored a lot of anger and resentment against him for a long time," he explained, reaching for a fresh, hot, homemade potato chip and dipping it in the ranch dressing. "That's what you saw in high school, but things changed rather abruptly when I was twenty."

"Oh?" Noah picked up a wing, but paused, looking interested. "I can imagine how that would make you pretty angry. So what happened when you were twenty?"

"My mom was diagnosed with stage four breast cancer," Andy replied, meeting Noah's gaze steadily. "It was pretty much a turning point in my life. I realized I could keep going like I was, or I could dump the baggage and enjoy my relationship with my mother while I still had it instead of letting my dad's desertion rule my life. So I dropped out of college, got a job in the stockroom at Kaufman's, and took care of Mom until her battle was over."

Noah looked back at him somberly and lowered the chicken wing back to the plate, looking a little pale. "I'm very sorry," he said quietly. "That must have been very hard for you, especially being so young."

"It was." Time had blunted the sharp edges of loss, but Andy saw no need to sugarcoat his story, not when it had changed the direction of his life. "But I don't have any regrets, and I'm grateful I got my head out of my own ass in time to develop a close relationship with my mom before I lost her. My dad and I still aren't on speaking terms, and I don't have any brothers or sisters, so I've tried to create my own family, which has given me a stronger appreciation for developing ties."

"I can understand that. I'm an only child, too, and so was Jeff... my partner. I think that's why Emily was so important to us both." Noah sighed, and reached for his beer. "We'd planned to have two or three kids, but things don't always work out the way you plan, you know?"

"Yeah, I know." Andy gazed at him, sympathetic to Noah's loss, which had to be much fresher than his own, given Emily's age. "But life keeps going even when we're standing there, staring at the rubble of our plans and dreams. It does suck mightily at times," he said with a wry smile. "How long has it been for you?"

"Five years this past September," Noah replied. His tone was matter-of-fact, as though it was something he'd had tell people fairly often. "Em was barely six months old, so she doesn't remember him at all, which I sometimes think is the hardest part for me to deal with. I have videos of Jeff with her, and she's seen them, but it isn't the same."

"I bet she'll love them when she's older, though," Andy said encouragingly. "She's a little young to get it right now, but when she grows up enough to be curious about her family, those videos will be invaluable. It sounds like you're doing what you can to keep his memory alive for her, and that's all you can do."

"I try." Noah drew in a deep breath, then smiled ruefully. "Wow, we got pretty heavy, didn't we? Sorry about that. I'm not usually such a downer, especially at Christmas!"

"Technically, it's after Christmas," Andy pointed out, smiling to help lighten the mood. "Since we're heading into a new year, what better time to air out our hearts and try to leave the heavy stuff behind?"

Noah seemed to consider that for a moment, then nodded. "Yeah, I suppose you're right. But I'm not usually maudlin, honestly. And Emily is a blessing. It's impossible not to be cheerful when she's around. Of course I'm a bit biased." He grinned suddenly. "You should have seen her on Christmas morning when she saw Susie Sunshine. She shrieked 'Santa really did find me!' and lit up brighter than the tree. It takes so little to make a child happy."

Andy couldn't help but grin back, delighted he'd been able to contribute to Emily's happiness, if only a little bit. "I'm glad. She seems like a great kid, and I loved talking to her. Getting to work with kids is one of my favorite things about my day job. I don't get to interact with customers quite as much as I used to since I got promoted, but suffice to say, I'm one of the most visible and accessible managers in the store."

"So you really like working there?" Noah asked, picking up his wing again. "I image it's a total zoo at times. Like kindergarten recess with the circus in town."

"That's a perfect description of the week or so before Christmas," Andy replied, chuckling. "The chaos is exhausting, but fortunately, it's not like that most of the time. I really do enjoy working there. Kaufman's is good to its employees, and for the most part, I can leave my work at work. They're good about giving me some flexibility when our band gets invited to an out of state festival, too."

"Sounds like a good deal for you, then." Noah wiped his fingers on his napkin and reached for the messenger bag he'd brought. "Oh, before I forget, while I was unpacking some things, I ran across my yearbooks. I brought the one from senior year."

"Great!" Andy studied Noah speculatively for a moment, debating how bold he ought to be. On one hand, Noah still seemed pretty affected by his partner's death, but on the other, it had been five years, and the fact that Noah had a daughter was in no way a deterrent. Andy hoped to have kids one day, and he didn't care whether they were his by blood or not.

Without giving Noah a chance to object, he got up and slid into the seat on Noah's side of the booth, reaching for his beer as he settled in.

"It'll be easier to point and laugh from here than across the table," he said casually. "I brought some photos from the ten year reunion we can look at too."

Noah looked surprised at first, but then he nodded, seeming to accept Andy's explanation at face value. He propped up the yearbook and opened it, and Andy could see the inside cover was filled with signatures. "So where do we start? How about Math Honor Society? Or wait... how about English? We were both in that."

"Sure, although to be honest, I can't remember if I deigned to show up for the group photo," Andy replied with a self-deprecating smile.

"Let's see...." Noah flipped through the pages, his arm brushing against Andy's. "Ah, here we are... and yes! You did!" He chuckled, pointing triumphantly at the black and white photo. "Although I don't know who looks funnier, you in your Goth regalia or me in my earnest preppie attire."

Andy was too distracted by the zing of awareness that shot through him at the fleeting contact to pay attention to the photo at first, but then he looked at the page and groaned at the image of his teenage self, all spiked hair and insolence radiating from the past. "At least you don't look like you're about to whip out a switchblade!"

Noah shook his head with a grin. "Nah, you weren't a street punk. You had a reason for your attitude, and you grew up. You were looking for where you fit, right? Isn't that what all kids do?"

"In my case, I tried to fit in by pretending I didn't fit in anywhere. Rebel without a clue." Andy chuckled as he reached out and stroked his finger over the photo, feeling both amused and frustrated by his younger self.

It occurred to him that if he hadn't been trying so hard to cultivate his loner persona back then, he might have had a shot with Noah much sooner, and he blinked, wondering where *that* had come from. Then again, it was true, he thought as he peeked at Noah from beneath his lashes.

"Yeah, well, I was eighteen going on thirty-five," Noah replied, his smile a little crooked. "Classic overachiever, too busy thinking about where I wanted to be to really sit back and appreciate where I *was*."

"Any particular reason for that?" Andy asked. "Or is overachieving just in your nature?"

"I think it was my way of trying to make up to my parents for being gay." Noah shrugged. "Not that they asked it of me, and I didn't even really come out until I was at Stanford, and they were very accepting, but... I guess I thought that if I was as perfect as I could be otherwise, it wouldn't matter so much to them."

"Were you worried you were going to disappoint them somehow?" Andy glanced down at the clean-cut, preppy young man in the photo and back up at Noah, who still had something of the All-American look about him. Only with sexy glasses.

"I suppose, in a way. You know, back when we were eighteen, things like marriage equality and surrogate mothers weren't exactly making the evening news. My parents were like everyone's, I guess, talking about when I got married, and when I had kids of my own...." He tapped the picture of himself. "I assumed I'd never be able to give them that, so I was trying to make up for it in advance."

"Poor kid," Andy said softly. "Funny, I thought you had a perfect life. From the outside, it seemed like you had your shit together and everything fell into place for you. I guess no one really escapes adolescence without an issue or two haunting them."

"Yeah, and fortunately we both got past them, right?" Noah smiled suddenly and bumped his shoulder against Andy's in a friendly way. "So in the interest of not boring you stiff with more of my own adolescent angst, you were going to tell me about everyone else? Come on, dish! I want all the gossip."

"Hey, I told you about my adolescent angst." Andy jostled against

Noah playfully in return. "I'm interested in hearing about yours -- or whatever else you want to tell me about. But if it's gossip you want, I've got plenty of that." He leaned over and snagged a packet of photos he'd left on the other side of the table, smiling gleefully as he opened it. "Wait until you see what happened to our prom king and queen!"

Leaning closer, Noah peered at the top picture. "Oh, my God! Kevin Russell is bald now?"

"As an egg! Considering how vain he was about his hair back in the day, the irony wasn't lost on any of us."

As they went through the reunion photos, Andy sneaked glances at Noah, admiring how his eyes crinkled at the corners when he laughed and how his smile lit up his whole face. Somehow, he was even more attractive now than he had been in high school, and he was down to earth as well. Andy had come into this meeting prepared to gain a new friend if the chemistry wasn't there, but he found himself drawn to the man Noah Coleman had grown up to be.

Their next meeting would be a real date if Andy had anything to say about it, and he could only hope Noah felt the same way.

4

"**M**s. Rachel says I can jump on a tramboleen today! It's gonna be fun!"

"I bet it will be, Princess," Noah replied, squeezing Emily's hand.

He smiled down at his daughter, who skipped happily along at his side as they entered the gym. He'd been a little hesitant at first to leave her with the Tumbling Tots group while he worked out, but when they'd toured the facility and Emily had spotted the group of children running around the gymnastics floor, she'd begged Noah to let her join. Parents were allowed to stay to watch, but the coaches had encouraged them to go do other things, since the younger children could be distracted by their parents' presence.

So after relinquishing Emily to Ms. Rachel, Noah went to the locker room to change, stripping down to the shorts and singlet he preferred for working out, then taking his towel and water bottle up to the main part of the gym. He'd been a distance runner on the track team in high school, as well as playing baseball, and while he hadn't had time at Stanford to go out for track, he'd still gotten in several miles a week, managing to keep it up even after Emily's birth and

Jeff's death. Running had provided a much needed physical outlet for him, and he'd even done a couple of marathons in the last few years. But Chicago in winter wasn't one of the most pleasant places to go running, so he'd decided to switch to a treadmill until the weather got warmer.

His preferred machine near the window was open, but as he headed toward it, he was surprised to see Andy Lane on another treadmill, dressed in sweatpants and a Chicago Bulls t-shirt. After debating for a few seconds, Noah moved to the machine next to Andy's. He'd really enjoyed the time they'd spent together the previous week, catching up on people they'd both known, and for some reason, knowing Andy had lost someone important to him too had made Noah feel like they had more of a connection than simply having gone to the same school. They seemed well on their way to becoming friends, and Noah hoped Andy wouldn't mind him butting in on his workout.

"Hey," he said, giving Andy a smile as he slung his towel over on of the bars and put his water bottle in the holder. "I didn't know you worked out here."

Andy glanced over, startled, and popped an ear bud out of his right ear, smiling warmly at Noah. "Hey! Yeah, I come in a few times a week. It's the most convenient gym to my place."

"Yeah, it is for me, too." Noah quickly punched in the program he preferred, which started with a brisk walk for warm up. He glanced at Andy again, his smile turning teasing. "I guess I never imagined Void doing anything so plebeian as sweating. He was too cool, right?"

"Oh, you know it." Andy chuckled wryly as he removed the other ear bud and draped the earphones over the treadmill console. "But Andy is getting older and wants to keep himself in good shape, which means working up a sweat once in a while."

Noah nodded. "Tell me about it. My father always said 'Just wait until you're thirty! That's when it starts, and then it just gets harder!'" He shook his head. "I thought he was joking, you know? But I really did notice a difference right about then. Muscle strains didn't seem to get better as quickly, things like that. Suddenly I needed glasses, too."

Andy gave Noah a frankly appraising once-over, a heated gleam in his eyes. "If you ask me, you look better now than you did back then, especially with the glasses. They're sexy as hell."

"*What?*" Noah stumbled clumsily and reached out to grab the sidebars of the treadmill to keep himself from falling. Of all the things he might have expected Andy to say, that sure as hell wasn't one of them. Drawing in a deep breath, he shot Andy an aggrieved look. "Oh, very funny, Lane! What are you trying to do, kill me?"

Andy reached out instinctively to help steady Noah, watching with alarm. "I wasn't trying to be funny. I definitely wasn't trying to kill you! I meant it. I think the glasses are hot." He smiled and shrugged sheepishly. "I've got a type. So sue me."

"Oh." Noah wasn't sure what to think of that, but he smiled and shook his head, getting back into the rhythm of the treadmill before speaking again. "Uh... thanks. You just surprised me, that's all." He paused for a moment, then decided what the hell, he could be honest. "You're not bad yourself, you know. Much better as yourself than as Void."

"You think so?" A pink flush stained Andy's cheeks, and he looked quite pleased by the compliment. "Thanks, but I hope I don't ruin my reformed image by admitting I still wear eyeliner when I perform."

"Yes, I think so." Noah was surprised by how much Andy seemed to appreciate the compliment. Maybe Andy didn't feel as self-confident about his looks and he should, so Noah decided it wouldn't hurt to bolster him a bit, especially since it was nothing but the truth. "I don't blame you for keeping the eyeliner. That's how I recognized you, you know. Your eyes. I... well, I've always had a thing for blue eyes. Even when accompanied by dyed black hair and a chip the size of Alaska on your shoulder."

Andy's smile widened, and his pale eyes grew warm as he gazed at Noah. "The dyed black hair and chip are gone, but the blue eyes remain," he replied, batting his lashes dramatically.

With a snort of amusement, Noah rolled his own eyes. "I smell ham." A change of subject was probably in order, and he pointed to Andy's left arm, having noticed the full sleeve tattoo on it. "Nice ink.

You didn't have that in school, did you? Not that I can recall seeing you in anything but long sleeves back then."

Andy held out his arm so Noah could get a better look at the tattoo, which was one continuous large image rather than a series of smaller designs. Although Noah couldn't see the top, which was obscured by Andy's sleeve, he got the impression that the image was of a European style dragon coiled around Andy's arm from shoulder to wrist done in shades of blue and blue-green.

"No, I got this done about eight years ago. It's an homage to some of the early influences on my life, including Tolkien and Dungeons and Dragons."

"It's gorgeous." Noah meant it, too. He'd seen a lot of tattoos while in California, some nice, some uninteresting, and some just plain weird. "I've thought about getting one from time to time. Nothing that big, but... I don't know. Maybe Emily's name or something. Was it very painful?"

"It wasn't nearly as bad as I thought it would be," Andy assured him. "I mean, it *did* hurt, but it was bearable. Watching him work was a good distraction, plus I've got a fairly high threshold for pain."

"Well, considering how many piercings you used to have, I'd think so." Noah chuckled and began to pick up his pace as the tread-mill's speed increased. "Remember Mr. Wentworth, the vice princi-pal? I remember him saying he wasn't sure which was worse: you having so many holes in your head or the fact that you'd put them there on purpose."

Andy snorted and rolled his eyes. "He said that to my face once, and I told him at least my brain hadn't leaked out of any of them, because I was still making As in all my classes. I ended up with a week of detention for that."

"Yeah, he didn't have much of a sense of humor, did he?" Noah was beginning to sweat, and he picked up his towel to wipe his fore-head. "He gave me the only detention I ever had. You remember the way the marching band had the covers for the Sousaphones, that spelled out 'Spartans'?"

"Yeah...." Andy shot him a dubious look, one eyebrow raised.

"I'm the one who rearranged them for the senior year home-coming parade to read 'Nap Ratss'." Noah grinned.

"I remember that!" Andy laughed and shook his head. "I'm surprised you didn't get in trouble more often with all of your pranks. I guess you lucked out and didn't get caught?"

"Most of the time, yeah." Pasting a virtuous smile on his face, Noah put his hands together in front of himself. "Most of the teachers thought I was Saint Noah, and butter wouldn't have melted in my mouth. But if there was a practical joke afoot, I was usually in on it. I'm probably lucky that cameras in the hallways and parking lot were after my time, or I would have spent most of my time in detention."

"Meanwhile, I never actually stepped a toe out of line, and my friends and I were the first group eyed with suspicion whenever anything happened. That whole judging books by their covers thing definitely applies -- or maybe 'appearances are deceiving' is more appropriate." Andy reached over and punched Noah's shoulder lightly.

"Yeah, probably." Noah sobered. "Sorry if you ever got blamed for anything I was involved in. We weren't trying to get anyone in trouble. It was just kid stuff, you know? We never hurt anyone or even damaged anything. I guess at the time we just thought we were being terribly clever."

Andy nodded, his expression making it clear he understood all too well. "It's the same with my crowd. We thought our music, our clothes, and our attitude set us apart. We thought we were oh so clever and cool and better than all you mundane plebes." He chuckled self-deprecatingly. "Ah, youth. Anyway, no, we never got in serious trouble for any of your pranks. They *tried* to pin it on us, but they couldn't prove anything, and we always had airtight alibis because we *weren't* there, and we *didn't* do it. I think that frustrated the hell out of Wentworth and company," he added with a wicked grin.

Noah was relieved that Andy didn't seem to hold a grudge about it; in fact, he really seemed amused. "Well, we're all grown up now, and I've not played a joke in years. But what I'm waiting for is the parental curse to come to pass. You know the one I mean? 'I hope you have one just like you!' God help me when Emily gets to high school!"

A wistful look flitted across Andy's expressive face, but he quickly masked it with a smile. "You're going to have double trouble. The possible pranking and dealing with a herd of smitten young men mooning on your doorstep, because if she's just like you, she's going to be a heartbreaker."

Noah was taken aback again. Was Andy *flirting* with him? It wasn't as though Noah hadn't been flirted with before, of course, but he tended to just let it roll off his back most of the time, since Emily was his first priority, and for a long time -- a very long time -- he'd been mourning Jeff. In the last year, though, he'd gone out a couple of times with guys from the office, but nothing had gotten serious, and there hadn't been anyone he'd even considered bringing home to meet Emily. In fact, "casual" didn't really seem to be in his nature. He dated a few times before and after college, but then he'd met Jeff and fallen fast and hard, and that had been it. It was more complicated now because he wasn't going to subject his daughter to an endless parade of men coming into and going out of her life. She needed stability, but Noah didn't know if he'd ever feel the same way about someone else as he'd felt about Jeff. He didn't know if he *could*, for a lot of different reasons.

Of course he could be reading far too much into a simple compliment. Maybe Andy just tended to say what he thought, and Noah didn't want to look like some overly sensitive or conceited idiot. And what was wrong with him, anyway? Just because Andy was good looking and seemed to really like kids was no reason for Noah to be looking for some deep meaning in casual comments.

"Yeah, well... I guess I'll just be waiting at the door with a shotgun," he said finally, managing a smile.

"I wouldn't expect anything less." Andy's expression turned questioning, almost hesitant. "So...are you doing anything this weekend? If not, maybe we can get together. My schedule is totally open. The band doesn't have anything lined up, and I don't work at Kaufman's on the weekends except during the holidays."

"You mean like a date?" So maybe Andy's comment *had* been flirtatious.

"Yeah, like a real date, unless you're seeing someone?" Andy looked a little concerned at that thought.

"No, I'm not seeing anyone," Noah replied. Really, there wasn't any reason not to go out with Andy, was there? It would probably end up like his other dates in California had -- a nice time, no real sparks, and a return to casual friendship. "Sure, we can go out. Did you have something particular in mind? I'm still relearning things about the city, and most of those have been fun things to do with a five year old." He smiled apologetically.

"It depends on whether you'd prefer an adults-only date or if you'd like to include Emily," Andy replied, visibly relaxing now that Noah had accepted his invitation. "I don't mind either way."

No one had ever suggested including Emily on a date before, and Noah wondered again if he'd misread Andy's intentions. Having his daughter along would certainly make it feel less like a *date* date, but maybe it was a good idea. Andy was around kids all day, it was true, but he might find that having Emily along made Noah himself less interesting in a romantic sense, which was fine with him. "Well, if you really don't mind, maybe we could take Emily somewhere. She loves going new places."

"Great!" Andy grinned, his entire face lighting up. "Okay, we've got lots of options, depending on what you think she might enjoy. There's a children's theatre doing a production of *You're a Good Man, Charlie Brown*. I know 'Lucy' and 'Snoopy', and they're really excited about it, so it should be good. There's the children's museum, and we've got an indoor waterpark in town now."

Noah considered. "I think she'd like the theatre," he said slowly, then gave Andy a lopsided smile. "If Snoopy is around, that would be a bonus. I've been considering getting Em a dog, in lieu of the baby sister she wants."

"Snoopy might be willing to follow you home. He's single and always looking, but I intend to make sure he knows I have dibs." Andy nodded firmly. "Anyway, there's a kid-friendly cafe near the theater with a small indoor play area. We could have lunch there and then hit the matinee?"

Apparently Andy had the unique and rather disconcerting ability to keep catching Noah off-guard with his comments, and Noah had to reassess what Andy seemed to want out of this date. Or maybe he was just overthinking things again; Jeff had always said Noah could think things to death, so he took a deep breath and told himself firmly to stop looking for hidden meanings under every word. He liked Andy, and they were going to have lunch and take Emily to the theatre, that was all. Andy definitely wasn't staking some kind of claim on him!

"Sure, that sounds great. What time Saturday, and where should I meet you?"

"If it's a date, shouldn't I pick you and Emily up, since I asked you out?" Andy quirked one eyebrow at Noah questioningly.

"I suppose, but...." Noah paused, then shrugged. "I could pick you up, since I already have Emily's safety seat strapped in my SUV. Trust me, the thing is hell to move around between vehicles."

"That works," Andy replied, nodding. "I'll text you my address, okay? How about noon for lunch? The matinee starts at two."

"Sure, that sounds great." In fact, Noah found that he really was looking forward to it. It was nice of Andy to include Emily, and it would make Noah feel less awkward about a "date". "Oh, but I'll warn you, be careful about mentioning you work at Kaufman's to Emily. If she finds out you're a manager at a toy store, I'm sure she'll have a million questions."

"Okay, I'll save that information for later." Andy flashed Noah an enigmatic smile as he turned off the treadmill and grabbed a towel. "I need to shower and change so I can get to work, but I'll see you Saturday at noon." He stepped off the treadmill and blew Noah a playful kiss. "I'm looking forward to it," he added as he sauntered away.

"Bye." Noah watched as long as he could, but he couldn't risk falling off the treadmill. He shook his head, wondering why Andy was able to keep surprising him. Maybe he'd just been around laid-back Californians too long, and Andy was different. Just as different as Void had been in a way, but more focused and mature. But he'd enjoyed the time he'd spent with Andy so far, and he was sure they'd have a nice time on Saturday. A nice, simple, uncomplicated time.

The apartment building where Andy lived was in a decent section of the neighborhood. It was nice but not new, one of those places where young families just starting out or single people who didn't own their own homes tended to live. Chicago wasn't nearly as expensive a place to live as Palo Alto, but decent places weren't cheap, so Andy must have been doing pretty well at Kaufman's to afford his own place without a roommate.

Noah had debated what to tell Emily about the excursion and about Andy. He'd settled on the simple truth -- Andy was an old friend from high school -- without going into detail about whether or not this constituted a date. Noah still wasn't quite certain about that himself, and while he usually didn't lack in self-confidence, he was rusty enough on the social front to not want to put his foot in his mouth.

Emily had accepted the explanation without question, and she'd been excited about the prospect of the play. She'd chattered all morning about going and insisted on wearing a sweatshirt with Clifford the Big Red Dog on it, so Snoopy would know she liked dogs and wasn't afraid of them. She skipped along at Noah's side as they walked down the hallway to Andy's apartment, begging him to let her ring the doorbell.

Noah gave in, and Emily pressed the button three times before stepping back and looking at the door expectantly. It wasn't long before Noah heard locks being turned, and Andy opened the door and smiled warmly at them both.

"Hi, you two." Andy stepped back and held the door open. "Come on in. I just need to shut down my computer and get my coat, and we can get going."

"Sure." Noah smiled. "Andy, this is my daughter, Emily. Em, this is Mr. Andy Lane."

Emily looked up at Andy, her eyes wide with curiosity. "I'm Emily Coleman-Davis," she said, smiling shyly.

Andy squatted on his heels, putting himself closer to her level, and held out his hand. "Hi, Emily. I'm Andy. It's very nice to meet you."

Emily seemed to lose a bit of her shyness as they shook hands. "Nice to meet you, Mr. Andy. Do you have a dog?"

Andy appeared to take the left field question in stride, but then, he worked with kids at Kaufman's, so he probably had a fair bit of experience with their random jumping from topic to topic. "I wish I did, because I like dogs a lot, but my landlord doesn't allow pets."

"I like dogs, too! I hope Snoopy likes me, I wore my Clifford shirt for him!"

Noah chuckled, impressed by Andy's demeanor with Emily. He'd known plenty of adults who weren't parents who simply didn't know how to relate to little kids. They tended to be either condescending or dismissive, but Andy's manner was putting Emily immediately at ease. "Why don't we let Mr. Andy get his coat, Em?"

They stepped inside, and Noah looked around, curious about Andy's home. It was clean and neat, although furnished in a "bachelor chic" style he remembered having in his own place before he and Jeff had moved in together. But there were unique touches, too, such as the framed posters of various music festivals and some autographed photos of musicians on the walls. One corner of the living room was obviously Andy's practice area, containing an armless chair and a music stand. A mandolin rested on the chair, and there was a banjo case propped against the wall as well.

Andy went over to his desk to shut down his computer, glancing at them with a sheepish smile. "Sorry, I was checking email and time got away from me. I won't be but a second."

"No rush," Noah said, looking at one of the posters, which was for the Grey Fox Bluegrass Festival. Emily moved to the mandolin. "Don't touch, Em. That's Mr. Andy's."

"This guitar looks funny, daddy," she said, pointing to the bottom-heavy, teardrop shape of the mandolin's body. "It looks like it's going to have a baby!"

Andy laughed as he finished powering down the computer and went to join Emily. "It does, doesn't it? It's called a mandolin."

"Man-do-lin," Emily repeated, then looked up at Andy. "Can I touch it, please?"

Andy sat down cross-legged on the floor and picked up the instrument, holding it out to Emily. "Sure, you can touch it. It's not fragile unless you drop it, but we won't let that happen, will we?"

"No!" Emily shook her head, her expression solemn, although Noah saw the excitement in her eyes. She reached out with one hand to stroke the wood of the case and brushed her fingers over the strings. "It sounds sorta like a guitar, though. But funny."

"It's kind of like a guitar," Andy explained, nodding at her observation. "But the shape of it makes it sound different." He flipped the instrument onto its side and played a few chords, his graceful fingers dancing on the neck. "See?"

Noah found himself watching as closely as Emily did. Andy really was a natural with children, and Noah could easily imagine him as a teacher -- or as a dad. The thought made him blink in surprise, and he chuckled quietly. Andy might not have minded being looked at in that light, but no doubt Void would have been horrified.

"Pretty!" Emily clapped her hands in appreciation. "I like it. Do you play other instruments too?"

"I play the banjo, and I play the guitar a little, but I prefer the mandolin and banjo. What about you?" Andy gave her a curious look. "Do you like music?"

"Uh-huh." Emily nodded. "I have a keyboard that plays Disney songs. I like to sing, and I like to dance, too!"

"When she isn't wanting to be a pediatrician, she wants to be a gymnast, or a ballerina," Noah explained with a grin. "Or maybe all three. Right, Em?"

"Yes!" Emily grinned and nodded. "Thank you, Mr. Andy. I like your man-do-lin."

"You're welcome." Andy placed the mandolin carefully back on the chair and stood up, grinning back at her. "You just let me know if you ever want a private concert."

"Yes!" Emily nodded again and looked at Noah. "Can we have a concert, Daddy? With Mr. Andy?"

Noah looked between the two of them, wanting to chuckle at the identically hopeful expressions on their faces. It was obvious that Emily had taken to Andy and possibly Andy had taken to her as well. That was a good thing, if he and Andy were going to be friends -- or anything more.

"All right, all right! I'm not going to be a party pooper. But we'll have to do it another time, Em. Right now we have an appointment with lunch and with Snoopy, remember?"

"Snoopy!" Emily clapped her hands. "Yes, let's go have lunch and see Snoopy!"

Looking pleased at the possibility of a future concert, Andy went to get his coat, hat, and scarf, and when he was bundled up against the cold, he ushered them to the door. "I'm ready if you are!"

"Ready," Noah said, as he and Emily stepped out of the apartment. Andy locked the door, and then, to Noah's surprise, Emily caught Andy by the hand. It was a gesture of trust she rarely gave other people.

"Do you like mac and cheese?" she asked, looking up at Andy.

"I love it." Andy smiled down at her and gave her hand a little squeeze. "Especially when it's extra cheesy."

"Me, too!" Emily kept up a steady stream of chatter as they walked out to the SUV, and Andy never showed any impatience with her, which Noah considered to be almost a miracle. There was definitely more to Andy than Noah would have ever thought, and he was impressed. He wondered if Andy had ever thought about adopting a child of his own; some men were just born to be fathers, and it seemed to him that Andy Lane was definitely one of them.

---

ndy watched as Emily settled into playing with a bin of oversized Legos over in the colorful indoor playground, which mostly offered things like board games and blocks instead of playground equipment, but there was a small slide that emptied into a pool of soft rubber balls for the more active, energetic kids. He envied Noah a little; he'd wanted kids for years, and he'd even thought about adoption. However, his friends in the social work and legal fields had made him aware of the difficulties he'd face in trying to adopt a child as both a single parent and a gay man, so he'd put that dream on the back burner.

He glanced across the table at Noah, who was still looking over the menu. "Emily looks so much like you except for the red hair. Is she yours biologically, or was Jeff blond and blue-eyed too? How did you decide who was going to father her?" He knew the questions were intrusive, and Noah didn't seem eager to talk about Jeff, but he thought they ought to be open and honest about their past if they were going to think about building a future together -- which Andy definitely wanted to do.

Noah lowered the menu, glancing over at his daughter with a soft expression on his face. "Jeff had brown hair and blue eyes. Actually, it was the surrogate who had red hair. We didn't decide who was going to father her; it was random chance." His gaze moved to Andy, his blue eyes having dimmed a bit. "We both donated, because we didn't want to choose, and it didn't matter, you know? Both of us were going to love our child, no matter who ended up being the biological dad. But after Jeff died, I had to know, because I had to make sure she was going to be... okay."

Andy didn't think it was too much of a stretch to guess that Noah was worried about genetic factors, and he reached across the table to touch Noah's arm sympathetically. "So it was a health issue, not an accident?"

"Yeah." Noah shook his head. "Are you sure you want to hear about this? God knows I don't want you or anyone else thinking I'm looking for pity."

"I'm sure," Andy said firmly. They had to start building trust somewhere, and he thought this seemed like as good a place as any to start. "I know you aren't fishing for sympathy. You're a strong man, Noah, and I respect how you've rebuilt your life and Emily's after such a huge loss."

A flush stole over Noah's cheeks, and he shrugged. "I don't know about how strong I am. I was a wreck after Jeff died, and only the fact that I had Emily to take care of kept me from falling completely apart." He drew in a deep breath. "I always knew there was a chance I might end up a single parent someday, because Jeff was a cop. California Highway Patrol. But it wasn't something I thought much about, because we all take a risk every time we step out of the house, or get behind the wheel of a car, or cross the street. God knows, being from Chicago, I was aware the world is a dangerous place, but that's something you just learn to live with. And we were in Palo Alto, not LA or San Diego. So intellectually, I'd sort of filed away the fact that Jeff could get killed on the job. But who expects a thirty-eight year old man in seemingly perfect health to die of a heart attack while coaching a soccer game?"

"I'm so sorry." Andy rubbed Noah's arm lightly as he listened. "That must have been a huge shock."

"Yeah." Noah grimaced and glanced over at Emily again. "I was at the game, watching. I had Emily with me, of course. I was holding her, and Jeff was running down the sidelines, calling out to the kids on his team, and then... he just stopped and fell over. There were a lot of people there, including other cops, you know, parents of the kids. Someone started CPR while I was running over, and someone else called 911. Everyone did everything they could, but it didn't help. I found out Jeff had something called Brugada Syndrome. It's a defect of the electrical system of the heart, where it just kind of short circuits. Most people don't even know when they have it, because often the first symptom is a heart attack. It usually kills people in their twenties and thirties, but sometimes people are as young as their early teens, and...." There was a huskiness to Noah's voice, and he cleared his throat a little awkwardly. "That's why I had to find out if Emily was at risk. I had a whole genetic profile done on her and on me too just to make sure there wasn't anything wrong with either of us."

Andy nodded, understanding the need, although he wasn't sure he wanted to know if there were potential killers in his own genetic profile. That might, he thought, be one area where a certain amount of ignorance was bliss. "Did it make you feel better?"

Noah shrugged. "Yes and no. I mean, it was a relief to know Emily was fine and there wasn't a chance I was going to lose her to something out of the blue that I didn't even know was a factor. And to know that I wasn't going to suddenly die, either, and miss watching her grow up. But it also meant I'd lost Jeff completely."

"I can imagine that was like grieving all over again for him," Andy said softly, his heart aching for Noah's loss.

"Pretty much." With a sigh, Noah picked up the menu again and stared at it blankly for a moment before glancing up at Andy, giving him a wry smile. "I haven't talked this much about it in a long time. I can't imagine why you want to hear all this depressing stuff, unless maybe you're worried I'm going to suddenly break down over something and you wouldn't have any idea why. I won't, though. Trust me, I got plenty of counseling back in California. Five stages of grief and all that, and I've been assured that my head is no more screwed up than most people. Except for a severe aversion to soccer."

"No, nothing like that." Andy squeezed Noah's arm one last time and released it, sitting back. "I want to hear about it because it's a significant part of your life. You listened to me talk about my mom, right?"

"Well, yeah, but...." Noah seemed to be trying to put something into words, and he ran a hand through his hair, disarranging the soft golden waves. "Sorry. I guess I'm just really out of practice at dating."

"It's okay, Noah." Andy offered a reassuring smile. "I know I've been nudging this along, so if you need me to back off, I will. I'm okay with going at your pace."

"I'm all right. I just don't--" Before Andy could find out what Noah seemed uncertain about, Emily came running up, giving her father a hug and whispering in his ear. Noah chuckled and nodded. "Yes, we're about to order lunch, then go to the play." Emily smiled and whispered in Noah's ear again, and he laughed. "Well, you'll have to ask Mr. Andy that, Princess." He looked at Andy, his eyes full of amusement. "I told her it can sometimes be rude to ask personal questions."

Curious, Andy turned his full attention on Emily. "What would you like to know, Emily?" he asked with a warm smile.

Emily smiled back. "Is that really your hair? Can I touch it?"

Andy was surprised by the question, thinking she'd wanted to ask something about the cafe's food or the play area, but working with the younger patrons at Kaufman's had gotten him accustomed to the unpredictable twists and turns of a child's mind. He didn't hesitate to tug out the elastic band holding his ponytail in place and let his hair fall loose. In his "Void" days, he'd considered his natural color -- light brown with gold highlights -- plain and boring, but he liked it well enough now, counting himself lucky that it wasn't starting to turn gray or fall out. It hung just past his shoulders, its natural body making it fall in soft waves.

"Yes, it's really mine, and yes, you may touch it," he said, leaning over so his head was within her reach. "Just promise you won't yank, okay? I don't want a bald spot," he teased.

With a giggle, Emily reached out with one small hand and stroked his hair gently. "It's soft," she said, her smile widening into one of delight. "It's pretty, too." She glanced over her shoulder at Noah. "Isn't Mr. Andy's hair pretty, Daddy?"

Noah had been wearing an indulgent smile as he watched his daughter, but at her question, he blinked, then a flush colored his cheekbones, as though he was flustered. "Um... yes, it is, Princess."

"Thank you both." Andy couldn't help but grin now that he knew Noah did indeed find something about him attractive. "I think your hair is pretty too," he added, looking at Emily again. "Red curls are my favorite."

Emily blushed, looking very like Noah, but she seemed pleased. "What do you say, Emily?" Noah's voice prompted his daughter gently.

"Thank you." Emily said the word softly, then threw her arms around Andy and gave him a quick hug before releasing him and backing up against her father, who reached out and caressed her hair.

Andy looked at Noah, elated at having made a connection with the most important person in Noah's life. He'd always been good with kids, but he'd harbored an irrational fear that his ability to connect with kids would fail with Emily somehow, and he was relieved that they were getting along just fine.

"You're welcome," he replied as he tied his hair back again. "So who's hungry? I have it on good authority from my bandmate's son that the chicken fingers and mac and cheese are excellent. For us adults, I can personally recommend any of the sandwiches."

"Sounds good to me," Noah said immediately, seeming grateful for the change of subject. "How about you, Princess? Would you like chicken fingers?"

"Yes, please," Emily replied, her tone almost prim.

Noah reached into the messenger bag he'd brought along,

removing a package of wet wipes. "Let me clean up Emily and then we can get the food, okay?"

Andy turned his attention to the menu, but his mind wasn't on food. Noah had opened up to him, and Emily seemed to like him. As far as he was concerned, they could eat sawdust and he'd still consider it one of the best dates of his life.

7

Over the next couple of weeks, Andy continued courting Noah at a leisurely pace. They had dates on the weekend, sometimes with Emily and sometimes not. One night, Andy invited Noah to see his band perform; he was eager to show off, proud of their skill and accomplishments. When he'd formed the Big Biscuit Bottoms with Russ six years before, he'd never thought it would take off like it had. Over the years, they'd picked up three other talented musicians, and while they might never be signed to a major record label or win a Grammy, they were well-known and well-liked enough that they were offered more gigs and invited to more festivals than they could handle. For Andy, success meant having to turn down gigs instead of praying for five minutes at an open mic night somewhere.

Sometimes he got to see Noah at the gym during the week if their schedules happened to overlap, but he didn't go out of his way to make it happen, not wanting to seem pushy. He always stopped by the Tumbling Tots area to say hi to Emily if she wasn't too busy and to get caught up on her latest adventures in kindergarten on his way out. He called or texted Noah once a week or so as well, just to touch base and send the unspoken message that he was thinking about Noah, which he hoped would help soothe Noah's apparent nervousness about dating.

For the most part, however, life went on as normal. Kaufman's had calmed down considerably now that Christmas was over. They were pushing Valentine's Day merchandise, but since that wasn't a child-oriented holiday, there wasn't much of a pre-holiday spike in business. After work, he met up with the band to practice and plan a set list for their Valentine's Day gig. One of the more popular bars in Chicago had booked them to perform two sets that night and had requested an anti-Valentine's Day theme for the music since the bar was billing itself as an escape hatch for the singletons of Chicago this year. It had been a challenge to come up with appropriate songs for the theme without going into heartbreak ballad territory, but he and the rest of the band had been taking evil glee in digging around for suitable options.

The last weekend in January, he and Noah had planned to catch a movie on Saturday night, but early Saturday afternoon, he received a phone call from a frazzled-sounding Noah.

"Hey, Andy. I need to ask you a really huge favor. An epic one, actually." Noah sighed. "I've been called in for an emergency meeting at work this afternoon. My mother has come down with the flu, so she can't take Emily for me, and I've not been able to find a sitter. Would it be a terrible imposition for you to watch Em while I go into the office for a couple of hours? Then, if you don't mind, we can watch DVDs this evening instead of going out."

Knowing how picky Noah was about Emily's babysitters, Andy gave a mental fistpump. That Noah was willing to give Andy that responsibility felt like a huge step forward as well as like a sign of how much Noah was beginning to trust him.

"It's not an imposition at all," he replied quickly. "All I had on my agenda was laundry and maybe a little housework until tonight. It's nothing that can't wait until tomorrow."

"You're a lifesaver. Would you prefer to come over here or have me bring her to your place?"

"I'll go over there." Andy thought it would be better to play it safe and stay in an environment that was familiar for Emily, plus knowing she was safe at home would probably help Noah relax more as well. "How soon do you need me?"

"They've called the meeting for an hour from now. Would that work for you?"

"Sure, I'll head on over there so you can get ready in peace. See you in a few minutes, okay?"

"That's great. Thanks so much. I owe you big time." Andy could almost hear the relieved smile in Noah's voice. "See you soon!"

As soon as he hung up, Andy changed out of his sweatpants and sweatshirt and into jeans and a charcoal gray sweater over a tee shirt, keeping his clothes more casual and kid-friendly than they would have been if he and Noah had been going out as planned.

When he arrived at Noah's house, Noah apologized, thanked him again, and handed him what looked like a small phonebook's worth of emergency numbers, a list of all the first-aid supplies and children's medicine along with where it was located, and a chart with CPR and Heimlich Maneuver instructions on it. Andy assured him everything was going to be fine and got him out the door with a minimum of worried hovering.

Once Noah was gone, Andy turned and looked down at Emily, who'd been trailing along behind them. He had given up the opportunity to snuggle up to Noah in a darkened theater, but he was gaining the opportunity to spend time with Emily, so the change of plans was fine with him. Noah had even promised a double feature for later: a kids' movie for Emily and then a movie for them once she was in bed.

"Looks like it's just you and me, Em. What would you like to do while we wait for your daddy to get back?" he asked, deciding that following her lead would probably keep things rolling along smoothly.

"I want to show you my dolly hospital!" Emily grabbed Andy by the hand and tugged him down the hallway toward her room. Andy stepped inside, and his eyes were immediately assaulted by the bright neon-pink of the walls. He knew it was Emily's favorite color, but it was a little overwhelming to see an entire bedroom painted in it. Fortunately the curtains and bedspread were white, and the dark wood of the floors kept it from overwhelming the senses. Almost.

There were shelves on the walls, all low enough for Emily to reach, and a huge toy chest with a royal carriage painted on it, sitting under the window. But Emily pulled him all the way to the far wall of the room, where a low table held Baby Betsy, Susie Sunflower, and a variety of stuffed animals, all in various states of being "doctored", if the amount of medical gauze wrapped around each of them was any indication. There was also a small toy doctor bag, stethoscope, and a clipboard "chart" with Emily's large, childish writing on it hanging from a hook installed on the wall.

"See? Susie broke her arm falling out of the tree house." Emily patted the doll gently on the head. "Baby Betsy tried to catch her and got squished."

"That's unfortunate." Andy nodded solemnly as he listened to the tale of the dolls' woe. "It's a good thing they have you to take care of them, though."

"Oh, yes. Daddy says I'm a really good doctor." She looked up at Andy, a proud smile on her face. "I putted a Band-Aid on Daddy when he cut his face shaving once. Do you need any Band-Aids on you? I can do it!"

"Well, I did hurt my finger at work yesterday." Andy held out his hand to show her the bruise on his pinky, the result of a heavy stack of boxes coming down on it while he was moving stock. "I could use a good doctor for that, I think."

Emily clapped her hands with excitement, and Andy found himself being ordered to take a seat on a low stool. Then she got her stethoscope and the doctor bag and proceeded to give Andy an "exam", even having him open his mouth and say "aah." Then he was gifted with a Dora the Explorer Band-Aid applied to his pinky, Emily taking as much care with the procedure as though she was performing open heart surgery.

"There! You have to leave it on for three days and take two aspirin, then come back to see me, okay?"

"Okay," Andy promised, trying not to chuckle over her "prescription". It was too bad she hadn't prescribed bed rest; he might have told Noah about it and tried to see if Noah would be his personal nurse.

After checking on each of the dolls and stuffed animals -- and giving Andy a running commentary about how they had come to be hurt -- Emily put away her stethoscope and returned to stand in front of Andy, her expression very serious.

"Can I ask you a question?"

"Sure, Em." He gave her his full attention, just like he would to any adult. "What is it?"

Emily bit her lip for a moment and drew in a deep breath. "Some of the kids at school say Santa isn't real, that he's just made up by parents. But you work at Kaufman's, so you get to see Santa, right? He's really real, isn't he?"

Andy didn't hesitate for a moment before replying, "Yes, he's really real."

It wasn't his place to tell Emily the truth; if anyone was going to do that, it should be Noah. But above and beyond that, he hated to see kids growing up fast and losing their belief in Santa and magic and all the other unseen wonders of the world. They had plenty of time to be grown up and cynical, and Andy didn't see any reason to hurry that along. He also wasn't about to disillusion her by admitting he was the one she'd confided her Christmas wish to.

A joyous smile lit up Em's face. "I knew it! I told them Santa even told me about my daddy being naughty when he was little, and Daddy said it was true, but they thought I made it up. But I didn't, and so he *is* real! And he's going to help me get my wish!"

Uh-oh... Andy forced himself to look curious rather than guilty as he pretended not to know what she was talking about. "I thought you got your wish. Didn't Santa bring Susie Sunflower and your doctor's kit?"

"Yes, but those were *little* wishes." Emily nodded sagely, as though she was an expert on the subject. "I have a big wish, too. A really big one, and I asked Santa, and he said he'd help. So if he wasn't real, he couldn't help me, but he *is*, so Tommy Neidermeyer is just a mean liar for saying he isn't!"

"You don't have to listen to Tommy," Andy assured her. "I can guarantee Santa will help if he can."

Which was true, he thought virtuously. He'd passed along her wish to Noah, who was the only one who could start that particular ball rolling.

"Good!" Emily smiled radiantly at him, then flung herself into his arms and hugged him tightly. "Thank you!"

Andy hugged her back, melting a little at her show of trust and affection. Maybe it wasn't smart to let himself get attached to Emily when things with Noah were still uncertain, but he couldn't help it. "You're welcome," he replied. "We're friends, right? So you can talk to me or ask me about anything you want."

"You're my best friend!" Emily said, beaming up at him. "I think you must be Daddy's best friend, too. You make him smile."

"Really?" That news made Andy absurdly happy, and he beamed back at Emily. "I'm glad, because you and your daddy are becoming my best friends too."

Emily hugged him, and gave him a smacking kiss on the cheek. "You know what best friends have together?" she asked, giving him an innocent look.

Andy had a sneaking suspicion the answer was going to be along the lines of "ice cream" or "cake", but he gave her a wide-eyed, credulous look as if he had no idea what was coming. "No, what?"

"Cookies and milk! Do you like chocolate chip? I helped make them!"

Andy wasn't sure Noah would approve, but dinner was still far enough away that he figured a couple of cookies wouldn't spoil her appetite. "I love chocolate chip cookies, and I think we deserve a snack now that you've made your rounds at the hospital."

Beaming, Emily took Andy's hand and urged him to his feet. "Cookies are good for hurt fingers," she said blithely. "Even Daddy says so."

After cookies and milk, Emily begged Andy to read to her,

handing him a well-worn copy of *Grimm's Fairy Tales*. Inside the front cover was printed "Jeff Davis" in childish letters, and Emily confided to him that it had once belonged to her "daddy in heaven."

After about two hours, Noah returned home, and he smiled at seeing Andy settled on the sofa with Emily on his lap. "Looks like you two didn't have any problems, I'm happy to see." He raised a brow at Andy. "Did she wear you out?"

"No, I'm good, so don't think you're going to get out of buying me pizza." Andy shot Noah a mock-scowl and wagged his finger. "We've already been planning our toppings, haven't we, Em?"

"Yes!" Emily jumped up and went to hug Noah around his thighs. "Pepperoni and sausage and bacon, please! And movies!"

"All right!" Noah laughed and tousled Emily's hair, then removed his tie and tossed it on the back of the sofa. "I suppose there's no use in trying to pretend pizza is healthy, anyway."

Noah ordered pizza and put in *Mulan*, and Andy sat on the floor and let Emily brush his hair and put sparkly pink barrettes in it while they watched the movie and waited for dinner to arrive.

"You know you spoil her rotten, letting her do that to you," Noah said, as he watched them from his position on the sofa. "She's now begging me to grow my hair long."

"I don't mind it," Andy replied, glancing back at Noah with a reassuring smile. "She's not hurting anything, and I figure I'm due some pink glitter in my life."

"To make up for all the black in your teens?" Grinning, Noah shook his head.

"Daddy! You're talking over the movie!" Emily turned and gave Noah a stern look. "You said it's rude to talk over the movie! Isn't it, Mr. Candy?"

Emily had gifted Andy with the nickname after he'd brought her some of her favorite chocolates at New Year's. They'd had a whole conversation once about what kind of candy they liked, and she'd hugged him and then walked around singing "Andy rhymes with candy and I like chocolate!" for the rest of the day. After that, the nickname had just stuck.

"It's *very* rude," he agreed somberly. "Especially when it interrupts beautification efforts."

"I beg your pardon!" Although his tone was grave, Noah's eyes gleamed with amusement. Then the doorbell rang, and he rose from the sofa. "Dinner's here! Why don't you pause the movie, Em, and we can start it back up after everyone has food?"

"Okay, Daddy!" Emily picked up the remote, and with her small tongue poking out in concentration, she found the button to stop the DVD player. Noah came back with the pizza, and soon they were settling down with their plates in front of the TV.

When Emily's bedtime rolled around, Andy trailed behind Noah and Emily, hanging back out of respect as Noah tucked her in and read a bedtime story. This was Noah and Emily's time, and while Andy hoped to close the circle one day, that time had not yet come. Instead, he stood back and watched and felt his heart lurch at the sight of Noah's tenderness as he bade his daughter good night.

"'Night, Daddy," Emily said, yawning widely. Her eyes fell on Andy, and she smiled a sweet, drowsy smile at him. "'Night, Mr. Candy."

"Night, Em." Andy smiled back and blew her a kiss.

Noah rose, then leaned over and kissed Emily's cheek before joining Andy at the door. He flipped off the light and closed the door, then beckoned Andy to follow him back toward the living room.

"She really must be tired. She didn't argue to stay up and watch another movie with us." Noah grinned. "And now would you like a beer?"

"I'd love one." Andy removed the barrettes from his hair as he followed Noah. "I need something macho to balance out the pink glitter," he added playfully.

"You're just lucky I don't let her play with makeup, or I bet you'd be all decked out. And not in Void's colors." Noah continued on into the kitchen, taking a couple of bottles out of the fridge and passing one to Andy. "So would you like popcorn? And we need to decide on a movie. What's your pleasure, Mr. Lane?"

Andy debated saying something about Emily wanting to learn to make ponytails and braids and to paint his fingernails in a couple of years or so, but he didn't want to spook Noah too badly. *He* was thinking about the future, but that didn't mean Noah was ready to face the idea yet.

"Popcorn and beer sounds great," he said instead. "Have you got anything with rugged men getting sweaty and maybe taking their shirts off to reveal rippling muscles? Wearing tight pants is an acceptable alternative to the ripped shirts. A couple hours of eye candy would do us both good, don't you think?"

Moving to a cabinet, Noah took out a package of microwave popcorn and got it going. "Uh, sure. Maybe *Bourne Identity*? Is Matt Damon rugged enough?"

"Oh yes." Andy nodded as he crossed the room and stood in front of the fireplace. He'd noticed the family portrait hanging over the mantel, but he hadn't had a chance to look at it closely before. In it, Noah was cradling bare baby Emily tenderly in his arms, holding her close to his chest while Jeff looked on protectively over Noah's shoulder, reaching around with one arm to touch Emily. Both men were bare chested, and the naked love in their faces directed to the infant in Noah's arms was breathtaking.

Jeff had been a handsome man, rugged and broad-shouldered, and for a moment, Andy marveled that Noah had given him a second look if Jeff was Noah's type. But if Noah didn't like him and wasn't attracted to him in some way, he wouldn't be here now. He'd made his interest and intentions clear and Noah had agreed to date him, so he didn't see a point to being intimidated by the past.

For all the beauty and love in the portrait, it *was* the past. Andy couldn't replace Jeff, and he didn't want to; he wanted to help build a future that would offer Noah and Emily a second chance at having a loving family. It might be different from what Noah had planned for his and Emily's life, but that didn't mean it couldn't be just as good.

"You guys made a gorgeous couple," he said, turning to look at Noah, "and a great family."

"Thanks." Noah walked over to stand beside him, looking up at the portrait. He smiled slightly, but Andy didn't see any sadness or even longing on his face. His expression was more like affection, as though he was recalling a pleasant memory. "There's a funny story about that portrait. We'd seen one like it at the photographer's studio, and we knew we wanted something similar. We hadn't thought about it much, only that it looked really cool. Then about two seconds after the photographer took that picture, Emily proved that her kidneys were working just fine."

Andy laughed, able to imagine the ensuing chaos all too well. "At least she waited until after he'd gotten the good shot, otherwise you'd have a very different family portrait hanging up there."

Noah's grin became wicked. "Oh, yes. A reminder of why diapers were invented in the first place. I've often wondered what I can extort out of Emily during those difficult teenage years in exchange for not relating that story to her suitors."

"I'd guess quite a lot." Andy grinned back, amused by the thought. "Too bad the photographer *didn't* get that shot. You'd have blackmail material for life."

"Definitely!" The microwave dinged, and Noah handed his beer to Andy. "Go ahead and get settled. I'll bring the popcorn and set up the movie."

Andy took the beer and headed back to the sofa, setting their beers on coasters on the coffee table and getting himself comfortable. As he watched Noah get the movie going, he couldn't help but smile, enjoying the simple, homey moment. With any luck, it would be the first of many more to come.

Once the DVD was in, Noah took a moment to turn down the lights, then joined Andy on the sofa, putting the bowl of popcorn between them. He picked up the remote and the opening credits started to roll. "I love action movies. As a kid, I wanted to be some kind of big, fierce hero type."

"I can see that." Andy tore his gaze away from Matt Damon and gave Noah a speculative look. "You'd be perfect for that. I think I'm more the snarky sidekick type. Definitely not leading man material, but good for a supporting role."

"What do you mean? You were a great Santa Claus!" Noah slipped off his shoes, then picked up his beer and propped his bare feet up on the coffee table. "Tell me that Santa Claus isn't one of the greatest of leading men! Everyone wants his attention, right?"

Distracted by the sight of Noah's sexy bare feet, Andy couldn't pull coherent words together at first. "Well, everyone under the age of about eight," he said at last. "After that, the enthusiasm tends to wear off."

"Oh, I wouldn't be so sure about that. I don't get the thing about snarky." Noah gave him a sideways glance. "I've never heard you be snarky. Or, I should say I've not heard adult Andy be snarky. Void is a whole different matter."

Andy chuckled wryly. "If we're talking about dream casting, then I'd rather be the snarky one than the little cute one, which is probably what I'm better suited for, but I can get my snark on when the occasion calls for it."

"Hopefully you won't have to be snarky with me." Noah put the back of one hand to his forehead in a melodramatic gesture. "After so many years in California among the yoga enthusiasts and tofu eaters, my delicate ears are no match for good old-fashioned Midwestern sarcasm."

"Just don't get me angry." Andy growled and gave him a mock-fierce scowl, indulging in a few theatrics of his own. It seemed like Noah was relaxing with him, and no matter whether it was due to growing familiarity or the beer, Andy was glad of it. "You wouldn't like me when I'm angry."

Noah lowered his head and peered at Andy over the top of his glasses. "Why is that, Mr. Lane? Are you going to get green and muscular and rip your shirt off? Now there's something that would make you *very* popular." He seemed to realize what he said and flushed a bit. "Er... with the kids."

Andy grinned and waggled his eyebrows. "Just the kids?" he teased. "I'd find a way to turn green and muscular if it made me popular with a certain adult."

The flush on Noah's cheeks deepened, and he lifted his beer, draining it. "You want another one?" he asked, rising to his feet.

Recognizing a cue when he saw it, Andy backed off the flirting and nodded. "Sure, as long as you're up."

With a nod, Noah moved toward the fridge. He was slow coming back, but he sank down beside Andy again and passed him one of the beers. Then he turned his attention to the movie, seeming absorbed in Jason Bourne's struggle.

Andy followed Noah's lead, focusing his attention on the movie rather than on how much he wished he could move the popcorn bowl, snuggle up close, and lean his head on Noah's shoulder, maybe even feel the warm weight of Noah's arm around him. Fortunately, it was a good movie and one he hadn't seen before, so it was easy for him to get engrossed.

After an hour or so, Noah shifted on the sofa and moved the empty popcorn bowl onto the table. He turned his head, looking at Andy, and lifted his arm, resting it along the back of the sofa behind Andy's shoulders. The movement was slightly hesitant, almost shy, but Andy could feel the warmth of Noah's arm, not quite touching him.

Andy held his breath for a moment, scarcely able to believe Noah was making what was, for him, a bold move. It was the most initiative Noah had shown, and Andy took it as a sign that maybe the walls were coming down a little. Or maybe the beer was kicking in. Whatever the reason, Andy wasn't going to waste the opportunity, and he slid over, closing the distance between them, and tucked himself comfortably under Noah's arm.

Noah let out a breath and seemed to relax, as though he'd crossed some hurdle. He moved his arm, bringing his hand down to rest on Andy's shoulder. Andy smiled and began to relax as well; he didn't look away from the movie, but he indulged in his earlier fantasy of leaning his head on Noah's shoulder, marveling at how comfortable and right it felt to be exactly where he was.

After a few minutes, Noah's hand moved, caressing Andy's shoulder very gently. Noah tilted his head, resting his cheek against Andy's hair, and Andy heard him sigh softly. Unwilling to break the spell, Andy didn't say anything, just kept looking at the screen even though he had no idea what was going on with the movie anymore. He rested his hand on Noah's leg, giving it a brief squeeze, but he didn't slide his hand up or make any other suggestive move, not wanting to risk causing Noah to retreat when they were finally making some progress.

They remained that way until the movie ended. The credits started to roll, and Noah stirred slightly, lifting his head. He didn't say anything, but he didn't remove his arm either, as though he was waiting to see what Andy would do. After about a month of slow and steady courting, Andy was too elated that Noah was finally *touching* him to break the contact just because the movie was over. He remained where he was, nestling a little closer to make it clear he wasn't planning to jump up and run any time soon.

"Andy?" Noah's voice was soft, as though he thought Andy might have fallen asleep.

"Hmm?" Andy lifted his head and looked at Noah questioningly. "Still awake. Still here."

Noah gazed at Andy, his eyes intent, as though he'd never really looked at Andy before. He lifted his free hand and brushed Andy's cheek with one finger in a fleeting caress before his gaze fell to Andy's lips. Moving slowly, Noah leaned forward, closing the distance between them, and pressed his lips to Andy's in a light, almost tentative kiss. Heat detonated in Andy's belly, and he couldn't hold back a soft moan at the touch of Noah's warm lips. He shifted, turning to face Noah to offer a better angle, and lifted his hand to touch Noah's cheek, cradling it in his palm. He parted his lips in a silent invitation; after weeks of longing, he was willing to give whatever Noah wanted.

Noah went very still, and he trembled slightly, as though he was waging an internal battle with himself. Just when Andy thought Noah was going to pull back, however, the arm around his shoulders tightened, and Noah deepened the kiss, exploring Andy's mouth, sliding his fingers into Andy's hair and tilting his head back. Andy slid his arms around Noah in response and eagerly surrendered to Noah's exploration. Never had a single kiss felt so good. Never had a single taste left him so hungry for more. In that moment, he knew he'd done the right thing by waiting and being patient, not only for Noah and Emily but for himself as well. He knew without a doubt now that Noah was the man he wanted to give his heart to.

The kiss went on for a long time, and somewhere in the middle of it, Noah groaned and pushed Andy slowly backward on sofa, pressing their bodies together. He twined his tongue with Andy's, stroking it seductively, as if trying to drive Andy out of his mind. Andy hooked one leg over Noah's hips, loving the welcome weight of Noah's body stretched out on top of his. Part of him wanted to hurry things along, but he refrained, letting Noah set the pace. There would be time for all the touching, groping, and writhing he wanted to do later, but right now, he didn't want to push Noah past his limits and ruin the progress they'd made.

At last, Noah raised his head, looking down into Andy's face. His breathing was none too steady, his eyes were dark, his face and lips flushed. "You taste good," he murmured softly.

"So do you." Andy caressed Noah's cheek tenderly, loving the sight of desire in Noah's eyes and knowing it was all for *him*. "I think you're right up there with chocolate."

"High praise indeed. But so are you." Noah leaned down to kiss him again, but it was swift and hard and over quickly, and Noah lifted himself up and away.

Obviously, the moment was over, and Andy let it go with only a little regret. He couldn't be upset when the last few minutes had given him far more than he expected out of the evening. He sat up and straightened his clothes, and then he brushed a quick kiss on Noah's cheek before he stood up.

"As much as I hate to make out and run, I should probably get going. I'm meeting the rest of the band for breakfast tomorrow morning so we can finalize our Valentine's Day set list and start practicing," he said, hoping to smooth away any awkwardness Noah might be feeling in the aftermath. He also wanted to make it clear he had no expectations about spending the night, since he doubted Noah was ready to deal with answering the inevitable questions from Emily.

Noah ran a hand through his hair and nodded. "Of course. I understand." He rose to his feet as well, looking a little dazed and even hesitant. "Um... I hope you have a good night."

Andy reached for Noah's hand and squeezed tightly. "Believe me, I already have."

After a moment Noah squeezed back. "Me too. I'll see you out."

"Sure." Andy didn't release Noah's hand as they walked to the door, wanting to enjoy the contact and connection as long as possible. Part of him wanted to fling caution to the wind and throw himself into Noah's arms again, but he refrained -- and decided he deserved something stronger than beer when he got home as a reward for his self-control.

Once they were in the foyer, Noah opened the door and released Andy's hand with another squeeze. "Hope your rehearsals go well tomorrow," he said softly, his eyes searching Andy's face.

"Thanks. Sweet dreams, Noah." Andy smiled warmly and waved as he headed out the door. He was wound up, his skin still tingling from Noah's touch, but it was worth any number of cold showers. His spirits were too high to be affected by a little sexual frustration, and he started whistling as he went to his car, needing an outlet for his good mood.

After weeks of moving at a snail's pace, he finally felt like he wasn't foolishly pursuing a relationship that was doomed to failure. Noah did want him, and knowing that was enough to keep him patient for however long it took to win Noah's heart.

8

After Andy left, Noah went to bed, but he couldn't fall asleep.

Turning from one side of the bed to the other, he punched his pillow and tried to find some position that felt comfortable, but the mattress might as well have been filled with rocks. Considering it was the very same mattress he'd had a perfectly acceptable night's sleep on twenty-four hours before, he knew that the problem wasn't with the bed but with himself.

Sighing, he got up and went into the kitchen, poured himself a glass of milk, and sat down at the table, staring at nothing. He tried not to think of Andy and of what had happened that evening, but his mind kept coming back to it, worrying at it like a dog with a bone. He groaned and pressed his hands to his eyes. He might as well just go ahead and face the fact that something was really wrong with him. Maybe once he did that, he could beat himself up and finally be able to sleep.

He shouldn't have kissed Andy; that was quite obvious. It was just that he'd wanted to do it, and... well, he thought all of Andy's flirtatious comments meant he'd be amenable, and though Noah didn't consider himself capable of doing a casual relationship, he didn't know what else to call what they had developed over the last few weeks. He'd tried to convince himself they were just friends and what they were doing was more hanging out together than dating, but Andy kept making comments about how he liked Noah's looks, and that he thought Noah was sexy, and other things that made it seem that Andy's feelings were definitely more than simple friendship. Things that kept Noah from thinking of Andy as only a friend in return and kept him looking at Andy's eyes, his hands, and his mouth in ways that you just didn't look at a *friend*.

It had been hard to concentrate on the movie, sitting there with Andy beside him and wondering what Andy really wanted from him. Andy had teased him about the Hulk comment, and it had made Noah wonder what he should do. He wasn't even sure what he really *wanted* to do, since there were so many things to consider, like Emily and what was right for her, and what was right for Noah, and for Andy, too. Finally he'd decided to test the waters a bit, and Andy hadn't hesitated to press up against him and rest his head on Noah's shoulder. Then when Andy had looked up at him, and Noah had found himself drowning in the blue warmth of Andy's eyes, he *had* known what he wanted. In that moment, he'd wanted to kiss Andy more than he'd wanted to breathe, and he'd done it, even if he had suffered a moment of near panic when he realized he had. But Andy had kissed him back, and the little moan he'd given had made Noah's toes curl with a pleasure he hadn't felt in years. So Noah had continued kissing Andy, lost in a haze of pleasure, the long-ignored needs of his body suddenly waking up and clamoring for attention. It had been one of the most intense kisses he could ever remember, and that included the ones he'd shared with Jeff. Maybe it was the years of celibacy, but that was only one part of it. The other part was... well, it was just Andy. Sexy, teasing Andy, who'd lured Noah out of his protective shell, keeping him off-balance until Noah couldn't help but want to kiss him.

But if the kiss had been more than Noah had dreamed, Andy's reaction afterward puzzled him and made him doubt himself, leaving him wondering if he'd misread everything and was only seeing what he wanted to see. Yes, Andy had kissed him back, but he'd not seemed at all disappointed when Noah had pulled away, and he'd neither suggested nor offered anything further. In fact, he'd left without even hinting that he wanted to see Noah again. Had he offended Andy in some way? Had the kiss been entirely different for Andy? Maybe the kiss that had shaken Noah so much had felt different to Andy. Maybe he'd decided Noah was a lot less sexy up close than he'd seemed from a distance.

That must be it. Andy had been really nice about it, but the kiss must have made him decide that Noah didn't really do it for him after all. Or maybe he hadn't wanted the kiss in the first place. He was just being a friend, letting Noah kiss him because Noah wanted to. At least he hadn't seemed offended, but Noah would have to be careful not to make Andy afraid he was going to jump him again. Even if Noah wanted nothing more than to see if he could coax another of those moans from Andy's throat.

Maybe it was for the best, anyway. They could stay friends, and things could go back to the way they had been. Noah would find a way to apologize and tell Andy it had been a momentary lapse, nothing more, and he didn't expect Andy to go to bed with him or offer up anything else in the name of friendship. Noah wasn't that needy, after all. He'd gone five years without sex, but that didn't mean he was going to push the first person he'd found attractive in all that time into something he didn't want. Everything would be fine.

Noah downed the milk, then rose from the table and rinsed out the glass before putting it in the dishwasher. He still didn't feel sleepy, but there were sleeping pills in the cabinet if he got desperate. Maybe he'd just try to relax and take a shower. A nice, cold shower. Maybe after ten or fifteen of them, he'd forget what Andy's body had felt like against his. Maybe.

When had things gotten so complicated?

A couple of days later, he still hadn't called Andy, and he was exhausted from the sleepless nights he'd spent reliving the kiss, trying to figure out what he'd done wrong, aching for the way Andy had left afterward, his manner friendly but remote. But he was spared the necessity because Andy called him, sounding as cheerful and friendly as ever as he greeted Noah.

"A friend of mine told me about a gallery that's got an interactive Dr. Seuss exhibit for the next month. What do you think if we take Emily one afternoon?"

"Uh, sure." Noah swallowed hard, wondering if he should offer an apology for what had happened. It was impossible to tell over the phone if Andy felt any trepidation about what Noah might do, but maybe the fact that he was suggesting an outing with Emily to a public place told Noah what he needed to know. "I'm sure she'd love that. Thanks. What day did you have in mind?"

"How about Saturday? I'm free all day."

"Sure, that's fine. How about two o'clock?" He and Andy had tended to talk a lot over meals, so maybe in the interest of not babbling and sounding like a totally needy idiot, maybe they should just keep it to the gallery trip. Why had he never realized Andy was so easy to talk to, until he couldn't really talk to him? "Where should I meet you?"

There was a pause on the other end of the line before Andy spoke again. "I thought we could go together, but I guess we could meet at the gallery if you don't want to have lunch first."

"I promised Emily a tea with her dolls and one of her friends from kindergarten." Well, he *had* promised, even if he'd not given a date yet; now it looked like Saturday was nominated. "So it's probably better to meet up there."

"Oh." It almost sounded as if Andy was disappointed. "Okay, well, is there any chance of us having dinner?"

"Um, sure, if you'd like. And assuming Emily is cooperative." That was probably safe enough, since no doubt Emily would monopolize the conversation. She adored Dr. Seuss, and there would probably be no end to her chatter until she fell into bed that night. That was probably for the best, too. Noah needed to see where he stood with Andy; maybe once he did, he could relax and act normally.

"Okay, great." The smile returned to Andy's voice. "I'd like that a lot."

"Sure." Andy gave him the address, and Noah thanked him, then said goodbye and hung up with the excuse that he needed to check on Emily. He drew in a deep breath and released it slowly, telling himself that everything would be fine. He could handle this, and if he couldn't, he could hide behind Emily.

By two o'clock on Saturday, Noah had given himself so many talkings-to that he thought he was in danger of repeating "Everything's fine, everything's okay" under his breath like a litany. Fortunately the tea party with Emily and her friend Allyson had gone very well, and she was very excited about the Dr. Seuss exhibit, skipping along at Noah's side and chattering a mile a minute. When they stepped inside the gallery, the first thing Noah saw was Andy waiting for them, and Emily dropped Noah's hand and went running to Andy, holding up her arms to be picked up.

Grinning, Andy bent and scooped her up, hugging her tightly. "Hi, Em. How was tea?"

"It was fun! Susie Sunflower had a new dress, and Allyson brought her dolly, and Daddy made sandwiches and cupcakes and tea!" Emily leaned back confidently in Andy's arms and grinned at him, revealing that the gap in front was wider. "Look! I lost another tooth!"

"Congratulations!" Andy inspected the gap as if he was quite impressed. "Has the tooth fairy collected it yet?"

"Uh-huh. I got a silver dollar!" Emily glanced over at Noah. "Daddy says it's real silver, from the year my other daddy Jeff was born."

"Then it's very special." Andy nodded, then glanced at Noah. "Ready to check out the exhibit?" he asked as he moved closer to Noah, bouncing Emily playfully. He dropped a smacking kiss on her cheek, and after a moment's hesitation, he leaned in and brushed a kiss on Noah's cheek as well, a flash of uncertainty in his eyes as if he wasn't sure how the gesture would be received.

Noah felt a tingle of awareness when Andy's lips brushed his cheek, but he told himself firmly that it was no big deal, just a friendly gesture, and he smiled reassuringly so Andy wouldn't feel like Noah was going to grab him and force him into a lip lock right there in the gallery. "Yeah, we're ready. Right, Em?"

"Yes! I love Dr. Seuss!" Emily clapped her hands, her face flushed with excitement.

"Me too." The smile seemed to help Andy relax, and his easy demeanor returned as he carried Emily over to the first exhibit area, which was devoted to the Cat in the Hat.

Emily was in heaven, being able to touch and interact with the characters in the exhibits. Some of them spouted recorded versions of their lines from the books, but others must have had microphones and people behind them, because they answered questions, much to Emily's delight. They moved from the Cat in the Hat to One Fish, Two Fish, then to the Sneetches, and Horton hearing his Who. At last they reached the final exhibit, which was Emily's favorite, The Lorax. There was a stuffed Lorax standing on his truffula stump, and Emily ran up to hug him and listen as he began to talk about the trees.

Noah glanced at his watch, surprised to see that it was close to five o'clock. That probably helped to account for how tired he felt. He'd had to make sure he didn't make any overly suggestive comments to Andy or touch him in any way that might be considered more than friendly, and he was ready for a break.

"Hey, Emily, are you hungry?" he asked, bending down over his daughter, who was whispering to the Lorax. "I think it's time we go get something to eat, don't you?"

"No!" Emily looked up at him, shaking her head and clinging harder to the Lorax, so that Noah began to worry she might actually pry the figure up. "I don't wanna go!"

Noah counted to five, reminding himself that it wasn't Emily's fault that he was feeling tired. He'd not been sleeping well, and it was making him irritable. But he'd had plenty of practice dealing with Emily in a wide variety of moods, and he kept his voice low and even.

"I know, Princess. You've had a great time, right? But you know how when something is over, it's time to go? The gallery will be closing, and you need to eat, and so do I. What do you say?"

"NO!" Emily's voice rose, and Noah could see tears coming to hear eyes. He gave a silent groan, realizing that she was over-stimulated and he probably should have made her take a break an hour ago. Normally Emily was an easy-going, happy child, but she had her moments when things got to be too much and she could yell and scream with the best of them.

"Hey, honey, please?" Noah recognized a note of pleading in his voice. "For me? Daddy's tired now. Maybe we can come back another time."

"I don't want to go!" Emily pressed her face against the Lorax and wrapped her arms and legs around it in a clear intention of not letting go.

Andy went over and squatted next to Emily, reaching out to stroke her hair soothingly. "I know the Lorax is really cool," he said, his voice quiet and gentle. "I don't want to leave either, but your dad and I want some chocolate ice cream. A whole scoop with sprinkles. But we have to say good-bye to the Lorax if we're going to have ice cream. You'd like some too, wouldn't you?"

"Chocolate?" Emily turned to look at Andy, sniffling. "*And* sprinkles?"

"*Rainbow* sprinkles," Andy replied somberly. He tugged one of her curls lightly. "What do you say? Can we tell the Lorax good-bye? I *really* want some ice cream."

Emily seemed to waver, then she gave the Lorax a final hug before turning and holding out her arms to Andy. Her face was still blotchy and her lashes were damp with tears, but she sniffled and looked at Andy with utter trust.

Noah watched this, a strange emotion causing his throat to go tight, and his heart began to pound. With surprise, he recognized it as jealousy, but it wasn't that he was jealous of Andy being able to comfort Emily when he couldn't. No, if anything, that proved what kind of man Andy was, that he could speak so patiently to a five year old having a temper tantrum. Noah could see Andy loved his daughter, and she had admitted Andy to the special circle of the people she loved, too. He'd make a terrific father one day.

But what Noah found himself jealous of was Emily. That Andy

could touch her and speak to her and accept her as she was, the good and the bad, without question or hesitation. Noah had that once with Jeff, but he'd almost forgotten what it felt like, especially when combined with the kind of hunger he'd felt when he kissed Andy. He'd thought he could put aside the desire he felt and be friends with Andy, but he knew he couldn't. He couldn't do uncomplicated, not when it came to Andy. He wanted more than friendship, but it looked like friendship was all he could ever have.

Andy didn't hesitate to pick Emily up, smiling warmly at her as he carried her back to Noah. He turned that smile on Noah, his eyes alight with hope. "So... ice cream?" he asked, leaning his cheek against the top of Emily's head.

Noah cleared his throat and looked at his watch, just as an excuse not to have to look at Andy holding Emily. "Sure. Where should we go?"

"There's an ice cream parlor a couple of blocks from here," Andy replied. "It's in walking distance, but we could drive over there if you're tired."

It wasn't snowing, so Noah shook his head, deciding that he might need the walk in the cold air to help him push aside the feelings he was having. "Let's just walk," he replied. "Do you want me to carry Emily?"

"No, it's cool. I've got her." Andy rubbed Emily's back gently and gave Noah a reassuring smile.

"Okay." Noah passed Andy Emily's coat, which he'd been carrying, then turned and headed for the door. He wished he had some time and space to himself so he could think of a way out of the mess he'd found himself in, but that wasn't an option. He was just going to have to go with it and find some way to tell Andy that they couldn't see each other anymore.

It was brisk outside, but that was fine with Noah, and he breathed in deeply, letting the air cool him. They made it to the ice cream parlor, and soon they were ensconced in a booth with dishes of ice cream. Noah had no appetite, but he forced himself to eat it, since it gave him something to do with his hands.

Meanwhile, Andy and Emily chatted about the exhibit, seeming oblivious to Noah's turmoil as they ate their ice cream, which was liberally topped with rainbow sprinkles. Andy darted questioning looks as Noah's silence stretched out, and Noah could see concern in his eyes, but he didn't say anything until the ice cream was gone.

"Mind if I stop by your house for a few minutes?" Andy asked. "I think some grown-up time might be necessary."

"I... I guess. If you want to." Noah pushed aside his half-eaten ice cream, then reached into a pocket, pulling out a packet with a wet napkin in it. He opened it and cleaned Emily's face. "Come on, Em. Time to go home."

"Okay, Daddy." She let Noah pick her up, and he turned and left the ice cream parlor, heading to where he'd parked his car.

Andy followed along since he'd parked in the same area, but he didn't try to start up a conversation as they walked, seeming a bit subdued. The drive was far too short for Noah's liking, and all too soon, they were home, and Emily was in her room, leaving him alone with Andy.

"Is something wrong?" Andy tucked his hands in his coat pockets, watching Noah intently. "Do we need to talk?"

Noah ran a hand through his hair, a betraying gesture, then sighed. "I... yes, I suppose we do." He looked at Andy somberly, trying to figure out what to say. How could he come out and tell Andy 'I want you, but you don't want me, and you'll be *nice* to me and I think that would kill me?' It wasn't a situation Noah had ever been in before, and it just seemed... humiliating. He didn't want a pity fuck, and he thought that's what it might end up being, because Andy seemed to like him, and it was obvious Andy loved Emily. Would Andy feel like Noah wanting to sleep with him was the price of admission for Emily's attention?

Not knowing exactly what to say, Noah cut to the heart of the matter and hoped he could come up with an explanation that didn't leave him sounding pathetic and weak. "I don't think we should see each other any more."

Andy gaped at him, looking stunned and stricken. "*What? But why?*"

Noah's throat grew tight. He knew he was hurting Andy, and he *hated* doing it. It wasn't right, and it wasn't fair, and he was the biggest jerk in the known universe for doing it. But he had to, for both their sakes, because Noah knew he'd end up wrecking everything anyway with wanting more from their relationship than Andy did. He was so tired, and right now, he felt he had no other choice.

"It's complicated." Noah looked away, fishing for any excuse to avoid revealing his true feelings. "I think we're at different points in our lives, you and I. You have your band and travelling, and I have Emily. I don't want her upset and confused. She's still adjusting to the move, and she needs stability. I have to focus on her needs before anything else."

"You realize I've been playing gigs like usual over the past month, right?" Andy folded his arms across his chest and fixed Noah with an unwavering gaze. "We perform out of state maybe three or four times a year at most. The rest of the time, I'm right here. How is that not stable enough for you?"

"It's not just that!" Noah looked back at Andy, wondering how he could make Andy understand without giving too much away. "I just don't think I can... handle this, okay? It's not your fault, it's mine. I guess there's something wrong with me that I can't..." *I can't stand being around you, knowing I can't have you. Just being friends, not touching you, knowing you don't really want me, and you will find someone else and then I'm just... the friend who gets left behind.* He couldn't put it into words, and he stared at Andy, feeling sick and miserable and more alone than he'd felt since Jeff had died. Defeated, he shook his head. "I'm sorry, Andy. I think... I *know* that kiss meant something different to me than it did to you. Like I said, it's not you, it's me, and I don't think we should make this harder than it needs to be."

"Oh." Andy stared at Noah a moment longer, his shoulders slumping in utter dejection, and there was a flash of hurt in his eyes before he turned away. "I see. Okay, well, I guess this is goodbye."

The pain Noah felt at those words almost doubled him over, and for a moment, he considered taking everything back, telling Andy he was wrong and begging his forgiveness. But this was for the best, it really was, so Andy didn't feel any pressure from Noah and Noah could go back into his familiar, protective cocoon and not have to deal with knowing Andy felt sorry for him.

"I'm sorry," he said softly, hating himself for putting Andy through this.

"Yeah, me too." Andy rubbed his eyes and drew in a shaky breath. "Tell Emily goodbye for me, okay? I don't think I should see her like this. It might upset her, and she won't get it. I don't care what you tell her about why I'm not around anymore. Just don't make me sound like too much of an asshole."

"I'm the asshole," Noah said miserably. It was so typical of Andy that he didn't want to upset Emily, and Noah found himself reaching out to Andy before making himself drop his hand. "Goodbye, Andy."

Andy nodded brusquely and headed for the door, making his escape from the house without waiting to see if Noah was going to show him out one last time. For a long time Noah stood and stared at the door, feeling an intense sense of loss, accompanied by a big dose of self-loathing. Knowing that he was trying to spare them both more pain in the long run didn't make him feel any better about what he'd done, and he wanted nothing more than to get good and drunk. But he couldn't; he had Emily, sweet Emily, who was going to end up hurting because "Mr. Candy" wouldn't be around anymore. He'd have to find a way to make it up to her somehow. If he could, which he doubted. Maybe someday when she was older he could explain it all to her, but for now, he'd just say Andy was busy. Maybe he'd keep her so active, she wouldn't have time to pine for Andy.

It was too bad Noah couldn't do the same thing for himself, but he suspected it would be a long time before he stopped feeling like he'd made the biggest mistake of his life.

9

———

"I want Andy! Can't you call him, Daddy? Doesn't he like me anymore?"

Emily's huge eyes welled with tears, and Noah felt like the worst father in the history of fathers. How could he have believed Emily wouldn't miss Andy that much? Just because Emily didn't cry over Jeff, whom she couldn't even remember, didn't mean she wouldn't feel the absence of someone who had become so close to her and who loved her as much as Andy did.

Emily had been all right for the first week or so; after all, it had often been a few days between visits and Noah had explained that Andy was busy. But after that, she'd started asking more often, especially when she didn't see Andy at the athletic club anymore. Over time, she started worrying something bad had happened to her friend, and now it had escalated to her worrying that Andy didn't like *her* anymore. All of which made Noah feel even more like shit than he had been anyway, and it didn't help that he missed Andy too. Funny how in only six weeks, he'd gotten used to Andy's teasing smiles and wry humor. He'd not realized just how much Andy had insinuated himself into his life -- and into his feelings -- until Andy suddenly wasn't there anymore.

"I know, baby." Noah wrapped his arms around his daughter and sighed, knowing what he had to do. If it were only for himself, he wouldn't have been able to bring himself to face Andy again, but Emily was innocent, and Noah felt horribly guilty for what he'd done to her and Andy both. So he would have to swallow his pride and find a way to fix this, for Emily's sake. Andy might tell him to go to hell, and Noah wouldn't blame him in the slightest, but he thought that asking Andy to visit Emily sometimes -- even if Noah took himself off elsewhere so as not to burden Andy with his presence -- might have a chance of success.

Which was how Noah found himself in his car on Valentine's Day, driving toward the bar where Andy's band was playing. He'd thought about simply calling Andy, but that was the coward's way out, and he remembered Andy talking about the gig he and his band were playing, an anti-Valentine's Day set at a popular bar. He'd fucked things up badly enough that he knew he owed Andy an abject personal apology, and he only hoped Andy wouldn't slug him too hard, even if he did deserve it. Besides, he *wanted* to see Andy, even if it was going to be hard. He'd thought about little else but Andy ever since the night they'd kissed, and it would be part of his penance to face Andy in person and be reminded of what he could never have.

He pulled up in front of the bar, a little surprised that the parking lot was jammed. Apparently there were enough single people in the area to fill the place up, and Noah sighed, realizing he could count himself among their number. He had only himself to blame for that, because *he* was the real reason he was -- and probably would always be -- alone.

It look a few minutes to gather his courage, but he finally got out of the car and walked toward the bar entrance. He stepped inside, hearing the music and immediately recognizing Andy's band on the stage at the far end. He looked toward the stage and stopped dead in his tracks as he caught sight of Andy.

The first time he'd seen the Big Biscuit Bottoms play, it had been at a smaller venue, and the band had been dressed more casually, but it looked liked they'd all stepped it up for the occasion. Noah didn't notice much of anything about the rest of the band; his gaze homed in on Andy. The only thing similar to Andy's usual wardrobe were his jeans, which were well-worn and hugged his ass in ways that ought to be illegal. He wore a red and black paisley brocade waistcoat over a crisp, white button-down shirt with the sleeves rolled up to his elbow, offering a peek at the dragon tattoo. To top it off, he also had a black bowler that he performed a little trick with, popping it off his arm and catching it on his head before launching into a new number, a high energy song with disturbing lyrics about a man drowning his lover in a river.

Andy was working the crowd with his usual flair, and if he was suffering over his separation from Noah and Emily, it didn't show in his performance, but then Noah didn't expect it to, given Andy's professionalism. He *did* sound a little...*vehement* with his anti-romance patter between songs, however. Noah winced, wondering if it had been such a smart idea to try to meet Andy here after all. Especially when Andy had his hair down and was wearing eyeliner, which made him even more ridiculously attractive than usual.

Reminding himself firmly that this was for Emily -- and hopefully for Andy, too -- Noah went to the bar, ordered a beer, then stood against the wall at one side of the room, watching Andy and waiting for his chance to apologize for his stupidity. Hopefully Andy was as forgiving as he was kind, and Noah said a silent prayer that he hadn't ruined things between them so badly that Andy wouldn't even want to see Emily again.

BY THE TIME the first set was winding down, Andy was pumped up from adrenaline and the energy of the crowd, who were loving the music. Instead of choosing songs about loneliness and heartbreak, he and the rest of the band had gleefully dug up the most over the top gruesome songs about romance that ended in death -- usually murder -- they could find. The result was a mix of folk songs, old country music, and even a couple of rock numbers, but the crowd was eating it up despite the unusual mix.

They'd started off with "Pretty Polly" and "The Banks of the Ohio", which were typical murder ballads, followed by "The Long Black Veil" and "Willie Taylor". After that, they'd taken a break from all the bloodshed with "Whiskey in the Jar" to get the crowd pumped up and in the mood for more drinks. Andy and Julie had sung "Where the Wild Roses Grow" as a duet, then Julie had sung "Single Girl" and "The Ballad of Pirate Jenny" on her own. They wrapped the set with Andy taking the lead again for "Gay Pirates", and by the time they left the stage, he was ready for a beer and a chance to rest his voice after all the singing and patter.

He stopped by the bar for the beer and lingered there, chatting with some of the patrons. A couple of young people even wanted to know if those were "real songs" and where they could get them, which amused Andy to no end. He cast his eye around for anyone potentially interesting; after two weeks of licking his wounds, he was ready to start moving on. Tonight, he'd dressed up a little, showing off his best assets in hopes of meeting someone new who could help him forget about Noah Coleman.

He still cringed with mortification when he thought about the night Noah said the kiss meant something different to him than it did to Andy. Obviously Noah had read his signals and decided he didn't want what Andy was offering after all. Maybe the kiss had been an experiment, and Noah hadn't felt the same kind of sizzling chemistry Andy had or maybe it hadn't been as good as the kisses he'd shared with Jeff. Whatever the reason, Andy was lacking *something*, and rather than put them both through the whole "I think we should just be friends" spiel, Noah had cut him off before things got too awkward.

He'd thrown himself into work, both at Kaufman's and with the band, to distract himself, but he still missed both Noah and Emily, and he couldn't help but wish for a different outcome. But if Noah wasn't interested and didn't feel the same kind of attraction, then nothing Andy did could *make* him feel more than he did. Looking back, Andy thought he should have taken Noah's reticence and snail-like pace as a bigger clue that he was trying too hard to make something happen, but he'd let hope cloud his judgment, a mistake he didn't intend to make again.

"Andy?" A voice spoke from behind him in a low, hesitant tone. "Do you have a moment?"

Andy turned, surprised to find Noah standing there, as though summoned up by his thoughts. He was dressed in black trousers and a long sleeved black shirt, but they did nothing to hide the fact that he looked as though he had lost weight. There were dark circles under his eyes as well, and he was sporting a day or two of stubble, which Andy couldn't recall him ever doing. He looked tired, and sad, and his blue eyes were dark with mute appeal.

Andy was tempted to say no and escape into the crowd; he couldn't imagine what they had to talk about, and he had no desire to relive the humiliation he'd felt the last time they had talked. But Noah's haggard appearance made him pause, and he nodded reluctantly.

"I guess. What do you want, Noah?"

"First, I want to apologize. I feel like crap for the way I handled things, and I'm hoping you can forgive me. If you can't, I understand completely, and I won't blame you. But... it's Emily." Noah swallowed hard, and his voice became rough. "She misses you so much. She's inconsolable, and I... I can't believe I deprived the two of you of one another. It was wrong, and I was hoping maybe you'd be willing to come and see her. Please?"

The apology got Andy's hopes up, but they were quickly dashed when Noah made it clear this was all about Emily. As much as it warmed his heart to know she missed him, Andy would have much preferred if Noah had come here because he'd realized he found Andy irresistible and regretted throwing away their chance for love.

"Sure." Andy mustered a smile, hoping his disappointment didn't show. "I've missed her too."

Noah drew in a deep breath and smiled at him in gratitude. "Thank you so much. I couldn't bring myself to tell her the truth.

Then she thought you didn't like her anymore, and... God. I've never made such a mess of anything in my life. I can make myself scarce when you visit her, if you find being around me to be too unpleasant." He lifted his hand and rubbed the back of his neck, looking away from Andy. "I don't want to make you uncomfortable."

As tempting as it was to take Noah up on that offer, Andy didn't think having her father scurry away every time Andy was nearby would send a good message to Emily. "You don't have to do that. I'm sure we can manage to act like mature adults for her sake."

"I know *you* can. You always have. I'm the problem." Noah shrugged slightly and grimaced. "I really am sorry. I thought you might get pretty sick of me mooning after you when you were just being friendly. I didn't want you to start avoiding me or thinking you had to take pity on me because I was a friend, so I thought it would just be easier... you know. A clean break, so you could get on with your life."

Andy frowned, trying to make sense out of what Noah had said, and he swiveled on his bar stool to face Noah directly. "What do you mean, you were mooning over me? You *dumped* me because that kiss didn't do anything for you."

"What?" Noah's eyes widened and he shook his head. "No! I let you go because it didn't do anything for *you*. I figured when you got up and left and then didn't call me for days, it was a pretty clear sign that you didn't find me... well. That you didn't feel what I did from that kiss. And you're a good person and kind, and I didn't want you to feel you had to give me anything just so you could be around Emily."

"Oh, for God's sake...." Andy groaned and covered his face with one hand. He could scarcely believe the level of misunderstanding going on between two grown, supposedly intelligent men, but at least the truth was coming out now. He grabbed his beer and downed it, feeling the need for some fortification for this conversation. "I got up and left because you were giving off 'moment of intimacy over' signals, and I didn't want to push you. I mean, we'd been seeing each other for *weeks*, and that was the first time you'd even touched me. I was starting to think maybe I was trying too hard to make something happen, but then you kissed me, and it was toe-curling and great. I figured you were just a really slow mover, so I left and gave you some space out of respect because I know the whole new relationship thing has to be hard for you in a lot of ways."

Noah blinked and frowned slightly, as though trying to make sense of Andy's explanation. "It took me a while to figure out if you were really flirting with me or if you were just being a friend, trying to bolster my confidence. I thought maybe you were interested in me, but, well, I admit to being ten years out of practice with dating, so I wasn't sure. I wasn't certain I was ready, either, because I've never really been into casual relationships, but while I was thinking we were just friends, you sort of... got under my skin. And I kissed you, and you were so *nice* about it, and I figured I was reading things into it that really weren't there. You were so good with Emily at the gallery, and you comforted her when I couldn't, and I was jealous that you were touching her, that you obviously adored her and not me. I knew friendship wouldn't be enough, and since I thought you didn't want me...." He trailed off, looking at Andy with hope in his eyes. "Was I wrong?"

"Are you seriously asking me that after everything I just said?" Andy gave him an exasperated look. "I was *trying* to get under your skin, and the only reason I was 'nice' about the kiss is because you couldn't even handle me flirting with you without shutting down and changing the subject. If I'd responded the way I wanted to, I was afraid you'd run off, clutching your pearls. So yes, Noah Coleman, you were wrong."

The fatigue seemed to melt away from Noah, and he put his beer down on the bar. Stepping closer, he stood between Andy's legs and wrapped his arms around Andy's waist. "How did you want to respond? Assuming you forgive me and will eventually let me live down the fact that I'm a total idiot and still *want* to respond."

Stunned by the bold move, Andy stared at Noah, trying to process this unexpected turn of events. His rational mind was telling him this was a risk; if Noah turned on an emotional dime once, he could do it again. But Andy's heart was telling him to give Noah a second chance and see what happened. He might get hurt, but then again, he might not if Noah meant what he'd said.

Tipping his bowler further back on his head, Andy slid his arms around Noah's shoulders. "If I'd responded the way I wanted to, there would have been a lot more groping," he said, searching Noah's face intently for any sign that Noah was withdrawing again as he had every other time Andy had spoken his mind about his interest. "Probably some thrusting too."

Noah smiled, baring his teeth. "Groping, like this?" Andy felt Noah's hands moving downward from his waist to his ass and squeezing. "See, I can be taught. Once I have my eyes opened, I'm not completely hopeless, I promise."

Andy's eyes flew open wide at the groping, and he felt a little zing of arousal, but he couldn't quite stop talking yet. "Just so we're on the same page -- *finally* -- I don't do casual either."

"Good. Because I have a responsibility to Emily, and if we're going to see where this goes, you will too." The smile disappeared, and Noah looked at him somberly. "Are you all right with that? I don't expect everything to be perfect, because both of us are human, but I want to try. I think we could have something special. *You're* something special, Andy. I think I realized that from the start."

Andy couldn't help but smile at that, a warmth blooming in his chest that had nothing to do with desire, and he tightened his arms around Noah. "I'm more than okay with that," he replied, wanting to reassure Noah that Emily was welcome in his life. "I've wanted to be a dad, but I wasn't sure it would ever happen. Emily might not be my family by blood, but she'll be my family by choice, if that's okay with you."

"Oh, yes. I can tell you love her, and she loves you. I know you'll be good to her, because you were born to be a dad." Noah leaned closer, brushing his cheek against Andy's. "If I kiss you, will it get you fired? Or put too much of a cramp in your anti-Valentine's mojo?"

His smile widening, Andy nuzzled Noah's stubbled cheek in return. "I'm willing to take the risk," he murmured.

He caught a glimpse of Noah's gleaming eyes just before Noah kissed him. There was nothing tentative this time, no hesitation or shyness as Noah claimed Andy's mouth hungrily. Noah's hands tightened on his ass again, pulling Andy closer against his body. A needy moan escaped Andy's throat as he parted his lips and moved willingly into Noah's embrace, clinging tightly to Noah's shoulders. This new aggressive side to Noah was a surprise, but a welcome one, and he responded to it eagerly.

Noah continued the kiss, taking his time about it, giving a hum of satisfaction as Andy surrendered to him. There was a vague, distant sound, starting softly, then growing louder, and Andy recognized it as applause peppered with some whistles and cat-calls. Noah pulled his head back, breaking the kiss with a little nip of Andy's lower lip, then looked around at the bar patrons with a grin.

"Don't worry, folks, I'm just trying to avoid getting murdered tonight," Noah announced as he looked at Andy with a playful grin. "Can I live at least until your commitment to entertain these fine people is finished?"

Andy pretended to consider the question despite the fact he was tingling all the way down to his toes. "Well, that was a pretty good kiss, so I guess I can spare you for now."

"There's more where that came from, once I get you home." Noah gave him a leer. "When does your next set start? I'll be good and not drag you out of here and ravish you the way I want to. Unless you *want* me to be bad."

Andy did want Noah to be bad -- very, *very* bad -- but he had a commitment to fulfill, and so he drew back regretfully and glanced at his watch. "I've got about five minutes, but as soon as the set is over, you can take me home and be as bad as you want." He leaned close and murmured in Noah's ear, "Whatever you want, it's all yours. I'm all yours."

"Then I'm a very lucky man -- and hopefully you'll feel as though you got lucky, too." Noah gave him another toe-tingling kiss, this one swift and hard, then reluctantly stepped back. "Sing fast, if you can. I'll sit down here and undress you with my eyes."

Andy had never wanted a set to be over so badly before in his life, but he didn't intend to shortchange the audience. Besides, he was proud to perform in front of Noah; he was good at what he did, and he wanted Noah to see that and be proud of him in return. Having Noah in the audience gave him another advantage in that he could try to drive Noah crazy from the stage, and he did, making sure his moves were a little more provocative and seeking Noah out in the crowd to give him some "come hither" looks.

Fortunately, the second set went even better than the first, probably because the patrons were drunker, and by the time it was over, Andy was riding another wave of performance euphoria liberally mixed with anticipation. Normally, he would have helped break down the stage and pack up their equipment, but he begged off this time. Once he explained what had happened with Noah, his band mates let him off the hook, and Russ agreed to take care of Andy's mandolin and banjo until Andy could pick them up.

"But if he hurts you again, we get to kill him, right?" Russ asked jokingly, although there was real concern in his eyes.

"I don't think it'll happen," Andy replied, feeling much more confident about his chances with Noah the second time around.

With a grin and a wave, he bade his bandmates goodnight and headed back to where he'd left Noah. The bar wouldn't be closing for another couple of hours, but he didn't intend to stick around.

"Your place or mine?" he asked, holding out his hand as he approached Noah.

Noah clasped Andy's hand and pulled him close, kissing him hard. It was impossible to miss Noah's arousal, and from the look on his face, Noah seemed to be considering throwing Andy over his shoulder and carrying him out.

"Yours. I texted my mother and asked her if she would mind staying with Emily overnight. She said she would be happy to, so I'm all yours."

"Great!" Andy tugged Noah's hand, practically dragging him to the exit. He loved that Noah was thinking about spending the night without Andy having to ask, and as much as he loved Emily, he was glad they wouldn't have to spend their first night together worrying about being quiet.

He'd gotten a ride to the venue with Russ, so he didn't have to be separated from Noah for even a few minutes, which made him happy, especially since he got to spend the trip teasing Noah with playful groping. Once they reached his apartment with the door securely locked behind them, Andy shrugged out of his coat, took off his hat, and sent it sailing across the room before launching himself into Noah's arms.

"Down the hall, first door on the right," he said. "Unless you want to stop for whipped topping."

Noah had tossed his own coat aside, and he pulled Andy close with one arm, lifting his other hand and running it through Andy's hair. "I don't think you need any embellishments. I'm already addicted to the way you taste." He punctuated the comment with another kiss, then wrapped his arms around Andy's waist, picking him up and carrying him to the bedroom.

Andy wrapped his arms around Noah's shoulders and his legs around Noah's hips, clinging tightly every step of the way and nuzzling Noah's ear.

"Mmm... feels good." Noah chuckled as he tumbled them both into the bed, rolling over so he was poised above Andy, looking down at him with an expression that mingled desire and affection. "Last chance to protest. Otherwise I'm going to do what I should have done weeks ago."

"Condoms and lube are in the top drawer of the nightstand." Andy rocked his hips up, wanting to show Noah how ready he was for *anything*. "Whatever you should have done then? Do it now!"

"Oh, I intend to, never fear." Noah took off his glasses and tossed them on the nightstand, then he began to press kisses all over Andy's face. He reached for the buttons of Andy's waistcoat, unfastening them quickly before he started in on Andy's shirt. Warm hands splayed on Andy's chest, stroking and caressing. "God, you feel good."

A low moan rose in Andy's throat, and he arched up, seeking more of the gentle touches. It had been a long time since he and his last boyfriend had gone their separate ways, and his touch-starved skin was waking up under Noah's hands.

"You like that?" Noah grinned and scraped his nails lightly over Andy's skin before brushing his thumbs over Andy's nipples, teasing them into taut peaks.

"God, yes," Andy groaned as he tugged Noah's shirt free from his waistband and slipped his hands beneath the hem. He was ready to do a little exploration of his own, and he slid his palms along the smooth expanse of Noah's back, relishing the feel of warm skin.

"Mmm..." The sound Noah made was almost a purr, and he pressed back into the slide of Andy's hands. He drew back just enough to unfasten his shirt and toss it aside. Noah's chest and abs were taut and toned, tanned and lightly sprinkled with golden hair. "May I assume that Big Biscuit Bottoms is a hint of sorts?"

Andy took a moment to admire the view and run his fingers through Noah's crisp chest hair. "Oh, yes. Russ and I founded the band, and we're both bottoms, so it was kind of a joke name. We never expected things would take off and we'd still be playing six years later," he admitted sheepishly.

Eyes gleaming with amusement, Noah tweaked Andy's nipples playfully. "Truth in advertising is a good thing. Lucky for you, my innate reserve gets left behind at the bedroom door."

Andy gasped and wriggled, arousal zinging through him at the teasing, and he slid his hands down to grope Noah's firm ass. "Definitely! I mean, I can switch it up, but if you prefer to top, that *won't* be a problem."

"We can switch it up sometime, if you like, but right now...." Noah leaned down, his lips close to Andy's ear. "I'm going to fuck you so hard, you won't remember your own name."

A delicious shiver ran down Andy's spine at the erotic promise in Noah's toppy tone, and he nodded, wide-eyed. "Sounds good to me," he said breathlessly.

"Good." Noah nipped the lobe of Andy's ear and moved his lips to the sensitive skin of Andy's neck, kissing him, then biting down. He worried the skin, not enough to be painful, but Andy knew he was going to have a mark. Meanwhile Noah's hands were busy, unfastening Andy's jeans, pushing them down until he could slide his fingers beneath the waistband of Andy's boxers, curling them around his cock, and stroking him lightly.

Gasping, Andy rocked his hips up, arousal building to an almost painful peak. It had been so long, and he wanted Noah so much; he wasn't sure how he could hold out against Noah's sensual onslaught.

"*Please*," he moaned, clinging to Noah. "I need you, Noah."

"I need you, too." Noah's voice was ragged, and he captured Andy's lips again, kissing him deeply, sucking on his tongue suggestively. Then he sat up and leaned over to open the nightstand drawer, pulling out the lube and condoms. "Too many clothes," he said as he tugged off his shoes and socks. "I want to see you naked."

Andy wasted no time in sitting up and taking off his boots and socks, tossing them over the side of the bed. He made short work of his waistcoat, shirt, and jeans, letting them join the growing pile of discarded clothes. After stripping off his plain white boxers, he reclined against the pillows with his arms over his head, putting himself on provocative display.

"Is this better?"

Noah's eyes were dark with desire, and he reached out to stroke Andy's hip. "Much better. You're gorgeous." He'd stripped away the remainder of his own clothing, and he moved over Andy, pressing down against him, their erections sliding together. "Do you feel what you do to me? Do you know how much I want you?"

Andy slid his arms around Noah, purring with pleasure at the press of warm, bare skin against his. "I've got a pretty good idea," he said with a wicked smirk. "If you want me so badly, why don't you take me? I'm yours, Noah, and believe me, I don't need a lot of warming up."

"Well, let's see about that." Noah reached for the lube, opening the bottle and coating his fingers. He nuzzled Andy's ear as he pressed against Andy's opening, slipping one finger inside. "I don't want it to hurt. Only pleasure. Besides, it's been a long time for me, and I don't want to disappoint you by lasting no longer than a teenager."

Andy wriggled impatiently. "You won't disappoint me unless you make me wait much longer!"

Chuckling, Noah distracted Andy with a kiss as he added another finger. Andy shamelessly fucked himself on Noah's fingers, hissing with pleasure when Noah brushed against the sweet spot. But he wanted more than Noah's fingers, and he groaned with relief when Noah finally tore open a condom packet. Noah rolled on the condom and coated himself with more lube, then moved over Andy again, lifting Andy's hips and positioning himself. He held Andy's gaze, giving him a heated smile as he slid forward slowly, claiming Andy's body in one smooth thrust.

With a heartfelt groan, Andy rocked his hips up to send Noah even deeper, savoring the feel of Noah sheathed within him. It felt right and perfect, like something he'd been waiting for his entire life had suddenly clicked into place. His heart soared as he gazed up at Noah, and he found the words spilling out unbidden.

"I love you," he murmured, reaching up to stroke Noah's cheek tenderly.

Noah's eyes widened, and he went still, staring down at Andy. Then he turned his head, pressing his lips to Andy's palm. "I don't know if I deserve it, but... thank you."

"You do." Andy craned up and brushed a light kiss against Noah's lips. "Or at least you will. You'll fall madly in love with me and be unable to live without me," he added, grinning wickedly.

He wasn't surprised Noah wasn't ready to say the words; they had started this journey in different emotional places, but he had utmost confidence in their future together, and he wanted Noah to know he was serious about their relationship and making it work.

Noah grinned back at him. "Well, I find you very hard to resist, I must admit."

He pulled back and thrust deep, and Andy clung to Noah's shoulders, crying out his pleasure. After weeks of waiting and longing, he wanted this -- *needed* it -- and he chanted a litany of "yes" and "more" as Noah groaned and began to thrust harder. Noah's skin became flushed, and his eyes were intent on Andy's face, as though he was committing every nuance of expression to memory. Then he reached between their bodies, wrapping his lube-slick fingers around Andy's cock and stroking him in counterpoint to the rhythm of their hips. Panting, Andy tried to hang on as his need spiraled out of control, wanting the pleasure of their joining to last, but Noah drove him relentlessly to the edge. With a wild shout, Andy bucked his hips up as he came hard, and he held nothing back, wanting Noah to see his desire.

"So perfect." Noah smiled, continuing to stroke Andy, wringing every nuance of pleasure from Andy's body. When Andy relaxed back against the mattress, he leaned over, pressing a tender kiss to Andy's lips.

Humming quietly, Andy slid his arms around Noah. "Yes, it was. Now let's have a little perfection for you, too," he said, smiling wickedly as he skimmed his hands down the length of Noah's back to squeeze his ass.

With a wicked grin, Noah began to move again, starting slowly, but soon quickening his pace until he was pounding Andy's willing ass and making the headboard bang rhythmically against the wall. Andy moved with Noah, his body pliant as he welcomed Noah's rough claiming, and he urged Noah on with soft cries and fingers digging into Noah's firm ass. Noah gazed into Andy's eyes until he threw back his head as he surged deep and came with a shout. After a few moments, he drew in a deep breath and moved away just long enough to dispose of the condom before collapsing beside Andy. He pulled Andy close and nuzzled his neck. "God. I think I've died and gone to heaven."

Andy rolled into the embrace and wrapped his arms around Noah, cuddling shamelessly. "Good. That means I shouldn't have any problem talking you into doing this again."

Noah ran his warm hands over Andy's back, seeming quite comfortable with Andy being wrapped around him. "No, I don't think you'll have a problem at all." He pulled back slightly so that he could look into Andy's face, resting his palm against Andy's cheek. "You're incredible, and I don't know if I deserve to have you feel the way you do about me. I know I've bungled things, but if you're willing to give me a chance, I promise to do better. I think we could have something good, if I haven't exhausted all your patience."

"Noah, you're hooked up with a grown-up geek boy who works at a toy store, plays the banjo, and masquerades as Santa." Andy regarded Noah with fond exasperation. "Believe it or not, there are some people who don't think I'm a catch. So let's put aside what we think we might deserve, okay? If you want me, you've got me, and if you fuck me like that on a regular basis, I can pretty much guarantee I'll have the patience of Buddha."

That announcement caused Noah to blink, then he threw back his head and laughed. "When you put it that way, it does cast a different light on things." Smiling, he kissed Andy on the nose. "I'm definitely out of practice on the fucking part, but I have no doubt you'll give me enough inspiration to get back in the game. So... we'll see how things go? I don't want to rush things too much, mostly because of Emily. She adores you already, but since we're a package deal, all three of us need to see how we get along. Is that all right?"

"That's fine with me," Andy assured him, giving him a little squeeze. "I know I've kind of nudged things along, and I launched myself off the emotional deep end before you did, but I think you know I can be patient, too. I've tried to follow your lead and not push too hard, and I'll keep on trying as long as you need me to. I don't want to rush you or Emily into something you aren't ready for."

"Thank you. I think as long as we're honest with each other -- and I mean all three of us -- we'll be fine. And you've been *very* patient." Noah smiled at him playfully. "I hope your Valentine's Day has turned out to be better than the songs you were singing. You're not going to kill me in my sleep, right?"

"Mmm... No, not tonight," Andy drawled and flashed a wicked grin at Noah. "I'm too tired and sated for homicide right now." With a contented sigh, he snuggled close again. "It's definitely been better than the songs. It's been one of the best Valentine's Days of my life, and there wasn't even a single box of candy involved."

"I'm rather enjoying it myself, truth be told," Noah replied, smiling warmly. "Maybe we should take Em some chocolates tomorrow, as a peace offering. We'll have to explain that Daddy and Mr. Candy are dating. I think she'll take it well." He laughed, a carefree sound. "I'll have to be careful, or she might decide she prefers you to me! Besides the fact that you're secretly Santa and you let her put sparkly barrettes in your hair, there is one very important thing you'll be able to do that I can't. Something crucial in every young girl's life. Something I will happily turn over to you."

Andy stared at Noah, puzzling over what he could do that Noah couldn't, but he couldn't come up with a single idea. "What in the world is that?"

Noah pulled Andy closer and rubbed his cheek against Andy's. "You're the one who'll have to teach her to put on makeup."

EPILOGUE

F our years later...

"...and you have our cell numbers, just in case, and don't hesitate to call, all right? Seriously, Mom, you're sure you're good with this?"

Allison Coleman rolled her eyes and shifted her three-month-old grandson on her shoulder, patting his diapered bottom. "Noah, I've told you it's fine. Your father and I did manage to survive eighteen years of you. You and Andy go on and have fun. Besides, I have the best assistant babysitter in the world. Don't I, Emily?"

"Yep!" Emily grinned at her grandmother, reaching up to caress Jonathan's soft cheek. At nine, she was already showing signs of promising to be tall and lanky, and in Noah's admittedly prejudiced opinion, she was going to be a stunningly beautiful woman one day. And a happy and well-adjusted one, too, thank God, even if their little family was anything but a traditional one. "Don't worry, Daddy. You and Dandy haven't gone out in months. Me and Grammy can do this. It's just one night!"

"Grammy and I," Noah corrected automatically, smiling at the nickname Emily had given Andy when they'd told her, two years before, that they were going to get married. She had been concerned about calling them both "daddy", then she'd decided that "Dandy" was better than "Daddy Andy" -- and Andy loved it. "Okay, right, you've got this."

"Of course they do." Andy smiled at the little group as he entered the room, dressed up in his usual natty, neo-Victorian style. It was one of the reasons he'd been so delighted over Emily calling him "Dandy". He moved to stand beside Noah and slid one arm around his waist. "If something comes up, we've both got our cell phones. Like Em said, it's just one night. We aren't running off to Tahiti for a month."

Noah chuckled, turning his head and nuzzling Andy's cheek. "Don't talk about Tahiti in the middle of February in Chicago! It's too tempting." Not as tempting as Andy, perhaps, but Noah had a sudden image of a naked, tanned Andy lounging on a beach, and he was glad he'd already donned his coat over his tuxedo. "I put our suitcases in the car, so we can go as soon as you're ready."

"Just let me say goodbye to two of my favorite people." Andy got a hug and kiss on the cheek from Emily, and then he tickled Jonathan, and Noah could see the look of wonderment in Andy's eyes that hadn't faded since their son's birth.

Noah had insisted on asking the same surrogate mother who carried Emily if she would be willing to carry a baby for them; fortunately, she had agreed, and this time, there had been no luck of the draw when it came to paternity. Since Emily was his daughter by blood, Noah had wanted this child to be Andy's. Jonathan had come out with a thatch of light brown hair and big blue eyes, and Andy had taken one look at him and exclaimed, "Oh, my God, I've got a mini me!"

The resemblance delighted Noah, and Emily was thrilled to have a sibling, even if she'd gotten a brother instead of the baby sister she'd once wanted. Noah looked past Andy at the portrait on the wall, which a few weeks ago had replaced the one of Jeff, Emily, and Noah. That picture was now in Emily's bedroom, and in its place was the new portrait of the Coleman-Lane family. It was done in the same style as the other picture, only Andy was holding Jonathan, while

Noah stood behind Emily. Jonathan held one of Emily's fingers tightly in his tiny fist, and Noah had one arm around Andy's shoulders and the other around Emily. Noah and Andy were bare chested, but Emily wore a simple white sundress, and Jonathan had on a diaper, just in case. All three of them were looking at the baby, and there was no doubt about the happiness and love on their faces. Noah could never look at the picture for too long without his throat tightening and feeling himself getting a bit choked up. But it was happiness that he felt -- happiness and wonder. Somehow he'd gotten a second chance for a love that most people were lucky to experience once in a lifetime. He'd almost screwed it up, and he knew just how lucky he was to have his family.

After kissing Emily and Jonathan as well, Noah looked at his watch. "I guess we should hurry. The restaurant said they won't hold the table for long, with it being Valentine's Day." He winked at Emily. "Dandy won't be happy if we end up having hotdogs for our anniversary dinner, right?"

Emily laughed. "Night, Daddy! Night, Dandy! Have fun!"

"We will," Andy replied as he returned to Noah's side, his face alight with anticipation; he'd been excited about an evening of dinner and dancing followed by a night to themselves at a luxurious hotel ever since Noah had presented the idea to him, and he'd been tormenting Noah with teasing hints about things he intended to pack for Noah's pleasure. "Thanks again, Mom. We really appreciate this."

"Just have a good time, and don't worry!" She made a shooing motion at them, and Noah chuckled, waiting while Andy donned his coat before wrapping one arm around him and leading him out of the house.

"Don't worry, she says!" Noah said once they were in the car, shaking his head in resignation. "From the woman who once told me she slept on a cot by my crib every time I had the sniffles. If I hover, I know exactly who I got it from!"

Andy laughed and reached out to squeeze Noah's knee before sliding his hand higher. "If you spend another second worrying about what's going on at home, I'm doing something wrong," he said, leering playfully.

Noah felt his body tightening in response to the teasing touch, and he wriggled slightly. "If you continue doing *that*, we really will be late for our reservation, as well as probably getting arrested for public indecency." He grinned. "If we spend the night in jail, I could maybe ask to borrow some handcuffs. Maybe it's a win-win situation after all."

"Oh, I've got the handcuffs covered." Andy smiled, a deceptively sweet and innocent expression that didn't fool Noah for an instant, but he did move his hand back to Noah's knee. "Since we're celebrating Valentine's Day *and* our anniversary, I wanted to make sure it was memorable."

"It sounds very promising," Noah said. He started the car, then leaned toward Andy, pressing a tender kiss to his lips. "I love you. Every day with you is memorable. Handcuffs are just a bonus."

Andy gazed at Noah with warm affection, practically melting at Noah's sentimental words. "I love you too," he murmured, returning the kiss tenderly.

Noah drew back and put the car in gear. "I guess we should go. It's hard when you look at me like that and there's a perfectly good bedroom not fifty feet away, but I'll contain myself. At least until after dinner and whatever dancing we do before I haul you up to our room and ravish you."

He pushed "play" on the CD player, and "My Baby's Got Two Daddies", an original song from the Big Biscuit Bottoms' first professional album -- released the previous year and written when the band found out about the surrogacy -- started up. Grinning, Noah pulled away from the house.

His babies did have two daddies -- and he wouldn't want it any other way.

HOLIDAY HOOTENANNY

1

J osh hummed as he wrapped up the remainders of the chicken casserole he'd made for dinner, then opened the fridge, looking for a clear spot among the cans of beer and soda and the Thanksgiving leftovers Clint's parents had insisted upon sending home with them, even though Clint had tried hard to refuse because he hated his mother's cooking. He moved a container of mashed potatoes out of the way, making just enough space for the casserole, and closed the door with a sigh of relief.

They would never finish the leftovers on their own, but he'd take the rest to work and leave it in the break room fridge, which was why Clint had deposited the leftovers in Josh's fridge instead of his own. Josh's coworkers at the studio would be quite happy to scarf it up, and Josh wouldn't have to feel guilty about wasting food. Having grown up in a huge family where there had been occasions on which they'd all gone to bed without having had quite as much to eat as they might have liked, it went against his nature to throw away perfectly good food when someone else might eat it.

He looked around the kitchen, satisfied he'd cleaned everything up well enough, and started the dishwasher before leaving the room. As he entered the living room of his apartment, he caught sight of

Clint, bent over as he looked at one of the lower shelves of DVDs next to the TV. The sight of Clint's firm ass in jeans could still make Josh's mouth go dry, and he admired the view before giving a wolf whistle.

"I think you do that on purpose," he said, walking over to Clint and patting what he'd just been admiring.

"Of course I do." Clint straightened and waggled his eyebrows at Josh. "Please tell me you threw away that God-awful tofurkey. The only reason I caved and took some in the first place is because I didn't want to get into another argument about my eating habits with my mother. She's convinced she can hear my arteries hardening."

Josh craned up slightly so he could nuzzle Clint's cheek, enjoying the rasp of stubble against his skin. "She loves you and worries about you," he replied diplomatically.

Clint's mother had always been very warm and welcoming to Josh, and Josh had been a little concerned when Clint insisted on carrying a turducken -- a de-boned chicken full of sausage stuffing inside a de-boned duck which was stuffed inside a turkey -- to his vegetarian parents' Thanksgiving dinner. He'd been secretly glad for it, however, when Clint's mother had served a tofu "turkey" to her fifteen holiday guests. She'd given Clint The Look but she'd served the turducken anyway, and Josh had felt sorry for her when there was no turducken remaining at the end of the meal, but there was plenty of leftover tofurkey.

"I'll take it in to work with me tomorrow," he continued with a smile. "There are several vegetarians. I bet they'd be quite happy to eat it."

Josh was a mechanical engineer working in special effects for Screen Gems, and the diversity of tastes among his coworkers pretty much guaranteed any food brought to the break room would be devoured almost instantly.

"As long as I don't have to eat it, I don't care where it goes." Clint nuzzled Josh's cheek in return and slid his arms around Josh's waist, pulling him close.

Josh couldn't help giving a little sigh of pleasure as Clint pressed against him. Clint was the definition of tall, dark, and handsome, and he'd turned Josh on from the first moment they'd met at Clint's veterinary practice. When Clint had walked into the examination room to take a look at Josh's cat, Schrodinger, Josh couldn't do anything but stare. It wasn't every day that six feet of lean, dark-haired, dark-eyed hunk walked into his life, and while Josh wouldn't wish suffering on any creature, he blessed Schrodinger's upset stomach to this day.

"You'll never have to look at it again." He wrapped his arms around Clint's shoulders, tilting his head back so he could look into Clint's eyes. "So what movie is on the agenda tonight? Something we won't mind missing while we make out on the sofa?"

"We could watch something like that, or we could watch something we could ogle together, like *300*." Clint smiled playfully at him and gave him a little squeeze. "It depends on whether you're in the mood for some serious eye candy or not."

"With you here, I already have eye candy." Josh wriggled against Clint's body. "I'm fine with anything, but I need about twenty minutes or so before we start it. It's the first of the month."

Josh had seven brothers and sisters, and each of *them* had at least three children, with his oldest sister Peggy having already produced six -- and she was pregnant again. Adding in his parents, his fourteen aunts and uncles and their spouses, and his grandmother, Josh sent an enormous number of birthday and anniversary cards throughout the year. After he'd left home, he'd designated the first of each month as "card day", and he sat down and made out the cards for each family member with a special event that month.

"No problem." Clint smiled easily, giving Josh's ass a teasing grope. "I'll get everything set up while you write out your cards." He raised a questioning eyebrow. "Are you including Christmas cards, or are you planning to deliver those in person?"

Josh wriggled happily at the groping. "No Christmas cards -- Christmas presents. I've been buying things here and there online as I have time, but I'll do a big shopping trip before I head home."

Clint gazed down at him, quiet and serious. "Just you? Not 'we'?"

Josh bit his lip, wondering what he should say. He'd only taken a boyfriend home to meet his family once, and it hadn't gone well. "My family is a bit... overwhelming. I'm not sure you'd enjoy spending Christmas in the chaos, that's all. Won't your folks expect you to spend it with them anyway?"

"I already let them know I hoped you were going to let me meet your family for Christmas," Clint replied. "That's why I made sure we spent Thanksgiving with them. I wanted you to meet my family because we've been together almost a year, and I can see us being together for a lot longer." He rested his palm against Josh's cheek. "I can see a lifetime with you. That's what *I* want, anyway."

The words and the loving look in Clint's eyes made Josh want to melt. He'd been thinking more and more lately about their relationship and about seeing if Clint was interested in them moving in together. At the moment, they alternated between Josh's apartment and Clint's condo, but Josh had been saving up long enough that he was considering buying a house, and he wanted Clint to share it with him.

"I can see a lifetime with you, too," he said softly, leaning his cheek against Clint's hand. He smiled wryly. "I just worry you might change your mind after meeting my family."

"I may be a city boy and an only child, but that doesn't mean I can't handle being around a large family on a farm." Clint gave Josh a reproachful look that was right out of his mother's repertory. "Your family produced you. I love you, so why wouldn't I love them too?"

How it was possible to feel happiness, guilt, and trepidation all at one time, Josh didn't know, but that was *exactly* what he felt. "I'm pretty sure you'll either love them or hate them, and I mean it when I say they're overwhelming. There will be fifty or more people coming and going all the time, with children underfoot constantly. You won't have any privacy, and there will be no respect for boundaries. No question will be off limits -- and no doubt you'll be asked the same one about two dozen times by different people. I've only taken one other person home to meet my family, and it wasn't even Christmas. He didn't last through dinner."

"Obviously he wasn't the right man for you," Clint replied, sounding confident. "Granted, it'll be a new experience for me, but I can handle it. I *will* handle it for your sake, because they're your family and they're important to you, just like you handled my mother grilling you about your recycling habits."

Josh laughed. "That was nothing, honestly. I like your parents, tofurkey aside." He sobered. "You have to understand what you're letting yourself in for. How many boyfriends have you had? What religion are you? And Lord, be careful on questions about the government and politics. It's a trap, no matter who is asking."

"You can coach me," Clint suggested. "Or give me a script. I don't care. I'm ready and willing to face whatever your family throws at me."

"Even if it's changing baby diapers or plucking a chicken? I'm not exaggerating, Clint. They're my family and I adore them, but sometimes they push even me to my limits." He sighed and shook his head. "But if you're absolutely certain you want to go, I guess we're going. I won't hold you to any thoughts of us taking our relationship farther until after we get back."

"Does that mean you'd like to talk about taking our relationship farther if I don't run away screaming from your family?" Clint asked, a hopeful note in his voice.

"If you're still speaking to me after spending Christmas with my family, then I think I'll have to keep you forever. And I really, truly mean that." Josh smiled wryly. "But let's see how it goes, all right? I sometimes think a saint would run screaming from my family."

"It's a deal." Clint looked quite pleased by their bargain. "But if I'm still speaking to you after Christmas, I'm holding you to that keeping me forever thing."

"All right, that's fair." Part of Josh was incredibly happy that Clint seemed eager for them to take the next step, but the specter of Christmas hung over him like the Sword of Damocles. "Let's kiss on it."

Clint's smile turned wicked as he pulled Josh closer and bent his head to brush a light, teasing kiss against Josh's lips before returning for a much deeper, warmer kiss, claiming Josh's mouth with the ease of familiarity. Josh sighed happily, giving himself over to the experi-

ence, burying his fingers in the dark silk of Clint's hair, feeling desire
rise with familiar swiftness. In the time they'd been together, he'd
come to realize how happy Clint made him and how well they fit
together in every way.

Now if they could just get through Christmas, the future could be
everything Josh hoped it could be. It was a big if, and he knew it. For
the first time in his life, all Josh wanted for Christmas was for it to
be over.

"WELL, THIS IS... RUSTIC." Clint stared out the window as Josh pulled
his SUV up in front of a house that was an architect's worst
nightmare.

There were additions and extensions added haphazardly everywhere Clint could see, without any obvious thought to design, unity,
or flow. The front porch was wide and fit around the front of the
house in odd lengths. The front yard was neat under its layer of snow,
and the house itself looked to be in sound condition, but it had a
distinct lived-in appearance.

"Yes, it is." Josh's green eyes were filled with anxiety as he gazed at
Clint. "Are you sure you want to go through with this?"

"I'm sure," Clint said firmly as he unfastened his seat belt.

He knew Josh was worried about this trip and how it would affect
their relationship, for which Clint blamed the asshole who'd run far
and fast the last time Josh had brought someone home. Clint thought
Josh had built the whole thing up in his mind as being far worse than
it actually was, but even if Josh's family was as large, loud, and intrusive as Josh claimed, Clint thought even a quiet, introverted only
child like him could find a way to cope for a few days. These were the
people who had shaped Josh into the kind and loving man he was,
after all, so they couldn't be all bad.

He put his hand on the door handle and looked at Josh, one
eyebrow raised. "Ready?"

"As I can be, I guess." Josh smiled crookedly, unfastening his own belt and opening the car door.

The front door of the house opened suddenly, and a tall, strong-looking woman came out, smiling widely. "Joshie! Oh, it's so good to see you!"

"Hey, Momma." Josh was smiling, too, and he skirted around the car and clasped Clint's hand, leading him toward the porch.

The woman came down the steps to meet them, and as they got closer, Clint could see her eyes were the same green as Josh's, and her hair the same sandy brown color, too, although liberally threaded with silver.

Grace Cash threw her arms around her son, hugging him tightly, and Josh hugged her back, letting go of Clint's hand. From Clint's perspective, it looked as though she was going to squeeze Josh to death. She finally pulled back, and Clint could see Josh's eyes were suspiciously bright.

"Momma, this is Clint Barker." Josh smiled, resting his hand on Clint's shoulder. "Clint, this is my momma, Grace."

She looked at Clint, smiling with genuine warmth. "Josh has told me so much about you. You make him very happy."

"I try, Mrs. Cash." Clint smiled back at her, feeling welcome already. "He makes me very happy, too."

"Call me Grace, please." She enveloped him in a big hug, her strong arms squeezing him tightly. "Anyone who makes my son happy is already family."

Clint thought he could actually hear his ribs creaking, and when he managed to get enough air to speak, his voice was strained. "It's a pleasure to meet you, Grace," he said, awkwardly returning the embrace.

She released him at last and stepped back. "Well, come on in! Your pa is with your Uncle Billy, Josh, but everyone else is inside. Might as well get the greetings out of the way and deal with your bags later. No sense fussing with them now. Oh, your Big Momma is going to be over the moon to see you."

Josh caught Clint's arm, holding him back for a moment as his mother continued up to the porch. "Are you okay?"

Clint felt his sides gingerly and gave an exaggerated wince to tease Josh. "I don't think anything is broken, so yes, I'm okay. So far so good, right?"

"It's early days yet," Josh replied, not losing the worry-line between his brows. "Come on, might as well see if we're going to make it through the introductions."

Clint followed Josh inside, and his first impression of the Cash house was of warmth. The temperature was blissfully warm, of course, helping thaw out the December cold that had crept into his fingers and toes, but it was more than that. As he followed Josh into the living room, he glanced around and saw everything from antiques that had probably been handed down for generations to finger paintings that looked like they'd been created by a child the day before. The decor wouldn't have lived up to his mother's magazine cover standards, but it looked cozy, inviting, and lived in.

His second impression was *holy hell, that's a lot of people.*

There were adults on every chair and sofa, and children were perched in laps or sprawled on the floor. There were at least twenty people in the room, and voices called out welcome in a cacophony that rivaled the crowd at a baseball game. Josh nodded and smiled at the greetings, but he took Clint's hand, and led him toward an old woman who was sitting in a beautifully carved rocking chair that looked at least a hundred years old. Her hair was completely silver, but her flashing dark eyes were bright and intelligent above high cheekbones. Josh had told him about Big Momma, and his description had included the fact that she was part Cherokee, and her striking looks reflected her heritage.

"Big Momma, this is Clint Barker," Josh said, squeezing Clint's hand hard. "Clint, this my grandmother, Mary Creek."

Sharp eyes looked Clint up and down, and Clint got the feeling that if she decided to take a dislike to him, things would be over before they'd even gotten started. The regard continued for several long moments, and the room fell quiet around them.

"Well, he's a looker," Big Momma said finally, and her eyes twinkled with amusement. "Much better'n that last one you brought home. He looked like a skeert rabbit."

Clint grinned, pleased he'd passed the test, and he held out his hand to her. "Thank you, Mrs. Creek. It's nice to meet you and, uh...." He looked around at the crowded room. "The rest of Josh's family."

"Call me Big Momma, child, everyone does. Lord a'mercy, this ain't half of Josh's family." She took Clint's hand and shook it, her grip surprisingly strong. Then her gaze moved to Josh, and Clint saw her deep affection for her grandson. "Come here and give your old granny a hug. Lands, if you don't look more like your grandpa every time I set eyes on you!"

Josh couldn't hide his relieved smile, and he leaned down and hugged his grandmother warmly. "Just don't try to pinch my tail the way I caught you pinching Grandpa's!" Josh said as he straightened up. "He always complained you gave him bruises so bad, sitting horseback was a pure misery."

Big Momma laughed, clapping her hands together in obvious delight, and Josh reached out to take Clint's hand again.

"Okay, since Big Momma isn't going to order him skinned and thrown down the well, everyone, this is Clint, my boyfriend. He's from a small family, so please don't overwhelm him all at once, okay? He's a veterinarian, as I'm sure Momma has told you, so dropping a chicken or a snake on him isn't going to send him running." There was a wry twist to Josh's lips as he looked around at the children in the room that made Clint wonder if *that* had been what had sent the last man running. "Don't try to confuse him by switching up names. It's going to be hard enough for him to keep everyone straight." He pointed to a set of twin boys with brown hair. "And you two, don't snicker if he calls the wrong one Brian or Billy, got it? I brought presents for everyone, but anyone who's mean to Clint just might get a lump of coal instead."

"He's not kidding. I saw him pack the coal," Clint said, looking at the younger kids solemnly.

That the crowd of people surrounding him didn't comprise even half of Josh's family was overwhelming; his own family barely hit the double digits when they gathered for holidays even when all of his aunts, uncles, and cousins showed up. He was going to approach this occasion like he approached the medical conventions he attended, where he was also surrounded by large groups of people he didn't know. He was going to smile, be polite, make small talk, and try not to offend anyone. If that didn't work, he'd find the nearest liquor store and stock up on liquid courage.

"It's nice to meet all of you," he added, waving to the room at large. "Thanks for letting me join you for Christmas."

Josh squeezed his hand and proceeded with the introductions. "Only" four of his seven siblings and their spouses and twelve of his twenty-eight nieces and nephews were present. Along with his mother and grandmother, there were twenty-four people in the crowded room, at least until Grace shooed the children out to go play in a back room. Josh had reluctantly admitted on the drive out to Possum Hollow (properly pronounced "Holler") that he had one hundred and seventeen first cousins at last count, so it was probably a good thing no more people had shown up to welcome Josh home.

"Cake and lemonade, boys?" Grace asked. "Or if you want something more substantial, there's leftover fried chicken from supper."

Josh looked at Clint with a smile. "Hungry? Momma makes wonderful fried chicken."

They'd eaten snacks on the drive from Wilmington to Possum Hollow, but Clint was ready for a real meal, and fried chicken sounded great to him. His mother hadn't made fried chicken since she became a vegetarian, and Clint wasn't terribly adept in the kitchen.

"I'd love some. I haven't had decent fried chicken in years."

"Then come on back to the kitchen and we'll get you both fed." Grace beckoned the two of them to follow her. Clint was led into an enormous kitchen, one that held two six-burner stoves, two refrigerators, and a sink almost as large as a bathtub. In fact, when they drew closer, Clint could see that it *had* been a bathtub at one point.

Grace shooed them toward a big table in the middle of the room.

"You're settling in right well, Clint. You're lucky only the ones who live here who are home tonight."

"I already told him Peggy and her brood and Beth Anne and Brenda Sue and their families have their own places." Josh leaned back in his chair, resting his hand on Clint's thigh under the table. "It does take a lot of hands to run a farm, which is why all my brothers still live at home."

Clint thought about the crowd in the living room and the number of children present, and he had to wonder how anyone managed to have sex in a house with this many people living in it. Either the walls were all perfectly soundproofed or everyone had really quiet sex.

"That's understandable. I don't have much experience with running a farm, but from what Josh has told me, it does sound like a lot of hard work," he said, covering Josh's hand with his own and giving it a little squeeze.

"Oh, it is, but it's honest work, too." Grace bustled about, preparing two plates of cold fried chicken and potato salad, which she placed in front of them with a smile, then added silverware and napkins. "Let me get you some lemonade. Or would you rather have iced tea? I wasn't sure if caffeine might be too much before bedtime."

"Lemonade is fine with me, thanks, Momma," Josh said, picking up his fork.

"It's fine with me too." Clint gave her a grateful smile before turning his attention to the chicken, which tasted even better than it smelled.

Grace poured them lemonade, then sat down at the table with them. "I told everyone to give you two a little space." She smiled wryly and looked at Clint. "I know we can be a bit much, taken all at once, and you might feel the need to escape. This house has five bathrooms, and one of them is 'adults only'. Josh can show you which one. If you need a little time out, go in there and lock the door. Trust me, I do it myself on occasion. Much as I love my family, sometimes a body just needs to breathe air no one else is breathing."

"Thanks, I'll make sure to note which one." Clint was relieved to hear there was a "time out" space for adults in the house, and he knew he'd be taking advantage of it. He liked Josh's family so far, but he wasn't used to being around so many people for long periods of time. A break would be welcome when all the noise and togetherness started to be too much for his introverted nature.

"I was thinking of taking Clint over to Marge's this evening. I want to make sure she meets him."

Grace raised one eyebrow, obviously surprised, but she nodded. "I suppose that makes sense. You boys just watch yourselves in there."

Clint gave Josh a questioning look, wondering what deep end he was about to be tossed into. "What is Marge's and why do we need to watch ourselves there?"

Josh finished off the chicken thigh he'd been eating and picked up his napkin to wipe his lips before answering. "Well, Marge's is a... I suppose the best way to describe it is 'honkytonk'. Momma's sister Marge owns and runs it. She's... different. But we'll be fine."

Grace gave a snort. "Just keep a hand on your wallet."

So it was *that* kind of place. Clint nodded, picturing a smoky dive with a lot of burly men in John Deere caps sitting at the bar with their ass cracks showing and a beer in hand, as well as some bikers at the pool table. He made a silent bet with himself that there would be country music playing when they walked in.

"I think I can handle it," he said, offering Josh a reassuring smile.

"I hope so." Rising to her feet, Grace nodded to them. "Just put the dishes in the sink when you're done and then fetch your bags from the car. Josh, I put you in the bedroom at the back, so you won't be disturbed by people going up and down the stairs all night."

"Thanks, Momma." Josh watched her leave, then looked at Clint, sighing in relief. "So far, so good, eh?"

"And you were worried I was going to run away screaming." Clint made a scoffing noise as he leaned over to brush a quick kiss to Josh's lips. "Silly man."

"You've been here all of thirty minutes. It's early yet." Josh groped Clint's leg again under the table. "But Momma must have the others cowed. I told her you were far more important to me than the last guy."

"Did you really?" Clint was inordinately pleased to know Josh had said that about him, and it made him doubly determined to survive the holidays with their relationship intact. He would get along with Josh's family if it killed him, damn it!

"I did, indeed." Josh leaned over to steal a kiss of his own. "Are you about done? We need to get those bags and the gifts inside before going to Marge's. I wouldn't like to leave anything valuable in the car while we can't keep an eye on it."

Clint polished off his chicken and potato salad, then got up to take his plate to the sink as instructed. "When your mom said she put you in the back bedroom, did she mean she put *you* in the back bedroom or did she put *us* back there? I don't want to dump my stuff in your room and cause a scandal."

Josh joined him at the sink. "She meant both of us. There's usually not a bedroom free with so many living here, but she sometimes farms out some of the older kids during the holidays to make room for me. When I told her you were coming, she asked if we'd mind sharing a room, since there are two babies in the house right now, and you can't put them in the same bedroom because if one wakes up and starts howling, the other will start crying too." He gave Clint a sideways glance. "You don't mind, do you?"

Clint raised one hand to his throat as if he was clutching a string of imaginary pearls. "Why, Mr. Cash, I just don't know! What will they think of me sharing a room with a man I'm not even betrothed to?"

Chuckling, Josh wiped his hands on a dishtowel and slid his arms around Clint's waist. "Since there's no chance of one of us turning up in the family way, I think the regular rules don't apply. Besides, I'm not the first homosexual in my family, remember? Big Momma's older brother was 'queer', as they called it back then, and he was her favorite brother. So she won't tolerate intolerance. She says Uncle Daw's ghost would haunt us all."

Clint was glad Josh had the support and acceptance of his family and that it extended to him as well. He couldn't resist teasing Josh some more, however, even as he wrapped his arms around Josh's shoulders.

"That doesn't mean I don't have my good reputation to consider," he said with a haughty sniff. "I assume you're prepared to defend my honor if anyone besmirches it."

"Oh, of course. I've been brushing up on my sword work so I can call any bastards out. I'll not have anyone ruining the reputation of my own true love." Josh's hands moved to Clint's ass, groping him playfully. "Is the real reason you wanted to come home with me was so my pa would force you into a shotgun wedding?"

"Would it work?" Clint's tone was light, but he found himself quite interested in Josh's answer. The whole reason he'd wanted Josh to meet his parents and to meet Josh's parents in return was to show he was ready to make a long term commitment. It seemed now he'd made that leap, he was ready to go all the way, up to and including marriage.

Josh tilted his head to one side, studying Clint intently. "I could probably arrange it, if you're still interested. After Christmas."

Clint smiled and shook his head, amused that Josh was still hung up on the idea that the holidays might tear them apart. "Haven't I already lasted longer than that other guy?"

"Well, yes, but you haven't met everyone yet. Now give me a kiss and then let's get things moved in. It'll be bath time for the kids soon, and I'm sure it's still just as chaotic as I remember. We'll want to be well away by then."

Clint leaned over and gave Josh a brief, chaste peck on the lips. "That's all you get until we're officially engaged. I won't have everyone in this house thinking I'm a man of loose virtue."

"What?" Josh's mouth dropped open and he stared at Clint. "Tell me you aren't serious. Please."

Laughing, Clint tightened his arms around Josh and bent his head to claim a deeper kiss. "No, I'm not serious, at least not about that. The shotgun wedding thing...." He made a back and forth gesture with one hand.

Josh licked his lips, as though wanting more of Clint's taste. "We'll talk about that on December twenty-sixth. Come on, quit stalling. Let's get going."

"Okay, okay." Clint laughed as he followed Josh back outside to the car. Obviously Josh still had doubts, but Clint was determined to prove a little family togetherness wouldn't be enough to tear them apart.

Once they got everything inside, Josh drove them to Marge's. Clint tried not to clutch the seat hard enough to rip the faux leather as Josh navigated the curvy mountain road. Born and bred on the flat end of the state, he wasn't used to being caught between a wall of solid rock and a plummet to certain death or to having his ears pop while navigating roads that had hills as well as curves.

Despite Clint's doubts they'd survive the trip, Josh turned into the dark parking lot of a one-story building with the car and its occupants intact. The lot seemed to be full of pickup trucks and motorcycles, and the glaring neon in the windows advertised at least four different kinds of beer and six different hard liquors. There was nothing to indicate the name of the place, but Josh had explained it was so well known, the building didn't need to be labeled. As Josh cut the engine, Clint could hear the sounds of a fist fight somewhere off in the darkness.

"This is it." Josh grinned at him. "I can't wait for you to meet Marge. She's my favorite aunt."

Clint unfastened his seatbelt and got out of the car, surveying the joint. The faint sound of a live band was audible even at this distance, and he wasn't surprised to recognize "Honky Tonk Blues".

"Oh my God. Please tell me this place sells moonshine. If it doesn't, I'm going to be disappointed."

Josh shot him a conspiratorial look. "Babe, this place sells the *best* moonshine in the Carolinas. Made by my uncle Billy. Remember Momma said Pa wasn't home because he was with his brother? That was a family code for them making a run to the still."

"*Seriously?*" Clint knew it was illegal, but he couldn't help feeling an illicit thrill at knowing his boyfriend's family ran an actual still. "Have you ever helped make it?"

"Oh, I've been out a time or two. Almost everyone in the family has. Pa grows corn for more than just feeding cattle, you know. His sisters Maybelline and Cora Beth own the bakery in town, which is a perfect cover for getting a lot of sugar without raising the interest of the ATF. Not to mention, Pa's brother Jim Bob is Possum Hollow's sheriff." Josh paused. "You might say it's a family affair."

Clint let out a low whistle. "Wow, your family has got it down to a science. I should probably be shocked or scandalized, but actually, I think it's kind of cool. Illegal, I know, but still kind of cool."

"Yeah, it is." Josh pulled him toward the door. "Now come on, city boy, let's get you a taste of real white lightning."

The inside of the place was so smoky, Clint almost felt like he was walking through a fog. There were tables close to the entrance, all of them full of some of the biggest men Clint had ever seen. A bar occupied the wall along one side, and there were pool tables in the back. The band was on a stage opposite the bar, and a few couples were dancing in the cleared space between. The clients reflected the mixture of vehicles in the parking lot, about equally divided between plaid shirts and cowboy boots and black leather and bandanas.

Clint looked around curiously, wanting to see if he could pick out Aunt Marge in the crowd. "Are you serious?" he asked, raising his voice to be heard above the band. "About the...." He mimed drinking in case mentioning the illegal liquor was frowned upon.

"Dead serious." Josh beckoned for Clint to follow and wound his way through the tables to the bar. He pushed in between two big guys and gave a low, three note whistle.

Over Josh's shoulder, Clint could see a woman at the far end of the bar turn, and her face broke out in a huge grin. "Josh! I shoulda known you'd come waltzing in here as soon as your momma cut you loose!"

So this was Marge, who owned the bar and tended bar as well. She was a tall woman, probably close to fifty with short blond hair that was spiked up with gel. She was wearing jeans so tight they looked painted on, with well-worn cowboy boots and a leather vest over a white t-shirt with the sleeves rolled up. There were tattoos on her arms, and a cigar was clenched between her teeth.

"Of course!" Josh said, as she strode toward them. There was nothing feminine about the way she moved, and when she reached Josh, she clapped her hand on his shoulder so hard that Clint heard Josh groan. "I can't resist coming to see my favorite aunt in the world, now can I?"

"Of course you can't, you sweet talker, you." She glanced over Josh's shoulder, and Clint found himself looking into a pair of green eyes just like Josh's. "Well hello, gorgeous. Are you the city slicker who's stolen my little boy's heart?"

"Yes, ma'am." Clint smiled and held out his hand. "I'm Clint Barker, city slicker and heart stealer at your service. It's nice to meet you."

Clint's hand was enveloped in a strong grip and squeezed hard enough to make him wince. "Don't you talk pretty, city boy. If you move those hips as sweet as you speak, no wonder Josh looks so satisfied. Don't got a sister at home, do you?"

"Unfortunately, no," he replied, trying to ignore the way his bones creaked in her grip. "I'm an only child, but if I did have a sister, I'd send her your way."

Marge grinned around the cigar and released his hand at last. "I like you, city boy." Her gaze moved back to Josh. "So I take it my charms aren't the only reason for your visit. You coming to sample the private family stock?"

"I think that would be appropriate, Aunt Marge. Thanks." Josh smiled and nodded, and Marge bustled off, returning a moment later with two glasses of clear liquid.

"On the house, boys." There was a light of unholy glee in her eyes that made Clint uneasy. "I won't make you pay, city boy, in case it comes right back up."

Clint swallowed hard as he accepted the glass, hoping he didn't embarrass himself and Josh by getting sick in the middle of Marge's bar, especially since he suspected she'd make him clean up after himself. He rarely had anything stronger than wine, and he'd certainly never had moonshine before, but this was an opportunity he didn't want to pass up.

"Thanks," he said and then looked at Josh. "You first, country boy."

With a laugh, Josh raised his glass in a salute, then raised it to his lips and took a judicious sip. "WHOOEE!" he exclaimed. "That's a powerful batch!" He looked at Clint. "Don't try to chug it. You'll die. Or wish you'd died."

Clint stared at Josh, wide-eyed, then glanced down at the glass in his hand, having second thoughts. He couldn't back down now, however, and so he raised it to his lips and took a sip -- and immediately felt his sinuses explode and his throat burst into flames simultaneously. When he managed to stop wheezing enough to take a decent breath again, he looked at Marge and Josh with watering eyes.

"Powerful is an understatement!"

Josh laughed and patted Clint on the back. "Good job! If it doesn't burn a hole in your stomach, you win!"

Marge was grinning. "Not bad. Not bad. Are you two going to stick around for a spell?"

"I think so. Right, Clint? You probably need to recover from the moonshine before we start back down the road." Josh's eyes were dancing with amusement.

"I could use a little recuperation time," Clint admitted, smiling sheepishly.

Country music wasn't really his genre; he preferred jazz and classic rock, but the band was good, and he liked Marge, so he was happy to stay and relax at the bar for a while.

"Okay. Looks like a couple of seats have opened up down the bar. Talk to you in a bit, Aunt Marge."

"Don't let city slicker fall off the stool and mess up his pretty face," Marge drawled, giving Clint a playful wink. She turned away and began to collect empty glasses as patrons called out for another round.

"She likes you." Josh pulled him toward the empty seats. Once they were ensconced, facing the stage so they could see the band, he tilted his head at the glass Clint still held. "You don't have to finish that. Would you rather have a beer or maybe a soda?"

Clint eyed the glass, waging a debate over whether the health of his digestive system was more important than his manhood. "Maybe a beer. I'm not convinced this stuff won't eat through my esophagus on the way down. I'll work up to two sips on my next visit." He grinned playfully at Josh. "Maybe I'll be up to a full glass by our tenth anniversary."

Josh smiled back at him, and there was nothing playful about the heat in his eyes. "Is that so?" he purred. "You still want me? Even knowing my family are moonshiners?"

"Of course I do." Clint leaned close and rested his hand on Josh's shoulder, feeling a spark of arousal as he always did when Josh looked at him like that. "I always will."

"Good." Josh leaned closer, closing his eyes and nuzzling Clint's cheek with warm affection. His free hand slid along Clint's thigh in a subtle caress.

"Are you fucking kidding me? That's sick!"

The moment was shattered by a belligerent voice coming from not two feet away from them. A big bruiser of a man, probably a biker if the black leather vest and bandanna he wore were any indication, stood glaring at them, his tobacco-stained teeth bared in a grimace of disgust.

Clint swiveled on his bar stool to face the man, glaring back. He refused to hide his feelings for Josh no matter where they were, and he assumed Marge would side with them rather than the homophobic asshole if a fight broke out. "Have you got a problem?"

"Damn right I have a problem! I didn't come out to see two men hanging all over each other!" The biker snarled at them, then spat on the floor. "That's what I think of folks like the two of you!"

The bar grew quiet around them, and the band stopped playing, making Josh's voice seem oddly loud. "Why? Are you jealous that my boyfriend is prettier than your girlfriend?"

It had to be the moonshine talking, because while Clint didn't hesitate to stand up for himself, he usually preferred to defuse the situation politely rather than escalate the problem by saying things like, "I think he's jealous that I get to hang all over you and he doesn't."

The big man gaped at them. Obviously their response wasn't what he had been expecting. Perhaps he thought gays were wimps, or maybe he'd thought his appearance was enough to intimidate them, because it took a moment before his face flushed red and he balled up his fists.

"You're gonna pay for that! I'm gonna mess up your face, and we'll see how pretty you are then!"

Before Clint could get off his stool and prepare to defend himself, he found a wall of tall, broad-shouldered men forming between him and Josh, and the redneck bully. There were three, although their sheer size made it seem like there were more of them; they had the burly strength of men who worked hard for a living, building their muscles in a field rather than a gym. Two of the men wore jeans and plaid work shirts and the third wore overalls over a white tee-shirt. All of them wore broken-in caps and identical ominous scowls directed at the bully.

"You want to repeat what you just said about our kin?" The man in the faded overalls asked, his voice deceptively pleasant.

The biker fumed at having the odds suddenly altered. With a snarl, he motioned toward one side of the room, and three more bikers came up to join him.

"Looks like we have us a rumble," the biker began, lifting his hands and cracking his knuckles. But before he could do anything else, the sudden, ominous sound of a gun being cocked came from behind the bar.

"There ain't going to be a rumble in *my* place. I suggest you fine, leather-clad gentlemen find somewhere else to drink."

Clint turned his head to see Marge holding a shotgun and glaring at the bikers. For a moment, the man who'd started the trouble looked like he was going to object, but several more of the locals moved up beside Josh's kinsmen, making it obvious whose side they were on. No other bikers came to assist the four troublemakers; either they were regulars, or they didn't want to get involved.

"Fine. This place stinks anyway," the biker muttered. "Shoulda known the bull dyke would stand up for the queers."

Things grew silent again, and Marge raised the gun, leveling it right at the big man's head. "That's *Ms.* Bull Dyke to you, asshole. You got until I count to three or you're going to be picking buckshot out of what's left of your teeth."

The man's eyes widened. Apparently the threat impressed him, or he suddenly developed a case of common sense, because he turned and headed quickly for the door with his three buddies right behind him.

Marge held the shotgun until the door closed, then she lowered it and grinned at Josh. "You are such a pain in the ass, Joshua. Good thing I love you."

There were snickers around the bar, then the band began another song, which Clint immediately recognized as "I Fought the Law and the Law Won." Laughing, he settled himself back on the bar stool and offered Marge an apologetic smile.

"Sorry, I don't usually go looking for trouble."

Marge waved it off. "No problem. Not the first time it's happened. Won't be the last." The shotgun had disappeared back wherever she'd gotten it from, and she turned back to work as though she hadn't just threatened to shoot a man sixty seconds before.

"Not your fault, city boy," the big man in the overalls said, grinning at Clint and holding out a hand the size of a ham shank. "I'm Jedidiah Cash, by the way. No relation to Johnny, but I am related to your little boy toy here."

Clint shook Jedidiah's hand, grinning back. "Pleased to meet you and thanks for your help. I appreciate it."

More than that, he was pleased by the show of solidarity from Josh's family. He hadn't expected this level of acceptance, much less protection, but it was good to know someone was watching his and Josh's backs while they were there.

"Don't let Jed fool you. He's a total softie." Josh laughed as Jed wrapped a huge arm around his head and rubbed it hard with his knuckles.

"What you saying about me, cuz?" Jed asked gruffly.

"Nothing! Nothing!" Josh replied. Jed let him go, and Josh ran his fingers through his hair. "Damn it, Jed! Do you know how long I had to spend with a blow dryer to get my hair perfect?"

"Oh, la de dah." Jed rolled his eyes. "Anyway, nice to meet you too, city boy. Josh is just lucky that most of the family is scared of Big Momma, or we'd have all kicked his sorry ass for being a pain in ours."

The other two men introduced themselves as Mason and Moss Creek. They were obviously brothers, and both had the green eyes that seemed to be a common trait of that side of Josh's family. They exchanged pleasantries, then things settled back down, and when they were alone again Josh brushed a kiss to Clint's cheek.

"Here you were saying I had to defend your honor, and you stood up for mine. My hero."

"The whole reason I took self-defense classes was so I would never have to take shit from assholes like that again." Clint reached out and rested his hand on Josh's leg, leaning into the kiss. "But that doesn't mean you get to besmirch my honor in the bedroom," he added with exaggerated primness.

"Far be it from me to compromise your maidenly virtue." Josh's voice was solemn, but the twinkle in his eyes betrayed his amusement. "But you see my kin would defend me, right? I may be a snotty little gay boy, but I'm *their* snotty little gay boy. Like Jed said, they know Big Momma would tan their hides if they let some asshole rough me up."

"So I see. I admit I was surprised by the wholesale acceptance, but after meeting Big Momma and Marge, I think I get it." Clint glanced over at Marge, wondering exactly how many asses she'd kicked some sense into when it came to the issue of accepting homosexuality.

"It's probably not quite as wholesale as it seems, but yeah, no one in the family is going to say anything. I knew from a young age what I was, and I went to Marge. She took up for me the way that Big

Momma and Uncle Daw took up for *her*." Josh shrugged lightly. "Big Momma says it's in the blood, and we can't help it any more than we can help having green eyes or freckles. Big Momma had to deal with discrimination in her younger days for being of mixed blood, and her brothers got in quite a few fights defending the family honor. Folk learned that family stood by each other -- and we have a *huge* family."

"That's an understatement," Clint replied dryly as he finished off his beer. "I feel like I'm about to be assimilated into the Borg collective."

"Really?" Josh looked at him pensively. "No one's going to try to change you, you know. I promise."

"No, it's not that," Clint hastened to assure him, giving his leg a squeeze. "I don't feel like anyone is trying to make me wear overalls or ride a tractor. It's just the sheer size, you know? It's completely foreign to my own experiences. It seems like it would be easy to get swallowed up and lost in the crowd. Maybe that's why a lot of your relatives have strong personalities, based on what I've seen so far. You've got to do something to stand out."

"I never really thought about it. Could be you're right." Josh smiled wryly. "I told you it was overwhelming, didn't I? I adore them, but absence makes the heart grow fonder sometimes."

"I can understand that." Clint chuckled and shook his head. "Anyway, do you want another beer or are you ready to call it a night? I'd ask if you could teach me to do some boot-scooting on the dance floor, but that might be pushing it."

"Dance lessons can be private." Josh finished his beer and stood. "Hey, Marge! Thanks for everything, but we're going to head back to the house. We had a long drive."

Marge came out from behind the bar and enveloped Josh in a bone-cracking hug. "I'll see you day after tomorrow at the hootenanny. You too, city boy."

Clint smiled warmly at her. "I'll be there with bells on."

She laughed and gave him a swat on the ass before sashaying back to work. Josh chuckled, taking Clint's hand and heading toward the door.

"She really does like you, to risk boy cooties like that."

"Good, I like her too." Clint laced his fingers with Josh's and flashed a teasing smile at him. "I like Jed, too. Think I'd have a shot with him if things don't work out with you? Brawny farm boys are a little outside my range of experience, but I think I could cope."

Josh stared at him for a moment, wide-eyed, then snorted with laughter. "Good luck! If you can get past his wife, go for it! She'd probably scratch your eyes out. Carter women are powerful jealous creatures, according to Big Momma."

"What about Cash men?" Clint gave Josh a wide-eyed, innocent look. "Would you scratch someone's eyes out if they made a pass at me?"

"Yep!" Josh grinned and squeezed his hand. "I'd even fight those brawny farm boys for you. I might get my ass kicked up between my ears, but then you'd have to nurse me back to health."

"Gladly. In sickness and in health, right?" Clint said once they were settled in Josh's car once more.

Josh fastened his seatbelt, then smiled as he started the car. "You're wearing me down, I must admit. I'm halfway tempted to take you up on it on getting married and *then* make you face my whole family. Then it would be too late to run, and my cousins would make sure you didn't. Lucky for you, I'm a fair-minded man."

Clint shook his head but said nothing, just smiled to himself. So far, he found Josh's family to be big, loud, and a little overwhelming, but he didn't feel like running for home. Not by a long shot. Obviously a few hours weren't enough to convince Josh that this trip wouldn't be the end of their relationship, but Clint was patient and he had nothing but time to show Josh he was here to stay.

2

J osh was always perturbed that being back on the farm meant he had a hard time sleeping past dawn. It wasn't any particular thing that woke him -- although he heard the damned rooster start crowing before there was even a hint of light through the curtains -- and he always chalked it up to his subconscious trying to guilt trip him into getting up and doing chores. But for the first time, he was waking up at home with a warm, firm body snuggled up against him, and even though he knew he wouldn't be able to get back to sleep, he felt absolutely no desire to get out of bed.

Clint was spooned up against his back, one arm thrown across his waist, and Josh nestled into the embrace happily, pressing back against him with a quiet hum of satisfaction. Josh loved cuddling, and Clint didn't seem to mind indulging his constant desire for touch. He placed his hand on top of Clint's, lacing their fingers, and sighed softly with satisfaction.

Releasing a sleepy hum, Clint nuzzled the back of Josh's neck, and Josh could feel Clint's morning erection pressing against him. Chuckling, Josh wriggled his ass; that was another thing he loved about Clint, the way he was willing to spend time on their lovemaking, not always rushing, desperate to reach orgasm. Clint had patience, and

Josh loved the times they woke up together and spent a lazy hour or two driving each other crazy with desire.

Clint pressed a kiss to Josh's warm skin and began nuzzling his way from Josh's neck to his shoulder. "Do we have anywhere to be this morning?" he murmured, his voice raspy with sleep.

"Mm... no." Josh's breath caught, his cock twitching in reaction to the slide of Clint's lips over his skin.

"Good, because I found something I want to do." A wicked note entered Clint's voice, and he tugged his hand free of Josh's grasp so he could stroke Josh's chest, slowly trailing his hand lower and lower.

Josh moaned and closed his eyes. Clint knew just how to touch him, and he felt the muscles of his stomach quiver in anticipation. "I sure hope it's me."

"Oh yes." Clint bit down lightly on Josh's shoulder as he brushed his fingers over the erection straining the front of Josh's boxers. "Can I interest you in a little early stocking stuffing?"

Sliding his hand around the jut of Clint's hip, Josh groped Clint's firm ass. "Oh, hell yes. Stuff anything you want anywhere you want."

Laughing softly, Clint wriggled provocatively against Josh's hand. "Did you pack the lube?"

"Yeah, I put it in the drawer of the nightstand. One sec."

Josh stretched out his arm, fumbling for the drawer. He had to roll a bit, and Clint moved with him, keeping his erection pressed firmly against Josh's ass. The distraction made Josh clumsy, but he finally managed to get the drawer open and grabbed the lube.

A sudden banging on the bedroom door made Josh freeze in place.

"Uncle Josh! Mr. Clint! Momma wants to know if you're awake and want pancakes!"

"Oh, shit...." Clint groaned and tightened his arms around Josh, burying his face against the back of Josh's neck.

At that moment, Josh would have happily fed whichever small child was outside their door to the pigs. He counted to three. "Well, we're awake *now*. We'll be down in a few minutes."

"But do you want pancakes?" the young voice persisted.

"Yes, dam-- Yes, pancakes are fine!"

The sound of running feet indicated their small alarm clock had gone away, and Josh sighed. "Sorry about that."

Clint gave Josh a little squeeze. "My guess is that if we aren't down in literally a few minutes, someone will be back at the door to tell us our pancakes are getting cold. Do I win?"

Josh turned his head, pressing his lips to Clint's, then pulling back. "I think we both lose out this time, damn it. I didn't even think this might happen, since I've never slept with anyone at home before."

Clint sat up slowly, releasing Josh with reluctance. "This is my dubious prize for surviving the night, I suppose." He gave Josh a wide-eyed look of appeal. "How high are the chances we won't be able to have sex until we're home?"

"Not high, if I have anything to say about it." Josh turned and pushed Clint back down, straddling his hips. "I don't think I can survive three more days without having you inside me."

That brought a look of smug satisfaction to Clint's face as he gripped Josh's hips and bucked up against him. "Good. We can both be on the lookout for the first opportunity to get on Santa's naughty list."

"I want to be naughty now," Josh murmured, licking his lips. Clint had an incredible body, and even after almost a year together, Josh never got tired of looking at him. He smoothed his hands over the warm skin of Clint's chest, brushing his thumbs over Clint's nipples.

Sucking in a sharp breath, Clint arched his back in response to the teasing. "Pancakes, remember?"

"I'd rather have beefcake." Rocking his hips, Josh rubbed their erections together through their boxers. "Just a snack?"

"Well...." Clint looked like he was on the verge of being persuaded. "Maybe a little something to tide us over wouldn't hurt."

That was all the encouragement Josh needed. He threw off the covers, not minding the cool air against his skin as he slid down between Clint's legs. He tugged down Clint's boxers and wrapped his hand around Clint's flushed, hard cock. With an evil grin, he lowered his head, licking the tip before engulfing Clint completely in the heat of his mouth. Moaning, Clint buried his fingers in Josh's hair and lifted his hips eagerly.

"Yes...yes...so good...."

Clint's familiar, musky taste was delicious, and Josh hummed low in his throat in satisfaction. He moved his head, and he could hear the blood pounding in his ears as Clint's arousal inflamed his own.

"Uncle Josh! Mr. Clint! Do you want eggs with your pancakes?"

Clint's moans of arousal turned into groans of frustration as he covered his face with both hands and let out a string of muffled but very profane words.

Josh moaned as well, pulling his head back as Clint's cock began to soften, the interruption obviously derailing things.

"No eggs!" he ground out, giving Clint an apologetic look. "We'll be down soon!"

"I'm already down," Clint muttered as he sat up and raked his fingers through his hair. Blowing out a frustrated sigh, he looked at Josh. "No quickie for us. Those had better be some damned good pancakes."

Josh understood how Clint felt, and he nodded, his own arousal fading away into disgruntlement. "Yeah." He raked a hand through his hair, then regretfully pulled Clint's boxers back into place. "I guess we might as well bow to the inevitable."

Clint leaned over and kissed Josh, lingering before pulling back and rolling out of bed. "Maybe later. Surely we can find some quiet time today."

"We'll find some time if it kills me," Josh said, rising to his feet. "Because it just might kill me if we don't."

He was probably spoiled, having gotten used to being able to make love any time they wanted, so this frustration was something new for Josh. He drew in a deep breath as he moved to the dresser to get jeans and a shirt.

Clint dressed swiftly in jeans, thick socks, and a North Carolina State University veterinary school sweatshirt, then he grabbed his toothbrush, toothpaste, and razor. "I'm going down the hall to the bathroom before I go downstairs. I won't take long if you want to hit it before you go down too."

"Thanks, I think I'll do that." Josh smiled as he pulled on a long-sleeved t-shirt. "Just let me know when you're done."

After Clint left the room, Josh occupied himself making the bed and straightening their things up. Once he'd done a quick shave and brushed his teeth, he and Clint finally went down to breakfast.

Grace greeted them with a smile. "Have a seat, boys. Pancakes and bacon, and there's some biscuits and gravy, too. Oh, and Josh, your pa needs to talk to you. He's taking a shower now, since he was out late last night with your uncle Billy."

Josh nodded as he took a seat at the table. "Sure, Momma." He greeted his older brother Jake and Jake's two sons, little Billy and Tommy, who were still at the table. "Is everyone else done?"

"Well, it's almost eight. They're out doing chores, and the kids are building snowmen," Jake said, adding more syrup to his own stack of pancakes. "I'm going to make a run into town, if you want anything."

All Josh wanted was thirty uninterrupted minutes alone with Clint, but that didn't seem to be on the table at the moment. He smiled and shook his head. "Not me. You need anything, babe?"

The heated look Clint gave him made it clear that Clint's thoughts echoed Josh's own. "No, I'm good."

With a smile, Josh forked several pancakes from the platter onto his plate before passing it to Clint. They were about halfway through when Clem Cash entered the kitchen.

Josh had his mother's coloring, but he had his father's height and slender, almost wiry build. Rising to his feet, Josh grinned as his father strode over and enveloped him in a hug.

"How are you, boy?" Clem asked.

"I'm good, Pa." Josh pulled back, looking into his father's familiar dark eyes, with the deep laugh lines showing as paler creases in his weathered face. There was more silver at his temples than when Josh had last seen him, but he was still full of the same solid strength Josh had always known.

Looking past his father's shoulder, he beckoned to Clint. "Pa, I want you to meet the love of my life. Clint, this is my father, Clem."

Clint stood up and held out his hand, his demeanor respectful. "It's nice to meet you, Mr. Cash. I've heard a lot about you from Josh."

Clem took Clint's hand, shaking it as he looked Clint over. "Nice to meet you, too. Gracie told me you were a handsome devil, and I reckon she'd know, since she married me." He grinned. "Hear you're a vet. That's a good, solid line of work. Says you ain't afraid of getting your hands dirty. I respect a man who works hard."

"Thank you, sir." Clint smiled, a flash of relief in his eyes at having passed muster with Josh's father. "I *have* worked hard to build a good reputation for my clinic. It helps that I love animals. I enjoy taking care of them."

"Well, we can always use a man of your talents on the farm." Clem flashed Josh a wink. "Reckon I could convince the two of you to leave the city and come out here? With Josh to take care of the still and you to take care of the animals, I might actually have time to put my feet up for a spell."

Josh laughed and shook his head. "Thanks for the offer, Pa, but I don't think you're going to get either of us to move to Possum Hollow. We're both spoiled by city living."

"I'm really more of a small animal vet, too," Clint added. "Now if you had a pack of shih-tzus running around, I'd be your man."

Clem lifted a brow. "Shits who?"

"Pa!" Josh rolled his eyes and chuckled. His father was a very smart man, but he wasn't above playing the "dumb hick" for laughs.

Clint laughed, although Josh knew he'd probably heard a variation on that joke for years. "You should get one. It would save Mrs. Cash lots of time if she had one to sweep the floor just by walking around."

"Got enough varmints running around underfoot," Clem replied, shaking his head. "Two legs, four legs, you name it, we got it. But speaking of being useful, I do need your help at the still, Josh. That condensing coil you set up for us has sprung a leak, and your Uncle Billy's patch ain't holding."

Josh looked over at Clint questioningly. Normally helping his father out would be a given, but he did have his lover to consider. "Would you mind? You could even come with us, if you'd like. Although if you'd prefer to stay here, I'm sure Momma would be able to put you to work on something for dinner tonight."

"I'd rather see the still," Clint replied, appearing genuinely interested. "I've never seen a real, functioning still before. Do you really help keep it running?" He gave Josh a dubious look. "Does that mean I might have to bail you out of jail if the revenuers ever catch you?"

Josh leaned over and brushed his lips against Clint's cheek. "My hero! I told you I helped with the still, didn't I? But I don't think you'll be having to do any bailing this trip. Revenuers tend to be soft city folk. Mountain winters aren't much to their liking."

"Ain't that the truth." Clem snorted and shook his head. "All right, then. Can you be ready to go in ten minutes? Dress warm, there's snow coming in."

"Ten minutes should be fine," Josh said, looking at Clint for agreement.

Clint nodded eagerly. "We can be ready. Thanks for letting me tag along. This will be something for the bucket list," he added with a delighted smile at Clem.

With a snort, Clem shook his head. "Meet me out front."

"Yes, sir."

Josh grabbed Clint's hand and hurried them out of the kitchen and back to their room. It only took a few minutes for them to put on thick coats, gloves, and boots, and grab warm hats. They were outside and standing by the truck by the time Clem came out, dressed as warmly as they were.

The old pickup truck didn't have much for shocks and the speedometer didn't work, but Josh enjoyed the opportunity to squeeze in close to Clint as they bounced their way up the winding mountain trail.

"You didn't know bucket list was literal, did you?" he asked, grinning at Clint.

"I had no clue." Clint used their cramped quarters as an

excuse to slide his arm across Josh's shoulders. "I'm up for a little holiday adventure, but I hope you're right about the revenuers. I'd rather not end the day with a high speed car chase."

"This truck can't go over about forty," Clem said easily. "If Jim Bob decides to take it into his damn fool head to chase us, we'd be better off on foot."

Josh chuckled. "That's if you can get Uncle Jim Bob out of the Waffle House and away from his cup of coffee."

"Well, yeah, there is that." Pa turned the truck off the nominally paved road and onto a rocky, pitted trail that didn't look passable on foot, much less by a vehicle. They continued upward, through ever denser evergreen forest.

Clem stopped the truck by a large, prickly looking bush. "We go on foot from here."

"Keep close," Josh told Clint. "It's a little rocky."

"You can say that again." Clem pulled a sawed-off shotgun from behind the seat, then got out of the truck. "Let's go, boys."

Clint got out, peering around at their surroundings with obvious interest, and once Josh climbed out and they got underway, he stuck close as instructed. "Are there wild animals in the area?" he asked, eying the shotgun with concern in his eyes.

"Sure. Bears, bobcats, wolves, coyotes. But the one you have to watch out for is wild boars." Josh made a face. "You would not believe how mean three hundred pounds of bacon can be."

Clint's eyes grew wide and round. "Three hundred pounds? Seriously?"

"Close to, some of 'em," Clem chimed in, looking back over his shoulder. "They're descended from domestic pigs that run off, and they went wild. They shot one in Georgia years back they called Hogzilla. The thing weighed eight hundred pounds and had tusks two feet long."

"It's true." Josh grinned at Clint. "Think about that next time you treat someone's Vietnamese potbellied pig at the clinic."

Clint let out a long, low whistle as he walked along, keeping up with Josh and Clem without any problem. "And that right there is the reason I specialize in small animals."

"Not that I'd call a Rottweiler small," Josh observed. Then he stopped and pointed ahead, where the trees thinned out a bit, revealing a sharp, rocky rise. The face had been undercut, although it was hard to tell if it had been natural or had some human assistance at some point. The result was an overhang, too wide and not deep enough to be an actual cave. There were screening boughs woven into camouflage netting draped over a large section, making a sort of shelter that would be almost impossible to see unless you were looking for it. "There's the still site. It's about as perfect as you could want. The hill and the overhang screen it from aerial observation, and there's a natural spring to provide water for the condensing coil."

Clem paused, looking around carefully. "Don't look like anyone's been around. Come on."

When they reached the site, Josh pulled Clint around the screening boughs, revealing the huge copper cook pot, the smaller thump keg, and the worm box with its coils of copper tubing. "There you go, city boy. A real Appalachian backwoods still."

"Wow...." Clint studied the apparatus with obvious fascination, moving in for a closer look. "This is *really* cool." He flashed a mischievous smile at Josh. "I feel like a bad boy just being here."

Clem had moved over to the worm box, and Josh slid close to Clint, taking the moment of semi-privacy to grope Clint's firm ass. It wasn't quite as satisfactory as it would have been if they'd had on fewer clothes, but beggars couldn't be choosers.

"You *are* a bad boy," he murmured, lips close to Clint's ear. "As soon as we get a moment alone, I'll give you a spanking."

Clint wriggled provocatively and gave him a look hot enough to melt the snow. "Promises, promises," he replied in a low voice, then he spoke again in at a normal level. "I know it's illegal, but it still feels like being part of history."

"It's definitely that." Clem beckoned them over to where he was, and Josh gave Clint a look that promised payback. "The Cash family has been making moonshine in these hills for two hundred years. Of course, it wasn't always illegal, but we couldn't let a little thing like the law interfere with our culture and traditions."

"Pa has been rehearsing that fancy speech for years," Josh said, peering down into the worm box. "Just in case Jim Bob ever failed to get re-elected as sheriff and we ended up with someone not so willing to turn a blind eye. We're going to need to drain the water, Pa, but I think I see the problem. The crack is bigger than Uncle Billy thought. I can cut this section off and solder in a new one."

"Good." Clem nodded and pulled the plug that drained the big barrel that held the condenser coils. "The tools are where they usually are. If you boys don't mind taking care of this, I'm going to run into town for more propane. Uncle Billy wants to start a run of mash the day after Christmas, so we have plenty of hooch for New Year's Eve."

"Sure, Pa, you do that." Josh beckoned to Clint. "Come on back here, you can help me with the tools, Doc. The patient is going to require surgery."

Clint leered at Josh as soon as Clem's back was turned. "Too bad it's too cold for me to slip into a nurse's uniform," he murmured. "But I'll be happy to assist in holding your tool."

The teasing words, on top of their interrupted interlude that morning, weren't doing much to help Josh's frustration. "You know how to work my tool better than anyone," he replied, giving Clint a heated look. "If we hurry up and get this fixed, we should have at least an hour free before Pa gets back from town."

"Really?" Clint's whole face lit up with hope. "Is there someplace relatively warm nearby we can go to? Although to be honest, I'm just about ready to risk frostbite."

"It's not so bad back behind the still." Josh grinned. "The mash inside is still warm. I think we could make do." He leaned closer and dropped his voice. "And I brought condoms and lube, just in case."

"And that is why I love you." Clint leaned in and kissed Josh, swift and hard. "Fine, let's get this 'surgery' done so we can have an illicit rendezvous behind an illegal still."

Josh moaned, the kiss only inflaming his desire. "Oh, city boy, you do talk purty." He glanced around the still, seeing that his father had departed, and he craned up for a slightly more lingering kiss. "There. That'll tide me over until we're done. I'm about to set a speed record for still repair."

With Clint's help, he got the worm box, which was just an old fifty gallon wooden barrel, removed, exposing the coiled "worm" of copper which condensed the alcohol vapor to a liquid. He'd helped build the assembly years before, so he was quite familiar with its workings. He carefully cut away the cracked part of the coils that his uncle had tried to patch, and got out spare tubing and a pipe bender to create a replacement.

"There's a reason we use copper, other than just tradition," he explained as he worked, having Clint feed the copper tubing in a bit at a time. "You can use stainless steel, but it takes a lot work if you need to make a repair, since you have to weld it instead of just soldering it. Copper is easier and more flexible, but it also reacts with any sulfides in the alcohol vapor and removes them. Makes the moonshine taste better." He chuckled at the memory of Clint taking his first sip of homebrew. "Speaking of which, did your taste buds ever recover?"

"I think they're starting to grow back," Clint replied dryly. "I may be ready for another sip around Easter."

Josh grinned. "You're tougher than that, city boy. There'll be special family eggnog tomorrow, and you've really got to try it." He held up the section of coiled copper, inspecting it for flaws. "There, that looks good. We'll solder it in place, put the barrel back, reconnect it to the feed from the spring, and then...." He wagged his brows suggestively.

"Sounds good!" Clint watched him with growing eagerness. "What else can I do to help speed things along?"

"Grab the flux and the soldering iron from the tool box back there, please. There should be work gloves, too. We can use those instead of our good gloves, in case anything splatters. Then you hold the tubing in place while I make the connection. Sound good?"

Clint executed a sloppy salute and hurried over to the tool box. It didn't take long for him to return with everything Josh had asked for, including the gloves. "I guess this is where my steady hands will come in handy."

"Steady hands are always welcome."

A few minutes later, the soldering was finished, and they quickly reassembled the still. Josh turned to Clint, wrapping his arms around Clint's waist and pulling him close with a grin.

"Well done, for a city boy. Our patient is going to live. What kind of reward do you want for assisting?"

"Preferably a naughty and naked one," Clint replied, sliding his arms around Josh's shoulders in return. "Didn't you say something about a warm spot around here somewhere?"

"Oh, yes." Josh slowly moved backward without releasing Clint, guiding him back between the still and the rough rock face. Here, the warmth of the fermenting brew in the still and the heat from the propane burners beneath it had created a comfortable little niche that was hidden from view. "Warm enough to be naughty, do you think? I don't think being totally naked is an option, but are you willing to make do?"

The answering heat in Clint's eyes made the little niche seem even warmer. "I'm more than willing to make any compromise necessary. We can do totally naked when we're home in a nice, warm, comfortable bed."

"Works for me!" Josh stripped off his gloves, letting them fall to the ground, then moved his hands to zipper of Clint's thick coat, pulling it down. He pushed Clint's sweatshirt up, running his palms over Clint's chest, eager for contact. "Mmm... you feel good."

Clint moaned and arched against Josh's wandering hands, and he reached for the fastening of Josh's coat in return, seeming as eager for contact as Josh was. "Feels so good having you touch me again. It's been too long!"

"Five minutes is too long," Josh replied, brushing his thumbs over Clint's nipples, then pinching them. "This time no kids are going to come pounding on the door. Instead, you get to pound me."

"Thank God." Clint groaned, although Josh wasn't sure whether it was due to the nipple play or the thought of pounding him senseless. Bending his head, Clint captured Josh's mouth in a fierce, demanding kiss that made the depth of his need clear.

Josh responded eagerly, wanting to make Clint desperate, drawing Clint's tongue into his mouth and sucking on it suggestively. His jeans were uncomfortably tight around his hardening cock, and he thrust his hips forward so that Clint would know he was just as aroused.

Clint reached down to unfasten Josh's jeans without breaking the kiss, working to push both his jeans and boxers down. Josh wriggled, helping him, needing to feel Clint's hand wrapped around his cock almost as much as he needed to breathe.

A sound reached him, and in his lust-filled haze, he ignored it, thinking the shuffling and the low grunt had come from Clint. But a clatter of something falling caused him to freeze, and he opened his eyes as he broke away from the kiss with a gasp. Moving one hand, he clamped it over Clint's mouth, stifling any objections as he tried to figure out who -- or what -- had entered the shelter.

Clint's muffled protests stopped abruptly when he heard the noise too, and he stared at Josh with wide, round eyes that flashed with alarm. Josh shook his head, slowly lowering his hand, not bothering to hide his frustration at the untimely interruption. He pulled his boxers and jeans back up, even as he listened to the snuffling and pawing sounds coming from the other side of the still.

It was the wrong season for bears, and the sounds were too clumsy for a bobcat or a coyote. He supposed it might be a deer or an elk, but they normally shied away from the smells of a still. Which left one possibility. A very *bad* possibility.

Motioning for Clint to stay put, Josh moved slowly around the bulk of the cook pot, careful to be as quiet as possible. When he rounded the end, he looked toward the source of the noise, barely refraining from yelling in frustration and fear at the sight of a huge boar snuffling and ripping at a half-empty sack of corn his father left just inside the shelter.

The boar was engrossed in its free meal, but Josh knew that would end if it decided he or Clint were a threat to it or if it thought they might try to fight it for the food. Moving slowly, he backed toward Clint, putting his lips close to Clint's ear.

"Wild boar. We need to get out of here."

Clint nodded vehemently, the alarm in his eyes escalating into panic, and he gestured for Josh to lead the way.

Josh took Clint's hand, giving it a reassuring squeeze before starting to move slowly and quietly toward the other end of the overhang. The camouflage netting had been secured to the rough stone of the wall with nails pounded into the rock, but Josh lifted it away carefully, motioning for Clint to duck outside.

Clint slipped outside, then reached back to hold the netting up for Josh in return, darting anxious glances in the direction of the boar. Josh ducked his head as he stepped outside, but as he turned to tug the netting back in place, he pulled a bit too hard, and a huge section at the top of the overhang pulled away, sending the fabric and its weight of branches crashing back against the end of the still.

There was a loud squeal of alarm from the boar, and Josh knew that things had just gone from bad to worse. "Run for that tree!" he yelled at Clint, taking off for the closest of the pines. Even though he hadn't climbed a tree in years, he hadn't forgotten how, and he grasped the lower branches, hauling himself up before turning and reaching a hand down to Clint. "Come on!"

Clint didn't bother grabbing Josh's hand, instead latching onto the lower limbs and scrambling up. He made the mistake of looking back, and seeing the boar closing in made him slip, but he clamored up the tree and perched on the sturdiest limb he could find, clutching the trunk like a lifeline.

"What now?" He shot Josh a panicked look. "Will it get bored and go away on its own?"

The boar, which was mottled brown and black and had to weigh at least two hundred pounds, squealed furiously and charged at the tree. It impacted on the trunk, ripping at it with his tusks and gouging the bark.

"I sure hope so," Josh replied, cautiously climbing up to a branch at the same level Clint occupied. "Being stuck up here is going to be a hell of a lot colder than what we were planning."

"We left the gun down there." Clint grimaced and tried to zip up his coat with one hand. When that didn't work, he gingerly let go of the trunk and did the fastest zip-up Josh had ever seen before grabbing the trunk again. He stared down at the boar with growing concern. "Um. Can that thing knock this tree over?"

"No, don't worry about that." Josh smiled reassuringly, reaching out to pat one of Clint's hands where he clutched the tree in a death grip. "We're safe enough up here. I wish I'd thought to grab the gun, but Pa left it by the entrance, so I'd have had to go past our grumpy friend to get it."

He sighed. So far this had been the worst trip home he could ever remember. He just hoped Clint wasn't going to get frustrated and disgusted enough to leave.

Clint relinquished the tree with one arm and grabbed Josh's hand, squeezing it tightly. "I guess this isn't the best time to reveal I'm afraid of heights," he said shakily, and Josh could see he was turning pale.

"What?" Josh stared at Clint in horror, his concern for his lover overriding everything else. "Oh, shit. Look, I'll climb down and run for the gun, okay?"

"No, no, no!" Clint shook his head wildly and tightened his grip on Josh's hand. "I don't want you going down there. Just don't let go, okay? I feel better when you're touching me."

"Okay, I won't." Josh scooted as close as he could, wishing he could risk getting on the same limb Clint occupied, but he was afraid it wouldn't take the weight of them both. He clasped Clint's hand tightly and offered a reassuring smile. "I won't leave you, I promise. We'll just wait for Mr. Pig to wander off, and then we'll climb down nice and slow, okay? Everything will be fine. You'll have a hell of a story to tell your patients, won't you? I think the dogs will laugh and the cats will be sympathetic."

"I'll definitely get sympathy from all the cats." Clint managed a shaky laugh. "They might even bro-fist me. The dogs will wonder why I didn't growl and bite it on the ass."

"Yeah, well, it's easy for the dogs to talk big, but I think they'd all whimper like puppies if they got a good look at our rampaging slab of bacon down there. Those tusks are mean." Josh ran his thumb over the back of Clint's hand, trying to soothe him. He hoped he was providing enough of a distraction that Clint wouldn't think about being up in the tree. If Clint passed out, Josh was afraid he'd fall. "I want to shoot that damned thing for interrupting when it did. I thought I was finally going to get laid!"

Clint's laughter was more genuine this time, tinged with wry humor. "So did I. Maybe your dad will come back in time to shoot that damned boar so we can have ham, pork chops, and bacon for dinner. I'm feeling vindictive enough to eat all three with a side of tenderloin and pickled pigs feet for dessert."

The laughter was a relief, and Josh relaxed slightly, although he kept a firm hold on Clint's hands. "Dr. Barker, that is a very unveterinarian-like thing to say! Although I'm in full agreement, I admit. If Pa does shoot it, maybe we'll have the head stuffed. It would make an interesting conversation piece mounted over the fireplace, don't you think?"

"At the very least, it could serve as a warning." Clint was smiling now, even as he pointedly avoided looking down. "This is what happens when you interrupt us during sex."

"It might give my nieces and nephews pause at that. Although maybe not. The Cashes are a powerfully stubborn lot, you know." Josh smiled wickedly. "We also don't hesitate to go after what we want. But you may have noticed that already."

"The trait is rather noticeable, yes," Clint replied dryly. "Not that I mind at all."

Josh could still hear the boar below them, so he kept talking, amusing Clint with stories about his childhood, including tales of skinny-dipping with his friends from high school and having to stay in the water so that no one would realize he was turned on by naked guys. In keeping Clint distracted, he distracted himself, so much so that he nearly jumped out of his skin when his father's voice called out from below.

"What in the hell're you two doin' up there? It ain't the season to go bird watching!"

Josh looked down and waved at his father. "Hey, Pa. No, we got treed by a boar. It must have wandered off while we were talking."

"Oh, thank God." Clint gazed down at Clem like he was an angel sent to rescue them. "Is it safe to come down? Are you sure it's gone? *Really* gone?"

"Must be, I don't see it," Clem replied with a shrug. "Come on down and help me get this propane unloaded and we can go home. I told you snow was coming, and we want to be down off the mountain before it hits."

Josh looked at Clint. "Do you want to go first or shall I?"

Clint was down the tree and on the ground almost before the words were out of Josh's mouth. He jumped from the lowest limb, landing a little unsteadily, and he appeared on the verge of falling to his knees and kissing the ground. Instead, however, he smiled gratefully at Clem.

"I definitely want to be off the mountain as soon as possible."

Josh climbed down and slid his arm around Clint's waist, kissing his cheek. "I don't blame you a bit. Too bad we didn't get to shoot that boar."

"I'll keep a look-out for it," Clem promised. "Don't need one thinkin' this is its territory."

"Thanks, Pa. Come on, lover, let's get this done so we can go home."

Josh led Clint back toward path out, wanting to unload the propane and hurry back home. There was going to be a big family dinner that night before the really big Christmas Eve celebration the next day. He and Clint probably wouldn't have a chance to be alone again until late, unfortunately, but Josh was determined that once they went to bed, nothing and no one was going to interfere with their lovemaking again. He just might bring the shotgun with him to guarantee it.

3

Despite his best efforts to relax and go with the flow, Clint was starting to get overwhelmed. It had started the night before during the family dinner, to which only Josh's siblings, their partners, and their children had been invited. By Clint's reckoning, the head count had neared fifty people, and apparently they had decided that twenty-four hours was enough of a respectful adjustment period for Clint. He hadn't been able to take a step without someone stopping him to talk, which led to questions. Lots and lots of questions.

He'd been hit with a non-stop barrage questions ranging from "How much do you make a year?" to "Can I watch you and Uncle Josh kiss?" One of Josh's sisters had drawn him aside and asked him in all seriousness, "So gay sex. How exactly does that work?" Some of the children had been eager to know if he'd had to perform any dissections in veterinary school and had exhibited a macabre interest in the "grossest" illness he'd seen. One young man had offered to take him to see some fresh road kill and seemed disappointed when he didn't accept.

Before the end of the evening, he'd had to take a time out in the designated adult's bathroom, giving himself five minutes of peace and quiet before facing the crowd once more. Josh had watched him with obvious concern and stuck close all night, offering support.

Between the encounter with the wild boar and the encounter with Josh's wild family, Clint was exhausted by the time the gathering dispersed at last. Josh seemed drained as well, and they fell into bed together, too tired to do more than cuddle each other to sleep.

Now it was Christmas Eve, and Clint stood just inside the main activity room of the local VFW hall, which was packed with people who were all related to Josh either by birth or by marriage. Grace had estimated about five hundred people would be in attendance, and Clem had boasted that they never had to hire a caterer or a band for the event. Long folding tables lined one wall, and Clint could practically see them groaning and sagging under the weight of countless dishes. Clint recognized some, didn't recognize others, and didn't *want* to know about a few.

Clem said enough people brought musical instruments that they could play in shifts and keep going all night. The current incarnation of the Cash-Creek family band was playing a song called "Pretty Polly" with a quick tempo that had coaxed a few people out on the makeshift dance floor. Clint found himself keeping time with the lively tune until he started paying attention to the words and realized it was about a woman being brutally murdered by her lover.

Josh had been given the honor of escorting his grandmother to her table, but he quickly returned to Clint's side, capturing one of his hands and squeezing it firmly. Like most of the family, Josh had "dressed up" for the event, although the Possum Hollow version of fancy dress seemed to mean jeans without holes at the knees. But Josh had donned black trousers and a green sweater that matched his eyes, and he smiled up at Clint a bit ruefully.

"Freaking out yet?"

"Uh." Clint couldn't summon up a glib dismissal of the whole freak out idea, mainly because he was still processing the fact that it was possible to be related to this many people all at once. "Not quite yet. I may need a couple of time outs or some really strong eggnog before the night is over, though."

"We'll make sure you get both," Josh promised. Clint could see Josh was trying to cover up the fact that he truly was worried. "Just... if you need to run, please let me go with you, all right?"

Even though stepping into this crowded room had taken monumental effort after the socializing overload the night before, Clint still didn't want to bail on Josh. "I'm not going to run."

"Good. Now tell me, would you like to eat first or dance?" Josh pointed to the huge Christmas tree that took up one corner of the room. "Or we could go look at the tree. I also happen to know where they like to hang the mistletoe."

Clint had visions of flashes from dozens of cameras going off if they went anywhere near the mistletoe, and he dragged Josh over to the tables instead. "Let's eat."

There was a line of people who all seemed to have the same idea, but it moved fairly quickly. Josh handed him a plate, then leaned close.

"Avoid the stuff in the big red bowl. It's squirrel. The things that look like chicken legs are actually possum."

Clint had been reaching for one of the "chicken legs", but he snatched his hand back quickly. "I think for tonight, I'm a vegetarian. Don't tell my mother," he murmured as he moved down the line, choosing what he thought were relatively safe vegetable dishes and several pieces of cornbread.

Josh chuckled, but Clint noticed he stuck mostly to the vegetables as well. "I sort of lost my taste for wild game since moving east." He gave Clint a wicked smile. "Let's get some eggnog. There should be enough White Lightning in it to help you relax, and the sugar and eggs will buffer your stomach."

Once their plates were loaded and they had both eggnog and sweet tea, Josh scouted out a small table that stood empty. It only had four place settings, and apparently no one else in attendance could get by with less than six, so for now, they had the table to themselves. Clint dropped into his chair with a sigh of relief. People didn't usually disturb others while they were eating, and he hoped he'd have enough moonshine in his system to get him through the inevitable after-dinner socializing.

Josh kept up a running commentary while they ate. "See the big woman over there in the red dress? That's my cousin Sephronia. We'll do our best to avoid her, because she's what we politely call a religious nut. She hands out tracts, even at events like this. Oh, and the guy with the eye patch is Uncle Dave. I guarantee you he was drunk before he arrived. Then that man over there, he's my brother Tom's father-in-law. He thinks the government is trying to read our minds and that alien abductions are happening all over the county. Don't ever mention the FBI or the CIA to him, or he'll think you're an agent sent to put a chip in his head."

"Do I need to be taking notes on all of this?" Clint asked, only half-joking. "I'm starting to feel like I need an instruction manual."

"Just stick by me, and I'll keep you safe." Josh smiled and surreptitiously patted Clint's leg under the table. Then he paused, eyes widening. "Oh, no. Here comes my Aunt Lucinda. She thinks she's 'open minded'."

A large woman in an eye-wateringly red and green flowered dress, with her graying brown hair pulled up in a bun, was approaching them purposefully, a large smile on her face. It was barely possible to see a resemblance to Clem in her features, and she was smiling in a rather frighteningly intense way.

"Joshie! My, my, how you've grown! And this must be your boyfriend I've heard so much about!"

"Hello, Aunt Lucinda," Josh said, rising to his feet politely. "Yes, this is Dr. Clint Barker."

"It's nice to meet you, ma'am," Clint replied politely, although he couldn't help but be wary of the look in her eyes.

"Oh, a doctor, do tell!" Clint could practically see her rubbing her mental hands together. "And from the city! So did you meet in a gay bar or on the internet?"

Josh's smile looked sort of congealed. "Neither, actually. Clint is a vet, and I took my cat to his clinic. Neither of us go to gay bars, as a matter of fact."

"I've never really been into the bar scene," Clint agreed, plastering a smile on his face despite the sinking feeling in the pit of his stomach that told him he wasn't going to enjoy this conversation.

"Really? But I thought that was the big thing in the city." Lucinda looked disappointed, as though she had actually *wanted* her nephew to have brought some anonymous hook-up from a bar to his family's holiday party. It looked to Clint as though she wanted their situation to be as sordid as possible in order to prove how "accepting" she was of her family.

"You've never been to the big city in your life." Clem suddenly came up beside his sister and took her by the arm, giving Clint and Josh a wink that Lucinda couldn't see. "Now why don't you come over and talk to Grace for a few minutes? She said she'd like you to help her with serving up the ambrosia."

"But...." Obviously torn between the desire to question them more and the lure of having been requested for help, Lucinda sighed. "Well, hopefully we'll get to talk more later, boys."

As soon as she was out of earshot, Clint turned to Josh with a horrified look. "For a minute there, I thought she was going to ask us about glory holes next."

Josh nodded. "I go out of my way to avoid her. She's not a bad person, really, but she's a little hard to take. Momma must have seen her coming and sent Pa to rescue us."

"Thank God." Clint grimaced and shook his head as he turned his attention back to his collards and fried okra. "Although I suppose it's not much worse than your niece asking me which one of us is -- and I quote -- 'the girl' last night."

A flush stained Josh's cheeks. "Hailey is only twelve, and she's lived on a farm her whole life. I think she was just trying to understand the mechanics of it."

"I figured as much." Clint smiled and gave Josh's thigh a reassuring squeeze under the table. "I told her she shouldn't try to compartmentalize human sexuality into such gender binary categories. Then I told her you're a big nellie bottom."

Josh's mouth fell open, and his flush deepened to a crimson that looked even darker next to his green sweater. "You didn't!" he said, his voice strangled. "Please, tell me you didn't!"

Clint laughed, delighted by the horrified look on Josh's face. "No, of course I didn't! I left it at gender binary categories. What we do in the privacy of our bedroom is our own business. Unless it's a bedroom in your parents' house, in which case we don't do anything, or if we do, I suspect it becomes other people's business via the walls."

"Bastard," Josh grumbled, although there was a twinkle of amusement in his eyes. "You're going to pay for that. If I make *you* scream, the family will think you're the nellie bottom!"

"At this point, I wouldn't care what they think, as long as an orgasm is actually involved," Clint retorted, sticking his tongue out at Josh.

"Don't show me that unless you intend to use it!" Josh smiled wickedly, then took a bite out of a buttered corn muffin, licking crumbs from his lips with deliberate slowness.

Clint watched avidly, wishing he could taste Josh right then and there. It felt like an eternity since they'd had any private time together, and he missed their intimacy. He missed being able to hold Josh without dozens of eyes watching their every move. He missed being able to kiss Josh without feeling like they were a sideshow attraction. He missed having time to make love *at all*, much less at their leisure.

With a sharp sigh of frustration, he turned his attention back to his collards. "Believe me, I'd use it if I could."

He felt Josh's hand on his leg, stroking his thigh slowly, but it was a gesture of comfort rather than seduction. "I know," Josh murmured softly. "Believe me, I feel your pain."

"I know you do." Clint offered a reassuring smile and covered Josh's hand with his own, giving it a squeeze. "But it's only a couple more days."

"That's right, and tomorrow is Christmas. Things will settle down a lot after tomorrow's dinner." Josh looked anxious to reassure him. "I think by then, everyone will be tired of everyone else, so we'll get some time alone."

"Maybe we can be extra naughty tomorrow night." The thought of the crowd dispersing enough that he wouldn't be surrounded by people made Clint feel better, especially since it meant he might be able to drag Josh to bed as well. Renewed by hope, he began to eat with more gusto.

All too soon, however, they had finished eating. After disposing of their plates, Josh slid an arm around Clint's waist. "Take a deep breath; I need to introduce you around more. Mostly to my aunts and uncles, but that's another couple of dozen people."

Inwardly, Clint quailed, his introverted nature urging him to run screaming into the night rather than face more people, but outwardly, he put on his polite "meeting new people" smile and slid his arm around Josh's shoulders. "Once more unto the breach," he murmured.

"First up is Big Momma's last surviving brother, Uncle Hezekiah." Josh's voice was low, although from the appearance of the elderly gentleman they were approaching, he wouldn't have been able to hear them anyway. The man seemed to be nodding off, although Clint didn't see how it was possible for anyone to sleep in the uproar around them.

"Uncle Hezekiah?" Josh spoke loudly and touched the elderly man on the shoulder. "It's Josh. I wanted you to meet my boyfriend, Clint."

The man opened his eyes, and there was a keen intelligence in them, much like there had been in his sister's. Obviously senility didn't seem to run in Big Momma's family. "Josh? Ah, good to see you, boy! Boyfriend, is it? Well, can't help what's in the blood." He looked up at Clint. "My brother Daw liked fellers, too. So did my son Jerome, lord rest his soul. Passed away in a car accident years back."

"I'm sorry to hear it." Clint offered his hand, and Hezekiah shook it with a grip that was still firm and strong.

The old man nodded. "You take care of Joshie here, or Mary will never let you hear the end of it. Dotes on the boy." He cast a sideways glance at Josh. "You got your granddaddy's looks, but you got Mary's eye for the good looking fellers, don't you?"

Josh flushed, but he lifted his chin. "Well, I'm with Clint for more than his looks, Uncle Hezekiah."

Hezekiah gave a laugh that sounded like a cackle. "You got your granny's pride, too! Go on, boy, I was only teasing." He looked back at Clint. "Watch out for the Carters in the bunch, you hear? Talk your head off. Now go on, boys, enjoy yourselves and let an old man rest."

"It was nice to meet you, sir," Clint said as Josh led him away, and he went along obligingly, ready to get the rounds of introductions over with.

The next thirty minutes or so went by in a blur of handshakes and thick Appalachian accents, and Clint felt dizzy from trying to remember all the names and faces. All he knew was there were at least two Earls and a Clementine in there somewhere. His smile was growing strained, but he kept up the polite small talk for Josh's sake, not wanting to give any of Josh's relatives a reason to think ill of him. Despite Josh's remarks about his family straining his patience, it was obvious to Clint that family meant a lot to Josh -- and that the family adored Josh. Making a favorable impression was important to Clint if only because he didn't want to give Josh any reason to doubt their relationship or that Clint could fit in.

Still, he could feel his inner resources depleting; he was growing mentally and emotionally tired, which was worse than physical exhaustion in a way. He was making a valiant effort to remain friendly and approachable, but what he wanted to do more than anything else was to run far away and find -- as Grace had so perfectly put it -- air that no one else was breathing.

Suddenly they were standing in front of a man who gazed at the two of them -- and at Josh's arm around Clint's waist -- with tight-lipped disapproval. He had graying brown hair and blue eyes, but Clint didn't see any family resemblance to Josh or any of the various Cashes, Creeks, Carters, Emersons, or other families that were part of the crowd.

"Ira." Josh's tone was almost wooden, with none of the friendly warmth with which he had greeted the rest of the family. "Clint, this is my Aunt Louella May's husband, Ira Jacobs. Ira, this is Dr. Clint Barker."

"Oh." Ira looked Clint up and down, then shrugged. "Well, I doubt he'll last longer than the last one you tried to foist on us, Joshua."

Josh stiffened, and it was obvious he was holding on to his temper with effort. "There's no need to be rude, Ira. If you'll excuse us, we'll leave you to your own company, which I know you far prefer to mine."

Clint reached out to clasp Josh's hand in a show of defiance. He supposed there had to be at least one bad apple in every bunch, and obviously, Ira was it. "Yes, excuse us," he said politely. "Although I suppose I should warn you that Josh will be foisting me off on the family regularly."

"I doubt that. Your sort doesn't really believe in long term commitments." Ira's tone was full of contempt.

Josh's fingers shook beneath Clint's. "Merry Christmas," Josh muttered, then tugged Clint away. He didn't stop until they reached the table where drinks were set up, and he took a cup of the fortified eggnog, downing it quickly, then grimacing.

"Ugh. Sorry about that," he said, looking up at Clint apologetically. "I didn't think we'd run into that creep, since normally he avoids me -- and Marge -- as assiduously as we avoid him."

Clint got a cup of spiked eggnog for himself, hoping the alcohol would take the edge off his temper, because he wanted nothing more than to go back and punch Ira in his smug, sanctimonious face.

"Sounds like a good plan to me," he growled, shooting a glare in Ira's direction.

"Yeah." With a sigh, Josh ran a hand through his hair. "He's a bigot and a jackass. He thinks he's better than the rest of the family just because he's got more money than all of us combined. God knows why my aunt married such a creep, but unfortunately we're stuck with him. Momma won't have him in our house, though. He insulted Marge in front of her and that was it."

"*Good.*" Clint downed half of his eggnog, still casting dire looks at Ira even though the crowd obscured his view. "I'd rather deal with Aunt Lucinda than him any day."

"Yeah, there's no comparison, believe me." Josh reached out, putting a hand on Clint's arm. "Let's not let him put a damper on the evening, though. You've held up great, and I appreciate it."

"I told you I could handle this." Clint could hear an edge creeping into his voice despite his best efforts to remain calm and collected throughout the holiday festivities. The last thing he wanted to do was upset Josh just because he was feeling the strain of too much socializing, however, and so he mustered a smile in hopes of softening his words.

A worried look came into Josh's eyes. "I know you did," he replied quietly. "But you see why I was worried, don't you? This is like the total opposite of your family. Just because you *can* handle it doesn't necessarily mean you *want* to handle it."

Frustration swelled inside Clint, threatening to break over the nearest target, which unfortunately was Josh. He knew he needed to keep a lid on his temper, but his nerves were frayed and his self-control was strained to its limit. Before he could stop himself, the words were out of his mouth.

"Is that what you *want*? I've been doing my damnedest to fit in with your family, and all you've done is forecast doom. Do you *want* your family to break us up?"

Josh's eyes widened, and he stepped back slightly, looking hurt and upset. "Of course I don't! How can you even think that? I just said I appreciate what you've put up with!"

"I know what you said." Clint grimaced, feeling guilty for snapping at Josh but his irritation at life in general hadn't abated in the slightest, so he wasn't inclined to apologize yet. He shook his head -- and the room suddenly began to move in unpleasant ways. Maybe that eggnog had been stronger than he realized. "I know *everything* you've said since we got here, most of it negative."

"Is that what you really think? That I'm being negative about you? About *us*?" Josh's green eyes darkened, and he held out a hand to

Clint, a gesture of appeal. "I'm not, I swear! I'm trying to make this work, too!"

"Well, you could have fooled me!" Clint snapped, then he scowled and turned toward the exit. He really didn't want to fight with Josh, especially not at a family gathering on Christmas Eve, and he needed to get out and cool off before he said or did something he would regret -- or he goaded Josh into it. "I need some air."

"All right." Josh dropped his hand and lowered his gaze. "Find me when you're ready to leave."

Clint nodded tersely and walked away before he said anything else to make the situation worse. Later, he would need to apologize, but right now he was too wound up to make sincere amends for being snappish. He dredged up enough courtesy to say "excuse me" as he headed directly for the door, eager for a breath of fresh, cool air away from the stifling crowd of people.

Most of the people outside were smoking, so he avoided the corner of the building where they'd congregated, stepping into the darkness of the parking lot, surrounded by the silent cars. It had begun to snow, fat, fluffy flakes that drifted slowly down from the dark sky. The air was crisp and cold, but since the wind was still for the moment, the chill was bearable.

After a minute or two, he heard footsteps crunching through the snow. He thought it was Josh, since the figure was the right size, but as the man grew closer, he realized it was Clem.

"Damn, city boy, what're you doing out here? It must be fate, because I sure could use your help right now!"

The cold air had helped clear Clint's head, and he was already feeling better now that he was somewhere quiet where no strangers were constantly bumping into him. "What do you need?" he asked, hoping whatever it was didn't require him to go back inside the VFW hall.

"My boy Andy stayed behind to keep an eye on our cow, Bluebell. He just called to say she's decided to give us a Christmas calf. I've got to head back to the house because he thinks it's a breech birth. Bluebell ain't young, and I ain't leaving no animal to suffer, party or not."

Clem smiled wryly, the expression very similar to the one Clint had seen countless times on Josh's face. "Seeing as you're a vet, and you just happen to be here, how about coming along to give me a hand?"

"Uh... I don't really have experience with large animals," Clint reminded him. "Are you sure you don't want your normal vet?"

"Doc Pritchert retired to Florida back in September, and we don't have a replacement yet," Clem explained. "I can't see as it matters whether an animal is small or big. A birth is a birth, ain't it?"

"But a poodle can't break my bones if it kicks me." Clint smiled wryly and shrugged, unable to say no when there was an animal that needed his help, no matter how big it was. "I don't have any of my equipment, not even a stethoscope, but I'll do my best."

"That's the spirit! Ain't seen a vet yet as would let an animal suffer without trying to help." Clem clapped him on the shoulder. "Come on, I have a jacket in the truck you can use, if you're feeling the cold. You must have been hitting the eggnog hard to be out here bare-headed and without a coat!"

Clint gave a self-deprecating chuckle, his smile turning sheepish. "I may have had a little more than I thought," he admitted. "I'm sober enough to help Bluebell, though, or I will be by the time we get back to the house."

"You sure will. Heater in the truck doesn't work so well. When you get chilled, that means the 'shine is wearing off."

Clem guided Clint to his truck, the same one they'd taken out to the still site the day before, and pulled out a jacket of some indeterminate color that smelled of fuel. "Here you go. Let's get on the road. Full moons and baby critters don't wait for no one."

Clint murmured his thanks and shrugged into the coat gratefully. He'd begun shivering a little, and the warmth was welcome. As Clem started the truck and pulled out of the parking lot, Clint felt a twinge of remorse for not ducking back inside long enough to let Josh know he was leaving, but it was too late now. His cell phone was in the pocket of the coat he'd left back at the VFW hall, but he'd give Josh a call from the farm after the calf was born.

Even though this was outside his usual realm of practice, Clint was looking forward to the challenge of tackling a calf birth. Clem was right when he said Clint couldn't sit idly by when there was an animal that needed tending, and he was already falling into his professional mindset even though he was supposed to be on vacation. A doctor's work was never done, and that included vets.

As Christmas Eves went, Josh thought this year's was just about the worst one he could remember.

After Clint had walked away, obviously needing space, Josh had fought down the almost overwhelming urge to run after him, to beg and plead for forgiveness, to tell Clint it was all a horrible misunderstanding. Josh didn't think he'd been nearly as negative as Clint was implying, but maybe his worry about what Clint thought of his family combined with the frustration of their normally active sex life being brought to a screeching halt was showing more than he realized. Whatever the reason, Clint needed space, and Josh was going to give it to him. No matter how much it hurt.

It was hard to keep from glancing at his watch every thirty seconds and even harder not to fret that all his nightmares about Clint's reaction to his family were actually coming true. He was trying to find some way to distract himself when Marge came up to claim him for a dance. He didn't feel much like dancing, but refusing his aunt was out of the question.

"You look lower than a booze hound in a dry county," she said, taking him by the hand and leading him into a two step. Marge always led, so he'd gotten used to it. "Saw you run into Ira. What happened to your city slicker? Did he go outside to lie in wait for the bastard and beat him up?"

Somehow Josh managed a smile, but it faded quickly. "Ira was Ira. It was irritating, but I'm used to it."

Marge's eyes narrowed. "And what about city boy? Don't tell me he's taking a mad at Ira out on you!"

"No. Or at least, I don't think so." Josh frowned. Clint wasn't the type to take his anger at someone else out on Josh, but maybe Ira had been the last straw after the general frustration with everything, plus Josh's "negativity" that Clint had complained about.

"He'd better not, or I'll mess up that pretty face of his."

Marge's tone was casual, but Josh was well aware the sentiment behind it was quite real. "No, nothing like that, I'm sure. He just needed some space. He's an only child from a small family, and we're... well." He shrugged. He didn't have to explain big families to Marge.

"We're overwhelming in small doses, and this ain't exactly a quiet, intimate family gathering?" Marge gave him a sympathetic smile. "He'll get used to us, Josh. Give him time. I actually like him, and I can see he makes you happy." She paused, looking at him closely. "Are you worried *he* isn't happy?"

"Well... yes." Josh wouldn't have admitted that to his own mother, but Marge had been his confidante since adolescence. "I'm worried that having me isn't worth the stress of dealing with all of us, and I love him."

"We always worry about the ones we love. But Josh, that boy loves you, too. I could see it. He's here, and he ain't run away screaming yet."

"I think he might be close." Josh sighed and shook his head. "I don't want to lose him, Marge. He's the one I want. Forever."

Marge smiled. "It'll be fine, darlin'. You'll see. Let him have a few minutes to breathe, then go out there and grab him and take him back to that big, empty house and screw his brains out. No one else will be leaving here for hours. You'll see. Everything will look different in the morning."

Josh felt his cheeks grow warm. "Aunt Marge! What if Momma heard you telling me to have illicit relations in her house?"

"She'd say you were a durn fool if you didn't." Marge grinned and winked at him. The dance ended, and Marge stepped back and patted his cheek. "You're a good boy, Josh. Clint is lucky to have you. Remember that, all right?"

"I will." Josh smiled, a genuine smile this time, then threw his arms around her and hugged her tight. "Thanks, Marge. You always seem to be able to make me feel better."

"That's what maiden aunts are for," she replied, returning the hug.

"Maiden. Ha!" Josh released her. "I'll go look for Clint now. I never even thought about the house being empty while everyone is here!"

"You'll learn. Merry Christmas, honey." Marge waved goodbye before melting back into the crowd.

"Merry Christmas!" he called after her, then turned and headed toward the exit. He didn't care if he had to beg and plead; he was going to get Clint back to the house and take Marge's advice.

He ducked out into the chilly night, looking around to see if he could spot Clint. Some of his cousins were smoking by one corner, and he knew Clint didn't like being around the smoke, so he wouldn't have gone that way. He walked out into the parking lot, shivering a bit at the cold, but he didn't see anyone -- and it was snowing, the thick flakes obscuring any trace of his own footsteps quickly. He kept searching, walking all the way to where they'd parked the car, in case Clint had decided to sit inside, but the SUV was empty and undisturbed.

Frowning, Josh went back inside, deciding he must have missed Clint in the crowd. He looked around, checking the quiet corners, the kitchen, and the men's room, but there was no sign of his lover. He pulled out his cell phone and dialed Clint's number. The phone rang, but then went to voice mail.

Growing concerned, Josh went to look for his parents. He found his mother and asked if she'd seen Clint recently, but she shook her head. He asked his brothers and sisters, and his nieces and nephews, aunts and uncles, but no one had seen Clint in quite a while. Several people remembered seeing him walk outside, but no one could recall seeing him come back inside.

Panic began to set in, but Josh kept himself from running around flailing his arms by sheer force of will. He didn't want to cause a scene and embarrass Clint, either, if it turned out Clint had just found a quiet place to relax, so he began a swift but thorough search of every nook and cranny of the VFW hall, checking every door, every closet, even the big walk-in freezer and the basement. But after over an hour of searching, one thing was obvious: Clint was not anywhere in the VFW Hall.

Surely he hadn't just left without saying anything! Josh pulled out his cell phone again and began calling Clint's phone over and over, hoping he'd get an answer. Even if Clint was mad, surely he wouldn't let Josh call and call without any response. He couldn't have been *that* mad.

Could he?

While making what had to be the hundredth call, Josh walked by the cloakroom and heard the familiar ring of Clint's phone. He almost sagged in relief. Clint must have hidden behind the rack of coats, maybe even fallen asleep. Josh rushed into the room and looked around, calling out for Clint, but there was no response. He called the phone again, and this time, he traced the ring to the pocket of a coat. Clint's coat, still hanging where it had apparently been all evening.

There was no sign of Clint.

Numb with shock and dread, Josh went back to his mother. "Where Pa?" he asked quietly. "I need him. I think... I think something has happened to Clint."

"What?" Grace's face went pale. "You still haven't found him?"

"No, and his coat is still hanging up." Josh felt tense, his stomach knotted with worry. "That's why I need Pa."

"Oh, honey, he went home hours ago, before he even got to eat. Bluebell went into labor." Grace rested her hand on Josh's arm. "Maybe Clint got a ride with someone who left already? He's probably back at the house."

If Clint had gone back to the house, it was just to collect his things and return to Wilmington, although that didn't explain why he'd left his coat and phone. But Josh was willing to work on that assumption, even though a call to the house yielded no answer. He was grasping at any explanation, trying to keep from worrying that

Clint had walked off into the wilderness without a coat and frozen to death.

He left the VFW Hall, taking Clint's coat with him and racing along the snow-covered roads at a reckless speed. When he got home at last, he opened the door and sprinted inside, calling out for Clint. He raced through the empty rooms, practically screaming, until he finally reached the bedroom they had shared, his heart pounding wildly. He hoped to find Clint inside, not caring if Clint was angry or upset, so long as he was *there*, safe and sound.

But the room was as empty as the rest of the house, although Clint's clothes and luggage were still there, and Josh walked slowly back downstairs. He needed to call Jim Bob, report Clint missing, and have the county call out search and rescue teams. Clint must have decided to walk somewhere and gotten lost or hurt, or maybe he'd been attacked. Those bikers they'd run up against at Marge's could have come back, spoiling for a fight. Something horrible must have happened, because Clint wouldn't just walk away without a word and leave Josh behind, no matter how upset he'd been.

He was in the kitchen when the phone in his hand suddenly rang, and his heart began to beat wildly. He didn't recognize the number on the display, but he didn't care, pushing the talk button with shaking fingers.

"Clint? Is that you?" he asked, knowing his voice sounded pitiful but not caring.

"No, it's your Uncle Jim Bob," came a deep voice from the other end. "Your ma is worried, Josh. I take it you didn't find your man?"

"No... No, I didn't." Josh's throat began to close up. "He's not here. I haven't found him anywhere."

"Don't fret, boy. I'm going to get the bloodhounds. You need to bring me a piece of clothing, but if he just wandered off and got lost, the dogs will find him."

"Yes, sir. Thank you, Uncle Jim Bob. I'll come right back to the hall."

He hung up, then suddenly his legs wouldn't hold him up any longer. Sinking down into a chair at the kitchen table, Josh felt overwhelmed, fear and grief and regret churning inside him and making him feel sick. If only he'd gone after Clint right away. If only he'd pushed the issue and not let Clint walk away in the first place. If only he'd just apologized for making Clint unhappy, none of this would be happening.

He needed a moment, just a moment to give into the shakes, and he crossed his arms on the table, lowering his head and moaning in pain.

Just then, the door to the mud room opened, and he heard someone stomping snow off their shoes, followed by the deep rumble of his father's voice. His heart sank -- until the door leading into the kitchen opened and Clint stepped through. His clothes were covered in blood, dirt, and mucus, and there was hay in his hair, but he looked proud and happy.

"It's a girl!" Clint announced, smiling broadly despite the fatigue etching his features, and he clapped his hand on Clem's shoulder when Clem entered the kitchen. "Bluebell and baby are doing great."

Josh was up out of the chair before he was even aware of moving, and he crossed the kitchen in a single, bounding step, throwing his arms around Clint's shoulders and clinging to him as though his life depended on it. He could feel himself trembling, but he didn't care. Clint was all right. He was *here*, and Josh felt tears of relief and joy pricking his eyelids.

Clint wrapped his arms around Josh, returning the tight embrace. "Whoa, babe... What's wrong? Did something happen at the hall?"

Josh raised his head, staring at Clint with red-rimmed eyes. "You disappeared! I've been looking for you for hours! Jim Bob is getting the bloodhounds because we thought you'd gotten lost in the snow without your coat!"

"Oh, shit! Seriously?" Clint stared at Josh, a flash of guilt in his eyes. "I'm sorry, I didn't mean to worry you like that. I ran into Clem when I went outside, and he wanted my help because Bluebell's calf was breech. I was going to call you once the calf was born, but I guess it took longer than I realized."

If Josh hadn't been so worried, he might have been angry at Clint for going off without a word, but under the circumstances, his sense of relief was so profound, he didn't care why Clint had left. All that mattered was that he was here now.

"I don't care. All I care about is that you are safe and you didn't leave me, and I won't have regrets for the rest of my life that my last words to you weren't me saying how much I love you." Tightening his arms again, Josh leaned his head on Clint's shoulder. "I love you. Never leave me again. Ever."

Clint pressed a kiss to the top of Josh's head. "I love you too, and I'm not going anywhere." A note of wry amusement crept into his voice. "I just spent the last few hours with my arm in a cow's uterus because your dad asked me to. If that doesn't tell you I'm here to stay, I don't know what will."

"He did really well, Joshie," Clem piped up, and Josh raised his head, favoring his father with a stern look.

"That's all well and good, Pa, but you took ten years off my life when you stole my boyfriend. I might have to put coal in *your* stocking tomorrow morning!"

Clem chuckled and shook his head. "Will you forgive me if I offer to call Jim Bob and go back to the VFW so the two of you can have an hour or so all alone?"

Josh raised a brow and looked at Clint. "What do you think? Are you willing to save Pa's Christmas by making me forget why I was so upset?"

"For an hour alone, I'd forget about sending a bill." Clint shot a mischievous look at Josh's father.

"It's a deal! Let me have ten minutes to clean up, and the house will be yours." Clem grinned and clapped Clint on the shoulder. "That was damn fine work, son. Any time you want to give up city life, you'd make a great country vet." He looked at Josh. "I'm sorry you were worried, Joshie. But it wasn't Clint's fault. He's a good one. I think you should keep him."

"Maybe I will... if you hurry up and let him make it up to me for scaring me half to death." Josh's words were tart, but he smiled. "Go on, Pa. You can celebrate Christmas with the woman you love, and I'll celebrate it with the man *I* love."

"Fair enough." With a wink, Clem left the kitchen, and Josh turned his attention back to Clint, resting his hand against Clint's cheek and looking up at him somberly.

"I really was worried," he said softly. "I thought something horrible had happened to you, and I have never been so scared in my life."

"I'm sorry." Remorse was clear to see in Clint's eyes as he gazed at Josh. "It happened kind of fast. I walked outside, and the next thing I knew, Clem was there, and we were already on the way back here before it occurred to me that I hadn't let you know where I was going." He paused and tightened his arms around Josh. "I'm sorry for the things I said to you too. I was tired and irritable from too much socializing, and I took it out on you. I guess I was trying so hard to prove I could handle your family that I didn't take enough time outs along the way, and it got to me." He smiled wryly and added, "The eggnog probably didn't help."

The apology soothed away the lingering doubts and hurt in Josh's heart, and he smiled up at Clint. "Yeah, you can't hold your liquor, city boy. I'll have to remember that. But later. All that matters right now is that you're safe, and you aren't breaking up with me. And we have an hour of time blissfully alone in which I can show you how much you mean to me."

"Can we spend a few minutes of that time in the shower?" Clint sniffed his clothes and grimaced. "I'm filthy, and I smell like cow. You could scrub my back, and I'll scrub whatever you want scrubbed in return," he added with a playful leer.

As far as Josh was concerned, he'd spend the time anywhere Clint wanted as long as it involved them both being naked. "I'm game for the shower." He stepped back and reached for Clint's hand, tugging him toward the stairs, eager to make up for lost time.

Chuckling, Clint clasped Josh's hand as he followed willingly; his fingers were still a little chilly, but they warmed up quickly in Josh's grasp. "I feel better. Helping a cow give birth was the respite I needed, oddly enough. It was just me, your dad, and Bluebell, and I didn't have to worry about making small talk. Clem makes a pretty good veterinary assistant," he added, casting a mischievous look at Josh.

"Oh? Well, he should. He's not only birthed animals, he had to deliver my two youngest siblings." Josh glanced at Clint somberly. "I'm glad you're feeling better, though. I was worried you really had left me."

"No, of course not," Clint replied vehemently. "It would take a lot more than a rowdy holiday party with two thousand or so of your closest relatives to chase me off. Haven't I been trying to tell you that ever since we got here?"

Josh squeezed Clint's hand, then pulled him into the "adults only" bathroom. "Yes, you have, and it's finally getting through my thick skull. But now we have more important issues at hand." He gestured at the old-fashioned claw-footed bathtub. "Such as... do you want a bath or a shower?"

Clint eyed the large tub with interest, a heated gleam appearing in his eyes. "I think that looks plenty big enough for two, don't you?"

"It should be, if you don't mind us being really close." Josh put the plug into the drain, then turned on the taps. "There, that'll take a few minutes, but I know what to do in the meantime." He smiled and began to unbutton Clint's shirt.

"Conveniently enough, I want to do the same thing." Clint reached for the hem of Josh's sweater and tugged it up eagerly.

Lifting his arms, Josh let Clint pull his sweater off, then stripped his undershirt off over his head and tossed it aside before returning to finish Josh's buttons. They couldn't get naked fast enough to suit him, and he tugged impatiently, popping off the last two buttons. He licked his lips as he looked at Clint's bare chest, reaching out to brush his hands over the firm muscles before circling Clint's nipples with his thumbs. "God, you're so gorgeous. It still takes my breath away."

Clint's chest hitched, and he sucked in a sharp breath at the teasing, his eyes darkening with arousal. "Let's hope you still think that in a decade or two."

"You're like fine wine, love. You'll only improve with age." Josh kept up the teasing for a moment, then trailed his hands downward, caressing as he homed in on the fastenings of Clint's trousers. "It's Christmas Eve, and I'm opening my first present."

"It's the gift that keeps on giving." Clint leered, reaching for the fly of Josh's jeans in return, brushing his knuckles over the erection straining against the fabric. "And look! Here's *my* present, and it's just what I always wanted."

Sucking in a breath at the teasing, Josh pushed his hips forward, seeking more contact. "Good, because it's all for you." He unzipped Clint's trousers and slipped his hand inside, cupping Clint's cock and squeezing lightly. "My, my... I think the present I'm getting is even bigger than the one I have for you."

Moaning, Clint shifted restlessly and fumbled with the zipper on Josh's jeans, his fingers uncharacteristically clumsy. "Let's just hurry up and get both of these presents unwrapped. I don't think I can wait much longer."

"Fine by me!" Josh quickly toed off his shoes, then left off teasing Clint to strip his jeans and boxers off before quickly removing his socks. He straightened, standing in front of Clint naked and aroused. "Come on, city boy. The water is warm and waiting. And so am I."

"Just what I need after my first bovine breech birth." Clint grinned as he swiftly stripped off the rest of his clothes, shoes, socks and all. He waved Josh toward the tub. "Do you want to dive in first or shall I?"

"I'll get in first, then you can get in front, so I can scrub your back." Josh delayed long enough to steal another grope, then grabbed several towels from the storage cupboard, placing them close at hand before snagging a couple of washcloths and climbing into the warm water. He moved as far back as he could, then grinned at Clint. "Come on in, it feels great."

Clint climbed in and settled in with his back to Josh, humming softly with pleasure as the warm water lapped over him. "It does feel great." He leaned back, settling comfortably against Josh's chest. "Now it feels even better."

"Mmm... yes, it does." Josh reached for the soap and lathered up a washcloth, then began to run it over Clint's chest in slow circles. "I never really appreciated this tub before, but I'm beginning to see how appealing it is."

Humming louder, Clint arched his back to meet Josh's gentle touches, and he let his head fall back on Josh's shoulder. "So am I. It's much more fun with you in here than it is alone. I can do things like this." He sneaked his hand behind his back, lifting up to put enough space between them so he could curl his fingers around Josh's cock, stroking it lightly.

Gasping at the contact, Josh had to hold back from bucking his hips upward. "Oh, you're naughty," he murmured, his lips close to Clint's ear. "Of course, two can play at that game." Curling his free hand around Clint's cock, Josh stroked in retaliation.

A shiver rippled through Clint's entire body, and the rhythm of his hand faltered momentarily before he got back on track, stroking Josh harder. "There's no way I'm going to last," he said, his voice ragged with need. "I hope you don't mind giving new meaning to the term 'quickie'."

Josh chuckled. "Let's concentrate on you. We'll take the edge off and go back for seconds later."

"We'll make the most of this hour," Clint promised. "But I want to focus on you, too. Unless you've been sneaking away for a quick jerk off when I wasn't looking, it's been just as long for you as it has for me."

"Alas, it really has been just as long for me." Josh brushed his lips against Clint's jaw. "Okay, we'll do it your way. As long as I can have a kiss."

Clint turned his head to meet Josh's lips in a warm kiss, deepening it as he continued to stroke Josh's cock at a leisurely pace. Parting his lips, Josh twined his tongue with Clint's, his arousal spiking higher with every caress of Clint's hand. He mirrored the motion as he stroked Clint's cock, hearing the water lapping at the sides of the tub as they moved together, warm wet skin sliding against warm wet skin.

Clint's hungry moans were muffled by the kiss, but he didn't try to break it, exploring Josh's mouth eagerly as if it was the first time. His body was growing taut with need, his muscles quivering as his arousal spiked with every touch of Josh's hand. No less affected than Clint seemed to be, Josh began to buck his hips, unable to hold back as Clint drove him higher and higher. Then he moaned as he fell over the edge, pleasure pouring over him in heated waves.

Pulling back from the kiss, Clint stroked Josh throughout his release, seeming intent on wringing every bit of pleasure from Josh's body as possible, and he smiled with fierce satisfaction over his shoulder at Josh.

"Perfect," he murmured. "I've missed that."

"Mmm... So have I." Josh smiled lazily, satiation washing over him and leaving him warm and relaxed. "But I know something else you've missed, and now you're going to have it. Lean back against me."

Clint withdrew his hand and relaxed against Josh's chest again, putting his trust in Josh completely. "Have your wicked way with me. I'm yours."

"Yes, you are." Josh put both arms around Clint and nipped his lover's ear playfully. He began to stroke Clint's hard cock again, and with his other hand he tweaked one of Clint's nipples, rolling the sensitive flesh between his fingers. "Let me take care of you, babe. I want to make you feel really, really good."

Clint groaned and arched up, his skin growing flushed. "You always do. Every time."

"Good. I love watching you come. I love to see you lost in pleasure because of me." Josh nuzzled Clint's cheek, and increased the pace of his hand on Clint's cock. "I love you so much."

"Love you too -- so much--" Clint sounded breathless, his words coming between short, shallow panting breaths, then his back bowed, a familiar sign that he was close to the edge. With a sharp cry, he snapped his hips up, making the water slosh all around them as he let go and surrendered completely to the pleasure Josh offered.

"Yeah, that's it." Josh continued to stroke Clint until he felt Clint relax limply against him, and he pressed his lips to Clint's cheek.

Giving Clint pleasure always gave him a rush, and he ran both hands over Clint's chest and stomach, enjoying their closeness. It had been days since they'd been able to be together like this, and he'd missed it.

Clint craned up and back to press a lingering kiss to Josh's lips, capturing one of Josh's hands and twining their fingers.

"This is the best Christmas present ever," he murmured, smiling against Josh's lips. "But next year, is there any chance we could stay at a hotel? I never want to go this long without you again."

"I think we can figure something out." Josh retrieved the washcloth and soap again. "But speaking of presents... I do have one for you, and I'd like to give it to you tonight."

Clint nodded and smiled, obviously pleased by the idea. "I'd like to give you my present tonight while we're alone too. It's not really something I want to give you with dozens of eyes watching our every move."

"That works. Let's get washed up and we can spend the rest of our freedom in our room."

They managed to get cleaned up, although there was plenty of groping and teasing during the process. Then Josh cleaned out the tub while Clint gathered up their dirty clothes, and, wrapped in towels, they made their way to their room.

Josh went to his suitcase and removed a small box wrapped in green paper with silver bells tied on top. He walked up to Clint, smiling a little pensively. "I may have seemed a little negative the last few days, but I want you to know I've got more faith in you and in us than you may have thought." He offered the package, hoping Clint would be happy with the contents.

Clint shot Josh a quizzical look as he accepted the package, but he didn't waste any time untying the ribbon and ripping off the wrapping paper. When he opened the small ring box and saw the white gold band, its inset of diamonds glittering in the lamp light, he gasped, and his eyes flew open wide.

"Does this mean...?" He looked at Josh hopefully.

"It means I love you, and I want to spend the rest of my life with you." Josh smiled. "For a couple of hours tonight, I thought I'd lost you, and I never, ever want to feel that way again. You complete me, Clint, and I want us to build a life together."

"I want that too." Clint's eyes were bright and a little watery as he removed the ring from the box and held it out. "Will you do the honors?"

"Nothing could make me happier." Josh took the band and slid it onto Clint's finger, then lifted Clint's hand to his lips to press a kiss on top of it. "Merry Christmas, love."

"Merry Christmas." Clint smiled, wide and happy, and he admired his new ring for a moment, then he held up his hand. "Wait here. It's your turn, and I'm feeling a lot more confident about my gift than I was two minutes ago."

He swiftly retrieved a small box wrapped in paper with candy canes all over it and brought it back to Josh, offering it with a light kiss on the cheek.

Josh raised a brow, accepting it and quickly stripping off the paper, hope making his heart pound. He opened the box with trembling fingers, then smiled joyously as he saw the band within, its gleaming surface dotted with diamonds set at regular intervals. "I love it. I guess great minds think alike, eh?" He held out the ring to Clint. "My turn?"

Clint took the ring and slid it on Josh's finger, then clasped Josh's hand tightly. "I bought it shortly before we left because I wanted to prove I'm not going anywhere, no matter how crazy it gets with your family. I knew it then, and nothing has changed. I love you, and I want to spend the rest of my life with you, even if it means having moonshine and squirrel meat for Christmas dinner."

"Momma would never serve squirrel for Christmas dinner!" Josh protested, stepping closer to Clint and pressing against him. He couldn't ever remember being happier in his life. "The moonshine, however, is a different story. But that's for tomorrow. We still have at least half an hour of blissful peace and quiet. Shall we climb into that big feather bed and see if anything interesting pops up?"

"Oh, I'm sure we can find something in need of attention," Clint replied archly, sliding his arms around Josh and holding him close.

Laughing, Josh went into the embrace. Tomorrow was Christmas, and there would be more family, more uncomfortable questions and embarrassing stories, kids underfoot, and things going wrong, and noise and chaos, laughter and tears, and all the other things that accompanied a big family. But now he knew Clint could survive it, and so could their relationship, so he wasn't facing it with worry and dread, but happiness in knowing he could tell his loved ones that Clint would now become one of them.

But they still had a little bit of time to themselves, and he tugged Clint toward the bed, eager to share his joy with the one he loved most of all.

ABOUT THE AUTHOR

Ari McKay is the professional pseudonym for Arionrhod and McKay, who have been writing together for over a decade. Their collaborations encompass a wide variety of romance genres, including contemporary, fantasy, science fiction, gothic, and action/adventure. Their work includes the Blood Bathory series of paranormal novels, the Herc's Mercs series, as well as two historical Westerns: Heart of Stone and Finding Forgiveness. When not writing, they can often be found scheming over costume designs or binge watching TV shows together.

Arionrhod is a systems engineer by day who is eagerly looking forward to (hopefully) becoming a full time writer in the not-too-distant future. Now that she is an empty-nester, she has turned her attentions to finding the perfect piece of land to build a fortress in preparation for the zombie apocalypse, and baking (and eating) far too many cakes.

McKay is an English teacher who has been writing for one reason or another most of her life. She also enjoys knitting, reading, cooking, and playing video games. She has been known to knit in public. Given she has the survival skills of a gnat, she's relying on Arionrhod to help her survive the zombie apocalypse.